Franklin Benjamin Hough, And others

Diary of the Siege of Detroit in the War with Pontiac

Also a Narrative of the Principal Events of the Siege

Franklin Benjamin Hough, And others

Diary of the Siege of Detroit in the War with Pontiac
Also a Narrative of the Principal Events of the Siege

ISBN/EAN: 9783337123598

Printed in Europe, USA, Canada, Australia, Japan

Cover: Foto ©Raphael Reischuk / pixelio.de

More available books at **www.hansebooks.com**

DIARY

OF THE

SIEGE OF DETROIT.

Munsell's
Historical Series.
No. IV.

DIARY

OF THE

Siege of Detroit

IN THE

WAR WITH PONTIAC.

ALSO A

Narrative of the Principal Events of the Siege, by Major ROBERT ROGERS;

A

Plan for Conducting Indian Affairs, by Colonel BRADSTREET;

AND OTHER

AUTHENTICK DOCUMENTS,

NEVER BEFORE PRINTED.

EDITED WITH NOTES

BY *FRANKLIN B. HOUGH.*

Albany, N. Y.:

J. MUNSELL, 78 STATE STREET.

M.D.CCC.LX.

TO

J. Carson Brevoort, Esq.

OF BROOKLYN, N. Y.

Sir :

THE Contemporary Records of the Hoftilities which followed the Surrender of Canada in 1760, muft ever poffefs an unufual Degree of Intereft, as illuftrating the Indian Charaƈter, and the Succefs of the Line of Policy adopted by the French in their Northern Colonies of America, as contrafted with that of the Englifh.

Having early acquired an intimate Knowledge of the Interiour, by a Series of enterprifing Explorations, the French adopted a rational Method of fecuring the Benefits to be derived from a Monopoly of the Indian Trade, and with fuch Succefs that the Friendfhip they gained could not be an-

A   nulled

nulled by Treaties, or readily affigned to a Nation whom they had been taught to hate.

Deceived by the Statements of zealous Partizans in the French Interefts, the Natives fondly hoped for the Return of their ancient Allies to Power, and in the Ardour of their Enthufiafm they fought to merit returning Favours by anticipating the Arms of France in the Reconqueft of the Country, and the Expulfion of the Englifh.

The Journal and Documents here printed, from their undoubted Authenticity and great Diverfity of Subject, are believed to offer a valuable Addition to our previous Knowledge of the Events attending the Indian Wars of 1763; *and the Publifher, by infcribing thefe Pages to a zealous and difcriminating Student of American Hiftory, has the Gratification of believing that his own Labours for the Extenfion of Hiftorical Literature have met with an intelligent Approval.*

CONTENTS.

CONTENTS.

INTRODUCTION.

OTWITHSTANDING the English found themselves Masters of Canada, by the Capitulation of Montreal in September, 1760, the French retained a Place in the Memory of the Indian Tribes which could not be alienated by Treaties; and this Regard, which was gained by a long Series of kind Offices and well-timed Presents, was strengthened rather than diminished by the Neglect and Ill-usage which these Sons of Nature received at the Hands of the English.

There was no longer any European Rival to contend against; no Competition existed for the Monopoly and Profits of the Indian Trade, and no Risk of an Alliance with any civilized Power, to molest the long Frontier which had through many Years been desolated with Fire, and kept in Mourning by the cruel Hand of a lurking Enemy. The Motives for cultivating the Friendship of the Indians, which had been dictated

by

by Policy, no longer exifted, and thofe of Humanity and common Juftice foon proved inadequate to fecure thofe Favours which the Natives had long been accuftomed to receive from the Whites, and which the Introduction of the Weapons and fome of the Arts, if not the Vices, of Civilization, had to a certain Degree rendered neceffary to their Comfort and Contentment.

It was impoffible for them to fall back upon the Ufe of the Bow and Arrow, and the Club, after having become accuftomed to Fire Arms, and the only Means of their procuring thefe Articles which had thus been made neceffary to their Exiftence, was from the Englifh, now fole Mafters of the Country, upon fuch Terms and with fuch Sacrifices as unprincipled Traders or haughty military Officers might exact or permit, and if any Grievance arofe there was no longer an Appeal to a friendly Ear, or Hope of better Times for themfelves or their Children.¹¹

It will be remembered that the French ftill retained Command of the Pofts upon the Miffiffippi; that moft of the Inhabitants of this Nation, who were fcattered around the military Pofts in the Interiour, garrifoned by Englifh Troops, were ftill living in Terms of Intimacy with the Indians, and although yielding a formal Allegiance to their new Mafters, were ftill national in Language and in Heart, and finally that French Miffionaries and Emiffaries were ftill living in the Indian Villages throughout the Country. The War between

France

France and England, although fettled in North America, was ftill raging in Europe, and a Series of fuccefffful Operations in the old World, might have ftill enabled the French to claim the Relinquifhment of Canada, as one of the Conditions of Peace, as had occurred but a few Years previous in the Refurrender of Louifburgh, upon the Ifland of Cape Breton, after its Capture by New England Troops.

If in addition to thefe we remember, that the Indians had been taught by their French Allies, that the Grand Monarch of France was fcarcely lefs Omnipotent than Deity, that he loved his red Children and would ultimately protect them,—and that greatly perverted Accounts of the true Relations exifting between the two Countries were circulated among the Indians, we fhall have fufficient Reafons to account for the War which devaftated the Frontiers in the Summer of 1763, and in which Pontiac, the great Ottawa Chief, acted fo confpicuous a Part.

Sir William Johnfon, whofe Opportunities for knowing Indian Affairs were unfurpaffed, and whofe Judgment is entitled to the higheft Refpect in every thing that concerns thefe People, thus wrote to the Lords of Trade at the Period under Confideration :

" Without any Exaggeration, I look upon the North-
" ern Indians to be the moft formidable of any unci-
" vilized Body of People in the World. Hunting and
" War are their fole Occupations, and the one quali-
fies

" fies them for the other ; they have few Wants, and
" thofe are eafily fupplied ; their Properties of little
" Value, confequently Expeditions againft them, how-
" ever fuccef{ful, cannot diftrefs them, and they have
" Courage fufficient for their Manner of fighting, the
" Nature and Situation of their Countrys require not
" more.

" As the French well knew the Importance of the
" Indians, they wifely took Advantage of our Neglect,
" and altho' they were not able to effect a proper Re-
" conciliation with the Six Nations, took Care to cul-
" tivate a good Underftanding with the Weftern In-
" dians, which the Safety of their Colony, and their
" ambitious Views of extending their Bounds, rendered
" indifpenfably necef{ary ; to effect this, they were at
" an immenfe Expence in buying the Favour of the
" Indians.

" On the Reduction of Montreal, whereby the Fron-
" tiers claimed by Canada were ceded to His Majefty,
" I thought it prudent to fend Mr. Croghan, one of
" my Deputys, with the Troops, who were to take
" Poffeffion of Detroit, etc., whereby I reconciled the
" Change to the neighbouring Indians, then in Arms
" againft us, and the next Year went in Perfon to
" Detroit, where I held a Conference with the feveral
" neighbouring Nations, the Particulars of which will
" appear from my Tranfactions laft Year tranfmitted
" to your Lord^{pps} ; but apprehenfive that our occupying

" ing thefe Outpofts would never be approved of,
" unlefs the Indians fhared our Favours, as they had
" been accuftomed to thofe of the French, I reprefented
" to the Commander-in-Chief, the neceffity of weaning
" them therefrom gradually, as well as the repeated
" Accounts I had conftantly tranfmitted me of the
" Uneafinefs amongft the Indians, and my Apprehen-
" fions thereon.

 " The Indians of the Ottawa Confederacy (& who
" begun the prefent War) and alfo the Six Nations,
" however their Sentiments may have been mifrepre-
" fented, all along confidered the northern Parts of
" North America as their fole Property, from the Be-
" ginning ; and although the Conveniency of Trade
" (with fair Speaches and Promifes) induced them to
" afford both us and the French, Settlements in their
" Country, yet they have never underftood fuch Set-
" tlement as a Dominion, efpecially as neither we, nor
" the French ever made Conqueft of them ; they have
" even repeatedly faid at feveral Conferences in my
" Prefence, that 'they were amufed by both Parties with
" Stories of their upright Intentions, and that they
" made War for the Protection of the Indians' Rights,
" but that they plainly found it was carried on, to fee
" who would become Mafters of what was the Property
" of neither the one nor the other.' The French in
" order to reconcile them to thefe Encroachments,
" loaded them with Favours, and employed the moft

B   intelligent

"intelligent Agents, of good Influence, as well as art-
" ful Jefuits, amongft the feveral weftern and other
" Nations, who by Degrees prevailed on them to admit
" of Forts, under the Notion of Trading Houfes, in
" their Country; and knowing that thefe Pofts could
" never be maintained contrary to the Inclinations of
" the Indians, they fupplied them thereat with Ammu-
" nition and other Neceffaries in abundance, as alfo
" called them to frequent Congreffes, and difmiffed
" them with handfome Prefents; by which they en-
" joyed an extenfive Commerce, obtained the Affift-
" ance of thefe Indians, and poffeffed their Frontiers in
" Safety; and as without thefe Meafures, the Indians
" would never have fuffered them in their Country, fo
" they expect that whatever European Power poffeffes
" the fame, they fhall in fome meafure reap the like
" Advantages. Now, as thefe Advantages ceafed,
" on the Pofts being poffeffed by the Englifh, and
" efpecially as it was not thought prudent to indulge
" them with Amunition, they immediately concluded
" we had Defigns againft their Liberties, which Opin-
" ion had been firft inftilled into them by the French,
" and fince promoted by Traders of that Nation and
" others who retired amongft them on the Surrender of
" Canada and are ftill there, as well as by Belts of
" Wampum and other Exhortations, which I am con-
" fidently affured have been fent amongft them from the
" Illinois, Louifiana and even Canada, for that Purpofe."
                                                        The

The Treatment which the Indians were accuſtomed to receive from the Engliſh Traders has been ſpecified by Sir William Johnſon.[1]

"The Frontier Traders, ſenſible they have little to "apprehend from their Conduct, went ſtill greater and "more dangerous Lengths than their Superiours; from "a Variety of unheard of Frauds, I ſhall ſelect a very "few Inſtances which will tend to ſhew to what Lengths "ſome of that Character will go when ſubject to no "Controul, and becauſe two of theſe Inſtances were "the Occaſion of our loſing the Trade and Affections "of ſome powerful Tribes of the Ottawaes, who were "perſuaded to come the Length of Oſwego to Trade 'with us, and the laſt Inſtances cauſed the Defection "of the moſt powerful Tribes of the Senecas.

"Several of the Ottawaes having traded for a con- "ſiderable Time at Oſwego, where they got ſome Arti- "cles which they could not procure from the French, "an Ottawa Chief of great Influence with his Family, "brought his Packs to a Trader there, in order to try "the Market; the Trader, after the uſual Practice of "deceiving him in the Weight, hurried the Peltry into "a private Room, telling the Indian that all Mer- "chandize was very dear, owing to the Severity of "Dutys (a ſtale, but dangerous Artifice ſtill practiſed). "deſired him to chooſe out what Goods he wanted; "the Indian having made a Choice, was aſtoniſhed to

---

[1] Col. Hiſt. of N. Y., vii, 955.

find

" find that his Skins produced not one third of what
" he had been accuftomed to receive for the like Quan-
" tity (for the Trader had befides his Extortion on
" the Goods reckoned the Peltry at only one third of
" its real Weight) went away difcontented, but return-
" ing faid, he was afhamed to go back with fuch fmall
" Returns, and begged for a fmall Keg of Rum,
" which the Trader gave him, as he faid, as a high
" Favour, but on opening the Keg foon after his De-
" parture it proved to be Water.\\ Another Trader for
" fome valuable Furrs, which he received from an Ottawa
" Chief of great Influence, who came likewife to try
" the Market, and defired to have his Returns in Rum
" for a general Feaft, gave the Indian 30 fmall Kegs with
" Directions not to open them by the Way, otherwife
" the Trader would be punifhed for letting them have
" fo much; but the Indian before his Return to Nia-
" gara, being defirous of fome Liquor, opened them
" and found them all Water. This has been often
" acknowledged by thefe Traders, and on its coming
" to the Knowledge of the French, they made fo good
" a Ufe of it, that thefe People and all their Friends
" were ever after our most implacable Enemies. The
" next Inftance is that of a Seneca Warriour, whofe Influ-
" ence and Abilities were fo well known, that I found it
" a very hard Tafk to bring them over, which however
" I at length effected in 1756, when he came to me
" with a large Party of Warriours, who were to fet out

on

" on public Service in a few Days, but having fome
" Furrs to difpofe of, I gave them at their Defire a
" Paffport to Schenectady, wherein I recommended it
" to a Merchant and Trader there, to ufe them very
" kindly, and to do them the ftricteft Juftice, notwith-
" ftanding which, this Enemy to the Interefts of his
" Country, impofed upon them in the groffeft Manner;
" it appearing from their Account, & his own Confef-
" fion fince, that as they were Strangers, he had doubled
" the Prices of his Goods and allowed them but half
" the Weight of their Peltry ; this was refented ac-
" cordingly, the Indians took another Route back, and
" the Chief fent me a Belt of Wampum with a Mef-
" fage informing me of the Impofition (the Particulars
" of each Article being marked on the Handle of an Axe)
" and affuring me that he fhould always continue to have
" a perfonal Regard for me, but not the leaft for the
" Englifh who had ferved him fo often, but the laft
" Inftance was of fuch a Nature, that he had accepted
" of an Invitation from the French, who knew how to
" treat them, and their Services ; he made his Words
" good ; in a few Days cut off a large Settlement, and
" continued our moft violent Enemy ever fince, par-
" ticularly at Niagara in 1759, whilft it was not in my
" Power to have the unworthy Author punifhed. To
" this I muft fubjoin an Inftance in the Cafe of the
" Chief of all the Senecas, a Warriour, whofe Influence
" and Capacity were, and are well known here, whom I
had

" had fteadily preferved in the Britifh Intereft, when
" we were almoft totally abandoned, this Man at the
" Eve of the late War, was thro' the Means of Liquor
" feduced by fome *Agents* at *Albany* to fubfcribe his
" Name to an Indian Deed for a Tract within the
" Bounds of Pennfylvania, but claimed by the Con-
" necticut People, in Virtue of their obfolete Charter,
" which extended their weftern Limits to the South
" Seas. This being a moft iniquitous Proceeding
" highly refented by the Six Nations; the few who fub-
" fcribed to it became obnoxious to the reft, particu-
" larly the Chief before mentioned, fo that he was
" obliged to fly to the French for Protection, who fo
" far won upon him, that he with a powerful Party
" who followed his Fortunes took up Arms fhortly
" after, attacked a Body of Provincials at Lake George,
" whom they totally defeated and killed 45. Since
" which he was concerned in the moft important Ser-
" vices againft us, cut off fome of our Settlements, and
" occafioned the Deaths of more than 400 of our
" People. Thefe, it is prefumed, will fuffice to fhew
" the Effects of the Refentment of a few Indian Indi-
" viduals."

Such being the Caufes of Difaffection, and fuch the
Motives ftill remaining with the French to encourage
Indian Hoftilities, there was wanting only a Leader
around whom to Rally and upon whom to rely for
Direction

Direction and Counfel, and fuch a Chieftain was found in the Perfon of Pontiac.

By Merit as well as by Birth he had gained the Pofition of principal Chief of the Ottawas, and his Achievements and Talents had gained him an Influence fcarcely lefs powerful over the Ojibwas, Pottawottamies, and in fact over almoft all the Races of the Algonquin Stock. The Seneca Tribe of the Six Nations were alfo brought into this Alliance, and led by this energetic, crafty and vindictive Enemy of the Englifh to unite in a Plan for the fimultaneous Deftruction of the Pofts along the whole Frontier, as the Prelude of a general War of Extermination.

Pontiac was about fifty Years of age. He was a Friend to the French, whofe Fortunes he ardently defired to retrieve in Canada, and from whom he had without doubt been promifed large Reinforcements and unlimited Supplies. The Merchandife ftored at Detroit and other Pofts in the Interiour, at the Time Hoftilities began, were alone fufficient to provoke the Cupidity of the Savages, with much fewer Grounds for Grievance than actually exifted, and at Detroit alone, the Value of Goods was eftimated at half a million Pounds Sterling.[1]

In the Code of Indian Warfare, that Meafure is honourable which is fucceffful, and Treachery, Craft and Force may be alike employed, as Circumftances favour

[1] Lanman's Hift. Michigan, p. 107.

one or another. With thefe People, a Parole of Honour or the Obfervance of a Truce, would have been faithfully kept only fo far as a Fear of Confequences compelled them, and the Incidents concerning the Detention of Col. Campbell and Lieut. McDougal, as related in the following Pages, furnifhes but one of a Multitude of Inftances which Hiftory affords in Proof of the Fact, that the Natives knew no Code of Honour where an Advantage could be gained by a Breach of Truft.

The Hatred felt by the Indians towards the Englifh, began to affume a centralized and efficient Form in 1762, in the Fall of which Year Pontiac fent Meffengers with War Belts far and wide, calling every where upon the Warriours of his Race to unite and at a concerted Moment to fall upon and deftroy the neareft Military Pofts of the Englifh, affuring them that their Father, the Grand Monarch, would fuftain them in their Effort, and that they would be able to drive thefe hated Englifh from their Land.

The Incidents which marked the Execution of this Defign are related in the following Pages, and the high Degree of military Merit which faved Detroit from the Fate of many other Frontier Pofts, will long remain a Subject of Admiration.

The Diary printed in the following Pages, we believe to be now for the firft time publifhed, and although its Author is unknown, we have Reafon to infer from

                                        feveral

feveral Allufions to himfelf, and References to other Records kept along with it, that he was the Secretary of the Commandant, and that he was fully in his Confidence. The Manufcript is all in one Hand-writing, and is written upon about half a dozen Sizes of Paper, which were evidently in loofe Sheets at the Time, and have fince been bound in one Volume.

It was purchafed from a Bookfeller in London, and its former Owner had begun to print it; but finding, after getting through thirty-two Pages, that the Sheets had not been bound up in Chronological Order, the Enterprife was abandoned, until it came into the Hands of the Publifher of the prefent Series. It bears conclufive Evidence of Authenticity, and is believed to offer new and valuable Contributions to our Knowledge of the Events to which it relates.

The Tribes, one by one, were gradually won back to Peace with the Englifh through the Addrefs of Sir William Johnfon and others, whofe Sagacity led them to this Pacification by Detail, rather than to attempt a general Treaty with all the hoftile Tribes, as this might lead to a Union among them that would be dangerous in its Tendencies and difficult to controul.

The Pride and Hatred of Pontiac long kept him aloof from thefe Negotiations, and many an ineffectual Effort he made to interrupt them; but the final and conclufive Intelligence of Peace between France and England, received from the French themfelves, at

C   length

length convinced them that the laft Hope of Succour had vanifhed, and that no Effort of theirs could Benefit their loved and cherifhed Allies, or controul the Progrefs of the Englifh.

Pontiac concluded a Peace with George Croghan, Deputy of Sir William Johnfon, at Detroit, in Auguft, 1765, and promifed to meet Sir William at Ofwego in the Spring following to ratify the Peace in Perfon, and from this Vifit he returned laden with Gifts to the Maumee, where he fpent the fucceeding Winter. In 1767, new Sources of Annoyance to the Indians were encountered by the Infults and Aggreffions of the Frontier Settlers, and a brief but bloody War enfued on the Borders of Virginia, in which Pontiac is not known to have been concerned. During the Summer of 1767, he went to the Illinois, and foon after repaired to St. Louis to vifit his Friend St. Ange, who then commanded at that Poft. He was treated with great Kindnefs, and two or three Days after, hearing that a large Number of Indians were affembled at Cahokia, on the oppofite Side of the River, for fome focial Purpofe, he refolved to crofs over and fee what was in Progrefs. He was advifed to the Contrary, but relying upon his own Courage and feeing no Danger, he went.

The clofing Scene of his Life we cannot fo well relate as in the Language of Francis Parkman, Jr., of Bofton, whofe beautifully written Hiftory of the Con-

fpiracy

fpiracy of Pontiac, evinces a great Amount of Refearch, and a high Degree of literary Merit.

* * " The Place was full of Illinois Indians ; fuch " a Scene as in our own Time may often be met with " in fome fqualid Settlement of the Border, where the " vagabond Guefts, bedizened with dirty Finery, tie " their fmall Horfes in Rows along the Fences, and " ftroll idly among the Houfes, or lounge about the " Dram-fhops. A Chief fo renowned as Pontiac could " not remain long among the friendly Creoles of Ca- " hokia without being fummoned to a Feaft ; and at " fuch primitive Entertainment the Whifkey Bottle " would not fail to play its Part. This was in truth " the Cafe. Pontiac drank deeply, and, when the " Caroufal was over, ftrode down the Village Street to " the adjacent Woods, where he was heard to fing the " Medicine Songs, in whofe magick Power he trufted " as the Warrant of Succefs in all his Undertakings.

" An Englifh Trader, named Williamfon, was then " in the Village. He had looked on the Movements " of Pontiac with a Jealoufy probably not diminifhed " by the Vifit of the Chief to the French at St. Louis ; " and he now refolved not to lofe fo Favourable an " Opportunity to defpatch him. With this View, he " gained the Ear of a ftrolling Indian belonging to the " Kafkafkia Tribe of the Illinois, bribed him with a " Barrel of Liquor, and promifed him a farther Reward " if he would kill the Chief. The Bargain was quickly made.

" made. When Pontiac entered the Foreft, the Affaf-
" fin ftole upon his Track, and watching his Moment,
" glided behind him, and buried a Tomahawk in his
" Brain.

" The dead Body was foon difcovered, and ftartled
" Cries and wild Howlings announced the Event.
" The Word was caught up from Mouth to Mouth,
" and the Place refounded with infernal Yells. The
" Warriours fnatched their Weapons. The Illinois
" took Part with their guilty Countryman, and the few
" Followers of Pontiac, driven from the Village, fled
" to fpread the Tidings and call the Nations to Re-
" venge. Meanwhile the murdered Chief lay on the
" Spot where he had fallen, until St. Ange, mindful of
" former Friendfhip, fent to claim the Body, and
" buried it with warlike Honours, near his Fort of St.
" Louis.

" Thus bafely perifhed this Champion of a ruined
" Race. But could his Shade have revifited the Scene
" of Murder, his favage Spirit would have exulted in
" the Vengeance which overwhelmed the Abettors of the
" Crime. Whole Tribes were rooted out to expiate it.
" Chiefs and Sachems, whofe Veins had thrilled with
" his Eloquence, young Warriours, whofe afpiring
" Hearts had caught the Infpiration of his Greatnefs,
" muftered to revenge his Fate, and from the North
" and the Eaft, their united Bands defcended on the
" Villages of the Illinois. Tradition has but faintly
preferved

" preferved the Event ; and its only Annalifts, Men
" who held the inteftine Feuds of the Savage Tribes in
" no more Account than the Quarrels of Panthers or
" Wild-cats, have left but a meagre Record. Yet
" enough remains to tell us that over the Grave of
" Pontiac more Blood was poured out in Atonement
" than flowed from the Hecatombs of flaughtered
" Heroes on the Corpfe of Patroclus ; and the Rem-
" nant of the Illinois who furvived the Carnage re ·
" mained for ever after funk in utter Infignificance.

" Neither Mound nor Tablet marked the Burial-
" place of Pontiac. For a Maufoleum, a City has rifen
" above the Foreft Hero ; and the Race whom he
" hated with fuch burning Rancour trample with un-
" ceafing Footfteps over his forgotten Grave."

The Papers which follow the Diary in this Volume
are now moftly printed for the firft Time, from original
Manufcripts in the State Library at Albany, and will
be found to have an interefting Relation to the Con-
fpiracy of Pontiac and the Wars of that Period. The
Alarms which thefe Events occafioned on the Frontier
were fcarcely lefs Diftreffing than actual Hoftilities, and
thefe were often greatly aggravated by Rumours of In-
vafions and Murders which proved groundlefs and ab-
furd. The Refources of the Country, and the Spirit
of the Inhabitants were, however, tefted by this Crifis,
and Hiftory is enriched with Details, which might not
have been otherwife preferved.

Albany, Feb. 1, 1860.   F. B. H.

DIARY

OF THE

SIEGE OF DETROIT.

DIARY

OF THE

SIEGE OF DETROIT.

HE 1ſt of May Pondiac, the moſt confiderable Man in the Ottawa Na- tion, came here with about 50 of his Men,[1] & told the Commandant[2] that in a few Days when the reſt of his Nation came in he intended to come and make him a formal Viſit, as is the Cuſtom with all the Na-

---

[1] The Pontiac MSS. quoted by Parkman and aſcribed to a French Prieſt, ſays the Party numbered *forty*. The Commandant in writ- ing to Sir Jeffrey Amherſt, ſtates the Number as *fifty*. They came for the nominal Purpoſe of dancing the Calumet Dance and declaring their Friendſhip for the Engliſh, but in reality to aſcertain the Strength of the Garriſon, and the Nature and Extent of their Means of Defence. While moſt of them were dancing, the others were ſtroll- ing about the Premiſes, narrowly examining everything.—*Parkman's Pontiac*, p, 201.

[2] Major Henry Gladwyn, had but a ſhort Time previous to this Date, ſucceeded Major Campbell in the Command of this Poſt. He had accompanied Braddock in his unfortunate Expedition in 1755, was made Captain in the 80th or Gage's Light Armed Foot, Dec. 25,

tions

tions once a Year.[3] The 7th he came with all the Ottawa and Part of feveral other Nations, but we faw from their Behavior & from Reports that they were not well intentioned, upon which the Commandant took fuch Precautions that when they enter'd the Fort (tho they were by the neareft acc[ts] about 300 hundred and arm'd with Knives, Tomahawks, & a great many with Guns cut fhort and hid under their Blankets) they were fo much furpriz'd to fee our Difpofitions that they wou'd fcarcely fit down to Council; however in about half an Hour after they faw that we were prepared for the worft, they fat down & made feveral Speaches which were anfwer'd as calmly as if we did not fufpect them at all, and after receiving fome Tobacco & Bread & fome other Prefents they went away to their Camp.[4] This Morning a Party fent by him for that Purpofe took Capt. Robinfon & Sir Robert

1757, and commiffioned Major of that Regiment, June 20, 1759. In December of the Year following, he became a Major in the regular Army.

He continued in Command at Detroit through the Seige of Pontiac, and until relieved, Aug. 31, 1764, upon the Arrival of the Army under Col. Bradftreet.

He was promoted to the Rank of Lieutenant-Colonel, Sept. 17, 1763, and to that of Major-General, Sept. 26, 1782. He died at Stubbing, near Chefterfield, County of Derby, England, June 22, 1791.

[3] Referring to the Ojibwa, Pottawattamie and Wyandot Tribes, who were leagued together in this Enterprife.

[4] Other Authorities ftate that but fixty Indians were permitted to enter the Fort. All the Troops and Employées about the Premifes were drawn up in military Array, and as Pontiac and his Men paffed on to the Council Houfe, he found Major Gladwyn and his Officers fitting armed with Swords and Piftols. It was evident that the Purpofe of the Vifit was underftood, and the crafty Savage was overawed. As he came to that Part of his Speech in which he was to have given the Signal for Attack, a roll of Drums and clafh of Arms at the Entrance confufed him, and he fat down. The Commandant has been cenfured for not detaining him, which he probably would have done had he fufpected the Extent of the Plot.

Davers

Davers in a Barge near the Mouth of Lake Huron, which Capt. Robinſon went to ſound. They with Part of the Boat's Crew were put to Death,[5] the reſt they took Priſoners as we were afterwards informed. The 8th Pondiac return'd with a Pipe of Peace in order to aſk Commandant leave to come next Day with his whole Nation to bury all bad Reports, but the Commandant wou'd not give him leave but told him if he had any thing to ſay he might come with the reſt of the Chiefs and he would hear them. However inſtead of coming the 9th in the after Noon he ſtruck his Camp and croſſ'd the River within ½ a Mile of the Fort,[6] but being inform'd by the Interpreter that he would not be permitted to come in, he embark'd again & he commenc'd Hoſtilities by killing the King's Cattle that were on an Iſland about 3 Miles from the Fort,[7] with the People that took care of them, and a poor Engliſh Family that had juſt built a little Houſe there,[8] as alſo another Engliſh Family that liv'd juſt behind the Fort.[9] He alſo cut of the Communication

9

[5] An anonymous Letter, dated at Detroit, July 9, 1763, and printed in the Pennſylvania Gazette, Nos. 1,807, 1,808, ſtates that the Body of Sir Robert Davers was boiled and eaten. Mr. Paully (whoſe Eſcape from the Enemy is elſewhere noticed) ſaw the Skin of Capt. Robertſon's Arm in uſe as a Tobacco Pouch. Theſe Murders occurred May 9, 1763.—*Parkman's Pontiac*, p. 207.

[6] The Ottawa Camp had previouſly been about five Miles above on the eaſt Side of the River.

[7] Iſle au Cochon or Hog Iſland, is now on the American Side of the National Boundary. It is two Miles long and one wide.

[8] The Perſon killed here was named James Fiſher, who had been a Sergeant of the Regulars. A further Account of this Murder is given in Rogers's Narrative in the ſubſequent Pages of this Volume. His Wife and four Soldiers are by ſome Accounts reported as having been murdered at the ſame Time.— *Thatcher, Lanman.*

[9] This Family was that of an

from

1763.
May.
from the Fort to the Inhabitants on each Side so that we cou'd not get the least Thing brought into the Fort. He told the Inhabitants that the first of them that shou'd bring us any Provisions or any thing that cou'd be of any Service to us, they wou'd put that Family to Death. They also surrounded the Fort & fired a vast Number of Shots at it and the Vessels which were anchor'd so as to flank the Fort both above and below.[10] The Garrison lay upon the Arms all Night, not being above 120 Men,[11] Merchants, Sick & Officers. The

English Woman, named Turnbull, who lived outside of the Fort on a distant Part of the Common. Major Gladwyn had given her a Piece of Land for her Residence.—*Lanman's Michigan,* 106.

[10] There were two small armed Vessels lying before the Fort at this Time, named the *Beaver* and the *Gladwyn.* They rendered efficient Service in the Siege, and kept the Enemy from approaching by Water.

[11] The Garrison at the Beginning of the Siege consisted of one hundred and twenty-two Men and eight Officers, besides about forty Fur-traders and Engagées, who were more inclined to the French and were willing to be neutral. The Fort was Quadrilateral, with one Side near the water's Edge, and consisted of a single Row of Palisades twenty-five feet high, with Block-houses over the Gates and at the Angles. It contained two Six-pounders, one Three-pounder and three Mortars, badly mounted and calculated rather to inspire Terror than to do Execution among the skulking Savages

who so assiduously watched the Fort, seldom venturing in Numbers within Range of the great Guns, but ready to take off the unlucky Person who might chance to show his Head above the Pickets, or his Body before a Port hole.

This Enclosure contained about 100 small Dwellings, closely built upon narrow Streets, a Council-house, a small Church and Barracks for the Troops. A wider Street, called the *Chemin du Ronde,* led around the Buildings adjacent to the Pickets. The Buildings were of Wood and very liable to be set on Fire by burning Arrows. The Church was particularly exposed to this Casualty, as it stood near to the Palisades, but the Indians were threatened by the French Priest with the anger of the Great Spirit, if they did not desist from their Attempts to fire this Building. The Garrison by keeping constant Watch and plenty of Water in Cisterns, prevented Fires from taking. The River is here half a mile Wide.— *Discourse of Lewis Cass, before the Hist. Soc. of Michigan, Sept.* 18, 1829, p. 29.

10th they furrounded it again and fired very brifkly till
about 11 or 12 o'Clock when they made fome Propofals for an Accommodation (which was lucky for us,
as it gave us Time to get Provifions in to the King's
Store as we had not above three Weeks at fhort allowance), and Capt. Campbell and Lieut. McDougal,[12]
with the principal Part of the French, who faid they
would be anfwerable for their Return, went out to hold
a Council with him, but as foon as Pondiac got them
in his Poffeffion, he chang'd his Mind & would not
come to Terms as he had a few Hours before promif'd
the French, who feem'd to do all in their Power to
make him difperfe his People, but on the contrary fent
Word to the Commandant that he muft leave the Fort

[12] Major Donald Campbell had been fucceeded by Gladwyn but a few Days before. M. Gouin, a friendly Canadian, finding that thefe Men were in great Danger, haftily fent a Meffage for them not to come out, but as they had already ftarted with La Butte, one of the Interpreters and fome other French, they would not heed the Warning and paffed on. When they came to a rifing Ground, beyond which the Indians lay, the latter ran yelling towards them, as if they were prifoners running the Gauntlet, but Pontiac allayed the Tumult, and led them to a Lodge, where fome few Words were fpoken, but on their propofing to Return they found themfelves Prifoners. They were quartered in the Houfe of M. Meloche, near Parent Creek, and clofely guarded, but otherwife well treated for the Prefent. Two Indians had been detained in the Fort a few Days before, and were ftill in the Hands of the Englifh, which doubtlefs prevented the Savages from Acts of Violence at this Time.

On the 4th of July following, a Nephew of an Ojibwa Chief, was killed and fcalped by a Party from the Fort. Upon hearing this News, the enraged Uncle ran to the Houfe of Meloche, feized Major Campbell, bound him faft to a Fence and killed him with Arrows. He was afterwards fhockingly mangled, and it was reported that his Heart was eaten by the Savages. Lieut. McDougall inftantly fled, and fucceeded in reaching the Fort in Safety. Some Authors have ftated that the Murder of Major Campbell was approved by Pontiac, while others affirm that he was highly offended, and that the Murderer was obliged to efcape beyond his Reach.— *Parkman's Pontiac,* 211, 260; *MSS. Sir Wm. Johnfon,* vol. vii.

as

as M. Bell Etre did, that was to fay to take Provifion
enough with him to carry him to Niagara, but to leave
all the Merchandife.[13]   To which the Commandant
anfwer'd that he cou'd not come to any Terms with
him until he fent back Capt. Campbell & Lieut. Mc-
Dougal, for whom he wou'd give up the two Pottawattamies that he had detained for them.   The Garrifon lay on their Arms all Night as ufual.   We were
at the fame Time told by fome French that they
thought the beft thing we cou'd do wou'd be to fave
ourfelves in the Veffels, as there was 1000, fome faid
1500 Indians ready to fall upon all Sides of the Fort,
but they got for Anfwer that if in cafe they were three
times a numerous there was not an Officer or.[14]

12   In the Morning Pondiac fent another Meffage defiring the Fort to be given up, as before, to which the
Commandant gave an equivocal Anfwer to gain Time,
to get Provifion, having for two Nights before employ'd fome French Men to put fome Corn and Pares
Geefe on board the Veffels unknown to the Indians.
The twelfth in the Morning they furrounded the Fort
& fired upon it and the Veffels for about four Hours
very brifkly, tho at fo great a Diftance that we had but
one Man flightly wounded in the Fort and another on
board one of the Veffels.   We kill'd three or four of
them and wounded nine or ten.   We fet fire to fome
out Houfes from behind which they annoy'd us.   The
Garrifon lay upon their Arms on the Rampart all
Night, as they had done for three Nights before.   The

---

[13] M. P. de Beletere was the laft
French Commandant at Detroit,
before its Surrender to the Englifh
in the Autumn of 1760.   He was
fent with the other Prifoners under
the Care of Lieut. Holmes and thirty
Rangers to Philadelphia.—*Rogers's
Journal*, p. 229.

[14] The Sentence in the Manufcript
thus ends abruptly.

thirteenth

thirteenth in the Morning we heard that the Hurons had interfepted one Chapman,[15] with five Battoes or Canoes loaded with Merchandize, amongft which they got fixteen half Barrels of Powder and fome Rum, & that they were all drunk with it, upon which Hopkins,[16] with twenty-five Men, among whom were Mr. Starling, Mr. Watkins and McCormick, Volunᵗˢ went on board the Sloop in order to go oppofite the Huron Village,[17] and under the fire of her Cannon to land and burn it with their Booty and their Corn, the Wind being favorable to go up or down the River, but unluckily before he got Half way there the Wind fhifted and he was obliged to return, but by the Fire that the Huron kept while the Veffel was under Sail it did not appear that they were Drunk or off their Guard. They conftantly fired on the Fort & Veffels till dark, but without doing the leaft Damage. This Afternoon

[15] Chapman was a Trader, who, without fufpecting Hoftilities, was approaching Detroit. Heckewelder relates (*Hift. Ind. Nat.* 250), of a Man of this Name, and perhaps the Perfon here referred to, that after being kept fome Time by a Frenchman, the Indians refolved to burn him alive. He was bound to the Stake, and the Flames were kindled, when in the Agonies of that Moment an Indian handed him a Bowl of Broth. Upon touching it with his Lips, it was found boiling hot, and in an Inftant he threw the Difh and its Contents into the Face of the Savage. "He is mad! he is mad!" fhouted the Crowd, and haftily quenching the Fire, they relieved him from his horrid Fate and fet him at Liberty. The fuperftitious Awe with which the Natives regarded Lunatics and Idiots, has been often remarked by Hiftorians, and aids in explaining fome ftriking Incidents in their Annals. Chapman was brought in and furrendered July 12th, 1763.

[16] Captain Hopkins had Charge of a Company of Rangers, and in the numerous Skirmifhes and Sorties that occurred during the Siege, he is often mentioned as having had the Command.

[17] The Huron Village lay Eaft of the River, a fhort Diftance below Detroit. A Miffionary of the Order of Carthufian Friars, by Permiffion of the Bifhop of Canada refided there,—*Carver's Travels*, p. 92.

burn'd

burn'd feveral out Houfes from behind which they annoy'd us. The Garrifon lay on Ramparts as ufual.

12   The twelfth in the Evening Pondiac fent in another Meffage demanding the Fort, at the fame Time faying that the firing fhou'd feafe until an Anfwer was fent; this was to get Time to bring of the Dead and Wounded that had fallen in the Morning as appear'd from about thirty or forty of them coming about the Fort without Arms immediately after the Meffenger arrived, but not fo near as to be taken; after this Meffenger ariv'd we found that the Corn, Flower & Bare's Greafe that we had put on board the Veffels & that we found in the Fort would laft us for upwards of three Months.

The Anfwer to the above Meffage is in the Memorandum of the 16th.

14   The fourteenth[18] they began firing at about eleven o'Clock and continued till dark, not daring to approach nearer than the neareft Houfes that cou'd cover them, which was upwards of two hundred Yards off. They fir'd a great deal but more upon the Veffels than on

[18] Major Gladwyn appears to have fucceeded this Day in getting off a Letter to Gen. Amherft, as appears from an Epiftle of the latter to Col. Bradftreet, Q. M. G., dated June 22, 1763:
* * * "Major Gladwyn writes me of the 14th May, that the Detroit was invefted by a large Body of Indians; but that the Garrifon was in high Spirits, and he was in Hopes of being able to defend the Place untill he received fome Succours from Niagara; & Major Wilkins acquaints me he had, immediately on the Arrival of the Schooner from the Detroit, fent off a Reinforcement of fifty Men with a Lieutenant and non-commiffioned Officers, which I truft will have arrived in Time to fave the Place. I well know that you are always ready, however I think it neceffary to acquaint you to be prepared for moving at a moment's Warning, as, if the Savages are not quickly reduced, I believe I fhall employ you on a Command which I am certain will be agreable to you."—*Bradftreet & Amherft Papers*, p. 140.

the

the Fort. We had this Day a Searjeant and one private Man wounded.

Laft Night thefe Indians made a kind of Breaftwork
between the Fort and Mr. St. Martin Houfe of fome
Pickets that he had for a Garden.[19] This Morning
we cut two Embrafures through the Stockades for two
four Pounders with which we intended to diflodge them
in cafe they fhould return again. But inftead of their
coming to fire in the Manner they had done yefterday,
there was only a few of them came and began firing
fcattering Shot at eleven o'Clock & continued fo till
the Evening which we did not mind. This Morning
a Party went out and burn'd the remainder of the
Houfes that was near the Fort from behind which they
annoy'd the Veffels. They day before yefterday we
were informed that Mr. Rutherford,[20] who was with
Capt. Robinfon, was not kill'd but remains a Prifoner
with the Indians.

The Garrifon lay on their Arms to night as ufual.

The Anfwer the Commandant fent to the verbal
Meffage that Pondiac fent the 12th in the Evening
was, That he was not fent here to give up the Fort to
Indians, and advifed Pondiac to difperfe his People
and take care of his Ammunition to hunt with.

This Morning at 11 o'Clock they began to fire fcat-

---

[19] St. Martin, a French Interpreter, lived near the Fort, and his
Houfe was a convenient Point from
whence the Indians might annoy
the Garrifon. The Owner appears
to have been very kindly difpofed
toward the Englifh, and on the 30th
of June withdrew with his Family
into the Fort.

[20] Mr. Samuel Rutherford was
subfequently purchafed by M. Cuefiere, from the Indians, for £80
worth in Goods, but Pontiac upon
learning the Fact went with a Body
of fifty Men and reclaimed him,
faying it was not a good Precedent
to fell Prifoners to the French. He
efcaped to the Fort on the firft Day
of Auguft.—*Lanman's Hift. Michigan,* 108.

tering

1763.
May.
16

tering Shot from Mr. St Martins Houfe & Mr. Babies,[21] and continued till Evening, but without doing
us any Damage.

The moft of the Inhabitants affembled themfelves
to day to fpeake to Pondiac, who told them before he
would give over his Defign he wou'd fend two Frenchmen and two Indians to the Illinois to inform himfelf
whether what we had told him with regard to the Peace
was true or not, & as to Capt. Campbelle & Lieut.
McDougal he wou'd take care of them, and deliver
them to the Commandant that he had fent for from
the Illinois.

This Day a few Shot were fired as ufual from Mr.
Babies & Mr. St Martins Houfes at the Veffels with-
out doing any Execution. The Garrifon lay on the
Ramparts.

17   This Day there was not above a dozen Indians appeared within fight of the Fort, who did not fire above
twenty Shot. The Garrifon lay on the Rampart.

18   This Day a few Shot were fired from St Martins &
Babie as ufual without Damage. The Garrifon lay on
the Ramparts.

19   This Day we were very quiet, not having ten Shot
fired at us. We were laft Night inform'd that there
was upwards of 150 Indians gone to the Mouth of the
River to interfept fome Party's that we expected from
Niagara, upon which the Commandant ordered the
Scooner to be got ready for Sea to fend her down to
cover t em in cafe they came fafe to the Mouth of the

---

[21] M. Babie, a Frenchman in eafy
Circumftances, evinced the greateft
Friendfhip to the Englifh, and fe-
cretly furnifhed them with Provifions, at a Time when they were
much needed. He came into the
Fort with his Family, July 3, bringing fuch of his Goods as he could
remove, and leaving the Remainder
at the Mercy of the Indians. His
Houfe was burned by the Englifh
as a precautionary Meafure on the
25th of Auguft.

River.

River. We alfo receiv'd fome Letters laft Night from
Fort St Jofephs by an Indian that we had fent from
here, every thing there feem'd quiet and the Indians
declar'd great deal of Friendfhip for the Garrifon.

This Evening a Man that was taken Prifoner fix
Days ago by fome Ottawas and Mingoes in the Huron
River ariv'd here by the Affiftance of two or three
Frenchmen that were coming down that River. He
inform'd us that he was hired with one Crawford a
Trader who was on his way Home, that about 15 Indians met with them and laid down their Arms and
call'd them Brothers, but after having reconnoiter'd
them and finding they had a great quantity of Peltry
fell upon them and took them all Prifoners and oblig'd
them to return with them to a carrying Place on a fmall
River that runs into the Miamis, from whence he
made his Efcape as the Indians took him from a
French Man, he fpeaking a little French.

The Garrifon lay on the Ramparts as ufual.

The 21. At eleven o'Clock the Scooner fail'd for
the Mouth of the River with a N. E. Wind.[22] No
Indians appear'd near the Fort to day till the Afternoon when a few came and fired fome Shot at the
Sloop.

At fix in the Evening it was reported the Scooner
was run aground, upon which all the Indians gather'd
themfelves together to attack her, but the foremoft
Cannoe having one Man kill'd by a Shot from her
frightened the reft fo much that they put afhore again.

This Morning at 8 o'Clock we were inform'd that

[22] Other Accounts ftate that the
Veffel which failed this Day for Niagara, was the *Gladwin,* the fmaller
of the two, and rated at about eighty
tons. Carver records the Fact that
fhe was afterwards loft on Lake
Erie with all her Crew, through
the Obftinacy of her Commander,
who could not be prevailed upon to
take in fufficient Ballaft.—*Carver's
Travels,* p. 99.

after

after the Indians had attempted to attack the Schooner
fhe carryed out an Anchor and hall'd off and this
Morning arriv'd at the Mouth of the River.

At 9 o'Clock Mr. St Martin came with a Meffage
from the Hurons, who defir'd him to tell the Commandant that they had been forc'd into the War by the
Ottawas, that they had taken Chapman & his Merchandize, as alfo a Cannoe with five Englifhmen coming from Sandufky yefterday, among whom were Mr.
Smallman & two Jews, who muft have all fallen into
worfe hands if they had not taken them, as they had
not killed any of them; they defired to know what
Opinion the Commandant had of them, that if he
wou'd make Peace with them they wou'd give up
their Prifoners and pay Chapman for the Part of his
Merchandife that fell to their Lot in the Divifion
of them with the other Indians; to which the Commandant defir'd the Interpreter, Mr. St Martin, to
anfwer that upon thefe Conditions he wou'd take it
upon himfelf to make Peace with them for the Prefent
and recommend them to the General,[23] who he made
no doubt wou'd make it a lafting one if their future behavior fhould merit it.   They alfo offer'd to get themfelves entrench'd on a fmall Ifland at the Mouth of
the River and protect all Merchants Boats from the
other Nations that fhould arive there.   But the Commandant did not afk that of them for feveral good
Reafons, but would rather they fhou'd perform their
Promifes & remain quiet, or ufe their Endeavors to
feparate Pondiac & his followers, who at this Time
had cut off all Communication between us and our
Outpofts, as alfo lay in wait at different Places to intercept all Merchants that might be on their way hither.

[23] Sir Jeffrey Amherft, then Commander-in-Chief of the Britifh forces in North America.

He reign'd at this Time with moft defpotic Sway over the French, making feveral of them plow Land for him to put Corn in the Ground, and after they had done wou'd kill their Cattle. Three Days ago he fent fix Frenchmen with fome Indians amongft fome other Nations to advertife them of what he was doing and to bring him Word from the Illinois wheather what we had told him with regard to the Peace was true or not.[24]

We had not one Shot fir'd at us to day, notwithftanding which the Garrifon lay on the Ramparts as ufual.

This Morning Pondiac being inform'd that the Scooner was on Ground, forc'd Capt. Campbelle to crofs the River with him in order to put him on board of a Cannoe to go and tell the Commander of her to give her to the Indians, but when he ariv'd at the Huron Village he was again inform'd that fhe was in the Lake, upon which he return'd. When Pondiac propofed this to Capt. Campbelle, he told him he might put him to death for he wou'd not go, but Pondiac told him he would not put him to death, but he would oblige him to go, and forc'd him.[25]

We had not one Shot fir'd at us to day.

The Hurons promif'd to remain neuter for five or

[24] The Commandant at the Illinois was at this Time M. de Neyon, who was ftationed at Fort Chartres, the principal Poft of the French in that Region. This was located near Kafkafkia, on the Miffiffippi, in the prefent County of Randolph, Ill. It was built in 1720, under the Aufpices of the Miffiffippi Company. The Capitulation of Montreal did not include the Remote French Pofts beyond the great Lakes.—*Brown's Hift. Ill.*, 165.

[25] Other Accounts ftate that the Schooner lay becalmed, upon difcovering which the Indians came out in their Canoes, with Major Campbell in the Prow of the foremoft as a Shield againft the Fire of the Englifh. The brave old Officer called out to the Crew to do their Duty regardlefs of the Confequences to him—*Parkman's Pontiac*, 230.

fix Days to try if they cou'd not by fome Means get
Pondiac to feparate his People, at the Expiration of
which Time they expected fome of the Delaware &
Shawany Chiefs who was to join with them & oblige
Pondiac to come to their Terms.

The Garrifon lay upon the Ramparts as ufual.

24   At about feven in the Evening the Indians furrounded us and began to fire on the Sloop and continued till about ten o'Clock, when the People on
board obferv'd a great Number firing from one Place
they pointed a fix Pounder and fir'd it, after which
they did not fire ten Shot tho they had fir'd upwards
of a thoufand before; at eleven they began to fire from
Mr. St Martins Houfe upon the Flag Baftion where
we are inform'd there was about two hundred who
brought Combuftibles to fet fire to the Fort, but none
of them dare approach nearer than where they cou'd
be cover'd, they kept a very hot Fire till after one,
which we did not mind, hardly ever returning a Shot,
till hearing one of them fpeaking louder than the reft
and a great many anfwering him, the Commandant
pointed a four Pounder at the Place loaded with a Ball
& Grape & fir'd it, foon after which they went off, not
firing twenty Shot after it, tho they had fir'd very
brifkly from 11. By the death Song that they fung
two or three times we imagine there was fome kill'd or
wounded. The Garrifon lay upon the Ramparts.

25   This Morning every thing was quiet till the Afternoon all which Time we employ'd in making a kind
of Cavalier[26] to flank the Bank between Mr. St Martins Houfe from whence they much annoy'd us, but at

[26] A Mound of Earth, ufually   an Enemy on an adjacent Height, or
built in the Gorge of a Baftion, and   to command the Trenches of the
feveral Feet higher. It is ufed to   Befiegers.—*Brande's Dictionary.*
defilade the Works from the Fire of

four

four in the Afternoon they furrounded us with Combuftibles as yefterday, which prevented our raifing the
Cavalier, inftead of which Mr. Watkins was fent out
to take with five Men to take Poffeffion of that Part
of the Bank that the Enemy annoy'd us from the yesterday, which not only prevented them from approaching but drove them away, fo that from 9 at Night we
had not a Shot fir'd at us. The Garrifon on the
Ramparts.

This Morning early we put up the Cavalier. At 9
o'Clock we were inform'd that laft Night a Party of
Ottawas ariv'd from Sandufky who brought Enfign
Paulle,[27] the Commandant Prifoner having enter'd
the Fort with a few that he thought were his Friends,
who fiez'd him and put the Garrifon to death. The
Ottawas that went there told the Hurons that this
Place was taken & that their Brothers and the reft of
the Hurons had taken up the Hatchet againft us, notwithftanding which the Hurons would not confent for
three Days.

This Afternoon we were inform'd that Pondiac
having underftood that the Veffel was ftill at the Mouth
of the River, took Capt. Campbelle by Force as before,
with an Intent to oblige him to go with them in order
to take her by Treachery. They alfo took M. La

26

[27] Enfign Chriftopher Paully, of
Sandufky, on the 16th of May was
treacheroufly feized while in Con-
verfation with feven Indians, dif-
armed and made Prifoner, moft of
the Garrifon under his Command
killed, the Fort burned, and himfelf
thruft into a Canoe and taken on to
Detroit. On the Way he was
threatened with being burned alive,
and upon arriving at Pontiac's
Camp he was affailed with the barbarous Treatment ufually beftowed
upon Prifoners. An old Woman,
whofe Hufband had died, chofe to
adopt him in Place of the deceafed
Warrior, and he accepted the Alter-
native to fave his Life, but watching the firft Opportunity efcaped
and reached the Fort at Detroit,
July 4th. He had been commiffioned an Enfign in the 60th Regiment, Feb, 8, 1761.—*Parkman's
Pontiac*, 238, 260,

Bute

1763.   Bute the Interpretor & a Frenchman that could fpeake
May.   Englifh. The Garrifon lay on the Ramparts.

27   This Morning at Day light we fir'd two Cannon to
advertife the Veffel that they might not be deceived as
Pondiac intended in making them believe it was Peace.
Every thing was quiet laft Night.

At 3 in the Afternoon Pondiac return'd with Capt.
Campbelle, and faid that he had demanded the Veffell,
but the Commandant wou'd not give her up, upon
which Pondiac told him they wou'd come & attak him,
& he anfwer'd they might.   Then he went & encamp'd
on a neighboring Ifland, but the Veffel weighed Anchor
& went off before Day.   This Pondiac fays.

A few Shot fir'd as ufual at the Veffel to day and a
few at the Fort.   The Garrifon lay on the Ramparts.

We were inform'd to night by M. St Martin that
the Hurons were ftill refolv'd to remain Neuter, &
that in cafe the Ottawas oblig'd them to take up Arms
they wou'd go off into the Woods.

That if the reft of their Nation which were at Sandufky wou'd-not defift they wou'd difarm them.

28   Nothing of Confequence to day.   Some Councils
were held between the French and Indians about their
Cattle.   Some few Shots as ufual were fir'd at the Veffel and Fort.   The Garrifon lay on the Ramparts.

29   This Morning we were inform'd that there was about
50 Ottawas who lay in Ambufh in a Hollow way behind M. St Martins Houfe all Day yefterday, immag-
ining that we fhould make a Sortee as we had done
two or three Days before to burn fome Logs that they
had made a Breaftwork of.   This we fuppofe was in
confequence of what fome of the French told them.

At 10 o'clock we were inform'd that two Batteaus
were cut off in the River Huron with 19 Soldiers & a
Woman which we fuppofe muft have been Serjeant
                                                Shaw

Shaw who went from this with Provifions to Michilimackinac, the 17th April.

At 3 in the Afternoon Mr. Sterling[28] rec[d] a Letter
from Mr. Rutherford informing him that on the 8th
Inftant they were inform'd that by fome French People
in the River Huron that the Indians were ill inclin'd
& beg'd them to go no further, but Sir Robert [Davers]
and Capt. Robinfon did not give much Credit to it
and went on, that on turning a Point at the Entrance
of the Lake they were fir'd upon by fome Indians
who kill'd Sir Robert, Capt. Robinfon & two Soldiers
the firft Shot, the reft they took Prifoners. This
Evening a few Shot were fir'd at the Veffel and Fort
as ufual, without doing any Damage. The Garrifon
lay on their Arms.

This Morning at 8 o'Clock we had the difagreeable
Sight of eight Battoes with Provifions that a Party of
Indians had taken belonging to a Party commanded
by Lieut. Scuyler,[29] the [28th] Inftant, about 14 Miles

[28] Mr. Sterling was an Englifh
Trader then at Detroit. After the
Receipt of the Treaty by which
Canada was confirmed to the Eng-
lifh, he was appointed to take Charge
of the French who were in the
Fort.

[29] This fhould have been written
Cuyler. He had left Fort Niagara
May 14th, with 96 Men in eighteen
Boats, and a plentiful Supply of
Provifions and military Stores. He
had met neither Friend nor Foe
until he landed on the 28th at Point
Pelée to encamp The Party was
furprized by a great Number of Indians in Ambufh. The Men threw
down their Arms and fled to their

Boats, five of which pufhed off, but
only two of which efcaped. The
following Letter from Niagara gave
the firft Intelligence of this Event to
the Superintendent of Indian Affairs
in America:

NIAGARA, 6th June, 1763.
Honoured Sir: By My Letter of
yefterday you'll be fully informed of
euery thing that come to my Hands
fince my laft of the Month of May. [1]
I fhall only fignify to you at Prefent
what Accounts have come here fince
laft Night: firft, that the Queen's Independents upon their way to the
Detroit, and a Serjeant and twenty

[1] This Letter relates the infolent Demands of the Indians for Rum, but no
Hoftilities had then been heard of,

4

from

1763.
May.

from the Mouth of the River; as the Affair happen'd in the Night we have no juſt Accounts of the kill'd & Priſoners, but Lieut. Scuyler with two Batteaus made their Eſcape. When they were paſſing the Fort at about 600 Yards Diſtance we call'd to them, as their was but a few Indians in ſome of them, & told them to puſh off towards the Veſſel & ſhe would cover them with her Fire, upon which the foremoſt, having four Soldiers & two Indians[30] in it put off, the Soldiers ſiezing the Indians & throwing them overboard and gain'd the Veſſel notwithſtanding the Fire of the Indians from the Shore. The Batteau had ſeven Barrels of Pork & one of Flower on board. One of the Soldiers fell overboard with the Indians whome after a great Struggle they tomahawk'd.

At three in the Afternoon the remainder of the Party that was at the Lake return'd and brought two or three Traders Batteaus, which they lay in weight for, being

Men of the 60th Reg't within 25 Miles of that Place, at 11 o'Clock at Night were attacked by a Party of Indians and out of 76 of the Independents only 36 return'd here.

That the Old Betts Daughter has been informed this Day by a Seneca Chachim to quit this Place, as they have rec'd a Belt from the Indians about Pittſbourg to take up the bloody Hatchet, and that all the ſurrounding Indians in them Parts are abſolutely determined thereupon. An Anſwer the Senecas have not given to thoſe who ſent the Belt till ſuch Times as all the Shachims muſt be firſt made acquainted of their Proceedings the likewiſe have ſent with the Belt one Scalp that they took in or about Pittſbourg. You may depend upon me to give you the moſt timely Notice of every thing that pertains to his Majeſty's Service in the moſt diſtinct Manner that my Capacity will permit & never ſhall fail meriting Honor'd Sir to be your faithful Servant.

DE COUAGNE.

The Honourable Sir Wm. Johnſon.
—*MSS. of Sir William Johnſon,* vol. vii.

[30] Other Accounts ſtate the Number of Indians in this Boat as *three.* The Soldier that periſhed was drawn overboard by the Indian he was throwing out, and ſome Authorities relate that they periſhed in each other's Embrace. Another Writer affirms that the Indian ſwam aſhore. —*Parkman's Pontiac,* 233.

inform'd

inform'd they were coming by the Prifoners they took of Mr. Cuylers Party. The Garrifon lay on the Ramparts as ufual.

This Morning two drunken Indians came up to the Fort without Arms, being hot brave, to fet Fire to it, but were fir'd upon one of which fell on the Spot and the other ran away but fell in our Sight, and we fince hear is dead. The Indians have been fo drunk this two Days paft that they did not fire five Shot at us. The Garrifon lay on the Ramparts.

This Morning at about 3 o'Clock two Men call'd from the Hill behind the Fort who told us they were two Traders that had made their Efcape from the Indians who we let in at a fmall Port. A Quarter of an Hour after a Man call'd to the Veffel for a Boat from the other Side of the River, but thinking it might be a Decoy, we got two Frenchmen in a Cannoe who went brought over a Man of Capt. Hopkins Company who made his Efcape from the Indians after Mr. Cuyler Defeat and croff'd the Country from Lake; he brought his Arms with him. This Day fome Indian Cannoes went down the River as we fuppofe to cut off fome more Traders Boats that is expected from Niagara. The Garrifon lay on the Ramparts.

This Morning about fifteen Cannoes went down the River as we imagine to intercept fome more Traders that are on the way between Niagara and this Place.

In the Afternoon a Frenchman brought in a Letter that was enclof'd to me from Niagara which Capt. Campbelle gave in, by which we were inform'd that the definitive Treaty was fign'd at London the 20th February. Not a Shot was fired to day. The Garrifon lay on the Ramparts.

This Afternoon a few Shots were fir'd at the Fort & Veffel as ufual. The Garrifon lay upon the Ramparts as ufual. This

31

June 1.

2

3

This Morning Mr. Cuefiere purchaf'd Mr. Ruther-ford from the Indians on Condition that he fhou'd keep himfelf. A few Shot were fired at the Fort and Veffel as ufual.

This Evening fome Indians ariv'd with four Prifon-ers and fome Scalps & reported that Miamee was taken,[31] & that the Shawanees & Delawares had com-menc'd Hoftilities at Fort Pitt.[32]

5   This Afternoon about fifty Indians fired for an Hour or two at the Fort & Veffel without doing any Execu-tion. The Garrifon lay on the Ramparts.

6   This Day we were inform'd that the Commandant of Fort St Jofeph was Prifoner with the Puttawattamies; we imagine that he was oblig'd to evacuate his Poft not having more than a hundred weight of Flour the 12 May and in attempting to come here was taken.[33] It

[31] Fort Miami, on the Maumee, under the Command of Enfign Holmes, was treacheroufly captured on the 27th of May. Holmes was enticed away from the Fort by a young Indian Girl who lived with him, and reprefented that a Squaw lay dangeroufly ill in a Wigwam not far off. He was fhot; the Sergeant who came out to learn the Caufe of the firing, was taken Prifoner, and the Remainder furrendered at Dif-cretion.—*Parkman's Pontiac,* 244.

A fimilar Verfion of this Affair is recorded in this Diary for June 8, and a further Statement June 15th.

[32] On the 27th of May a Party of Indians approached Fort Pitt and encamped. The next Day they came to the Fort with Pack Horfes laden with valuable Furs, with which to purchafe Ammunition. Tidings of murders and burning were foon after brought in, and the Country around was fpeedily vifited by a diftreffing warfare in which many Perfons were killed, and Commu-nication with the reft of the Pro-vince was entirely cut off. On the 28th of July it was vigoroufly be-fieged, but on the 1ft of Auguft the Enemy withdrew to Attack Gen. Bouquet, by whom they were de-feated in the memorable Fight at Bufhy Run.—*Parkman's Pontiac,* 359.

[33] The Poft at St. Jofeph in Charge of Enfign Schloffer with fourteen Men, was furprifed on the Morning of May 25th, by a large Number of Pottawattamies, who came into the Fort in an infolent and diforderly Manner. At a given was

was alfo reported that Miamees was taken, but it was
reported fo many different ways that we did not believe it.   Some Days ago Mr. Cuefiere purchaf'd Mr.
Rutherford from the Indians, but a Miffiffagy Indian
ariving the Day before yefterday and informing Pondiac that they nor the Six Nations had not ftruck nor
would not ftrike if the Peace was made, alarm'd him,
upon which he went with fifty Men & took back the
Prifoner, faying that it was not a good Prefident[34]
to fell their Prifoners, that when things come to be
accommodated they cou'd exchange them or give them
up as they faw occafion.   Every thing quiet to day.
The Garrifon lay on the Ramparts.

This Day the Indian Chiefs had a Council at the   7
Puttawattamees but for what end we know not.   A
few Shot were fir'd at the Veffel & Fort as ufual.   The
Garrifon lay on the Ramparts.

Yefterday Pondiac took two Prifoners from Mr.
Babie that he had purchaf'd from the Indians, telling
him the fame that he told Cuefiere.

The Council held yefterday as we are inform'd was to   8
conclude upon a Method to attack the Veffel, which
they intend by fiting up eight Batteaux and lining them,
with which they are to fall down the Stream and board
her, while a great Number keeps a hot Fire upon the
Fort.   This to be done in a very dark Night.   All
quiet to day except a few Shot from St Martins Houfe.
The Garrifon lay on the Ramparts.

This Afternoon three Batteaux paff'd up the River   9
that were taken by the Chippawas near the Place Mr.

Signal, thofe within rufhed to the   at Detroit, on 15th of June.—*Park-*
Gate, killed the Sentinel and ten   *man's Pontiac,* 240.
other Men, and took the Com-   Schloffer's Statement is recorded
mandant and the three furviving   in this Diary for June 15th.
Men Prifoners.   He was exchanged   [34] Precedent.

Cuyler

Cuyler was defeated. There was eleven Perſons in them, two of whom were kill'd, the reſt they brought here Priſoners.

We were alſo well aſſured that the Miamee was taken, as a Frenchman ſpoke to the Corporal of that Garriſon who was Priſoner with the Indians, who told him that Mr. Holmes had been inform'd of the Deſigns of the Indians & that he had ſhut the Gates of the Fort, which the Indians ſeeing found they cou'd not take it but by Treachery, accordingly they employ'd a Squaw that Mr. Holmes kept to bring him out of the Fort to bleed her Siſter who was ſick in a Caban, and as ſoon as he came there three or four Ottawas who had hid themſelves on purpoſe fired at him and kill'd him, then took one Welch whome they had Priſoner and went to the Fort & made him tell the Men if they would lay down their Arms they ſhould be all ſav'd, upon which they open'd the Gates. We hear they have carried them towards the Illinois. The Garriſon lay on their Arms.

10   This Day the Puttawattamies ſent Mr. Gamelin with a Meſſage to the Commandant deſiring to change Mr. Schloſſer for one of the Indians we have in Cuſtody. To which the Commandant anſwer'd that they muſt firſt let him know how many Priſoners they had taken & what they had done with them, and gave leave to four of the Chiefs with Mr. Gamelin to come within thirty Yards of the Fort to ſpeake to the two we had in Cuſtody, at their Requeſt. In a Hour afterwards the whole Nation came to Mr. St Martins Houſe (when the Garriſon was order'd on the Ramparts), where they halted and ſent forward four Chiefs, who told they were led into the War by Pondiac, &c.; to which the Commandant anſwer'd he believ'd it, & therefore adviſed them to diſperſe & mind their hunting & planting

planting, for if they perſiſted it wou'd end in their utter Ruin.   To which ˈthey hung their Heads & one of them ſaid he believ'd it.   They ſaid they had fourteen Priſoners & Mr. Schloſſer, all of whome the Commandant demanded, as one of the Indians we had in Cuſtody was one of the firſt Men in the Nation.   To which they did not give a poſitive Anſwer but went to hold a Council.

Every thing quiet to day.   The Garriſon lay on the Ramparts.

This Day we permitted ſome more of the Puttawattamees to ſpeak to the two we had in Cuſtody.

11

All quiet to day.   The Garriſon lay on the Ramparts.

Yeſterday one Cavalier ariv'd from Montreal who inform'd us that at Grand River, within thirty Miles of the End of Lake Erie, ſeven Engliſh Battoes with Merchandize was attack'd by ſome Indians, five of which were taken, the other two made their eſcape; that there was one Laſcelle with him from Montreal at the ſame Time who return'd to Niagara.

At five o'Clock about thirty Indians ariv'd at Pondiacs Camp from Saggina, who made with what he had in Camp 168 Indians beſides 250 that went down the River a few Days ago as it was ſaid to cut off the Communication at Niagara.   Neither Cavalier nor young Laſcelle, who ariv'd two Days before him, are yet come into the Fort altho Laſcelle ariv'd two Days before the other, they ſay the Indians have threatened to kill them if they come nearer than a certain Diſtance.

All quiet to day.   The Day before yeſterday and to day made Sorties and burnt ſome out Houſes and Gardens.   The Garriſon lay on the Ramparts.

Yeſterday and to day we buried five Corps that we took up in the River, two of whom we knew but the
reſt

reſt was ſo mangled that it was impoſſible for any body to have the leaſt Knowledge of them.

13 Nothing extraordinary to day. Three of the Puttawattamees came and ſpoke with the two we had in Cuſtody, who declar'd to us that they knew nothing of this Affair till they ariv'd at their Village below the Fort, when much to their Surprize they heard a great firing. That they never had any Meſſage ſent to them about it, nor was they conſulted in any Manner whatever, but was forc'd into it by the Ottawas. Upon which the Commandant aſk'd them if they were the Slaves of Pondiac, at which they hung their Heads ; he then told them what he had told them before with regard to their diſperſing, and that they wou'd ſee in the End that the Ottawas wou'd kill Pondiac for bringing them into ſuch an Undertaking, for that they, and every one that join'd heartily with them, wou'd be ruined; as they wou'd forfeit their Lands and be depriv'd of all the Neceſſaries of Life. Upon which they promiſ'd to go to their Camps and ſend in their Corn, &c. The Garriſon lay on the Ramparts.

14 Yeſterday we heard that Ouattanon was cut off and the Garriſon taken to the Illinois.[35]

Every thing quiet to day. The Garriſon lay on the. Ramparts.

15 This Morning between eleven and twelve o'Clock one of the Chiefs of the Puttawattamees (named Waſhee) who took St. Joſephs, came with four or five others to change ſome of their Priſoners for the two tnat we had

---

[35] Ouatanon was a Fort on the Wabaſh, a little below the preſent Town of Lafayette. It was then under the Command of Lt. Edward Jenkins, who was taken on the firſt of June, by Stratagem, with ſeveral of his Men, when the Remainder of the Garriſon yielded without Reſiſtance. The Indians, however, apologized for their Conduct, by ſaying that they acted under the Influence of other Tribes and againſt their own better Judgments.—*Parkman's Pontiac*, 243.

1763.
June.

in Cuſtody, and after talking near two hours, the Commandant got them to confent to give Mr. Schloſſer and two Soldiers that they brought with them for one of them that he had, and promiſ'd them that when they brought the reſt of the ·Priſoners he wou'd give them the other. They did not feem to be well contented as they expected the Man of the moſt Confequence in return for the Officer, but the Commandant was almoſt fure that if he gave him up they would not give above one of the eleven that remain'd with them for the other, and therefore detain'd him. The Account Mr. Schloſ-fer gives of the way he was taken is, that about feven-teen Puttawattamees came into his Fort under a Pre-tence of holding a Council, after they had engag'd the young Men of the Nation about him to join with them, to whom they promiſ'd all the Plunder after they were in the Fort, Waſhaſhe the Puttawattamy Chief went into his Room with three or four others, to whom he had prefented a Belt, as he cou'd fpeak a little of their Language himfelf, for they had detain'd his Interpreter on the other Side of the River till every thing was ready, but before they had made him an Anfwer a Frenchman came in and told him their De-fign, upon which the cry was given in the Fort & they fiez'd him immediately & the young Men that agreed to join him ruſh'd into the Fort, knocking down the Centinel and before the Men cou'd get to their Arms put ten of them to death, which Waſhſhe tryed to pre-vent but in vain, the remaining three and himfelf they took Priſoners. After this was done all the Chiefs of the St Jofeph Indians came to Mr. Schloſſer and told him that they knew nothing of the Affair, that their young Men croſſ'd the River in the Night unknown to them, & defir'd him to acquaint the Commandant here that they were not concern'd in the War, nor would not be.

One

1763.
June.
One of the Soldiers we got to day was taken at Miamee who gives the fame Account of its being taken as we have already heard, with this Difference, that the Serj. after he heard the Shots that were fir'd at Mr. Holmes went out to fee what it was & was taken Prifoner, after which they brought one Walch whome they had Prifoner to tell them what has been already mentioned, upon which they deliver'd up the Fort, and French Colours was immediately hoifted in it, but does not know wheather it was the French or Indians that hoifted them.　This Evening we were inform'd from good Authority that Saggina Indians had been with Mr. Labute to defire him to fpeake to the Commandant to make Peace with them, that they had not yet enter'd into the War, that is they had neither kill'd any body nor did they take any Merchants.　To which Mr. Labute anfwer'd they knew well enough he dared not go to the Fort, that if Pondiac knew he fpoke to the Englifh he would put him to death, and told them they muft come themfelves.

All quiet to day.　The Garrifon lay on the Ramparts.　We are affured that all the Chiefs of the Hurons are peacibly inclin'd but there is a Band of 25 young Men that they cant bring over Part of whome are gone to Niagara with the Ottawas.

16
This Day at twelve o'Clock Wafhfhe with two other Puttawattame Chiefs, & two Saggina Indians[37] came with a Flag to fpeake to the Commandant.　After they enter'd the Fort one of the Puttawattamees got up with a String of Wampam & defir'd to be heard, That what they had already told him was true, & that what they were going to fay was from their Hearts, upon which he prefented the Wampam.

[37] One of the latter was Mindoghquay.　He returned to the Fort Dec. 12th, tendering his Friendfhip.

He

He then took another String and told the Commandant that the two Saggina Indians were fent in the Name of all their Chiefs, that they were Brothers, and their Hearts inclin'd the fame way. That they the Puttawattamees knew nothing of the Commencement of the War, but were hurried into it by the Ottawas, but they had now buried the Hatchet and it fhou'd never rife again. Upon which they prefented the Wampam. Then took another String & faid they had fent Meffengers for the reft of their Prifoners who fhou'd be all deliver'd up as foon as they came in. Then one of the Saggina Indians got up with a String of Wampam & faid he was fent in the Name of their Chief and defir'd he might be heard. That their Hands and ours had always been join'd fince we took Poffeffion of this Country, and they never fhou'd be parted; that they had not enter'd into the War at all, that their Hearts were the fame as the Puttawattamees, and intended to remain fo; that he fpoke the real Sentiments of the Hearts of all their Chiefs, which he defir'd we fhou'd believe, knowing that if he told lies the great God wou'd be offended at him, upon which he prefented the Wampam. Then the Commandant took a fmall Belt and defir'd to know before he gave them an Anfwer, wheather the Puttawattamee Chiefs that were there fpoke only for their Bands in particular or for the whole Nation, to which they anfwer'd for the whole Nation. He then told them that he was glad they had open'd their Eyes and did not intend to perfift in a thing that muft end in their Ruin, that the only thing they cou'd do to convince him of their good Intentions wou'd be to give up the reft of their Prifoners and go to their Villages and tend their Corn & hunt. That he wou'd then recommend them to the General, and that they wou'd find every thing he told them was true.

true. That the Peace was actually made between the French and us, and if they perfifted in a Thing of this kind we fhould not only fight againft them, but the Canadians (the People they thought they were fighting for) wou'd alfo take Arms againft them as we were all one. That he knew they were made to believe there was no Peace & that there was an Army coming from the Illinois, but thofe that told them fo, told lies, & were their Enemies, which they wou'd foon fee. That if they took his Advice & did as he defir'd them they might live for the Future in Tranquility as they had done before, and fee the Ottawas ftarving in the Woods for want of the Neceffaries of Life that they cou'd no ways get but from us. Then prefented the Belt.

The Saggina Indians further faid that the Michili-mackinac Indians wou'd not ftrike and if Pondiac attempted to go towards that Poft they would prevent him.

The Commandant then took another String and told the Saggina that he was glad to hear they were fo well inclin'd & that they had more fenfe than to be lead into a thing by the Ottawas (that wou'd be their Ruin). That he never intended any thing but Peace with them, that the Ottawas began the War without any Reafon, that he was well pleaf'd with their Behavior and would alfo recommend them to the General if they continued at their Villages in the fame Tranquility that they faid they were then in. That they might be fure every thing he faid was true which they wou'd find in the End, and defir'd them not to give Ear to any Lies that might be fpread amongft them. Then gave the Wampam. Upon which the Saggina Indian faid he was glad to receive it, that the Chiefs wou'd believe when they faw his Mouth (as he call'd the Wampam) they were pitied. All quiet to day. The Garrifon lay on the Ramparts.   All

All quiet to day. This Evening we was told that a
Cannon was heard at the Mouth of the River about 11
o'Clock this Morning, which muſt have been the
Veſſel ; a little after Sunſet we fir'd another to anſwer
her. Upon the Report of the Cannon in the Morning
ſeveral Indians were ſent off to ſee if ſhe was there or
not. The Garriſon lay on the Ramparts.

Since the firſt Information that we had of the Indian
Intention of attacking the Veſſell with Batteaux, Capt.
Hopkins lay on board of her every Night.

This Day the Jeſuiſt ariv'd from Michilimackinac,
with the diſagreeable News of its being cut off by
Treachery. The Particulars not yet come to Hand.
All quiet to day. The Garriſon lay on the Ramparts.

This Day the Jeſuiſt came into the Fort, and brought
a Letter[38] from Capt. Etherington by which we were
inform'd, That the 2ᵈ June the Chippawas were playing at Croſſ[39] at Michilimackinac (three Days after
they had a Council with him and profeſſ'd a great deal
of Friendſhip. That upon the arrival of a Canoe from
Saggina, one Mr. Tracy a Merchant went to the Water-
ſide to ſpeak to them which the Indians ſeeing ſaid to

19

[38] This Letter, dated June 12th, is publiſhed in *Parkman's Pontiac*, p. 596, from the Original, as pre-ſerved in the State Paper Office of London. It is ſubſtantially the ſame as that of Capt. Claus, given on the following Pages. The Jeſuit refer-red to was Father Jonois, then ſta-tioned at L'Arbre Croche.

[39] The Game of La Croſſe, or Baggattway, is played with a Bat and Ball ; two Poſts are planted in the Ground, about a Mile apart, and each Party having its Poſt, the object is to propel the Ball, which is placed in the Centre, toward the Poſt of the Adverſary. In the Ar-dor of Conteſt, if the Ball can not be driven to the deſired Goal, it is ſtruck in any Direction by which it can be diverted from that deſigned by the oppoſite Party.

A Game much ſimilar is ſtill played by the Iroquois of New York and Canada.—*Carver's Travels*, 201 ; *Smith's Hiſt. Wiſconſin*, i, 137 ; *N. Y. Senate Doc.*, 1850, *No.* 75, p. 81.

themſelves

1763.
June.

themfelves now is the Time, for if thefe People enter the Fort they will tell our Defign, upon which they tomahawk'd Mr. Tracy and gave the Cry, & in an inftant fiez'd Capt. Etherington & Lieut. Leffley who were at the Gate of the Fort looking at them playing, forc'd by the Centry and enter'd the Fort where they found their Squaws (who had been previoufly plac'd with their Tomahawks) with which they forc'd the Guard before they cou'd get under Arms, kill'd thirteen Men on the Spot with Lieut. Jamet who fought with his Sword againft five for a long Time, but after receiving thirty-fix Wounds fell in their Hands after which they cut off his Head and kill'd fix of their Prifoners; they pillag'd all the Merchants and got fifty Barrels of Powder with Lead in Proportion. The Ottawas took the Officers and eleven of their Prifoners from them whome they keep at the Priefts Houfe. Capt. Etherington then gave a written Authority to Mr. Langlad[40] to Com^d in the Fort till further Orders, and recommended him Mr. Langlad and one Mr. Farli to the Commandant

[40] Sieur Auguftine du Langlade, about 1750, became the Owner of moft of the Lands around Green Bay, and his Defcendants ftill refide there. He was a Man of Character and Education, and retained the polifhed Manners of the French Metropolis. His Son, Charles Langlade, was a Native of this Country and in 1760 was commiffioned by Louis XV, and appointed Second in Command at Michillimackinack, where he was refiding at the Time of the Maffacre. The Narrative of Alexander Henry, the Trader, gives an unfavorable impreffion with regard to the Humanity of M. Langlade.

At the Time of the Attack, as the Indians were purfuing the Englifh from one Retreat to another, Henry rufhed into his Houfe and befought him to afford an Afylum. The Frenchman, who ftood at his Window watching the Slaughter, looked at him a Moment and then turned again to the Window, fhrugging his Shoulders and remarking, *Que voudriez-vous que j'en ferais?* "*What would you have me do?*" He afterwards willingly fubmitted the Keys of his Houfe to allow the Savages to fearch his Premifes for Englifh.—*Smith's Hift. Wifconfin,* i, 346; *Henry's Travels.*

here

here as good Men & who did all in their Power for
the good of the Service, as alſo the Jeſuiſt who has a
great deal to ſay among the Indians.[41]

All quiet to day.   The Garriſon lay on the Ramparts.

[41] The Circumſtances attending the Attack upon Michillimackinack and its Capture by the Indians, on the 4th of June are alſo ſet forth in the following Extract from a Letter written at Montreal by Capt. Daniel Claus to Sir William Johnſon:
"* * * 6th Aug. Whilſt I am writing this, my Landlord tells me that Capt. [George] Etherington and Lieut. [James] Leſſley paſſed the Door coming from Miſſilimakk who I heare with all the Traders except one Traſey [Tracy] who was killed by the Enemy Indⁿˢ were eſcorted here by the Ottawas as living near that Place.   I followed them immediately to the Govˢ, and there learned the News of them Parts, which is that a Parcell of Chippeways to the Number of 100 aſſembled near the Fort as cuſtomary in the Beginning of Summer, and diverted themſelves playing Football, and Capt Ethrington and Mr. Leſſley (not ſuſpecting the leaſt Treachery, having then not heard a Word of Detroit being beſieged by the Enemy Indians) ſtood out of the Fort to ſee the Indians Play; that on a Signal given by a Yell, they both were ſeized and bound, and that the ſame Inſtant the Centries were tomahawked, likewiſe Mr. James, who was Officer of the Day in the Fort, together with 18 Soldiers killed and taken.   Then the

Traders were plundered and taken Priſoners; that afterwards themſelves were dragged to the Chippeways' Encampment where the Spoil was divided, and a Council held, in what Manner the Officers were to be put to Death.   In the mean Time the News reached the Ottawa Town 30 Miles from Miſſilimakinak, who without any Delay ſat off armed to Miſſilimakinak, and inquired into the Reaſon of the Chippeways Behaviour.   The latter had nothing to ſay hut that a few Days before the Blow, they received Belts of Wampᵐ from Pontiac, the Ottawas' Chief at Detroit, in conjunction with yᵉ Chiefs of their Nation living there, informing them of the Rupture with the Engliſh, and deſiring them to cut off Miſſilimᵏ. The Ottawas were ſurpriſed and chagreend and inſiſted upon the Chipways delivering up the Priſʳˢ, &c.
The latter to reconcile themſelves with the Ottawas, made up a Heap of Goods and put Mr. Laſſley & 2 Soldiers by them as their Share of the Prey, but they would not accept of it, and demanded all the Priſʳˢ.   The Chipways at laſt gave way and delivered over Mr. Laſſley and the Soldiers and demanded a Ranſom for the Traders, which they agreed to, and being every one exchanged they took them into their

This

1763.
June.
20

This Morning the Commanding Officer gave the Jefuift fome Memorandum of what he fhould fay to the Indians & French at Michilimackinac, as alfo to Capt. Etherington, as he did not choofe to carry a Letter faying that if he was afk'd by the Indians if he had any he would be oblig'd to fay yes, as he never told a lie in his life. He gave him a Belt to give to the Ottawas there, defiring him to tell them that he was very well pleaf'd with their not meddling in an Affair that muft end in their Ruin.

That if they fend their Prifoners to Montreal, it will convince the General of their good Intentions for which they will be probably well rewarded.

To give his Compliments to Mr. Langlad and Mr. Farli and thank them for their good Offices which he exhorts them to continue. To defire them to try and prevent as much as poffible all Commerce with our

Care and afterwards efcorted them fafe to this Place. The Officers and Traders can not fay enough of the good Behaviour of thefe Ottawas and Genl Gage is refolved to ufe and reward them well for their Behaviour. As Capt. Etherington is going to Gen. Amherft, you will doubtlefs hear the Particulars of the whole Affair. By what I can find none but the Chipeways at Miffilimk and thofe of the fame Nation & Ottawas at Detroit, are concerned in the prefent Breach. All the reft of the weftern Nations, and even fome Chipways living at the Falls of St. Mary would not engage or receive the Belts fent by Pontiac, and on the contrary are very well inclined to our Intereft, in particular the Nations living at La Bay, and the Sioux, who are always at War with the Chipways; and if the Indns now here (among whom there are fome other Nats as they come here in behalf of 8 Nats to the weftward who affure us of their Friendfhip) leave this fatisfied; it may be of infinite Service wch I intend to reprefent to Gen. Gage, and I believe you will approve of making them handfome Prefents as an Encouragement for their good Behaviour, and the only Means of chaftifing thofe villainous Nations who are the Occafion of this unhappy Event. * * *" —*MSS. of Sir William Johnfon,* vol. vii.

The Circumftances of the Capture of Michillimackinack, have been related with great Minutenefs by Alexander Henry, an Eye witnefs, who narrowly efcaped the Maffacre.—*Henry's Travels.*

Enemies

Enemies, above all Ammunition & Arms. That he authorizes Mr. Langlad to Command in the Fort according to the Orders given him by Capt. Etherington till further Orders.

To defire Capt. Etherington to try to advertife the Governor of Montreal of what has happened as foon as poffible, and to fend back all Merchants that may be on the way, Englifh or French, if they find from Circumftances of Affairs it is neceffary. To tell him all the News that he has heard from us that might be depended upon regarding the Pofts that has been furpriz'd and murdered, and that the diffinitive Treaty was fign'd at London the 20th of February according to the Articles of the Sceffation of Arms.

This Day we heard that fome Shawanees were ariv'd at the Hurons who fay that all this Nation (except a few who watch the Motions of the Army near Fort Pitt) are feveral Leagues below on the Ohio, who remain there to intercept the Army that is coming from Foit Pitt.

That upon their receiving the Belt, they were order'd to ftrike againft the Englifh, upon which they commenc'd by killing fifteen Merchants that was amongft them in different Towns.

Yefterday a Saggina that was in the Fort with the Puttawattamees was here & rec^d a Belt from the commanding Officer which he was to prefent to the Nation to tell them that it was his Advice that they fhould remain quiet as they faid they had done, as thofe that enter'd in the War wou'd furely be ruined in the End. Some few Shots fir'd to day at the Veffel at a great Diftance. A Sortie was made to day to cut down & burn fome Pickets between Mr. Babies & the Fort. The Garrifon lay upon their Arms.

This Morning fir'd two Guns down the River, being

22

6

ing

ing inform'd that the Veffel was there.   Made a Sortie
and pull'd down a good many Pickets and cut an
Orchard that was near the Fort.

At eleven o'Clock about fifty Indians came to Mr.
Babies and fir'd brifkly at the Veffel and Fort, they
kill'd one Man on board the Veffel & wounded another.

Two Hours after which they went over the River
and the Hurons join'd them & the Puttawattamies to
attack the Veffel, but we do not know yet whether
the Veffel is there, or wheather that was their real Defign.   The Garrifon lay on the Ramparts.

23   This Day a few Shot were fir'd at the Fort and
Veffel as ufual.

This Evening we were inform'd that the Veffel was
not at the Mouth of the River, but that the Indians
thought fhe was and went & made a kind of an En-
trencht at the Ifle au Deinde[42] where the Channel is
narrow in order to fire upon her as fhe paff'd.   The
Garrifon lay on the Ramparts.

24   Some few Shots were fir'd at the Fort this Morning.
Capt. Hopkins with twenty Men made a Sortie this
Afternoon, imagining there was fome few Indians in
the neighbouring Houfes but did not find any.   The
Garrifon lay on the Ramparts.

25   A few Shot fir'd as ufual at the Veffel & Fort to day.
The Garrifon lay on the Ramparts.

26   [Sunday.]   This Day Pondiac went to Mafs on the
other Side of the River & after it was over he took
three Chairs that belong'd to the People for himfelf and
his Guard to ride in to look for Provifion making the
French his Chair men.   He gave Billets to the People
for their Cattle fign'd with his Mark, with the Imita-

---

[42] Turkey Ifland, on the eaft Side   of the main Channel, and now included in Canada.

tion

tion of a Coon drawn on the Top of each Billet.[43] 1763.
Nothing Extraordinary. The Garrifon lay on the June.
Ramparts.

Pondiac fent another Meffage to the Commandant 27
telling him there was nine hundred Indians affembled
at Michilimackinac, and that as he had Compaffion on
him defir'd him to furrender himfelf, that the Garrifon
wou'd be well uf'd, but if he waited till thofe Indians
ariv'd he wou'd not be anfwerable for the Confequences.
That the Roads were all fhut up round us and we
cou'd receive no Succour.

To which the Commandant anfwer'd as he had done
before, that he wou'd not give him an Anfwer to any
thing he afk'd till he fent back Capt. Campbelle and
Lieut. McDougal, whome he kept contrary to all the
Laws of even Savages. That he might fave himfelf
the Trouble of fending any more for he wou'd not
anfwer to any thing till thefe two Gentlemen were return'd. Soon after Pondiac fent Word by one that
was paffing, that he had too great a Regard for Capt.
Campbell & McDougal than to fend them to the Fort,
for if he did that, as the Kettle was on the Fire he
fhou'd be oblig'd to boil them with the reft.

A few Shot fir'd at the Fort and Veffell as ufual.
The Garrifon lay on the Ramparts.

This Afternoon at five o'Clock we were inform'd 28
that the Scooner[44] enter'd the River at 10 this Morn-

[43] Thefe Bills of Credit were drawn on Birch bark, and were promptly redeemed by Pontiac. Rogers ftates that they bore the figure of an Otter. The great Indian Chieftain was evidently affifted to the Idea by fome of the Canadians. The Contribu-tions were all collected at the Houfe of Meloche near Parent's Creek, and a vain and conceited old French-man, named Quilleriez, acted as Commiffary.——*Parkman's Pontiac*, 225.

[44] This was the Schooner *Glad-wyn* that had failed for Niagara on the 21ft of May, and was now re-turning with Lieut. Cuyler and the

ing

1763.
June.

ing; at 6 she came in Sight after paffing the Ifle au Deinde where there was at leaft 160 Indians hid in Holes who fir'd upon her all the while at a little Diftance, as the Channel is not above a hundred Yards wide. The Wind failing her she drop'd Anchor about four Miles from the Fort.

A few Shot were fir'd to day at the Veffel & Fort as ufual. The Garrifon lay on the Ramparts.

As it was imagin'd the Indians wou'd attack the Scooner, the Commanding Officer made a Feignt as if he wou'd land fome Troops in Batteaux which the Indians hearing fo alarm'd them that they guarded the Edge of the River and dropp'd their Intention of attacking the Scooner.

29

The Wind contrary all Day till about 6 o'Clock, when it came a little favorable for about Half an Hour, of which the Scooner profited, weighing Anchor and coming in Sight of the Fort beyond the Huron Village.

This Day we heard that the Indians that went from this about twenty Days ago had taken Prefque Ifle, that they loft three Men there, that the Way they took it was by fetting fire to a fmall Houfe that was clofe to the Fort & which communicated the Fire to it, that they kill'd but three, & the Officer with feveral Prifoners was given to the Nations near that Place.[45]

remainder of his Company, together with fuch Troops as could be fpared from Niagara, in all numbering about fifty Men. To encourage an open Attack from the Indians who fwarmed upon the Shores of the River and the Iflands which divided its Channel, the greater Portion of her Men were kept out of Sight, ready to appear at a moment's Notice.—*Parkman's Pontiac*, 253.

[45] The Fort at Prefque Ifle, was a large Block-houfe of folid Timber, the upper Story projecting on all Sides and roofed with Shingles. It ftood on the Shore of Lake Erie, a little below the prefent bufinefs Part of Erie, Pa. It was affailed on the Morning of June 15th, by 200 Indians, chiefly from around Detroit, and after a Refiftance of three Days, which prefents few Parallels in defpe-

This

This Day a few Shot fir'd from over the River, &c., as ufual. The Indians guarded the River fide to night fearing a Sortie. The twenty-fifth at Night it was fo Cold here that there was a very white Froft. The Garrifon lay on the Ramparts.

At 12 o'Clock the Wind fprung up favourable for the Scooner when fhe weigh'd Anchor and reach'd this about 3, with a Detachment of twenty-two Men from the 30th Reg.ᵗ and Lieut. Cuyler and twenty-eight Men of Capt. Hopkins's Comp.ʸ of Rangers, with 150 Barrels of Provifion and fome Ammunition. Lieut. Cuyler informs us that Prefque Ifle was burn'd the 22d Inftant after being attacked three Days.

30

We were inform'd this Evening that Pondiac had been demanding of the Inhabitants to affemble to dig Trenches, that if they refuf'd it he wou'd put them to the Sword. The Hurons fir'd upon the Scooner all the while fhe was paffing and a great Number from Pondiacs Camp affembled at Mr. Babies & fir'd at the Boats that went & came from her after fhe came to an Anchor.

One Serjeant and four Men were wounded in the Scooner a coming up the River. The Garrifon lay on the Ramparts, except thofe that came in the Scooner, who lay in their Quarters.

The Garrifon was employ'd this Morning in unload-ing & puting Ballaft on board the Scooner. Mr. St. Martin & his Family came into the Fort to day, he being inform'd that the Hurons intended to take him to their Town to interpret for them. This Afternoon

rate Labor and unavailing Courage, the little Garrifon under Enfign Chriftie furrendered on Condition that they fhould be allowed to with-draw to the nearest Poft. With Characteriftick difregard of this Treaty, the unfortunate Men were feized and fent Prifoners to Detroit.

Chriftie was brought in by the Hurons and furrendered with feveral other Prifoners, July 9th.

the

the Puttawattamees came with a Flag to fpeake about giving up their Prifoners, five of whom they faid they had at their Village and whom they promif'd to bring in the next Day.

The Commandant recommended to them to bring them in as foon as poffible & retire to their Villages, as he fhould now make Sorties with great Bodies of Men, and if he fhould meet with them fhould treat them as Ennemies as it was not poffible for him to diftinguifh the Nations one from another.

A few Shot were fir'd to day at the Fort & Veffels. The Garrifon lay on the Ramparts.

2   At three o'Clock this Morning Lieut. McDougal with an Albany Trader ariv'd at the Fort, having made their Efcape from the Indians; about Half an Hour afterwards, another Prifoner ariv'd at the Scooner that made his Efcape from the Hurons, who had been taken with one Crawford a Trader fome Time ago.[46] Lieut. McDougal inform'd us that the Council the Indians held yefterday to demand the French to join them & make Trenches, which was promif'd by one in the Name of all the young People. A Party was fent out to Mr. St. Martins Houfe to cover a working Party near the Fort, which the Indians came to fire upon, and upon our fending out a Reinforcement all the Hurons croff'd the River & came running up as far as Mr. Gamelins and after firing a few Shot at the Fort went back.

This Morning took Poft in the two Block Houfes on the Hight that commands the Fort, and from which a Chief of the Saggina's was wounded in paffing by the Edge of the Woods an Hour after.

This Evening we were inform'd that Pondiac had

[46] Crawford's Capture is related in this Diary for May 20. See p. 11.

taken

taken away Mr. Navarre, Mr. Hecotte and all the
Heads of Familys on that Side of the Fort, but no
body knew for what.

This Evening threw a Shell to try a Mortar that we
had enlarg'd about Half an Inch. All the Garrifon
except the old Guard lay on the Ramparts.

This Day Mr. Navarre wrote a Line to the Com- 3
mandant informing him that the Inhabitants were
oblig'd to write to him in Pondiacs Name for the laft
Time to furrender the Fort, and to let him know that
if he wou'd not give it up they wou'd oblige all the
Inhabitants to take up Arms. Accordingly Mr. Louis
Campo came in with the Meffage in the Evening, and
at the fame Time afk'd Permiffion to come into the
Fort, which the Commandant agreed not only to him
but every one that cou'd bring Provifion with them.
Mr. Babie & Mr. Recme who liv'd oppofite the Fort
came in with their Familys between eleven & twelve
at Night, abandoning all they had except a few Move-
ables that they brought with them.

All the Garrifon lay on the Ramparts except twenty
Men that were finifhing a fmall Ditch round the Fort.

This Day the Commandant collect'd the Inhabitants
of the Fort and read the Articles of Peace to them &
fent a Copy of it over to the Prieft on the other Side
of the River.

This Morning early made a Sortie with thirty Men 4
to cover a Party to bring in fome Powder & Lead that
was in Mr. Babies Houfe, after which we deftroy'd an
Entrenchment that the Indians had made, from which
they annoy'd us. The Indians being advertif'd that
we was out came down and Capt. Hopkins was fent
out with a Party of twenty Men more, who with nine
or ten Frenchmen and the Party that was firft out,
purfued them as far as it was fafe ; we took one Scalp
and

and wounded two or three more,[47] we had one Man wounded.   While we were at Dinner Dr. Paulli enter'd the Fort having made his Efcape in open Day light, by whome we were inform'd that the Indian we kill'd this Morning was the Son of the moft confiderable Chiefs of the Chippewas, and that we only wounded another.   That upon their Arrival at the Camp he was inform'd that they were gone to look for Capt. Campbelle to kill him, upon which he form'd a Refolution to attempt to fave himfelf.   He was dreff'd fo like an Indian, his Hair being cut and painted in their Fafhion that no body knew him when he was brought in.   This Evening we were inform'd that there was 140 Frenchmen gathered at the Hurons who had made an Agreement to defend one another againft all Ennemies.   Mr. Navarre publifhed the Articles of Peace both to the French & Indians.

The French were affembled to day by orderd of the Commandant, who all rejoic'd to take up Arms to the Amount of about forty, and chofe Mr. Sterling to com^d them.

The Garrifon lay on the Ramparts.   Yefterday we wounded an Indian with a Grape fhot from the Veffel behind the Breaftwork at Mr. Babies Houfe.

5   This Morning Mr. Labute came into the Fort, and inform'd us that as foon as the Chippewas were inform'd that we had kill'd the Son of their great Chief they went to Pondiac and told him that he was the Caufe of all their ill look, that he cauf'd them to enter

[47] The Sortie of this Day was led by Lieut. Hay.   One of his Men had long been a Prifoner with the Indians and had acquired in fome Degree their ferocious Habits. Coming up to a wounded Savage, he tore off his Scalp and fhook it with an exulting Cry towards the Enemy.   This Act coft the unfortunate Major Campbell his Life.— *Parkman's Pontiac*, p. 260.

into

into the War and did nothing himfelf, that he was very brave in taking a Loaf of Bread or a Beef from a Frenchman who made no Refiftance, but it was them that had all the Men kill'd and wounded every Day, & for that Reafon they wou'd take that from him which he intended to fave himfelf by in the End, then went and took Capt. Campbelle, ftrip'd him, & carried him to their Camp, where they kill'd him, took out his Heart & eat it reaking from his Body, cut off his Head, and the reft of his Body they divided into fmall Pieces.

He likewife inform'd us that in a Quarter of an Hour after Mr. Paulle made his Efcape upwards of a hundred Ottawas left their Camp in fearch of him.

This Evening we were inform'd that the Ottawas found one of their Men dead in the Edge of the Woods oppofite the Fort, who we fuppofed muft have been kill'd from one of the Cavaliers. The Garrifon lay on the Ramparts.

This Morning we were inform'd that we kill'd three Indians and wounded one in the Affair of yefterday.

At 12 o'Clock the Commandant fent the Sloop up to Pondiacs Camp under the com^d of Capt. Hopkins and Enfign Paulli, but the Wind being very weak they had Time to remove almoft all their things out of their Cabans & fend their Women and Children away before fhe ariv'd, however they fir'd near fifty Cannon at thofe that were there, and threw feveral Shells amongft them, we have not heard what Number was kill'd or wounded.

The Puttawattamees came with a Flag while the Sloop was battering their Camp, and after telling the Comm^t that they had heard the Peace between the French and us proclaim'd, & that they believ'd it, and the feveral Chiefs with their Bands were gone & going

6

to

to leave Pondiac, they afk'd him to give them the Indian we had for two of our Prifoners that they wou'd
bring in.   Upon which the Commandant told them
that he wou'd ftill ftand to what he had told them before
with regard to changing Prifoners, that notwithftanding
all they had promif'd the laft Time they were with
him, they went down the River and fir'd againft the
Scooner when fhe was coming up, and a few Days before ftole two Horfes from him, notwithftanding all
which, to fhow that he pitied them if they wou'd bring
in all their Prifoners & the Horfes, & promife not to
do any more Mifchief either to the French or Englifh,
as we were now one, he wou'd give up the Indian he
had, and wou'd recommend them to the General, but
if they made the leaft Difficulty in it he wou'd not hear
them any more and they muft take the Confequences
of his Difpleafure, upon which they hung their Heads
and faid they found every thing that he had told them
to be true, and could not deny what they were accuf'd
with, and not only promif'd to do all he afk'd of them,
but that none of their Nation was to come nearer the
Fort than Mr. Campo's Mill, about a Mile from it.

Pondiac who always told the French that we were
all dead Men that were in the Fort, cou'd not help
acknowledging to day that we were come to life & that
he was ruin'd.   The Garrifon lay on their Arms.

7   This Day the Puttawattamees came with a Flag for
a Belt of Wampam that the Commandant promif'd
them to carry to the reft of their Nation at St. Jofephs
& to the Miamees to tell them what they had done &
how much they were pitied by the Commandant whofe
Advife they muft always follow; which Belt they got
with a Letter to the Interpreter there defiring to tell
the Indians what he had promif'd the Puttawattamees
here as they were the firft that offer'd to make Peace,
                                                    viz.

viz. if they continued quiet for the Future and minded their hunting he would recommend them to the General, who he made no doubt wou'd forgive them, as he be- liev'd they had no hand in the War, further than that fome of their young men were led into it before they knew what they were doing.

The Hurons came at the fame Time and told the Commandant that neither they nor the Puttawattamees knew any thing of this Affair at the Commencement, for Pondiac never confulted them about it until he had got fuch a Number of Men together that over- power them both, and then he told them his Defign & threatened them that if they would not join with him he would cut them to pieces. That notwithftanding which they never did any thing but fire one Day againft the Fort except a Band or two of their young Men whome they cou'd not then command.

The Commandant told them he believ'd it, and afk'd them if they did not now fee that every thing he told them was true, which they cou'd not deny. He then promif'd them the fame he had done to the Puttawat- tamees, if they would give up all their Prifoners & behave well for the Future. He told them he cou'd not make Peace with them, but as he told the Putta- wattamees wou'd recommend them to the General.

They promif'd to do all he defir'd of them, but told him it wou'd take them two or three Days, as all the Prifoners that were adopted in the Room of the People they had loft muft be given up by the Confent of thofe that had them, as they were given to them by the Nation.

We imagine that the Reafon of the Hurons coming to day was in Confequence of the Commandants fend- ing the Sloop yefterday to batter the Camp of the Ottawas & Chippewas, by which they faw how much they

1763.
July.
they were in our Power. The Garrison lay on the Ramparts.

8

All quiet to day except a few Shot being fir'd as usual at the Fort & Vessel at a great Distance. Several of the principal Inhabitants brought in their Goods yesterday & to day, and one Maisonville brought five Pittiaugers[48] loaded with 10,000 weight of Lead & Peltry into the Fort tho the Indians knew he was coming with it; if it had fallen into their hands it wou'd have been a fine Prize, but he being resolute & acquainted with their Manners & Customs took such Opportunitys that he ariv'd safe. He was at Outattanon when it was taken. The Garrison lay on the Ramparts.

9

This Morning six of the Huron Chiefs came in and brought Ensign Christie, a Soldier of the R. A. Rangers, a Woman & Child and five other Prisoners, and after telling the Commandant that they were drawn into the War before they knew where they were and many things to the same Purpose of what they had told him the 7th Instant, they ask'd him if it was not advisable for them to retire until such Time as we receiv'd Succours enough to assist them in case they should be attack'd, which he told them to do, and when the Army ariv'd desir'd them to come back that they might show their Sincerity.

They intended to go and join the Puttawattamees & build a kind of Stockade upon the River Huron to defend themselves against the Ottawas in case they should declare War against them. All quiet to day. The Garrison lay on the Ramparts.

10

Last Night at twelve o'Clock the Enemy made a large Float with Four Batteaus, which they fill'd with Faggots, Birtch Bark & Tar, and other Combustibles

---

[48] Perigua, a narrow Ferry boat, carrying two Masts and a Lee-board.—*Webster's Dict.*

which

which they brought into the Middle of the Stream about
a Half a Mile above the Veffels & fet on Fire, but the
Veffels being properly moor'd let go one of their Cables and fheer'd off from it, letting it pafs at about a
hundred & fifty Yards Diftance.

This we fuppofe was not entirely the Invention &
Work of Indians.

At 4 o'Clock fome of the Miamee Indians came
within three hundred Yards of the Fort with a Flag,
with an Intention to fpeake to the Commandant about
one Levy they had Prifoner, but not daring to come
any nearer they fent in a Lift of Things by a Frenchman that he had promif'd them if they wou'd give him
up. But the Commandant fent them Word he wou'd
not give them any thing.

The Garrifon lay on the Ramparts. Not a Shot
fir'd to day.

This Day the Hurons brought in the Goods (that 11
had fallen to the Share of three or four Bands)
that belong'd to Chapman & Levy & others, as alfo a
Panee that had been adopted in the Family of one
Babi, which was a very extraordinary thing, as they
feldom give up a Prifoner that is adopted.

Yefterday Pondiac was at the Huron Village with
fifteen of his beft Warriors compleatly arm'd to frighten
them, but it had no effect with Babi & Theata & two
or three other Chiefs as appeared from their Teftimony
to day. They told the Commandant that they had
not yet brought the reft of the Nation to Reafon, but
hop'd in a little Time to do it, when they wou'd give
up their Prifoners & their Merchandife; they alfo told
the Commandant the Name of a Frenchman who had
bought a gold Watch of them for 2000 Wampam.

The Commandant told them that if they cou'd not
bring the reft of the Nation to do as they did they
muft

1763.
July.

muft abandon them, as by & by when the Army came it wou'd be too late for them to make any offers.

We heard to day that the Miamee Indians were gone off with Mr. Levy.

This Night & between 12 & one o'Clock the Indians fent down another large fire Float which paff'd without doing any Damage.   They had made two, but Capt. Hopkins, who was on board the Sloop, fir'd a Cannon at them as foon as he perceiv'd the firft & frightened them fo that they jump'd out of their Cannoes & let the other go without being light'd, which we tow'd on fhore.   The Garrifon lay on the Ramparts.

12   This Morning the Puttawattamees came again with Mr. Chapman, one Crawford & another Prifoner of Capt. Hopkin's Company, & promif'd to bring the reft as foon as they arriv'd.   Accordingly at 4 in the Afternoon they came with four Royal Americans two of the Rangers & one of Mr. Crawford's Men, & demanded their Brother, but the Commandant told them what he told them before, that when they brought in all the Prifoners he would let him out, knowing by our Prifoners that they had fome more, they promif'd to bring them the next Day or as foon as they cou'd be got together, & wou'd bury every thing that had paffed in their next Speech.

They brought an Ottawa with them which the Commandant was inform'd of, and upon enquiry found that he came to fee where the Fort was moft acceffable, that they might fet Fire to it, upon which he told the Puttawattamees that they had an Ottawa with them. They then feeing he was difcover'd faid he was left with them by a Band that was gone home, to bring them the News of the finifhing their Peace with us, but the Command^t told them if he let him out again
                                                        the

the Ottawas would laugh at him & defir'd them to afk
him in cafe he fhou'd fend one of his to their Camp if they thought their Chiefs wou'd not do the fame.

He then defir'd the Interpreter to tell them that he wou'd not ufe him as they had done Capt. Campbelle & the reft of our Prifoners, but would guard him for the Security of the reft until they brought them all in.

At 4 o'Clock this Afternoon the Scooner fet fail for Niagara, but the Wind failing fhe drop'd Anchor about 4 Miles off.

Since the Proclamation of the Peace, the French that were in the Fort were put under the Command of Mr. Sterling. The Garrifon lay on the Ramparts.

This Morning at about Half paft two, our outlying 13 Centrys fir'd upon two or three Indians that were cralling to the Fort, but one of them being a Frenchman & afraid got up and run away, calling out Je fuis François, at which Time the Indians fir'd at them & fhot him through the Body, but he is not yet dead.

At one o'Clock the Puttawattamees came in with a white Belt and made many Profeffions of Friendfhip, but their chief Errant was to try to get the Ottawa that the Commandant detain'd yefterday. But the Commandant told them they wou'd do better if they wou'd not even fpeake to that Nation, as they only fought their Ruin.

They promif'd to bring in all the Prifoners they had to the Number of fix belonging to their Village if the Commandant would give them their Man, which he told them he would do, as he thought they were fincere.

They gave him a white Belt as a Token of their Fidelity & Friendfhip & he promif'd them another when they came back, as he had not any then made that was proper. The Garrifon lay upon the Ramparts.

This

    This Day an Ottawa from Michilimackinac came into the Fort and after a long Story was going to say something about the Indian that the Commandant detain'd the 12 Inftant, but he finding what he was going to say told him something that ftop'd him from making any Demands. All quiet. The Garrifon lay on the

15

Ramparts.

    This Day one Clermont who was formerly Major in the Militia came into the Fort and inform'd the Commandant that moft of the young Men in his Departm^t were going to Illinois, and afk'd if he thought proper to fend an Order to them not to leave the Settlement without his Permiffion (though he had already given a general one) which the Commandant did with Power to him or any of the Officers of Militia to bring them back with a Party of Men in cafe they fhould go off. This Day we were inform'd that the Ottawas & Chippawas had quarrel'd and were going to feparate.

16

All quiet. The Garrifon lay on their Arms.

    The 13 Inftant the Wind blew frefh at N. W. and continued till the 14th when it was eafterly till the Evening fhe came about wefterly and blew frefh all the next Day and to day S. W. fo that we imagin'd the Scooner muft have been at Niagara fome Time laft Night, or at furtheft to day.

    All quiet to day. We heard this Morning that the Ottawas were encamp'd on a Plain about a League off.
The Garrifon lay on the Ramparts.

    This Afternoon we were inform'd that the Indians had broke down two Barns to make fix large Rafts, which they were to tie together to burn the Veffel but they did not fend them. At 11 o'Clock two Frenchmen came to the Fort for Arms & Flints, informing us that the Jefuift had fent Word from the other Side of the River that the Hurons & Puttawattamees intend

tend to fall upon the French on the south-weft Side of
the Fort. But they did not. The Garrifon lay on
the Ramparts.

Yefterday the Wind S. W. to day N. E. This Day
we were inform'd that the Float they were making was
300 Foot long. We were alfo inform'd that all the
young Men towards the Grofs Point intended to go
off to the Illinois as they were afraid of being hang'd.

18

At about 11 o'Clock fome Ottawas came down oppofite the Sloop and call'd out to them feveral Times
to go over to them with fome Rum, &c. which they
anfwer'd. When the Garrifon call'd all was well, they
were very angry & fir'd over the River, which the
People on board obferving fir'd three or four Mufquets
in return, & by Accident wounded one of them. The
Garrifon lay on the Ramparts.

This Day about fixty Indians as neer as we cou'd
guefs, came within about 350 Yards of the Fort in
fome Orchards and fir'd upon the Fort. We threw a
Shell amongft them but unluckily it did not break,
which gave them great Joy by their crying; however
we prepar'd another, and while they were taking the
firft one up we fir'd it & it fell directly amongft them
& burft about three foot from the Ground, and as they
run away fir'd another after them, but have not yet
heard wheather any of them was kill'd or wounded,
tho every body imagin'd there was, as they went off
without making one Cry.

This Evening we were inform'd that the Enemy
were making twenty-four Rafts of about 30 Foot long
each, four of which were finifh'd. The Garrifon lay
on the Ramparts.

This Day we fited up a large Batteau with a Patta-
raroe that carried a three pound Ball.

We were inform'd that there was one Indian wounded

8   with

with the Shell yefterday. The Garrifon lay on the Ramparts. The Wind wefterly & frefh.

21　　This Day fitted up a fecond Batteau as the one mentioned yefterday. The Wind S. W. all Day & pretty frefh. The Garrifon lay on the Ramparts.

22　　This Morning Mr. L. Campo inform'd us that about the Middle of June the Ottawas of Michilimackinac brought off the Garrifon at LaBay,[49] without doing any further harm than killing one Man, who was kill'd by the Chippewas; the Renards[50] and Folls a voines[51] Nations came with them to Michilimackinac, but finding them well difpof'd turn'd back.

The Ottawas of Michilimackinac fay that they brought off Mr. Gorrel & his Garrifon fearing the Chippewas wou'd kill them. The Wind S. W. all Day & pretty frefh. The Garrifon lay on the Ramparts.

23　　The Wind S. W. and frefh the moft part of the Day. The Commandant & feveral Officers went out of the Fort, fome on Horfeback & fome on Foot, at whom

[49] The Poft at Green Bay, was then garrifoned by Lieut. Gorell, who, upon receiving a Letter from Captain Etherington of Michillimackinack, informing him of the Events at that Place, and advifing him to withdraw and join him, fummoned the neighboring Indians, ftated to them that the public Service required him to leave them for a while, and committing the Fort to their Care during his Abfence, he departed.

The Dacotahs were hereditary Enemies to the Ojibwas, and in Cafe of Hoftility would have been active Auxiliaries of the Englifh.—*Parkman's Pontiac*, 321.

[50] Renards, the Foxes. This Tribe belonged to the Ottawa Confederacy and numbered about 320 Warriors.—*Sir William Johnfon's Report*, 1763.

[51] The Volles Avoines (Wild Oat) Tribe, according to Sir Wm. Johnfon's Report to the Board of Trade, dated Nov. 18th of this Year, numbered 110 Warriors, and formed a Part of the Ottawa Confederacy. In 1736, they numbered 160 Warriors, refided North of Lake Michigan and bore as their armorial Device the large tailed Bear, the Stag and a Kilion (a Species of Eagle), perched on a Crofs.—*N. Y. Col. Hift.*, vii, 582, ix, 1055.

the

the Indians fir'd a good many Shot but without doing
Execution. The Garrifon lay on the Ramparts.

The Wind S. & S. W. the moft part of the Day.
This Day the two Batteaux were fent up the River to
look at the Situation of the Enemys Camp & try to
bring off any Cannoes or Fire Floats that might be convenient, but there was none to be come at without running a Rifk of lofing more Men than they were worth;
however they oblig'd them to throw away their Ammunition, as they lin'd the Sides of the River & fir'd very
brifkly from each Side without even wounding a Man.
The Batteaux now falling down with the Stream & then
rowing up again, on purpofe to draw their fire, as we
were well inform'd they had not much Ammunition.

24

This Day we were inform'd that there was about 70
Chippawas ariv'd from Michilimackinac, among whome
were 5 of the Foles a voines but not one Ottawas.
The Garrifon lay on the Ramparts.

The Wind S. & S. wefterly all Day, but not ftrong.
Nothing Extraordinary to day. The Garrifon lay on
the Ramparts.

This Morning Mr. Nauvarre fent in fome Letters
that were brought from the Illinois in confequence of
fome that were wrote by the Inhabitants of this Place
fome Time in May. The Meffengers alfo brought
fome for Pondiac.

This Morning were inform'd that yefterday there
was a Council at the Huron Village with the Shawanees that are come; that one Andrew, a Huron who
undertook to go to Fort Pitt fome Time ago, came
with them & fays he was hinder'd by them to go on,
that he was at Venango when it was taken & that all
the Garrifon was put to death without Exception; it
was taken in the fame Manner with the reft, fifteen
went in to fpeak to the Commandant & forty remain'd
                                                    without

1763. without, & while they were in Council the forty rush'd
July. in & put the Garrison to death.[52]   The Wind westerly.

The People in general seem'd to be a little cast down
on the Return of their Meffengers from the Illinois,
from which we imagin'd they had not receiv'd fuch
Answers as they expected.   The Letters they wrote
were fent from this about the Middle of May, unknown to the Commandant.   The Garrison lay on the
Ramparts.

27   This Morning André the Huron came into the
Fort, who told us that he was not at the taking of
Venango & that the Reafon he faid to the Ottawas
that he was there, was becaufe they would fufpect him,
but that all the Indians that he faw near the Ohio told
him fo.   That he was ftop'd upwards of twenty Days
by different Party's of Indians and that in trying to
crofs a River to get from one of them, he loft his Letters, that he did not dare to go into the Fort as he
wou'd have nothing to fhow, & knowing that the Indians had commenc'd Hoftility's there, altho he was on
the oppofite Side of the River.   He likewife inform'd
us that the Delawares had kill'd all their Prifoners in
confequence of the Prophecy's of one of their Nation
who pretended that he had been to Heaven and was
told by God that they muft put all the English to
death, but not to burn any as was fometimes their
Cuftom, otherwife we fhou'd overcome them.   He alfo
inform'd us that all the Hurons except the Bands of
Babi, Theata & another Chief, with Part of the Put-

---

[52] Venango was garrifoned by a
fmall Party under Lieut. Gordon,
and as every Man within it perifhed,
we have no Hiftory of the Details
except the Narrative of Indians, and
the Traces of its Ruins.   The Men
were all flaughtered on the firft Attack, except Lieut. Gordon, who
was referved for the moft refined
Tortures by Fire that Savage Inge-
nuity could invent.   This done,
they burnt the Place and departed.
—*Parkman's Pontiac,* 337.

tawattamees

tawattamees had fung the War Song again, but that
the Hurons, or Wiandots told the Ottawas that notwithftanding that, they wou'd not fight.

He alfo told the Commandant that as he was fufpected, being fo long away & not being at Fort Pitt,
if he would give him Letters again he wou'd go & return in twenty Days. Upon which the Commandant
told him he did not fufpect him, and as Proof wou'd
fend him again & defir'd him to come the next Day in
the Evening & he wou'd have every thing ready for
him, tho at the fame Time he cou'd not be otherwife
than fufpected, but as he was a very knowing fellow &
had a good deal to fay among the Indians it was thought
beft by the Interpreter and every body that was prefent to try him again, as he might change feeing the
Confidence we put in him, tho he had been acting the
Knave before. The Wind foutherly.

This Day we were inform'd by Mr. Sterling that
Madamoifelle Cuerfiere told him that Godfoy told
Pondiac when he return'd from the Illinois that he
cou'd not fend him any Succours yet as they had heard
by a Spanifh Veffel that the Peace was made, but that
as foon as his Couriers ariv'd that he had fent to New
Orleans if he found the News to be falfe he wou'd fee
what he cou'd do, & defir'd that the Inhabitants fhou'd
not appear in it at all, but keep themfelves quiet.

This Morning fix Frenchmen fet off in a burch
Canoe for Niagara with Letters from the Commandant.
This Evening Andre came in & took the Command-
ants Letters for Fort Pitt. The Wind foutherly.

This Morning at Half paft four o'Clock, it being
very foggy, we heard the Report of feveral Mufquets
& now and then as we thought Swivels at the Huron
Village, which we [thought] to be fome Indians firing
at the Scooner, as fhe might have come that far up the
                                                    River

28

29

1763.
July.   River without our feeing her in the Night, but in
about Half an Hour to our great Surprize, we faw
about twenty Batteaux, which upon their coming near
we found to be Englifh Boats, with a Detach[t] of about
260 Men under the Comm[d] of Capt. Dalyel.[53]   They
came the fouth Side of the Lake & burn'd a fmall
Indian Village near Sandufky that the Indians had
abandoned.   They had fourteen Men wounded in
paffing the Huron Village.

In the Evening we faw fome Fires at the Huron
Town which was faid to be fome Cannoes that they fet
on fire as they were gone away.   It was given out by
the French to Pondiac (as we were inform'd) that it
was not a new Detachment, but that the Commandant
had fent out his young Men as they cou'd under the
Cover of the Fogg, and row'd up the River again to
make them believe it was Succours that ariv'd.   The
Wind S. wefterly all Day.

30   The Wind S. wefterly.   This Morning André fet
off for Fort Pitt.   Nothing Extraordinary to day.
Two Prifoners fav'd themfelves to night from the Indians.

31   This Morning at three Quarters after two a Detach-
ment of 247 Men under the Command of Capt.
Dalyel march'd out with an Intention to furprize the
Indian Camp about three Miles & a half from the
Fort.[54]

[53] James Dalyell (fometimes written *Dalzell*) had been appointed a
Lieutenant in the 60th Regiment or
Royal Americans, early in 1756,
and in 1760 obtained a Company
in the 2d Battalion of the Royals,
or the 1ft Regiment of Foot.   He
perifhed in a brave but indifcreet
Attack upon the Enemy foon after
his Arrival at Detroit, as ftated in
the following Pages.

[54] The following Paragraph had
been written in the MSS. next following this, and erafed:
"It was given out yefterday
Morning by the French that we
intended to attack them, but they

But

But whether the Enemy were inform'd of it or dif-cover'd them in marching out is not known, but when they were within a Half of Mile of their Camp they were fir'd upon by a great Number of Indians from behind Orchards, Fences & Entrenchments that they had pofted themfelves in for that Purpofe, which put them a little in Confufion at firft, but they foon re-cover'd their Diforder and forc'd the Enemy from their Lodgements. They then finding that their Scheme cou'd not be put in Execution, they thought of making the beft retreat they cou'd, the Enemy being twice as numerous as they were, and knowing they cou'd not expect any more Succours from the Garrifon, for which purpofe they took Poft in feveral Houfes that was moft advantagious for to prevent the Enemy as much as poffible from getting between them and the Fort. Capt. Dalyel, who behav'd with all the Bravery in the World, was unluckily kill'd ; after receiving the fire from the Enemy, tho' Capt. Grant beg'd of him either to pufh on immediately, make a retreat without lofs of Time, he remain'd almoft in the fame Place for at leaft three Quarters of an Hour, foon after which he was kill'd, and Capt. Grant then with the Affiftance of the two row Galleys made as good a retreat as was poffible for any body to do, after fending off all the Wounded & all the Dead except feven.

did not know when. Their Reafon for thinking fo was, becaufe we were mending fome old Canoes, but we gave out we fhould not want them in lefs than four or five Days, imagining that News would be car-ried to their Camp with everything elfe, as we never could do anything in the Fort without their knowing; for even if the Gates were fhut and nobody permitted to go out, yet they knew everything we did, as one may fee from the other Side of the River every movement made infide of the Fort. The Detach-ment was three Quarters of an Hour from the Fort before we heard any firing, when it commenced and con-tinued four to five Minutes very heavy, at which Time our People were approaching the Bridge on the Side of the River."

We

1763.   We loft in this Affair, Capt. Dalyel kill'd, Capt.
July.   Gray, Lieut. Luke & Lieut. Brown of the 35th wounded, one Serjeant & 13 Rank & File kill'd and one
Drum^r and 25 wounded. 60 Reg^t one Private kill'd
& feven wounded. 80 Reg^t two kill'd & three wounded. 2 R. A. Rangers 2 kill'd & one wounded, & a
Traders Servant wounded. Total, Officers included,
kill'd & wounded, 61. The Indians fay they had five
kill'd and eleven wounded.[55]

Auguft 1   Laft Night about ten o'Clock a Prifoner was brought
in that was wounded at Mr. Cuylers Affair.

The Wind S. & S. wefterly all Day, and at Night
chang'd all round the Compafs.

This Day we were inform'd that Part of the Hurons
were Encamp'd on the upper End of the Grofs Ifle,[56]
where they had fome Corn, that they had fent their
Chief who was wounded in yefterday's Affair to the
Grand River with a Belt to defire the Puttawattamees
to join them.

This Morning about two o'Clock Mr. Rutherford
ariv'd at the Sloop, having made his Efcape from the
Indians about nine Mile from the Fort, feven of which
he came by Land, when finding a Cannoe he embark'd
in it & came to the Veffel.

Young Mr. Campo brought in the Body of poor
Capt. Dalyel about three o'Clock to day, which was

[55] Parents Creek, ever fince this
memorable Affair called *Bloody
Run*, enters the Detroit River about
a Mile and a Half above the Site of
the Fort, and near its Mouth was
croffed by a narrow wooden Bridge.
The Surface beyond was broken by
Ridges parallel with the Stream,
and Pontiac, forewarned by Canadians in his Intereft, had ample
Time to remove his Camp, and
conceal his Warriors along every
Hollow and behind every Building
and Tree along the Route of the
devoted Band.

[56] An Ifland about twelve Miles
below Detroit and ftill known by
this Name. It is feven Miles long
and about two wide at the wideft
Part.

mangled

mangled in fuch a horrid Manner that it was fhocking 1763.
to human nature; the Indians wip'd his Heart about
the Faces of our Prifoners.

Since the Detachment ariv'd the Garrifon has been
lefs fatigued than before, as inftead of every body lying
[upon] the Works, a Capt. Picket of 80 Men & three
Subalterns took their Place every Night.

The Wind wavering to day, but moftly S. and fouth-   2
wefterly.

Since the laft Sortie the People have brought in
feveral Cattle for the King, & offer'd any thing they
had, which we imagine was partly owing to fome Dif-
orders that the Soldirs committed the 31ft in the Morning by plundering feveral Houfes, and partly as they
fee we are fo ftrong that we can defend ourfelves both
againft the Indians & them, that is to fay to maintain
the Poft without their Affiftance.

The Commandant has not yet been able to get a
Copy of the Letter that the Inhabitants wrote to
the Illinois, nor a Copy of the Anfwer that Mr.
Noiyon fent back to them, by which it appears they
had a great Share in the Affair, tho they try to hide it.

The [Wind] N. Eafterly and pretty frefh. This   3
Day we began to fit up another Batteau for a four
Pownder.

Since the Sortie there has been every Night as we   4
are inform'd at leaft two hundred and fifty Indians difperf'd in Party⁵ round the Fort to watch our Motions.
About two o'Clock about fifteen were feen at a Houfe
about a Quarter of a Mile from the Fort, upon which a
Party was fent out, but whether they were feen in going
out or no we cant tell, but the Indians went off immediately.

This Morning at Half an Hour paft three o'Clock,   5
Capt. Grant with fixty Men of the Picket was fent out

9   to

1763.
Auguſt.
to take Poſt in ſome Houſes near the Fort that the Indians made a Practice of coming to in the Day time, where he reſted till one o'Clock, but none came near enough for him to hurt them.

The Wind S. Eaſterly & pretty freſh.   At four this Afternoon the Scooner appear'd in Sight.

6   This Morning at 8 o'Clock the Scooner anchor'd before the Fort; ſhe brought but eighty Barrels of Proviſion, a good deal of Naval Stores, & ſome Merchandiſe.

At 3 in the Afternoon a Frenchman came in from Michilimackinac which he left 15 Days ago and informs us that Capt. Etherington & his Garriſon, with that of Fort Wm. Auguſtus[57] and all the Engliſh Merchants were gone down to Montreal guarded by the Ottawas, a Detachment of one Subaltern, four Serjeants, four Corporals, one Drummer & ········ as alſo Commodore Lorain with ſixteen Sailors.

This Day unloaded the Scooner & made the Sloop ready to ſail.

7   This Day the Commandant recᵈ a Letter from Capt. Etherington dated at Michilimackinac the 18 July, who with his Garriſon & that of Fort Wm. Auguſtus

[57] This Fort was near the Grand Portage on Lake Superior and ſubſequently became an important Station of the Northweſt Fur Company under the Name of Fort William. Another Fortreſs of this Name ſtood on an Iſland in the St. Lawrence, at the Foot of Sloop Navigation, three Miles below the preſent Village of Ogdenſburgh. This Iſland was named by the French Iſle Royal, and by the Indians Oraconenton. From the Ruins of its Barracks and other Buildings, it is now known as Chimney Iſland. This Iſland was fortified in 1759 under the Direction of Chevalier Levi, and from him was named Fort Levi. In the Summer of 1760, while under the Command of M. Pouchot, it was attacked and reduced by Lord Amherſt and its Name changed to Fort William Auguſtus. This was the laſt Reſiſtance made by the French againſt the Engliſh in Canada.

was

was then going into the Boats to go to Montreal, as
alſo all the Engliſh Merchants, for whome he had obtain'd Permiſſion of the Indians to carry all their Merchandize.

This Morning at two o'Clock Capt. Hopkins and   8
two Subalterns with 60 Volunteers went down in Boats
with an Intent to ſurprize an Indian Caban at the
Puttawattamee Village. We went down undiſcover'd
to the Place we intended to land, and in turning in the
Boats to the Shore the Row Galley which was commanded by Lieut. Abbot being heavy did not follow
ſo near as could be wiſh'd, by which Means, it being
foggy & dark under the Land, ſhe loſt Sight of us and
drop'd down with the Current ſo far that before Capt.
Hopkins got her up again it was broad Day light &
we was diſcover'd & oblig'd to return back without
attempting any thing. The Fogg continued ſo thick
that my Boat & the Row Galley was loſt again; the
Row Galley at laſt threw out her Anchor and lay there
till it began to get clear, but the other Boats cou'd
neither do that nor go to the Shore, as the Enemy
follow'd us on each Side of the River.

The Wind has been up the River ever ſince the   9
Veſſel ariv'd that ſhe cou'd not go from this.

Both Veſſels were made ready to ſail to day, fifteen   10
of the Wounded were put on board the Sloop to be
ſent to Niagara as they cou'd be of no uſe here this
Year, & it ſav'd Proviſion, as alſo fourteen or fifteen
Merchants that had been Priſoners with the Indians.

The Wind ſtraight up the River alday. This Day   11
we were inform'd that the Puttawattamees & Hurons
were all coming back.

This Night one Jacob Taylor a Trader came in,
having made his Eſcape from the Indians.

The Wind almoſt Weſt, the Veſſels cou'd not ſtir.   12
The

1763.   The Wind a little to North of W., the Veſſels weigh'd
August. Anchor at 10 o'Clock & in two Trips got below the
  13   Huron Point, from where they had a large Wind to
         Sanduſky.[58] The Indians did not fire one Gun at them.
  14   This Morning the Wind W. and freſh.
  15   The Wind Weſt and freſh all Day with a good deal

[58] The Arrival of theſe Veſſels was announced to Sir William Johnſon in the following Letter :
" NIAGARA, 24th Auguſt, 1763.

Sir : Being allways glad to ſelebrat all oppertunityes of giving you the earlyeſt Inteligence of any thing perticular intreduces me to trouble you with this.

The Commodore arrived here on the 22d Inſt. and allſo the Schooner and the Sloop from Detroit. By them we have the following Account of the grate Luck and ſafe Arrival of Capt. Duel [Dalyell] and his Armiment at Detroit being ſomewhat remarkable, as the Indians was lying in Ambuſh for him which he knew of, but the Night and Morning that he arived being fogee Weather he got in to the Garriſon without the Knowledge of the Indians, who were ſoon made acquainted with it, not only his Arrival but his Intentions, which was the next Morning he march'd about two Miles Diſtance from the Garriſon being informed of ſome Intrenchments they had there, where he was fired on very warmly by a Party of Indians, as he was croſſing a wooden Bridge which was behind ſome Pickquets, notwithſtanding which the brave and undaunted Capt. Duel [Dalyell] march'd the

Men on to the Breſt work or Trench which the Engliſh ſoon got Poſſeſſion of, and the Indians retreated to another Trench they had ſome Diſtance in the Rear of the Intrenchment where Capt. Duel behaved with the greateſt Courage and Reſolution imaginable, but ſoon told Capt. Grant he was wounded, notwithſtanding which his Bravery in the Command was the ſame as before, but ſome Time after Lieut. McDougle informed Capt. Gray, belonging 55th [35th], that Capt. Duel [Dalyell] was wounded again and dead.   Then Capt. Gray took the Command and being informed that the Indians were ſurrounding them faſt by the Directions of their Sachem Pondeack and takeing Poſſeſſion of the French Houſes. Upon this News the Engliſh thought proper to Retreat. · Some Partys were detached to drive them out and take Poſſeſſion from the Indians, which they ſoon did, at which Time Capt· Gray was wounded taking Poſſeſſion of a Mill, but hope he will recover. Alſo Lieut. Brown of the 55th was wounded at the ſame Time.   Then Capt. Grant had the Command, who marched the Men very regular on the Retrait into the Fort. About fifteen Men with Major Rogers got in a Houſe who was to bring up
of

of Rain.   This Day threw a Coehorn Shell to the other
Side of the River.

16

The Wind weſterly all Day with Rain.   This
Day we were inform'd that Pondiac had given out
that the Commandant only ſent the Veſſels out into the
Lake to make the Indians believe that they went to
Niagara, but he knew better for they neither brought
Proviſions nor Men.   That when they ariv'd oppoſite
the Fort we always ſent two or three Batteaux along
ſide of them full of Men who were all hid except thoſe
that row'd, and as ſoon as they got on board huzza'd,
by which Means we made them believe that we receiv'd
Succours.

17

The Wind ſtill weſterly and N. W. with Rain.
Laſt Night there was 150 of the Enemy within about
three Quarters of a Mile of the Fort, 50 of whome
were conſtantly Centry; the Night was extremely bad.
They themſelves ſay that two or three of them ſwimed
down cloſe to the Fort, but obſerving ſome Soldiers
that was in a Batteaux anchor'd above the Fort with a
Patteraroe[59] in it, to put up their Heads, they went
back as faſt as they cou'd.

the Reare and Cover the Retrate, which was ſoon ſurrounded by the Indians and had no other way to get clear of them but by ſhowing them a clean pair of Heels, which he did, and a Corporal of the 55th had a fair Tryal for, and got ſafe in the Fort.

There is killed and wounded in this Engagement about thirty Engliſh, the Number of Indians is not known.

The have murdered Capt. Duel [Dalyell] in a barbarous Manner by Schelping him, cutting of one of his Arms and one Leg and takeing out his Bowels, his Body was brought in and buried in the Fort.   Laſt Night arrived here ſeventy of the 46th Regt.

I am Sir
Your moſt Humble Serv't.
T. DE COUAGNE.

P. S. By the Priſoners we have Account of the Seneckees, it is ſuſpeéted that they have joyned the Dellawares.

[59] Paterero, or Pederero, a ſmall Cannon mounted as a Swivel.

The

1763.
Auguſt.
18

The Wind N. W. Laſt Night & this Morning before Day the Ottawas chang'd their Camp from behind the Grand Marais to the River Rouge,[60] where they will be very convenient to harraſs any Party that may be coming up; or the Veſſels, as they will have early Intelligence of it, and Time to poſt themſelves in the moſt convenient Places for that Purpoſe.

Laſt Night Mr. Watkins with about eighteen Volunteers lay in Mr. Babi's Houſe as the Indians had paſt it two Nights before in order to try how near they cou'd come to the Fort. But he did not get an Oppertunity of firing upon any of them as there was Cry given as ſoon as he got there, which we imagine to have been one of their Centrys.

This Evening the Commandant recᵈ a Letter from one Waſſong, the Chief of the Chippawas, to this Effect: That if he had a Mind to leave the Fort he might do it peacibly at preſent, but if not that the River would ſoon be ſtop'd up. That he had never yet fought againſt him, for that if he had the Fort wou'd have been burn'd long ago, with a great many threats & very inſolent Expreſſions. The Commandant ſent Word to the Indians that if they had any thing to ſay to come to the Fort; that he knew they cou'd not write & therefore might be impoſ'd on by thoſe that wrote for them, & deſir'd the Meſſenger to tell the French that the firſt that wrote another Letter of that Kind might expect to be hang'd; which we ſuppoſe was in conſequence of ſome Batteaux that were ſent up the River in the Morning to ſee what the Enemy were doing, as it was reported they were making a large Raft.

19

The Wind eaſterly, but not much of it. This Day finiſh'd another Batteau for a four pownder.

[60] The River Rouge empties into the Detroit River from the Weſt, four Miles below the Site of the Fort.

The

The Wind N. eaſterly in the Morning & weſterly in the Afternoon, but not much of it.

20

This Morning at Half an Hour paſt three Capt. Hopkins, Enſign Perry & Enſign Kiggel and forty Men of the Piket, with Capt. Roger & four or five of his Men, & Mr. Watkins & Mr. Cornwell and ſome other Volunteers went to waylay the Road that the Indians generally take to paſs from the Puttawattimy Village to the Camp up the River, to favour which the Commandant ſent up four Batteaux, two with a four Pownder in each, and two with Patteraroes, they went as far as the upper End of the Iſle au Cochon,[61] and drew a good many of the Indians that way, but Capt. Hopkins being diſcover'd return'd without being able to do any thing.

The Wind S. & S. eaſterly, but very little of it. This Day part of the Picket was out about four hundred Yards from the Fort lodg'd in Houſes to try to catch or kill ſome Indians that daily came near the Fort, but their Intelligence was ſo good that they always knew of it and never came near enough. A Woman was wounded through the Arm by Accident at the Door of a Houſe behind which were two Indians.

21

The Wind ſoutherly in the Morning, from 12 till Night S. E. pretty freſh, then more ſoutherly. This Day part of the Picket was out as yeſterday and fir d a great many Shot at the Enemy, but was ſo far off that they cou'd not do any Execution. On their going out they ſaw two Indians whom they follow'd in purſuit of whom we had one Man ſhot through the thigh, for the Indians ran away (as is their Cuſtom) as ſoon as they ſaw our Men, and when they return'd the Indians return'd alſo and generally got a Shot at our Men without expoſing themſelves, however we heard

22

[61] Nearly five Miles from the Fort.

that

that one of the two that ran away this Morning was
ſhot through the Body.

At Half paſt nine this Evening a Negro made his
Eſcape from one Marſacks who had bought him from
the Indians.

23   The Wind S. & S. weſterly all Day.   This Morning we were inform'd that one of the Indians died laſt
Night that was wounded yeſterday & that two others
are wounded.

This Day the Picket was at Mr. Barrois & a little
beyond it ſkirmiſhing with the Indians the moſt Part
of the Day, we fir'd a good many Shells in the Garden
where ſome of them was & fir'd ſeveral Shot through
the Houſes they were in, ſo that we imagine they receiv'd a good deal of Damage.   About Half an Hour
before Sunſet the Party was order'd in, and as ſoon as
the Rear of the Party was well in the Fort they were
impudent enough to come to Mr. St. Martins Houſe
and fir'd ſeveral Shot in at the Gate & ſet Fire to two
or three little out Houſes that we had Poſſeſſion of all
Day, which the Commandant thought ſo inſolent that
he ſent out Major Rogers with the Picket to take
Poſſeſſion again, and upon his appearing the Indians
run away & he remain'd there all Night.   We had
three Men wounded to day.

24   The [Wind] S. & S. weſterly but not much of it;
in the Afternoon Rain, the Wind changing all round
the Compaſs.

This Night the Commandant ſent out an Officer &
thirty Men of the Picket to keep Poſſeſſion of Mr.
Brarrois's Houſe & Barn to protect it & Mr. St.
Martins, which the Indians ſaid they wou'd burn,
which he intended to do till they had thraſh'd their
Corn, &c.   This Day we had two Men wounded, but
one of them very ſlightly.

This

This Day a Bennickee[62] Indian came into the Fort for a Paſs to go to Montreal, being the third time within this five Days ; he ſaid he had been at War againſt the Cherokees, & that his Brother who came with him laſt Winter with Mr. Ferguſon went a hunting when he went away and he had not heard of him ſince. But one ——— an Albany Trader who was taken with one Meldrum between Miamee & Ouiattanon, came in this Evening and inform'd us that he had been four Days in the Woods without any thing to eat, having made his Eſcape from one of the Puttawattamee Villages about forty Miles off, where he heard the Indians ſay that in Capt. Dalyels Affair there was ſix Ottawas, two Chippewas and one Bennickee Indian kill'd, which Bennickee we ſuppoſe to be the Brother of this one that is in the Fort.

At ten this Night the Indians ſet Fire to a ſmall Houſe that we had Poſſeſſion of all Day from which we gall'd them. It was too far from the other Houſes that we had Poſſeſſion of to keep Men in, as they were always liable to be cut off.

This Day in the Afternoon the Indians came to 25 their Poſt & fir'd a good deal at our Men that keep'd Poſſeſſion of Mr. Barrois Houſe &c., but without doing any Harm.

This Morning Mr. Cecote & Mr. Forville came to 26 the commanding Officer in the Name of four of the moſt principal Chiefs of the Ottawas to aſk Mr. Labute to come to ſpeak to them, but Mr. Labute did not chooſe to go, & the Commandant wou'd not order him. In the Afternoon they fir'd a great deal & expoſ'd themſelves more than uſual. At four o'Clock they ſet Fire to Mr. Babi's Houſe which burn'd to the Ground in

[62] Abenaque.

1763. a few Minutes.   This Day we had one Man wounded.
Auguſt. The Wind S. & S. weſterly.

27   The Wind S.   This Morning we were inform'd that
there was one Indian kill'd yeſterday & three wounded.
This Day did not fire ſo much as yeſterday, wounded
one Indian.

28   The [Wind] S. W.   Very little firing to day at the
advanc'd Poſt.

29   The Wind weavering from S. S. E. to W. N. W.
This Day by Accident found two Keys that had been
lately made, one of which open'd one of our ſmall
Gates & the other a large one.   Yeſterday about fifty
Indians ariv'd here, 30 of whom had been oppoſite to
the landing Place 9 Mile up the River, & ſay they ſaw
a great many Engliſh carry'g Proviſion on their Backs
and otherwiſe, are likewiſe inform'd that the Indians
that [went] to Montreal with Mr. Lerond by Pondiacs
leave are come back, who met Cap. Etherington &
Garriſon about 25 Leagues from thence.

30   The Wind chang'd all Day from S. E. to S. & S. S. W.
This Evening we were inform'd that four Hurons
ariv'd from Sanduſky to inform the Indians here that
there was an Army of two thouſand Men between that
& Fort Pitt on their way hither, that the Indians had
been neer enough to fire upon them, & the Engliſh
returning the fire kill'd ſeven of the Miamee Nation.

The Indians fir'd a good deal from their Breaſtwork
at the outlying Picket to day.

31   The Wind chang'd all round the Compaſs.   This
Morning we were inform'd that a Chief of the Miſſeſagys was badly wounded yeſterday.

Sept. 1 The Wind almoſt due Eaſt all Day.   This Day we
were inform'd that the Chief of Miſſeſagys who was
wounded the 30 Auguſt died yeſterday.   This Day
the Nephew of a great Chief of the Ottawas was kill'd

at

at their Retrench^t that they were trying to open again,
as Mr. Brehm deftroy'd it yefterday Morning.

The Wind Eaft & a little to the fouthward of Eaft
all Day. The Indians fir'd a good deal to day at the
advanc'd Picket. .

The Wind a little to the fouthward of Eaft. This
Morning we were inform'd that the Scooner was in
the River near the lowermoft inhabitants & that there
was fome Mohawks in her, as four of them had landed
and fent for Babi^{63} & Theata of the Hurons to come
& fpeake with them & then went on board again.

At one o'Clock the Indians came and fet Fire to a
Windmill about three hundred Yards from the Fort.
At Half an Hour apaft 2 one Mr. Petet & another
Frenchman ariv'd from the Illinois by way of Fort St.
Jofeph, who inform'd us that 28 Days ago Mr. Neyon
the Commandant there had not rec^d the acc^t of the
Peace from Authority but expected it every Day. He
had heard it from New Orleans by an Englifh Mer-
chant that was ariv'd there from Martinico.

That the Oueattanon Indians had been with Mr.
Neyon for Ammunition and he had given them about
three Barrels of Powder & Lead in Proportion, enough
to keep them from ftarving a little while.

The Wind Eaft the moft of the Day. Laft Night
at about 9 o'Clock 340 Indians embark'd in Cannoes
and went to board the Scooner. The Merchants were
on Shore. The Channel where the Veffel lay not being
very wide and Rufhes growing on each Side of it,
they came within a little more than a hundred Yards
of her before they were difcover'd & then rufh'd in at
once upon her furrounding her with Cannoes & Bat-

---

[63] Babie, the Huron Chief, figned Odinghquanooron, and he appears
the Treaty at Fort Niagara, July to have poffeffed confiderable Influ-
18, 1764. His Indian Name was ence among his Tribe.

teaux

teaux and under a very brifk fire attempted to cut
holes in her Stern & the Cable.   The Cable they cut,
but notwithftanding there was but twelve on board,
two of whome Mr. Horfey and another was kill'd
& four wounded at the beginning, they never was able
to board her, but oblig'd to fly with the lofs (as the
French tell us) of eight kill'd & twenty wounded.
When the Commanding Officer was inform'd that there
was Indians on board and but twelve Men, he fent off
an Exprefs with a Letter to Mr. Horfey, but they
did not get down till the Attack began, and confequently cou'd not get on board, and this Morning, the
fifth, when we were inform'd that fhe had been attack'd,
the Commandant fent down four Row Galleys.

5   The Wind S. E.   At 9 o'Clock the Row Galleys
return'd, Capt. Hopkins & about twenty Men including fome Volunteers remain'd on board.

At 11 the Wind fpring up a little & the Schooner
came in Sight and at Half apaft three caft Anchor oppofite the Fort.   She brought 47 Barrals of Flour &
160 of Pork.

6   The Wind S. W.   This Day we heard that the Indians were watching near the Mouth of the River to
pick up thofe that were kill'd.   The Mohawks fay that
the Hurons kept them Prifoners after they went on
Shore, but from all Appearance they are great Rafcals
& came with an Intent to betray the People in the
Veffels.

7   The Wind S. W.   This Day we were inform'd that
feven Indians died of their Wounds.   The Commandant being inform'd by the People in the Schooner
that there was two more Indians coming in the Sloop,
who with thofe that came in the Schooner might have
laid a Scheme to come on board with other Indians
as Friends and endeavour to take her by Treachery,
                                                    thought

thought proper to fend a Man with a Letter to the River Cannard (as if he was going a hunting) with Orders to remain there till the Sloop came into the River, and then to go on board of her and give the Letter to the Commander, to whom he gave Orders for preventing any Treachery that they might think to practice againft him.

This Morning the Commandant was inform'd that 8 it was realy the Intention of the Mohawks to betray the Sloop if they cou'd & for that Purpofe they were gone to the Mouth of the River, upon which the Wind coming about he order'd the Schooner to make ready to fail, and wrote a fhort Letter to the General telling him the Reafon of his being oblig'd to fend her away before he had Time to write all that he intended, and wrote a Letter to the Commander of the Sloop with Orders & Directions how to behave in coming up the River. The Wind N. W. when the Schooner fail'd at Half paft one and continued fo till about Half after four, when it came about to Eaft and continued all Night.

The Wind E. Laft Night at about 11 o'Clock the 9 Indians burn'd the Barn of Mr. Reaume[64] on the other Side of the River with about 1000 Bufhels of Wheat in it, fome Peas & fome Hay.

This Morning we were inform'd that feventy Puttawattamys ariv'd from St. Jofephs.

The Wind S. W. Nothing Extraordinary to day. 10

The Wind wefterly all Day, & at Night blew pretty 11 frefh.

The Wind wefterly. 12

[64] In 1777, one Pierre Reaume was a prominent Settler at Detroit, and the next Year Charles Reaume was a Captain in the Britifh Indian Department at that Place. The latter fettled at Green Bay in 1790, and after holding a civil Office many Years died between 1818 and 1824. —*Firft An. Rep. State Hift. Soc. Wifconfin,* 61.

The

The Wind S. & S. Weſt. This Day we were inform'd that there was a Veſſel ſeen at the Mouth of
the River yeſterday Morning.

One of the Sailors that was wounded in the Scooner
told us yeſterday that the Sloop was going to land 200
Men and Proviſion at Preſque Iſle & was then to return to Niagara for Proviſion for this Place, which if
true is very ſurprizing, as they knew we had but ſix
Weeks Proviſion in Store when ſhe went away, and
the Scooner was ſent loaded with Pork, all to about
forty Barrels of Flour.

14 The Wind S. W. This Day we were inform'd that
forty Puttawattmys were gone to their Village at St.
Joſephs.

15 The Wind W. & S. W. For two or three Days
paſt we have had Accts of the Veſſels being at the
Mouth of the River & of Boats being at Sanduſky.

16 The Wind weſterly. To day we heard that the Indians were making ready their Cannoes to go off.

17 The Wind S. & S. W. Laſt Night a Soldier that
was taken the 29th May coming from Michilimackinac & a Merchant made their Eſcape & came into the
Fort. The Soldier ſays that he was told by a Frenchman that the Reaſon that the People aſk Billets or
Certificates from Pondiac for their Cattle was because
the People in Canada were to pay Half their Loſſes.
That he ſpoke with Aaron the Mohawk, who told him
he was ſent here by Sir William Johnſton to find who
were the Cauſe of the War.

18 The Wind S. & S. W. This Day we were inform'd
that the Ottawas, Puttawattamys & Wiandots were to
go off to morrow. That a Cannoe with ſome Hurons
was ariv'd from the Eaſt End of Lake Erie who ſaid
that they ſaw a Number of Troops embark'd on board
the Sloop and a great Number of Batteaux on their way
hither.
                                                      The

The Wind W. & N. W.   Very freſh all Day & laſt
Night from 8 o'Clock it blew very hard Squawls from
the ſame Quarter with a great deal of Rain.

This Day we were inform'd that the Puttawattamys
were all gone, & that the Ottawas were angry at Pondiac for propoſing to go, & they choſe one Manitoo
for their Chief in his Place.

The Wind W. & N. W., very freſh all Day and   20
very cold for the Seaſon.   Laſt Night twelve Frenchmen got a Paſs for Montreal & took ſome Letters with
them.

The Wind W & N. W. and very Cold.   We were   21
inform'd a few Days ago by Monſʳ Fortville that
Baptiſte Deriverre with his Party who came from the
Illinois with Monſʳ Sabole fought in Conjunction
with the Indians againſt the Veſſel when Mr. Horſey
was kill'd.

The Wind Weſt till 12 o'Clock when it changed to   22
the Eaſtward of South, and continued all Day a light
Breeze, the Air not being ſo cold as it had been for
two or three Days before.   Yeſterday the Indians ſent
word to all the Inhabitants not to offer to go into the
Fort for three Days, and if any came out of the Fort
they were to tell them to go back & inform thoſe
within not come out during that Time, under Pain of
having their Houſes & Barns burnt.

The Wind S. & a little to the Eaſtward of S.   23

The Wind S. E. and E. S. E. all Day.   Laſt Night   24
at about a Quarter after eight o'Clock Serjeant Fiſher
in paſſing from the Fort to Mr. St. Martins Houſe
was fir'd upon by two Indians as we ſuppoſe & was
kill'd, which gave Reaſon for us to think that it was
ſcheme laid by the French & Indians to get an Officer
Priſoner, as they knew the Commandant and many of
the Officers walk'd there (ſince we took Poſt at Mr.
Barrois's

1763.
July.

Barrois's) after Night, and for that Reason the French was neither to come in nor go out of the Fort; as otherwise they might fire upon some of them instead of us.

This Day at about one o'Clock Baby the Huron came into the Fort but brought nothing extraordinary. He said that the most of his Errant was to see the Major & pay him his Respects, it being the first Oppertunity he had since he was in before, as the Ottawas & Puttawattamys were always being along the Road to watch our Motions.

25   The Wind S. & S. E. till twelve of Clock then chang'd to the West with Rain.

This Evening we were inform'd that the Enemy intended to attempt to surprise the advanc'd Post. The Night was very bad, it raining very hard & the Wind shifting with hard Squawls from South to West.

26   The Wind pretty fresh from the West with Rain. This Day we were inform'd that some Indians came in last Night that had been to see whether there was an Army on the Lake or no, who reported that there was a vast Number of Boats between this & Sandusky which they imagin'd wou'd be here this Night or to morrow.

27   The Wind westerly all Day with Rain. This Day Aron the Mohawk sent word to the Commandant that he would come into the Fort to night or to morrow night.

28   The Wind N. W. & N. all Day.

29   The Wind W. all Day, hazy weather. Last Night at seven o'Clock Aron the Huron [Mohawk] came into the Fort with his Pass from Sir William [Johnson] & five other Mohawks who were to join Capt. Dalyell, who said that he was sent to find out the Reason of the War, and that he was convinc'd the French were great
Rascals,

Rafcals, yet the firft Belts came from the Five Nations, and that the Mr. Horfey fent him afhore before the Schooner was attack'd, Contrary to his own Judgment, to buy Vegetables ; that the Veffel was attack'd in Confequence of the Intelligence that was given the Indians by the two Frenchmen that went on board of her, & not from any that he or his People gave, and that the People on that Side of the River furnifh'd them with Cannoes & every thing they wanted. That many of the Inhabitants were going off to the Miffifippi with Quantitys of Merchandize that they had bought of the Indians, that they had taken from our Merch^{ts}. He promif'd to return in three or four Days.

The Wind S. to N. E. 30

The Wind N. & N. E. & fome Part of the Day Oct. 1 N. W.

This Morning a Frenchman crofs'd the River a little above the Fort with his Goods on his way to a Houfe down the River that he had hir'd, but being call'd to, to come in Shore, and not obeying was fir'd upon, which he did not mind but went on. The Commandant then ordered a Boat to bring them back, which they feeing coming after them oblig'd them to put in Shore oppofite the Fort. But as no Enemy was to be feen, the Boat went in under the Bank to bring her off, but before they got thirty Yards from the Shore two Indians came running down and fir'd upon them & kill'd one Man.

The Wind N. E. This Morning, at 10 o'Clock, Lieut. 2 Brehm, Lieut. Abbot, Enf^n Riggell & myfelf were fent up the River with four arm'd Batteaux to Reconnoitre an Ifland in the Mouth of Lake St. Clair to fee if it was poffible to bring Wood fiom it for the Garrifon & to try to bring off a Ships Boat that the Indians took from Capt. Robinfon, when we were about four

11 Miles

Miles from the Fort the Indians began to fire upon us from Holes they had made on the Side of the River, and two or three Times attempted to put off in a Batteaux & two or three Cannoes as we imagined to crofs the River to fire upon us from each Shore, but we drove them afhore as foon as they were well on board, but at laft feeing we only loft Time with them, pufh'd on to perform what we were fent about, when we had gain'd the upper End of the Hogg Ifland we faw them pufh off with nineteen Cannoes & Batteaux & feem'd to follow us, & when we were in the narrow Part of the River furrounded us under a brifk Fire from each Shore; upon which we turn'd to attack them, they ftill pufhing on with great Bravery all open to our Fire, making a great Hallowing; at length Lieut. Brehm got a good Shot at fome of them with a four Pownder charg'd with Grape at about forty or fifty Yards Diftance, which he fo difabled that out of about 15 or 16 that were in it we cou'd not fee but two that paddled. They then put on Shore fome on one Side of the River and fome on the other, & cry'd two death Hollows; we then rowed up and down in the fame Part of the River & call'd to them to put off again, that we were waiting for them. But they were then very quiet & did not Hollow as in the Beginning, & chofe rather to fire few ftraggling Shot from Shore than attempt coming off again. Then finding it too late to proceed we return'd to the Fort. We had one Man kill'd & three wounded, two of which were very flight. We have not yet heard what Number of them were kill'd or wounded. Upon our Return we were inform'd that one of the Veffels were in the Mouth of the River.

3   At 12 o'Clock, the Wind being almoft South, heard firing of Cannon & fmall Arms down the River, & at one or Half paft, the Schooner came in Sight; about
Half

Half paſt three ſhe arriv'd at the Fort, in which came Capt. Montreſor, who inform'd us that the Sloop was loſt the 28th of Auguſt between Preſque Iſle & Niagara,[65] the Proviſion and Guns were all loſt except 185 Barrells, which they brought in the Schooner ; the Rigging was all carried to Niagara.

The Wind S. W., pretty freſh with Showers of Rain. Laſt Night the Enemy ſet Fire to a Barn about ſixty Yards from the Poſt occupied by our outlying Picket, and crawl'd about the whole Night to try to get a Priſoner & kill a Centry, but they did not ſucceed if that was their Deſign, but on the Contrary had one Man kill'd as our People fir'd at every thing they ſaw move. Another had a ſpeer run through his Body by one of their own People, and we hear is like to die.

The Wind Weſt & very freſh. This Day the

4

5

[65] Letters to Sir William Johnſon:
NIAGARA, 8th Sepr, 1763.
Sr: In my laſt I wrote you that ye Sloop was loſt upon Lake Erie, ſince ye have been on Shore they have been attacked by a few ſtragling Indians, we have loſt three Men in ye Breaſtwork and one out that was ſcalped. Danl & ye Reſt of the Indians behaved very well.
DE COUAGNE.
CAT FISH CREEK, 9th Septm 1763.
14 Mills on Lak Eria.
Dr: According to Daniel Oughnour's Deſire I now take the Freedom to write to you. The 8th ultm we have been caſt away at this Place which detained him from Proſeiding to Detroit, but he ſays he'll go forward and deliver your Belts and bring you an Anſwer from the different Nations according to your Directions. The 3d Inſt we

had 3 Men kill by a ſmall Partey of Indians. Daniel ſpoke to them at little Diſtance from the Breaſtwork but they would not tell what Nation they were, he ſays he believes they are Cinices [Senecas]. We expect the Scooner from Detroit dayly. Aaron & 5 Indians went in her to Detroit. Daniel gives his Comps to you & Familey and deſire the Favour of you in caſe you ſee his Wife to tell her that he is well. Sir excuſe my Freedom in writing in ſuch a maner for I have had the Fever & Eague thoſe ſeveral Days.
I am Sir your moſt
obt Humbl Servant,
COLLIN ANDREWS.
P. S Capt. Coghran gives his Complements to you, he has uſed Daniel extremely well.—*MSS. of Sir William Johnſon*, vol. vii.

This

Schooner was made ready to fail.   This Day we were inform'd that there was two hundred Indians & twenty five Cannoes when they attack'd the Boats.

6   The Wind Weft.   Aron the Mohawk came in to day to fee his Comrades that came in the Schooner, who told us that there was three Chippewas kill'd & feven wounded the fecond Inftant.   That the Hurons were fickly with a bad Feever.   That feven or eight had died within five or fix Days paft.

7   The Wind E. & N. E.   The Schooner fail'd at twelve o'Clock, in which went Capt. Grey, Lieut. Brown & Lieut. McDonald.

This Day Mr. Campo came to the Commandant in the Name of Wabicommigot a Toronto Chief to know his Sentiments about a Peace, to which the Major gave no direct Anfwer, but told Mr. Campo that he might bring him to the Fort & he wou'd fpeake to him.   He ariv'd here laft Sunday with twenty four Men as he fays not to make War, but to try to accommodate Affairs.

8   The Wind E. & N. Eaft.   This Day 60 Miamees ariv'd; we hear that the Chippewas are preparing all the Boats & Cannoes they can to attack the arm'd Boats when they go up the River again.

9   The Wind Weft & N. W.   Laft Night a Soldier, a Trader and a Cherokee that was Prifoner with the Indians made their Efcape & came into the Fort.

This Day we were inform'd that the Indians had taken all the Cannoes they cou'd get from the Inhabitants but know not for what End.

10   The Wind E. to N. E. in the Morning, in the Afternoon wefterly.

12   The Wind wefterly.   Yefterday was held a Council with the Miffifagues, and this Day another with the fame.

The

The Wind from W. to N. W., pretty frefh all Day. 1763.
The Wind Weft & a little to the North of Weft all O^{ct.} 13.
Day & pretty frefh.
                   14
The Wind W. & N. W. with Snow in the Morn- 15
ing.
The Wind chang'd from one Point to another all 16
Day with now & then Snow.
The Wind S. & S. E.   17
The Wind Eafterly.   18
The Wind Eafterly. The Councils that has been 19
held thefe few Days paft has been attended with this
good Effect, that we have been able to get in fome
Wheat & fome little Flower, without which we fhou'd
not have an Ounce of Flower in the Garrifon ten
Days paft, as the Men for upwards of feven Weeks
paft have had only five Pounds of Flower p^r Week, &
for the other two Pounds Half a Gallon of Wheat
each.

 This Day a Soldier fav'd himfelf by running off 25
from a Chibbawa who brought him to Cuefieres to fell.

 This Morning Capt. Grant with a Party of 150 29
Men was fent to the Ifle au Couchon to cut Wood for
the Garrifon, the Commandant not choofing to let
more Time pafs in waiting for the Troops that he expected fome Time ago.

 Laft Night Mons. Dequendfe a Cadette ariv'd from 30
the Illinois and was in Council with Pondiac and the
Chiefs of all the Nations here, and this Morning
brought a Letter to the Commandant from Mon^r Da-
neyon Commandant of the Illinois Country, with a
Speech which he fent addreff'd to all Indians with
three Belts of Wampum & four Pipes of Peace, which
he diftributed to the Nations as he came along. In
the Speech he let them know that Peace was made between England & France & exhorted them to live in
                 Peace

1763.   Peace with us, telling them that fighting againſt us at
Oct.   *Preſent* was fighting againſt them, and deſiring them to
eſteem their Brothers the French that remain'd amongſt
us, as they wou'd never be abandoned by them.   That
they chang'd their Situation as the King order'd, & that
they had given up thoſe Parts of the Country that belong'd to the King & not theirs, and deſir'd an Anſwer
to his Speech telling them they ſhou'd allways receive
Succours from them at ſuch & ſuch Places.   That their
Villages would be full of Amunition & Merchandize.
Upon which Pondiac ſent in Word to the Commandant that their Hatchet was buried & deſir'd to have his
Anſwer in writing. To which the Commandant anſwer'd that if he had begun the War it wou'd be in his
Power to end it; but as it was him, he muſt wait the
Pleaſure of the General, to whome he wou'd write &
inform him of his pacific Inclination in caſe he committed no more Hoſtilities.   Pondiac then ſaid he
wou'd not commit any more & wou'd come when he
was ſent for.

The News of the diffinitive Treaty ariv'd at the
Illinois the 27 of September.   In another Letter to
the Inhabitants of the Peace being concluded, he mark'd
five Places on the South Side of the Miſſipi that any
of the Inhabitants might retire to that had an Inclination where they wou'd receive all the Succour that was
in his Power to give them.   From which one may
imagine that if one word cou'd prevent all the Nations
from committing further Hoſtilities it was in their
Power with a very few to do all they have done & that
they will always remain in their Intereſt as long as they
have any Footing on the Continent from whence they
can ſuccour them.

31   [66] This Day Mr. Jadeau was in the Fort & in talk-

[66] The following Extraɛt from a   Letter of Wm. Edgar at Detroit,

ing with Major Gladwin about Provifion, he told him that ever fince the Beginning of this Affair, the Inhabitants in his Diftrict had receiv'd Orders to give Pondiac a Bufhel of Peas or Wheat pr. Family, under Pain of difobey'ng the greateft of Orders, & that when the Indians were afk'd who gave them the Orders they faid fometimes Mons. Cecotte & fometimes Baptift Campo. Once in particular one of the Inhabitants upon being told that it was Cecotte that gave the Order tore it & told him he did not mind the Order nor Cecotte and then went away. The next Day the Indians came & it was much as all the reft of the Inhabitants cou'd do to prevent them from taking every thing he had in the World & pulling down his Houfe.

The following Names are thofe People who went from the Settlement & from his Diftrict within thefe three Weeks without Leave:

Grenon, an Inhabitant.
Millehomme Do.
Brifar & his Family.
De Roen.
Jean Faies.
Des Cheine, Labourer, & one Lizott Do.

Three Days ago Aron went from the River Huron on his way to Fort Pitt with Letters.

dated Novʳ 1ˢᵗ, 1763, ftates the Progrefs of pacific Overtures as then underftood:

"I have lately recᵈ a Letter from Hornlach, which came by an Officer from Illinois, who brought a Belt & Letter to the Savages, with the Account of the Peace between England & France which neither the Savages nor the French, *here* believed till now. In Confequence of which, our moft implacable Enemies, the Ottawas who were the only Nation here difpofed for continuing the War (all the reft having begged Forgivenefs for what they have done of our worthy Commandant) are now with the others, fuing for Peace, in the moft abject Manner.

Mr. Prentice is very well at Sandufky, as is Mr. Winfton at St. Jofeph's, and from the prefent Difpofition of the Savages I apprehend they will foon bring them *in*."

This

1763.
Nov.

This Day by the Returns from the Commiſſary it appear'd that we had upwards of 9000 weight of Flour & Wheat equal to about 23000 more, which would have been enough for to keep 250 Men here all the Winter, as the Commandant had given over any thoughts of Boats coming & imagin'd the Veſſel was loſt, as ſhe had been gone from this upwards of thirty Days.

This Evening Mr. Jadeau came in with a Letter from the Schooner dated at Iſle au Boiſblond, informing us that the Troops had left Niagara the 20th October.

Mr. Jadeau in Converſation happen'd to tell before Mr. Duquindſe that Pondiac had ſaid he was going with 9 of his Men to the Illinois with him, & that he, Pondiac, had been inform'd that Mr. Dequindſe was to take a good many French with him, which a little ſhock'd Mr. Duquindſe as he had given out that he was to paſs by St. Joſephs.

11

At three o'Clock the Schooner ariv'd, in which came Mr. Willeᵣ° of the 80th, who brought us the diſagreeable Acc't of a Party of about 70 Men being cut off at the Carrying Place at Niagara by a large Body of Indians, as alſo the loſs of moſt of the Carriages & Bullocks, which undoubtedly prevented the Army from coming ſo ſoon as they otherwiſe wou'd have done.[67]

[67] The Affair here alluded to, is the Surpriſe and Maſſacre at the Devil's Hole, three Miles below Niagara Falls and on the Road then recently conſtructed from Fort Niagara to Fort Schloſſer.

In September, twenty-five Wagons loaded with Proviſions and Supplies for Detroit, and eſcorted by fifty Soldiers and their Officers, were ambuſcaded at this Point by Seneca Indians, and with two exceptions the whole were killed, or driven off a frightful Precipice of a hundred and eighty feet. The Wagons and their Contents, with the ox Teams attached, were alſo hurled down the Chaſm. William Stedman, the Contractor, narrowly eſcaped on horſeback, and a drummer Boy, named Matthews, was caught by his Belt in the Limbs of a Tree, which broke the Force of his Fall, and he fell in the River

This

This Morning two Indians ariv'd from Point au Pain, with a Letter one Half wrote in Erfe & the other in Englifh, from Major Montcrife, giving an Account of the Batteau being caft away the feventh Inftant at the Highlands beyond the faid Point, where they loft 20 Boats & 50 Barrels of Provifions, with two Officers and a Surgeon drown'd, as alfo 70 Men, near the Shore. He lived many Years afterwards near Queenfton.

The following Letters, addreffed to Sir William Johnfon, relate to thefe Events on the Niagara Frontier:

NIAGARA, October 17th, 1763.

Sir: I have acquainted you of the fad Ufage of the Savages to the Detachment of our Forces that turned out at lower Landing fometime paft, where the Officers and Men were almoft totally deftroyed by them together with the King's working Cattle. Our Endeavor fince in tranfporting Provifions to little Niagara, intended for Detroit, has been fafely hurried on without their offering to difturb the Troops, but a few Days ago they killed a Man on the Race that dropped behind and fcalped him. There are four Men more of the Flankers miffed, all this without the Noife of a Gun. The Man that was fcalped was between Starlings Houfe and the Fort. They gave one fire at the Troops, Fort, or in the Air, uncertain, none being hurt or any Damage done. I have no more to acquaint you of but conclude Sir,

Your moft obt Servt,

DE COUAGNE.

I forgot there were fome Cattle fent here from Ontario fince which we had up at Work and now they are all taken, ftole by the Savages or ftraying in the Woods.

NIAGARA, Novr 11th, 1763.

Honble Sirs:

My laft to you was to acquaint you of Daniel, &c., which I hope came fafe to your Hands, fince which a fmall Party went out from the Lower Landing to cut Wood, when a Body of Indians furrounded them & killd & fcalped nine, one of which had his Head cut off within Sight of that Poft, it is fuppofed that the Indian who did this Murder was wounded from the Fort, as he was feen go off lame with the Head in his Hand, all which happen'd on the fifth Inftant.

I am in hopes of a Line from you the firft Oppertunity wherein fhould be glad to know how Affairs go down the Country, I mean in regard to the Indians, &c.

I am Sir

Your obdt Humle Ser.

DE COUAGNE.

P. S. Sir here is two Sifters of Silver Heells at this Place who would be glad to know where he is. One of them is the lame one, the other is the young one. Neither of them dare go to the Caftle.

&

1763.
Nov.

& that all their Amunition, even the Mens Cartridges, were wet, & that they had wifely (not knowing our Circumftances) take na Refolution to turn back to Niagara. But from the Steps Major Gladwin had taken fome Time before he was in a Situation to keep a tolerable Garrifon here with Provifion till the Month of May, & was in a good way of getting in enough till the Month of July, tho at the Expence of liftening to the Demands of Peace the Indians had fome Time before made, which notwithftanding he did not grant them. But put them off by telling them they muft wait the Generals Pleafure, &c., as will appear from the Councils he held commencing about the Middle of October.

Dec. 5.

This Day two Mohawks went from this by Land to Niagara with Letters; they came from Sandufky to this Place, having come with a Pafs from Sir William Johnfton when the Schooner was attack'd.

7

This Day Andrew the Huron got 6000 of Wampam & a good deal of Vermillion for the Voyage he made laft to Fort Pitt. The Reafon he took fo much of thefe Commoditys was (as he fᵈ) to fend the young Men of Sandufky to War againft the Cherokees.

Mr. Jadeau told Major Gladwin that Lafontaine, an Inhabitant near his Houfe, told the People that the Peace was not yet made, and that the Army was only come to fave the 200 Men who departed from hence under the Command of Major Rogers to reinforce the Garrifon at Quebec, he likewife took the Oppertunity of robbing the Merchants Batteaux that were brought in by the Indians when they were Drunk. He declar'd before Mon. Legrand that he had no more than 17 Yards of Chapmans Linnen, but Mr. Jadeau has found that he had 69 Yards. He broke open fome Cafes and ftole a Box with filver Trinkets which the Indians afterwards got from him.   Prud'homme

Prud'homme Senr is a dangerous Man & animates the Savages. He underftands their Language & told them not to go off, for if they did the Englifh wou'd hang the French, and as for Provifion they (the Savages) fhould never want.

Michael Campeau told the Indians of two Barrels of Powder that were hid in Mr. Jadeaux Houfe, he likewife animated the Indians very much. Buxton, an Ottawa Chief lodg'd in his Houfe.

St Louis, an Officer of the Militia on the South Side of the River, faid, when Mr. Jadeau was in Council with the Hurons, engaging them not to ftrike againft the Englifh, and gave them three Days to confider of it. What! faid St Louis, four Days? it muft. be refolv'd immediately; fhall we let our Throats be cut for the Sake of the Englifh? which fignified, fays Mr. Jadeau, that they fhou'd rather ftrike againft the Englifh than have the ill will of the Savages. He alfo faid it wou'd be a luckier thing for them to be with the Indians than the Englifh. Another Time he told the Informer that he did not know what Dominion he was under.

This Day Mindoghquay (a Chief of the Sagginaws who was in the Fort the 16 June & afk'd the Commandants Friendfhip, &c. as he had not enter'd into the War) ariv'd here with three Prifoners of the 60 Reg^t & one Sailor who was brought from the Chibbawas by one Beaulieu, and demanded the Continuation of the Commandants Friendfhip as he had promif'd in the Summer and gave him a Pipe of Peace & feveral large Belts. He was very well rec^d by the Commandant, as he had obey'd all his Orders from the firft Time he came into the Fort, retiring with his People and not committing Hoftillities as others did.

Laft Night one Mackoy ariv'd here, having made his

12

22

1763.
Dec.
his Efcape from the Puttawattamees about fifteen Ligues from this.

23   This Day Mr. Cicotte came to the Fort & told the Commandant that the Puttawamees intended to have brought the Man in that made his Efcape two or three Days ago, and that they intended to come in hoping he wou'd pity them.

25   This Day Mr. Marfac inform'd us that he was afur'd that there was four or five of the Puttawattamys of Naintaws Family that intended to come and take a Scalp if poffible, & defir'd the Commandant wou'd not let any body go out of the Fort, as fome of the Merchants had ftraggled out in the Country fome Days before.

27   This Day a Mohawk with one David Vanderhiden ariv'd Exprefs from Niagara, which they left two Days after the Arival of Major Rogers, who was only fix Days in going from the Detroit River to the Niagara.

31   This Day fix Indians (originally of the Saqui[68] Nation) but at prefent of the Puttawattame came in with a Prifoner, & told the Commandant that they came in Hopes of receiving Mercy. That if they pretended entirely to excufe themfelves from being concern'd in the late War they wou'd lye, but that did not fignify, tho' they were living amongft the Puttawattamys they were not of that Nation, nor like them. That what offence they committed was through fear, as they had been oblig'd to afk liberty to live amongft them, having been oblig'd anciently to fly from other Nations, who had this Summer made War againft their Brothers.

That they knew their Brothers the Putts had lied, & even come & fpoke to their Brother & the fame Day fir'd againft his Fort, but begg'd he wou'd not

[68] Sacs.

think

think that they had an Inclination to do the fame, but
that they fpoke from their Hearts, & came to offer
one of his Flefh which had fallen to them by Lot, &
to demand Mercy. That their Familys were ftarving.
That they cou'd not come into the Fort in the Summer as the Fort was every Day on fire. That in fine
they beg'd that they might live in the fame Friendfhip
with their Brother that they had done when he took
Poffeffion of the Country. That they hop'd, nor
they wou'd not return Home fhamefully, fuppofe their
Brothers did not liften to them, as what they did was
their Duty & which they wou'd have done before but
had not an Oppertunity. That notwithftanding they
were Orphans & had no Chiefs, & knew that the other
Indians wou'd laugh at them, & afk'd them how their
Brother rec^d them at his Fort, they wou'd not be
afham'd as it was their Duty they were doing, but
neverthelefs expected their Brother wou'd take them in
Compaffion.

The Prifoner being afk'd if he knew of their going
from Home during the Summer faid they always ftay'd
upon their Land the whole Time, except the two that
was at Prefq Ifle where he was taken, & they never
went abroad to War after he came amongft them, but
once in the Summer came as far as Mr. Gamelins with
him to give him up, & the other Nations told them
not to go to the Fort as they wou'd be kill'd.

This Day Baby & Theata with four or five more of
their Relations came in to wifh the Commandant a
happy new Year, as is their Cuftom, whom he rec^d very
well.

This Day fome of the Puttawattamys came to the
Settlement & fent in Word by Mr. Cicotte that they
wanted to come & fee their Brother the Command^t but
Mr. Cecotte was told that the Command^t had nothing
to

1764.
Jan.

to fay to them & they wou'd do much better to ftay at their hunting Ground.

12   This Day Vanderhiden & Jacob the Mohawk left this for Niagara with Letters.

13   This Day one of the Chibbaways came to the Settlement & fent for Mr. Labute to defire him to afk the Commandant leave to come in & fee him, which Mr. Labute inform'd him of, but the Commandant told Mr. Labute not to make him any Anfwer, but let him, the Indian, return as he faid he intended to do the next Morning.

14   This Day the Huron Chiefs (Baby, Theata & the Doctors Son) went to fee the Command^t before they went away, & after talking of the Beginning of this Indian War, &c., Mr. St. Martin faid it was fure that it took its rife from the Belts that paff'd amongft the Indians two Years ago, & that it was commenc'd in Confequence of the Succours that the Indians were made to believe they might expect from the Illinois. That one Sibbold that came here laft Winter with his Wife from the Illinois, had told at Mr. Cuellierrey's that they might expect a French Army in this Spring, & that, that Report took rife from him. That the Day Capt. Campbelle & Lt. McDougal was detain'd by the Indians, Mr. Cuellierry accepted of their Offer of being made Commandant, if this Place was taken, to which he fpoke to Mr. Cuellierry about and afk'd him if he knew what he was doing, to which Mr. Cuellierry told him I am almoft diftracted, they are like fo many Dogs about me, to which Mr. St. Martin made him no Anfwer.

20   This Day two Michilimackinac Chiefs came in to fee the Commandant, with one or two Wafhtinon Chiefs from the Grand River who were here in the Beginning of the Summer about fifteen Days, but went away

away.   They brought in a Prifonner that was given to
them by the Ottawas.

This Day Wabagommigot, a Chief of the Toronto   1
Indians who came in laft Fall, return'd and afk'd a
Certificate which the Commandant at that time pro-
mif'd him of his Behavior, which he gave him.

This Day fome of the Saky's came in with the other   14
Prifoner they promif'd to bring in the laft Time they
were in the Fort.

This Evening Aron the Mohawk ariv'd from Fort
Pitt with Letters from the General.

This Day fome of the Ottawas of the Grand Rivierre   20
ariv'd with a Prifoner whom they bought from fome
other Indians.

This Morning the Gunner going his Rounds found   Mar. 12
a Brand's end that had been fet up againft the Magazine Door the Night before, which appear'd to have
been on fire but was gone out.

This Day a Cow belonging to one Moran came in   14
from the Woods with ten Arrows fticking in her,
which were fuppof'd to be fhot by fome Party of Indians that was lying about the Fort.

This Day two or three Frenchmen faw a fmall Party   18
of Indians back of the Fort going loaded with Meat,
which muft be the Cattle that was kill'd & miffing for
two or three Days paft.

There has been a Party of Puttawattamys in the
Settlement every Night fince the 15th Inftant.

This Day the Commanding Officer was inform'd   21
that one Mintiwaby, an Ottawa Chief of the Grand
River, was to come in under a Pretence of Trade &
endeavour to furprize him & put all the Officers to
Death.   M. Informer.

This Day two Saky's came in and inform'd the   23
Commandant that the Chibbaways of the Ifles about
Michilimackinac

1764. Michilimackinac had fent Belts this Winter to their
March. Nation, to the Folavin & Puante, to ftrike againft us
this Spring, but they wou'd not receive them.   That
Waffong & Mafhoquife had tried to prevent that Party
from coming from towards St. Jofeph that was here
fome Time ago, but they wou'd not be advif'd, they
faid they had loft a Man laft Year & they wou'd have
Revenge.   That if they had known it fooner they
wou'd have advif'd us of it before they arriv'd, but
they [knew] nothing of it till they were gone.

That the Delawares & Shawanys had fent Belts
during the Winter towards St. Jofeph & La Bay to
invite the Nations thereabout to take up Arms againft
us in the Spring.

27   This Day France Ruiard fet off with two other
Frenchmen Exprefs to Niagara.

29   This Day the Commandant being inform'd that
there was thirteen Indians in the Woods behind the
Settlement, who were come to make War, fent out a
Party commanded by Lt. M'Dougal of twenty Men
to try to fall upon them by furprize; they fet off a
little after Dark & went through the Fields guided by
a Frenchman to the Place where their Fire had been
feen, but not finding them there, they return'd towards
a Houfe that they had been at the Night before, &
fell in with them on their way, but the Indians finding
they were difcover'd run off, after receiving the Fire of
the moft of the Party, but it was fo dark that they
cou'd not fee to ajuft their Firelocks & don't know
whether they kill'd any or no.

30   This Day an Indian was feen at the Edge of the
Woods behind the Fort.

April 12   This Morning at ten o'Clock the Schooner fail'd
for Niagara, in which were fent the two French Prifoners, as the Commandant was inform'd that the In-
                                                     dians

dians had faid they fhou'd not long be Prifoners, and
as it was imagin'd if any thing was intended by them,
it was through the Influence of the Friends of thefe two.

Laft Night at about 8 o'Clock [a] Prifoner came in   15
from Sagginaw who reported that the Day before he
came away the Indians kill'd and eat a young Girl they
had Prifoner & that he was to been kill'd that Day
himfelf, but they fent him out to bring in fome Wood
& he run off; he was eight Days a coming, but when
he was afk'd if he was hungry he faid no, that for the
firft two or three Days he was fainty, but fince he found
no great alteration though he had not eat a mouthfull
of any thing the whole eight Days.

This Day Andrew a Huron & two others from   27
Sandufky brought in one Mr. Prentice whom they
had Prifoner fince laft May. They told the Commandant they were not fent by any Chief, but as he
(the one that fpoke) looked upon Mr. Prentice as his
real Brother, he told him in the Winter he wou'd
bring him in, for he chofe to fee him content at this
Place than difcontent with him, which was the Reafon
he brought him in. But he imagined that Mr. Prentice cou'd have other no Reafon for leaving them, than
becaufe he cou'd not get Bread amongft them.

Mr. Prentice faid that he never wanted for any thing
they had during the whole Winter, & notwithftanding
this Man never got any of the Plunder that the Indians took from him when they made him Prifoner,
he gave him two Packs of Beaver & twenty Dollars
when he gave him up.

This Day a four in the Afternoon the Commandant   28
thought he heard a Cannon down the River & fir'd
another.

This Morning at Half paft four Mr. Jadeau ariv'd   29
from the Veffel with Letters and inform'd us that they
fir'd

fir'd a Gun from the Veſſel about the Time the Commandant thought he heard one.

This Afternoon eight Huron Chiefs & two or three
young Men came to ſpeak to the Commandant.
Theata ſpeaks:

My Brother, we beg you may take Pity upon us &
hear us, that the Words we now ſay may be as a Car-
pet for your Succeſſor to walk upon.

Brother, we beg you to have Pity upon us and be
aſſured of our good Intentions, as we have moſt faithfully repented of all the Ill we may have done, & do
ſincerely promiſe never to be guilty of any bad Thing
for the Future, having thrown ourſelves into the
Hands of God, if any Evil happens to us it muſt be
from him, as you may be perſuaded let the Earth turn
how it will, we ſhall never be adviſ'd to a bad Thing
again.

This, Brother, we beg you will inform the General
of the firſt Oppertunity.   Gave a large white Belt.

Another Chief got up with a ſtring of Wampum and
ſaid :

Brother, ever ſince the Engliſh have had Poſſeſſion
of this Place we have been uſ'd very tenderly, agreeable to the Promiſe you made us when you firſt came
here, for which Reaſon we hope our Brother will grant
us the ſmall favour we are going to aſk.

Brother, as Wood & Bark is very unhandy to us at
our old Village we hope you will give us leave to make
a new one up a ſmall Creek near the Bottom of the Settlement, where every thing will be more convenient.
Granted.

Brother, when you firſt came here you told us you
had conquer'd our Father & ſent him over the Great
Lake, & that all that then belong'd to him was yours,
but that we ſhou'd remain in our former Poſſeſſions

and

and be allowed the Jesuist, and now as we are going to 1764.
alter our Village we hope you will not prevent him May.
going with us. Gave a string of Wampum.

Granted by the Commandant.

This Evening four Indians sent by Sir William 6
Johnston ariv'd here with a Speech to the Nations
hereabout.

This Day we were inform'd by Mr. Jadeau that one 8
Rainbeau & his Family with one L'esperence went off
to the Illinois.

This Morning at Half past six the Schooner sail'd 15
for Niagara, in which went Peter & the three other
Indians that came here with a Speech from Sir William
Johnson.

This Afternoon some of the Saky's came in and inform'd us that one Lagesse and four other Puttawattamees were some where in the Woods near the Fort,
and intended to try to take a Scalp.

This Morning the Schooner anchor'd off the Fort June 2.
after having been kept at the Mouth of the River
three Days with contrary Winds.

This Morning a Band of Chippawas who were at
the Gross Point dividing themselves amongst the Inhabitants, ask'd at several Places for Provision, &c.,
one of them being refus'd a Cock by a Farmer had a
Dispute with him, & because he wou'd not let him
have it fir'd at him and shot him through the Body.

This Day the Band of Chippewas who fir'd at the 3
Frenchman headed by a Chief they call'd the Great
Spoon, came with a Belt & Pipe to Mr. Marsack, telling him they were very sorry for what they had done,
which Belt & Pipe he brought to the Commandant
next Day with a Prisoner they had sold him who was
taken at Presq' Isle. The Man they fir'd at died of
his Wounds last Night.

They

1764.
June.
They then fent in a Frenchman to tell the Commandant they had always been Fools, but that their Senfes
were now come to them and beg'd he might receive
them, to which he fent them Word that when they return'd the Goods that Mr. Marfac gave them for the
Prifoner & brought in the reft as they had promif'd
the Fall before, he wou'd fee them, but not till then.

4
Being his Majefties Birthday, the Garrifon was
under Arms at 1 o'Clock & fir'd three Volleys with
three Difcharges of the Cannon in the Fort & one of
thofe in the Schooner; after which His Majefties
Health was drunk upon the Parade by all the Officers
& feveral Frenchmen who were afk'd there by the
Commandant who afterwards din'd & fup'd with all
the Officers of the Garrifon together. At nine at
Night almoft the whole Town was eluminated.

6
Mr. Marfack after going to the Priefts came in
hafte to the Commandant to tell him that the Indians
had return'd him his Merchandife that he had given
for the Prifoner two or three Days before, & wanted
to come in. To which the Commandant fent the fame
Anfwer as he had done two or three Days before, that
when they brought in all the reft of the Prifoners &
their Chiefs came in a proper Manner, he wou'd receive them.

7
This Morning Mr. Marfack came in and inform'd
the Commandant that there was a fmall Band of Chippawas from beyond Saggina to come in, who came with
a Belt & Pipe of Peace, and after they had fmok'd &
told the Commandant they were come to open a new
Road between him & their Nation, as the old one had
been fhut up for fome Time; he enquir'd what they
were & who fent them, & found that they were from
the fame Place & Village with thofe that fold the Prifoner to Marfack a few Days before, and had no Authority

thority for coming nor had no Chief with them, but
they were Part of a Party that came to the Settlement
about feven or eight Days before, confifting of forty
Men, who told the Inhabitants they did not come to
make Peace but to make War. All which they could
not deny. The Commandant then took a String &
Wampum & told them to take that to their Chiefs &
tell them when they brought in the other Prifoner they
had in Poffeffion & came & afk'd Peace in a proper
Manner he wou'd hear them, and until then one of
them muft ftay with him, as perhaps they might to fell
the reft, & at the fame Time told them to tell their
Chiefs if any thing happen'd to his People amongft
them, he knew what to do with thofe he had. When
they saw this a fecond offer'd to ftay to keep the firft
one Company ; he is a Son of

The Coll. then afk'd them if he had three or four of
his Nation Prifoners, & wou'd fend two or three of his
People to their Village wheather they would not keep
them, to which they faid they wou'd. Then faid he
you wou'd undoubtedly think me a Fool to let you all
go when you have Prifoners of mine. They then f'd
perhaps it wou'd be hard for them to get thofe Prifoners, as they did not belong to their Relations. Yes,
but faid the Commandant, if they have an inclination
for Peace as you told me a few Minutes ago, they will
bring them in without any Difficulty. They then f'd
they were a little Band of fix or feven, every one for
himfelf; then f^d the Interpreter how came you here to
make a new Road for the whole Nation and fight in
alliance with them all laft Summer ; to which they
hung their Heads & cou'd not fay any thing.

This Day the Schooner fail'd with a head Wind for 10
Niagara and got below the Hurons Point.

This Day the Schooner return'd the Wind being 11
freſh

frefh ahead, and as Teata the Indian Chief ariv'd at their Village with Aron & two other Mohawks who came into the Fort and gave the following Intelligence annex'd in two Sheets of Paper:

DETROIT, June 9ᵗʰ 1764.

This Day a fmall Party of Puttawattamees ariv'd here who inform'd, that an Indian was come from the Illinois to St. Jofephs who inform'd them that he was in Council with Pondiac there.

That Mr. Deneyon told him he was glad to fee him & hoped that his Senfes were come to him.

Pondiac then took a large Belt and laid it before him faying, my Father the Reafon of my Journey is to get you and all your Allies to joyn with me to go againft the Englifh, upon which Deneyon took the the Belt & told him, your Speech much furprizes me, as I doubt not but you have receiv'd my Meffage wherein I inform'd you that the French and Englifh were but one, then return'd the Belt. Pondiac took the Belt again and importun'd Mr. Deneyon on the fame Subject. At laft Mr. Deneyon grew angry & kick'd it from him, afking him if he had not already heard what he f'd to him. He then addreff'd himfelf to the Illinois Indians & told them they faw him that Day in the Fort, but perhaps they wou'd fee their Brothers the Englifh the next, and exhorted them to live in amity with them, which he made no doubt of as their Sentiments were very good.

Pondiac then afk'd for Rum & Deneyon gave him a fmall Barrel, which he took to one of the Illinois Villages & with a red Belt exhorted them to fing the War Song with him, which fome of them did, but were forry for it when they were Sober. The Indian that brought this Account fays that before he left the Illinois he faw three Englifh Officers who were fent on
before,

before, the Army being but a little way behind with a
large Body of Indians.

DETROIT, June 10ᵗʰ 1764.

This Day Teata a Wiandott Chief ariv'd here from Sanduſky, where he had been to carry Sir William Johnſon's Speech, who ſays that after he deliver'd it and left it to their deliberation, the great Chief Bigg Jaco got up and thank'd him for the Trouble he had been at to bring it, and immediately the whole went out. After he had deliver'd the Speech he ſays he adviſ'd them to come to their Senſes, but in caſe they did not it was their Affair. Aron ſays they made great Game of Teata on ſaying ſo to them.

Four Days after, they came back and aſk'd Teata to come and hear what they had to ſay in Anſwer. The firſt Belt they gave him was a Repetition of Sir Williams Speech. Then they took another ſaying, Sir William aſks the Reaſon why we ſtruck againſt the Engliſh, we think he ought to know better than any body ; yes, ſaid they, it is Sir William that ought to know, but ſince the Senecas have made Peace with him & the Engliſh, tell him it was them that firſt embroil'd the Earth, & were the firſt Cauſe of what has been done. Gave the Belt.

They then took another Belt & ſaid, Sir William & the Six Nations want that we ſhould own our Folly & find words to excuſe ourſelves that we may be again ſet right. You'll tell him by this Belt, which you are charg'd to deliver to him, that for what is paſt, its paſt, that we have yet done no Harm ſince laſt Summer, we have kept our young Men quiet, for which Reaſon we think the Breach may be eaſily mended ; and tell him alſo we ſhall keep them quiet this Summer, when we think we ſhall be reconcil'd.

The two Mohawks who are come with Teata, ſay that

that they were told by the Hurons of Sandufky, that they wou'd not tell Teata the Refult of a Council they had had with the Shawanies, which was that they were to try to take Fort Pitt by Treachery, & if they fail'd there were to go ag^t the Inhabitants on the Frontiers. That the Onondagoes that Sir William fent againft the Shawanies came to one of their Villages, where they were afk'd what they came for, they faid we come to fcalp you ; then one Kayoughfhoutong faid here, take thefe, giving them two old Scalps that he had newly painted, go home & tell Sir William you have fcalp'd fome Shawanies. Upon which they return'd ; that the above mentioned Indian was the Caufe of their not ftriking againft the Shawanies. But it was not fo with the Tufcroras, for they loft three Men.

One of them further fays that before he left the Delaware Towns he faw thirty fmall Party's go out who were all intended to go to our Frontiers. They both fay, alfo, that the Hurons at Sandufky laugh'd at Teata behind his Back, & call'd him a Fool for believing what Sir William fayd and bringing fuch a Meffage.

That tho' he faid they wou'd be Friends, it can never be until all the Englifh, except Traders go from this Place, meaning Detroit, & then we believe we fhall agree. That their God tells them they muft make War & Peace for feven Years, at the End of which by force of Treachery during that Time, all the Englifh will be drove away & then they will have Peace and not till then.

That the Delawares & Shawanies and Hurons of Sandufky all fay the Englifh are Fools, that they can make Friends with us when they pleafe, and next Day tomahawk us. That the Englifh allways told them they had as many Men as there was Leaves on the Trees, but wee look upon one Indian as good as a
thoufand

of them, and notwithſtanding we are but Mice in com-
pariſon to them, we will bite as much as they can.
The two Mohawks father ſays that the Hurons at
Sanduſky told them they were very ſorry that Sir
William was coming here, as they imagin'd by that he
wanted to leave his Bones here.

They alſo ſay that while they were at the Shawanie
Village the French from the Miſſiſſippi ſent them a
Preſent of Powder, of which he ſaw three Barrels.

Mr. St. Martin, Interpreter, told Coll. Gladwin that
Hurons of this Place told him many Times that if
a Peace was made with the Delawares, Shawanies &
Hurons of Sanduſky, that it would not be good, nor
laſting.

The Schooner ſail'd at about four in the Afternoon, 12
and run out of Sight from the Fort before dark.

This Day Teata & ſeveral Hurons came to the Fort 13
& aſk'd the Commandant if they might not go once
more to the Hurons of Sanduſky, as perhaps tho' their
Ears had always been ſtop'd till now yet they might be
open at preſent.

The Commandant told them they might do as they
pleaſ'd, that he had ſent their Anſwer to Sir William
Johnſon with their Belts, that it was not intended to
force a Peace down the Throats of the Indians, nor
was it intended for any but thoſe who had ſincerely
repented of what they had done, & was realy reſolv'd
to remain our Friends for the Future. That in his
opinion they ought not to go, as they only laugh'd at
the Meſſage taken by Teata, & him for carrying it.

This Day a Huron promiſ'd to ſet off with his 14
little Band of about twelve to bring in ſome Delaware
or Shawany Scalps.

This Day Wabagommigot came in with ſome Chip- 15
pawas & two Priſoners & after repeating a good deal
of

of what paff'd in Council laft Fall, faid that as the
Commandant had defir'd him feveral Times go to his
old Village & to fee him yet here, would perhaps make
him think that he had no Intention to do what he had
order'd him, but the Reafon was, that he had been
trying to get all the Prifoners that was among his
Nation & to gather his Band together, which he had
now almoft affect'd ; he did not fpeak for the whole
Nation, but for thofe who were with him who had
heartily repented of what they had done & hop'd to be
receiv'd as he himfelf was. That there were fome
whom he advertifed of what he (the Commandant) had
told him with regard to their quick Repentance & of
the Council that was to be held at Niagara, but fince
they did not come in it was their Affair. He then
afk'd for the two Prifoners, faying it was nothing, but
this War, that fepperated him from the reft of the
Nation, who were neverthelefs part of his Body, for
which Reafon hop'd they wou'd be given up, as he then
wip'd away all the Blood that had been fpilt with the
two Prifoners he brought in. That he hop'd in going
home to his old Village he might not hear it faid that
things went ill at the Detroit becaufe Wabigommigot
was refuf'd that Favour. That fince the Malefactors he
then fpoke for (meaning People he had with him)
were come to their Senfes, & heartily repented of what
they had done, & as they were fet on by the Six Nations, hop'd they wou'd be forgiven & no more
thought of it.

The Commandant then afk'd him if he came in the
Name of the whole Nation, he f'd no, but in Part.
Then f'd he if you'l take my Advice you'l go to
Niagara before the Council is over & make Peace for
yourfelf & Band ; you have no Time to lofe as it will
be over in twelve Days. And as to the Prifoners I
                                                    fhall

fhall keep them till I get all mine in, as they belong to a Band that has not as yet afk'd for Peace nor brought in all my flefh. As to what he (Wabbigomigot) might hear of things going ill here, nothing cou'd go ill with us, but if any body did any thing that they ought not to do, it wou'd be them that wou'd fuffer ; that we were out of their Power. He then repeated to him that it was neceffary he fhou'd be at Niagara at the Council, for which Purpofe he wou'd give me a Receipt, that he had deliver'd two Prifoners, &c. ; that the Time was fhort & the fooner he went off the better.

The Frenchman that danc'd the War Dance at Sandufky this Spring with the Indians is named Thefault.

This Day Mindockquay came in with about 70 of his People & about thirty Chibbaways who brought in two Prifoners, being the laft they had amongft them, for whom the Commandant gave them the two Indians he detain'd fome Time ago.

The Puttawattamefs after all the Promifes did not go to Niagara, nor Wabbigomigot neither.

This Day the Schooner Victory return'd from Niagara with another new Schooner, the Bofton.

This Evening at about ten o'Clock one Reaume, a Frenchman, ariv'd from Michilimackinac with 18 Cannoes of Savages who came from the Bay the 3d June to go to Montreal, but when they ariv'd at Michilimackinac they were inform'd that ten Cannoes that were going there and an Exprefs with a Belt informing them that they fhou'd go to Niagara where they wou'd meet a great Englifh Chief, upon which they took their Route this way, & feveral Cannoes from the Nations thereabouts went acrofs Lake Huron by way of Lake Ontario. They brought four Englifhmen

men with them with all their Packs, who had been amongſt them ſince laſt Spring was a Year.

3

This Day ſome of greateſt of the Huron Chiefs of Sanduſky came in with five Priſoners to throw themſelves at the Commandants Feet, as they ſaid, and after telling him that what they had done was in conſequence of what Meſſages and Lyes the Ottawas ſent them, ſaid that if he wou'd have pity on them, he wou'd ſee they were ſincere, as his Will was theirs.

The Commandant told them the only way they had to get a Peace, and if they did not benefit of what he ſaid, it was their Affair.   He gave them a Certificate that they had deliver'd five Priſoner and that they had aſk'd for Peace, which they ſaid they wou'd take to Niagara with all the reſt of the Priſoners they had amongſt them.

This Afternoon the Michilimackinack Chiefs & Folle Avoines came in told the Commandant they came to take him by the Hand & let him know they were glad to ſee him, & wou'd come to morrow to ſpeake to him.

4

This Morning the above Indians came in to the Amount of fifty & told the Commandant that they, the Renards, the Sieus, the Saky's, Puants & Pians, were one Body & one Heart, and that, that Heart was as well intentioned as it had always been ; that he'knew himſelf from their Behavior laſt Year, that their & ours cou'd be but one; that they were invited by the General laſt Year to come to Montreal this Spring, but that when they were aſſembled at Michilimacinac they received a Belt from him, telling them that he ſtop'd up the Paſſage that way as the Small Pox was amongſt his People which they might catch & carry Home to the Deſtruction of their Wifes & Children, but if they wou'd go to Niagara they wou'd find all
they

they were in need of, for which Reaſon they beg'd the Rivers & Lakes might be open to them as uſual, ſhewing the Belt they receiv'd.

This Day ſome of the Hurons of this Village came in with the Chiefs of Hurons of Sanduſky who were in the Day before yeſterday & brought with them ſome Hurons that ariv'd the Day before to join their old Village & brought in five Priſoners, whom they ſaid they wou'd not have brought in till their Chiefs return'd from Niagara,[69] had it not been to encourage thoſe of Sanduſky to do the ſame, as the Commandant knew he was always ſure of them, but neverthelefs, tho they had, had ſome of them ſince they ſuck'd, yet that the Chiefs from Sanduſky might be witneſs of their good Intentions they brought them in ſooner than they promiſ'd.

The Huron that went to ſtrike againſt the Delawares & Shawanies return'd this day without doing any thing.

This Day Mr. Jadeau in repeating to the Commandant ſomethings that had paſſ'd between him and one Clermont (who had been ſent with a Letter to the Illinois, but went no further than where the Ottawas are in the Miamee River) ſaid that Clermont told him, you do very well in ſerving the Engliſh, but I have my Reaſons for what I do, and you will ſoon be oblig'd to ſave yourſelf in the Fort. Another thing ſaid he I'll tell you that you don't know, the Engliſh are all

---

[69] Theſe Chiefs had gone to Niagara to hold a Treaty with Sir William Johnſon. The Treaty was ſigned July 18, 1764, and bound the Hurons to deliver up all Priſoners, Deſerters and Negroes or other Slaves among them; to maintain a friendly Alliance and to do their utmoſt to preſerve His Britannic Majeſty's Intereſts and promote Peace among the weſtern Tribes. They were promiſed Pardon for all paſt Miſdeeds, and a free, fair and open Privilege of Trade.—*N. Y. Col. Hiſt.*, vii, 650.

defeated

defeated in the Miffiffippi and there will be fourteen hundred Men foon here, and all the Indians that are going to Niagara have agreed with the Ottawas to return with the Army, & the Ottawas are to meet them on the Lake & try to deftroy them. That Merchandize & Powder was in the greateft plenty at the Miamee River.

That one Borgard who came from St. Jofephs brought them a Barrel of Powder & fome Corn, Flour, &c. That there was one Clincincourt a French Officer, who was fent by Mr. Deneyon with Letters for the Commandant here, was ftop'd by the Ottawas, where they keep him, neither giving him Liberty to return nor come forward.

This Afternoon a Saggina Indian who had been fent by his Brother, as he faid, to the Miamee River to fee what paff'd came in and inform'd that while he was there a French Officer ariv'd there from the Illinois who was coming here with Letters, but the Ottawas ftop'd him & took his Letters from him, and fent for Cufieres Son to read them. After which one of the Ottawa Chiefs told him that Cuefliere had told them that it was a Letter from their Father the French King, who defir'd his Brothers the Englifh to make hafte & go away from this Place, for he was coming in a great Body & had a great many of his Children with him, whofe Inclination he was not Mafter of, & wou'd not anfwer for what harm they might do. The Officer they keep there & will neither let him go back or forward.

10   This Day Part of the four following Nations ariv'd here, the Saky's, the Renards, the Puants, and the Saulteux of Lake Superior, fome of whom came from the Forks of the Miffiffippi (and from all Appearance, and what they faid) they came in Expectation of getting Rum. They were upwards of two Months a coming;

coming; they brought upwards of fixty Packs of
Beaver.

This Day at 2 o'Clock the two Schooners left this
for the eaſt End of Lake Erie.

This Day Mr. Clinencourt ariv'd from the Miamee,
who had been detain'd by the Ottawas.

This Day at about 4 o'Clock in the Afternoon the
Schooner Gladwin ariv'd from Niagara.

This Day Waſſong, a Chief of the Chibbaways came
in with a Priſoner that he had promiſ'd to bring in,
in the Winter, but who had got Froſt bit and was not
able to come. After telling that he was not concern'd
in the Beginning of the Inſurrection and aſking Pardon
in a moſt ſubmiſſive Manner ſaid: he did not pretend to excuſe himſelf, that as he had told Mr. LaBute
in the Spring he would behave as a Dog that had offended his Maſter, that if he was puniſh'd & was miſ-
erable he had no body to blame but himſelf, and wou'd
ſtill fawn till he was taken into Favour again, for that
he was as a Dog that had been beaten and was running
round his Maſter with Fear & Reſpect, and wou'd
continue till he was pardonned, having ſince laſt Fall
reſolv'd to die rather than diſobey his Brothers Will.
And aſked what were the moſt ſalutary Means to be
well received by the General, ſince he had not been
inform'd that he ſhou'd have gone to Niagara. At the
ſame Time begging Mercy in the moſt ſubmiſſive
Manner and ſaid if his Brother cou'd ſee the Diſtreſs
their Familys were in, he wou'd have Pity upon them
& think they were puniſh'd enough.

The Commandant told him the Reaſon of the Inſurrection was becauſe they had ſomething then in their
Power which they wou'd never have again, for if they
had they wou'd act the ſame Part over again.

In the Evening we were inform'd that the Sloop
Royal

1763. Royal Charlotte was aground on this Side [of] the
July. Whitewood; at 2 in the Morning a Detachment was
sent with four Batteaux to lighten her & get her off,
which they did next Day by four in the Afternoon,
and the 24th she ariv'd here.

27   The Schooner Boston arived from Niagara.

29   This Morning at 11 o'Clock the Sloop Charlotte
set Sail for Niagara with Wind at N. W.

In the Afternoon Manitoo, an Ottawa Chief, with
five other Ottawas, four of whome were from the
Miamee River, came in with three Prisoners. The
Speaker said that God had been speaking with him a
great deal this last Winter, & that what he yn said was
the Sentiments of all the Chiefs, and beg'd to be pitied
& heard. He then beg'd Pardon for what they had
done in a most submissive Manner; the Reason of
their beginning he did not know, but he that set them
on (Pondiac) was return'd from the Illinois, but was
no more heard by any body in the Nation; that God
had told him he had done wrong, that he had made
this Earth for them & us to live quietly together in, &
that Pondiac the Causer of its being disturbed wou'd
not die but wou'd burn in Hell eternally, as all those
wou'd do who did not follow the Advice & obey the
Will of their Brother. God also told him he must not
lie, steal, nor covet another Mans Wife, all which
Commands they would strictly adhere to for the Future,
and that their Brother should see that what they said
was true & sincere in the End, & hop'd he wou'd have
Pity upon them. That they wou'd return to Sandusky
to where their Corn was planted, and after it was
gather'd wou'd come and ask'd Liberty to stay there
another Year, and that after that if their Brother was
convinc'd of their Sincerity they hop'd he wou'd give
them Liberty to come & settle their antient Village.
                                                    The

The Commandant told them if they did not know the Reafon of their beginning he would tell them. The Reafon was, faid he, that you had at that Time fome-thing in your Power that you will never have again, for if you had I am fure you would make the fame Ufe of it you have already done, but if you bring in all thofe who fet you on, black or white, I fhall tell the General what you fay, and it may be a Step toward your getting Peace, but it does not look as if you were very fincere, fince this is the firft of your Appearance. But I fuppofe the Reafon of your coming is becaufe your vain Hopes of an Army from the Illinois is vanifh'd & you fee yourfelves without Succour.

To which the Speaker faid the Reproaches their Brother made them were very juft, but it was not the Chiefs Fault that they did not come fooner, but his, for God had told him to remain quiet & not mind any more bad Belts for that he wou'd be forgiven when they proftrated themfelves before their Brother. And as a Proof of their fincerity they wou'd go and en-deavour to bring in the People he mentioned.

This Day the Schooner Victory ariv'd from Niagara 30 loaded with Baggage for the 17th; fhe left Niagara the 20th, but had very bad Weather. She fprung her Bowfprit and broke her Gaft.

Yefterday fome of the Hurons came to dance before 31 the Commandants Door, & after they had done were going away, when one of them who ftay'd a little be-hind was ftop'd by a Royal American near Mr. St. Martins Houfe, where he coax'd him in and murder'd him as it appears from all the Circumftances of the Affair; the Soldier was immediately put in Irons, and the Commandant was going to fend for the Chiefs, when two of them came into the Fort, having been in-form'd of it by two other Indians who ftay'd behind a
15   little

1764. little Time with him that was murder'd, who tho they
July. did not fee the Stroke, was near enough to hear it, as
was alfo a Corporal of the Artillery.

Aug. 5   This Day *the little Chief* came in and inform'd Mr.
Labute that Seckaho had deceived the Commandant,
that he was gone back to the Miamee River to where
his Corn was, & that after it was ripe, he heard that
Seckaho & what People of his Band would go with
him, with thofe of Pondiacs Band were going off to the
Illinois.

8   This Day Mintiwaby from Saggina came in with fix
or feven of Mindochquays Band, and brought a Prifoner that he had had all the Winter, who Mindoch-
quay told the Commandant in the Spring, would have
then been brought in, but Mintiwaby was gone to
Michilimackinac. He faid that the Chippewas at Sha-
guomigan had fent a Pipe to Mindochquays Band, &
defir'd him to fend it to Machoquifh who wou'd fend
it to the Shawnies & Delawares with the following
Anfwer, to the Invitation they gave them to join with
them to ftrike againft the Englifh laft Fall as Mocho-
quifh had fent the Belt from the Sha. & Dele. namely,
That they had no Complaints againft their Brothers
the Englifh, & they had a greater Regard for their
Wives, Children & young Men, than to enter into fo
bad a Thing.

10   This Afternoon at about four o'Clock, the Sloop
Charlotte & Schooner Gladwin ariv'd here, Commodore Loring & Capt. Grant came in the former.

11   This Day Mafhoquifh, a Puttawattamy Chief, fent
in a Turkey & fome Venifon & defir'd the Commandant would except of it, as he was unworthy of coming
into the Fort, but neverthelefs he & the Chiefs of the
Puttawattamees of St. Jofephs were getting the Prifoners they had together to bring them in, in two or
three

three Days in cafe they would be received. And that
if the Commandant had not a Mind to ftarve him,
he beg'd he wou'd fend him two or three Charges of
Powder and Ball.

This Day *the little Chief* told Mr. Labute that Pon-   12
diac continued his ufual Difcourfe & was as ill intentioned as ever; that he had tried to animate all the
Nations about here, by telling them that there was
abfolutely a French Army on the way here, from the
Illinois, but that the Commandant there could not
come with them untill he had received a Letter from
their Father, which he expected every Day. That
Seckaho had fent three young Men on to the Poft
Vincent[69] to meet them & bring him News.

This Morning a Puttawattamy came to the Settle-   14
ment & fent for Mr. Labute, to whome he told that
he was fent by one of their Chiefs to put his Brother
upon his Guard, as the Shawanees & Delawares were
come to join Pondiac at the Miamee River, to come
and attack this Place, that they were not yet arived,
but one of their Chiefs had feen fome Runners that
came before to inform they were coming.

Mr. Labute was further inform'd by the little Chief
of the Chibbaways that Pondiac had much threatened
the Ottawa Chiefs who brought in fome Prifoners a
little Time ago & told them that his Father was on
his way March & as foon as he came he would have
them all hang'd that tried to make up a Thing that he
(Pondiac) had begun.

The Sloop fail'd for Niagara.   15

The Schooner Bofton ariv'd in the Mouth of the   17
River from Niagara.

This Day at about one o'Clock the Schooner Glad-   19

[69] Now Vincennes, on the Wa-   bafh in Indiana.

win

1764.
Aug.
win fail'd for Niagara. At three o'Clock Mr. Marfack came in and inform'd that he had been told by fome Indians that fome of the Hurons of Sandufky were gone to meet the Army with the Belts that were fent them by the Six Nations to take up the Hatchet againft the Englifh, for that they might at leaft let the Englifh fight their own Battles, which they would tell them when they met them & defire them to return by the fame Belts that they defired them to take up the Hatchet. That they were all ready to receive the Englifh at Lake Sandufky.

20
This Morning Mr. Campeau came in & inform'd that he had overheard an Ottawa & two Folsavoines fpeaking about the Army, & the Ottawa afk'd where they were & which way they were coming; the others told him they were coming on the fouth Side of the Lake. What to do? f'd the Ottawa. To cut off the Hurons at Sandufky, f'd the others. O, faid the Ottawa, they are all ready to meet them, the Miamees & all the Puttawattamys are affembled there, & they have fent their Wives & Children back in the Woods, & have prepared their young Corn & Squafhes on purpofe that they may keep. That a Chibbaway was foon after fent off as he imagined to go to the Miamee.

Mr. M'Dougal was told this Morning by an Indian that most of the Chibbaways & all the Puttawattamys were on the Miamee River with the Ottawas & Miamees, and a good many other Indians.

This Day & laft Night all the Ottawas & Folsavoines, &c., that came from Michilimackinac this Spring to go to Niagara return'd.

21
This Afternoon the Schooner Bofton ariv'd. Laft Night Mr. Jadeau came with a Letter informing us that the Schooner Gladwin was aground near Ifle Bois Bland

Bland[70] upon which Mr. Grant was fent off with fome 1764.
Men to get her off.   Aug.

This Night Mr. Colville, one of the Mafters of the
Veffels, came up to get a Grapling and fome other
things for the Schooner Gladwin, as fhe had loft her
Anchors in getting off.

Commodore Loring left this in the Barge to go on   24
board the Schooner Bofton at the Mouth of the River,
for Niagara.

This Afternoon the Army ariv'd under the Com-   27
mand of Coll. Broadftreet.[71]

A Party of Men were fent to cut Timber upon Ifle   29
Cochon for Barracks, &c.

All the Inhabitants were ordered to appear at nine
next Morning from fifteen Years old upwards to renew
their Oaths of Allegiance, which ran in the Terms following.[72]

This Morning the Schooner Victory fail'd for Nia-   31
gara, with Coll. Gladwin on board.

This Evening the Hurons came to fee the new
Commandant, and after their ufual Compliments gave
him the Name of the little Deer.

This Afternoon fifty-five Ottawas, including Women Sept. 2
& Children, ariv'd here according to their Promife

[70] Ifle Bois Blanc, or White-wood Ifland, lies in Front of Amherft-burgh, on the Canadian Side of the Channel and 18 Miles below Detroit. It is a little over a Mile in length, and to one defcending it is the laft Ifland on the left-hand Side before entering Lake Erie.

[71] Col. John Bradftreet had ferved with great Reputation in the Wars with France in America. He re-ceived a Commiffion as Colonel in Feb. 1762, and held at this Time the Office of Quarter-Mafter General. In 1772 he was promoted to the Rank of Major-General. He died at New York, Sept. 25, 1774, aged 63 Years. *Maff. Hift. Coll.; Army Lifts; Dunlop's Hift. N. Y.; Parkman's Pontiac.*

[72] A Blank here occurs in the MSS.

made

1764.
Sept.
made to Coll. Broadſtreet, when he left the Miamee River.

3   This Morning the Ottawas came to Coll. Broadſtreet to give him their Hands & told him they only came to tell him that the Chibbeways & Puttawattamys were to come in next Day & then they would ſpeake for the Whole. But without their ſaying any thing about making Peace, he told them that *if they were as well inclined for it as him* there would be one juſt at the Mouth of the Miſſiſſippi.

5   This Day a Council was held with the Ottawas and Chippawas, the Puttawattamees not having come in.

6   This Day the Puttawattamees ariv'd.

7   This Day the Ottawas, Chippawas, Puttawattamees, Miamees & Hurons ſign'd the Articles of Peace given them by Coll. Broadſtreet, the Contents of which is in the Book of Councils. Yeſterday the Sloop Charlotte, the Schooner Boſton & Schooner Gladwin enter'd the River.

10   This Day the Schooner Victory ariv'd from Niagara.

11   This Morning the Schooner Gladwin ſail'd for Michilimackinac.

13   This Morning Mr. Crofton arived from Niagara in a Batteaux.with Deſpatches for Coll. Bradſtreet.

This Afternoon News came by Indians, that the Shawanies & Delawares would not make Peace, & that they had detain'd Mr Paulie & the People with him, & were reſolv'd to defend themſelves.

14   This Morning at 8 o'Clock the Army embark'd to go to Sanduſky.

16   This Morning the Schooner Victory ſet ſail for Sanduſky, where ſhe was to wait Coll. Bradſtreets Orders.

17   This Morning the Sloop ſail'd for Niagara.

This Evening Capt. Morris ariv'd here, having been ſent by Coll. Bradſtreet to try to go to the Illinois, but

but was ftop'd by the Miamees who were going to
burn him.

This Morning an Exprefs was fent to overtake Coll.
Bradftreets with Letters from Coll. Cambell & Captain
Morris.

The Schooner Victory return'd from Sandufky for
Provifion; in which came Mr. Cheppoton with Orders
from Coll. Bradftreet.

This Morning the Schooner Bofton arived after laying four Days in the River with contrary Winds.

This Morning Minechefne arived from Coll. Bradftreet with fome Indians, who brought Orders for Mr.
Cheppaton to fpare no Expenfe in getting fome Indians of each Nation to take up the Hatchet againft
the Shawanys & Delawares & for Minechefne to bring
the *little* Chief of the Chippawas in particular. As
alfo Orders to Coll. Campbell to fpeak to the Hurons
to fend as many of their People as poffible; his Speech
& Anfwer to it is in the Book of Councils of this
Date.

This Morning the Schooner Bofton fail'd for Fort
Erie.

This Morning Mr. Cheppaton left this for Sandufky with thirteen Indians, who had taken up the
Hatchet againft the Shawanies & Delawares.

This Morning Mini Chefne left this with eight Indians who had taken up the Hatchet againft the Delawares & Shawanies.

This Day we were inform'd by a Man who came
from Lake St. Clair that Mr. St. Clair[73] enter'd Lake

[73] This was probably James St. Clair who was commiffioned as a Captain in the 45th Regiment, March 10, 1761, Arthur St. Clair had previoufly been in the Regular Service but was then refiding in Pennfylvania,

Huron

Huron the thirteenth with the Schooner Gladwin, &
was foon out of Sight, the Wind being very good.

This Morning the Sloop Charlotte arived from Fort
Erie.

20   This Day the Sloop Charlote fail'd for Fort Erie,
with 121 Packs of Peltry, being the laft of 1464 Packs
that were fent from this fince laft April.

21   This Day fome Indians with Maifonville & J.
Reaume arived from Sandufky, who brought Letters
informing us that the Army had left that Place the
18th Inft.

22   This Day André the Huron arived from Sandufky,
who inform'd that he had been fent out on a Party
from Sandufky with twenty Englifhmen & nine Indians to cut off a Shawanie Village confifting of four
Cabans.   That the Morning after his firft Days March,
four of his Indians who were of the Six Nations chofe
to ftay awhile behind, and at mid day when he halted
he enquired for them, & was told by one of the Englifhmen who ftay'd a little while with them that they were
return'd to the Camp, upon which he pufh'd on without them.   The fourth Day, knowing he was near the
Village, he fent two of his young People on before,
who in a fhort Time return'd & told him they faw two
Indians coming on Horfeback, who foon after arived
& told him they knew his Defign, but that the Village
was increafed to ten Cabans, & if he went on would be
cut to Pieces, & moreover that the Shawanies had afk'd
Peace from Coll. Boquet & were gone with all their
Prifoners to meet him to the Amount of two hundred,
upon which feeing they were apriz'd of his Defign &
were going to make Peace he fent back his Party &
took two Indians & proceeded to the Village, where
he was inform'd that the four Indians that return'd
from the Party inform'd a Huron Chief who had made
                                                    Peace

Peace with Coll. Bradſtreet, who immediately ſent off an Expreſs on Horſeback to the Village, & that one of the two Indians that met him was the Brother of a Mohawk Chief. That he was ſure in caſe that his Deſign had not been diſcovered, the Indians that were with him would not have fought. That in paſſing by the Head of the Sanduſky River he ſaw a Huron of San-duſky who told him he was ariv'd from the Frontiers of Virginia where he had been at war with a Party of Shawanies & Delawares, who had taken thirty Scalps, and that if he would not believe him he would give him two, that were pretty freſh to ſhow to his Father the Commandant at this Place, which Scalps he ſaw.

This Day the Militia return'd from Michilimacki-nac.

This Day the Schooner Boſton ariv'd at the Mouth of the River after been eighteen Days from Niagara, & the Schooner Victory, who came out with her, they ſuppoſe was drove back.

This Morning Capt. St. Clair arived here from Michilimackinac after laying up the Schooner Gladwin in a ſmall River near the Head of the River Huron.

This Evening the Sloop Charlotte, the Schooner Boſton & Schooner Victory arived oppoſite the Fort.

This Morning André & five other Hurons left this on a ſcout againſt the Shawanies & Delawares & were to encamp at the River Rouge for to night.

This Afternoon a Soldier was kill'd and ſcalp'd on the Road between the River Rouge & the Fort.

This Morning a Soldier was kill'd & ſcalp'd behind the Fort near the Edge of the Woods.

Andrew return'd this Morning & promiſ'd (as he imagined it was Indians from Sanduſky that took the two Scalps) that he would fall upon the firſt Indian he ſaw from the other ſide of Lake Erie.

16   This

1764.   This Day we were inform'd that it was fome St.
Nov. 25 Jofeph Indians that took the Scalps as they had feen
          them.

26   This Day two Puttawattamies of this Place came in
          & inform'd that it was the St. Jofeph Indians that
          took the Scalps at the Inftigation of a Saky who had
          been with them near twenty Years, & whofe Son was
          kill'd this Time twelve Months at this Place.

          This was confirm'd by many Informations from
          many Indians.

Dec. 14   This Day Machioquiffe a Chief of the Puttawatta-
          mees of this Place arived from St. Jofephs with a Let-
          ter from one Chevallier to the Commanding Officer,
          who inform'd the Commandant that Chevallier told
          him the King of France had fent over fome Merchants,
          whom he had order'd to fell Things to the Indians at
          the following Rate, viz: if the Englifh fold a Blanket
          for four Beaver they were to fell it for three; if they fold
          it for three, they were to fell it for two, & if the Eng-
          lifh fold it for two they were to fell it for one, and
          every thing elfe in Proportion. That there was five
          Cannoes of that Merchandize already at St. Jofephs, as
          much at Ouiattanon & a good deal gone to the Sha-
          wanies & Delawares.

          After a good deal of Difcourfe with the Command-
          ant about the Scalps that was taken the 23d & 24th of
          Novem. he afk'd him in cafe the Murderers could be
          brought before him to make a proper Submiffion,
          wheather he would not forgive them; to which he faid
          if they were brought before him & made proper Sub-
          miffions he would not ufe them as they merited.
          Upon which Machioquiffe promif'd to go and get fome
          Sauteux & ufe all the Means in his Power to bring the
          Murderers in & with the Englifh Prifoners that was
          at St. Jofephs.

                                                  January

January 21ft, 1764 [1765].

This Day Andrew the Huron arived from Fort Pitt, with Letters, for being inform'd that Peace was made with the Shawanies & Delawares, he proceeded to that Place inftead of ftriking againft them as he was directed when he left this. He faid the Shawanies & Delawares told him there was three Battoes & two Perriaugres arived at the Mouth of the Oenentois, from the Illinois, & they fent them a large Belt of Wampum defireing them to go immediately out of their River. That they had made Peace with their Father the Englifh, and would not have any more to do with the French.

Andrew the Huron left this for Fort Pitt with Maifonville.

Feb. 27

A fmall Party from the Miamees took a Prifoner that had ftraggled from the Veffel at the River Rouge.

Mar. 11

Mr. Jadot was fent from this to the Miamee to bring one Clermont & his Family & fome others to this Place, as we had been inform'd they fpirited up the Indians to ftrike here, but the Indians met him before he ariv'd there & difarm'd his Party, and fent him back.

17

Coll. Campbell fent them a Meffage by fome Chibbawas (who offer'd themfelves as Volunteers) to let them know if they did not give up every Prifoner they had & the Arms they took from Mr. Jadots Party, he would declare them his Enemys ; & the Chibbawas who carried this Meffage had Orders from their Chief Seccaho, that in cafe they did not comply with this Demand they might look upon them as their Enemies as they wou'd immediately ftrike againft them.

15

The Schooner Victory fail'd for Niagara, in which went Lt. Stewart & Sir Edward Pickering.

This Day the Chibbawas return'd from the Miamee and

May 8

and brought Word they wou'd foon be in with their
Prifoners & defir'd their Father not to be impatient;
but by private Intelligence we were inform'd quite
otherwife.

16   This Day the Sloop Charlot ariv'd from Niagara,
in which came Lt. M'Dougal.

17   This Day fome of the Ottawa Chiefs from the
Miamee River came in & deliver'd a Meffage to the
Commandant which they f'd they receiv'd from Col°
Croghan, inviting them to Fort Pitt, begging he
wou'd write to Col° Croghan & tell him in cafe they
did not come at the Time appointed that it was becaufe they were emploied in trying to bring in the
Miamees to make a proper Submiffion to ther Father
& with their Prifoners.

And defiring if he their Father chofe they fhou'd go
to the Miamee he wou'd get one or two of the Hurons
Chiefs to go with them.

In the Afternoon one   a Mohawk who had
been fent laft Fall by Sir Willm Johnf^n as a Spy among
the Indians came in with two Bennakees & inform'd
the Commandant, that as their was frequent Reports
at Sandufky that a Body of French & Indians were
coming by way of the Miamee, they fent fome young
Men as far as the Miamee to fee whether it was true,
& as the above mentioned Indians were on their way
here they met the Hurons returning from Miamee, who
told them that the 9th Inft. Pondiac's Nephew ariv'd
from the Illinois who inform'd them that while Pondiac & the great Saalteur from Michilimackinac was
there, fix Englifhmen, with one Maifonville a Frenchman, a Delaware, a Mohawk & a Huron from this
Place ariv'd there from Fort Pitt, whom Pondiac
caufed to be feized and brought them as far as Ouiattanon, where they were all burnt but two whom he was
                                                    bringing

bringing to give to the Miamees. That Pondiac had
feven large Belts for to raife the St. Jofephs, the Miamees, the Ouiattanons, the Pians, Mafcoutons, and the
Illinois, who were to affemble with fome Nations to the
northward & make what Efforts they could againft this
Place the Beginning of next Month, for which Purpofe Pondiac had befides the above Belts a very large
one which was for the Hatchet from the French. That
this undertaking was to be entirely by the Indians
without any Affiftance.

St. Vincent, one of the above Indians further fays,
that being at the Shawanee Town about twenty Days
ago, a French Trader from the Illinois told him that
he had receiv'd a Letter from Maifonville when he was
going down the Ohio, who inform'd him that he had
been fent by the Commanding Officer at Fort Pitt, to
go to the Illinois with fome Englifhmen.

Three Chiefs of the Ottawas with fome young Men 20
left this with a Meffage from the Commandant to the
Miamees and one for Pondiac.

This Morning the Sloop Charlotte fail'd for Ni- 21
agara.

This Afternoon one of the Chibbawas who were fent
to the Miamee the 15th March, came here & brought
back the Belts which the Miamees would not receive &
told quite a different Story from what their Chief Seccaho told on the Return of the reft.

This Day the Indians from St. Jofephs came to the 24
Settlement with a Prifoner, & a Belt from their Chiefs,
but the Commanding Officer wou'd not receive them
as there was no Chief with, and as they had not fulfil'd
their Promife.

The Prifoner they fent in by two Puttawattamy
Chiefs of this Place with the Belt, which the Commandant receiv'd & fent them Word, when their Chiefs
fulfill'd

fulfill'd their Promife he wou'd receive them as his
Children, but not till then.   This Prifoner was gave
to them by the Shawanies & Delawares two Years ago,
whom we new nothing of, being one more than they
f'd they had.

25   This Day the Huron Chiefs with two Onondagoes
came in & told the Commandant that they came to
fpeake to him upon the fame Subject they had done
the 17th Inftant, faying they had fince been inform'd
by fome people from towards the Illinois that they
were in Danger, that the Indians the laft Time had
only taken up the Hatchet againft the Englifh, but
that now they would take it up againft the French &
them, as they liv'd near the Englifh and lik'd them ;
& that they fhould perifh with them.   They then defir'd they might give the Commandant a little Advice,
which if found good he wou'd have Pitty upon them
& do.

They then f'd that as the Indians depended entirely
upon what they could get or take from the Inhabitants
for Subfiftance, they thought it advifable that they
fhould joine in fmall Partys & gather together their
Corn & Cattle & make at different Places fmall Stockades where eight or ten Families might fecure themfelves in, with their Effects ; that in propofing this to
them the Commandant would fee whether they were
inclin'd to be faithfull or not, for if they objected againft
it, they were certainly inclin'd to fight, as the Indians
would render themfelves Mafters of them & would
oblig'd them to do what they pleaf'd & ftrip them of
every thing, in cafe they remain'd in the undefenfible
Condition they were then.   They beg'd the Commandant would defire the Inhabitants on the South
Side of the River to join with them to make a Stockade at the Huron Point near the Priefts Houfe, that
they

they might put their Wifes & Children in for Security, for notwitftanding they were a fmall Number they would then Laugh at any thing the other Nations cou'd do, but if they were to remain they would be in their Power & perhaps be oblig'd to do thing they had not Inclination to do, for faid they, what will not a Man do to fave his Life, & when we fee a Knife at our Throats we fhall perhaps commit Faults, for thefe and many other Reafons they beg'd the Commandant wou'd propofe to the People to put themfelves in fome kind of Defence. They further faid they new the Inhabitants would be very angry at them if they new they propof'd fuch a thing, but they new on their Side that if they did not comply with it they wou'd foon repent it, and perhaps wou'd be very glad to take Refuge in their little Fort, in cafe they got one built. They faid there was no Time to loofe, the fooner it was done the better.

In the Afternoon the Commandant fent for the Officers of the Militia, and acquainted them of the News he had heard & propofed to them to put themfelves in the beft ftate of Defence they cou'd, agreeable to which he gave them fome Propofals in Writing, a Copy of which is amongft the Orders iffued to the Militia.

This Day the Schooner Vi&ory ariv'd, having been fent from Niagara with Capt. Simpfon of the Artillery to take up the Cannon left by Col⁰ Bradftreet laft Fall near the River au Roche, but was oblig'd to put in here for Want of Provifion, having had a great deal of bad Weather & not being able to go to the Place. The Veffell in very bad Condition.

The Schooner Vi&ory.

[The Diary thus ends abruptly in the Middle of a Page in the Manufcript.]

26

June 6

JOURNAL

OF THE

SIEGE OF DETROIT,

BY

Major ROBERT ROGERS.

INTRODUCTION.

MAJOR Rogers arrived at Detroit on the 29th of July, 1763, with the Detachment under the Command of Capt. Dalyel, and fhared in the gallant but unfortunate Sortie made under the Command of that Officer a few Days after, in which the Leader and many of his Men perifhed. The Information contained in the following Narrative is entirely from hearfay, and only brings down the Chain of Events to the 4th of July, although dated nearly a Month later. It is probable that Maj. Rogers began to write an Account of the Siege foon after his Arrival, and that this was only partly finifhed when the failing of two Veffels (mentioned on Page 59) offered a convenient Opportunity for fending it to Sir William Johnfon. At the Clofe of the Volume of Journals publifhed by Major Rogers in 1765, is an Advertifement of a fecond Volume to contain, among other Things, an Account of

the

the Indian Wars in America fubfeqent to 1760. Sub-
fcriptions were folicited and the Book was promifed
within a limited Time, but from fome Caufe unknown,
it was never printed. It is reafonable to infer that the
following Pages were intended to form a Portion of
the Book, and that this Fragment, now firft printed,
may be the only Part that has been preferved. It was
found among the Manufcripts of Sir William Johnfon
in the New York State Library.

F. B. H.

JOURNAL

OF THE

SIEGE OF DETROIT.

JOURNAL of the Siege of Detroit, taken from the Officers who were then in the Fort, and wrote in their Words in the following Manner, viz:

The 6th of May; when we were privately informed of a Conspiracy formed against us by the Indians, particularly the Tawa[1] Nation, who were to come to council with us the next Day, and massacre every Soul of us. On the Morning of that Day, being Saturday the 7th of May, fifteen of their Warriors came into the Fort and seemed very inquisitive and anxious to know where all the English Merchants' Shops were.

At 9 o'Clock the Garrison were ordered under Arms and the Savages continued coming into the Fort till 11 o'Clock, diminishing their Numbers as much as possible by dividing themselves at all the Corners of

[1] Ottawa.

the

the ftreets moft adjacent to the Shops.   Before 12
o'Clock they were three hundred Men, at leaft three
times the Number equal to that of the Garrifon; but
feeing all the Troops under Arms, and the Merchants
Shops fhut, imagined prevented them from attempting
to put their evil Scheme into execution that Day.

Obferving us thus prepared, their Chiefs came in a
very condemned like Manner, to Council, where they
fpoke a great deal of Nonfenfe to Major Gladwine and
Capt. Campbell, protefting at the fame Time the
greateft Friendfhip imaginable to them, but expreffing
their Surprife at feeing all the Officers and Men under
Arms.   The Major then told them that he had certain
Intelligence that fome Indians were projecting Mifchief, and on that Acc^t he was determined to have the
Troops always under Arms upon fuch Occafions:
That they being the oldeft Nation, and the firft that
had come to Council, needed not to be aftonifhed at
that Precaution as he was refolved to do the fame to
all Nations.

At 2 o'Clock they had done fpeaking, went off feem-
ingly very difcontented and croffed the River half a
League from the Fort, where they all encamped about
6 o'Clock that Afternoon.   Six of their Warriors' returned and brought an old Squaw Prifoner, alledging
that fhe had given us falfe Information againft them.
The Major declared fhe had never given any kind of
Advice.   They then infifted upon naming the Author
of what he had heard in regard to the Indians, which
he declined to do, but told them it was one of themfelves, whofe Name he promifed never to reveal; whereupon they went off and carried the old Woman Prifoner with them.   When they arrived at their Camp,
Pondiac their greateft Chief feized on the Prifoner and
gave her three Strokes with a Stick on the Head,
                                                which

which laid her flat on the Ground, and the whole Nation affembled around her and called repeated Times kill her, kill her.

Sunday the 8th, Pondiac and feveral other of the principal Chiefs came into the Fort, at 5 o'Clock in the Afternoon and brought a Pipe of Peace with them of which they wanted to convince us fully of their Friendfhip and Sincerity, but the Major judging that they only wanted to caggole us would not go nigh them nor give them any Countenance, which obliged Capt. Campbell to go and fpeake with them, and after fmoaking with the Pipe of Peace and affuring him of their Fidelity, they faid that the next Morning all the Nation would come to Council where every thing would be fettled to our Satisfaction, after which they would immediately difperfe, and that that would remove all kind of Sufpicion.

Accordingly on Monday Morning the 9th, fix of their Warriors came into the Fort at 7 o'Clock, and upon feeing the Garrifon under Arms went off without being obferved. About 10 o'Clock we counted fifty-fix Canoes, with feven and eight Men in each, croffing the River from their Camp, and when they arrived nigh the Fort, the Gates were fhut, and the Interpreter went to tell them that not above fifty or fixty Chiefs would be admitted into the Fort, upon which Pondiac immediately defired the Interpreter in a peremptory Manner to return directly and acquaint us that if all their People had not free Accefs into the Fort none of them would enter it : that we might ftay in our Fort, but he would keep the Country, adding that he would order a Party inftantly to an Ifland where we had twenty-four Bullocks, which they immediately killed. Unluckily three Soldiers were on the Ifland and a poor Man with his Wife and four Children
which

which they all murthered except two Children, as alfo a poor Woman and her two Sons, that lived about half a Mile from the Fort.

After having thus put all the Englifh without the Fort to death, the ordered a Frenchman who had feen the Woman and her two Children killed and fcalped, to come and inform us of it, and likewife of their having murthered Sir Robert Davers, Captain Robert-fon and a Boats' Crew of fix Perfons two Days before, being Saturday the 7th of May, near the Entrance of Lake Huron, for which Place they fet out from hence on Monday the 2d Inft. in order to know if the Lakes and Rivers were Navigable for a Schooner which lay here to proceed to Michilimackinac. We were then fully perfuaded that the Information given us was well founded, and a proper Difpofition was made for the Defenfe of the Fort, although our Number was but fmall, not exceeding one hundred and twenty, includ-ing all the Englifh Traders, and the Works were nigh Mile in Circumferance.

On Tuesday the 10th, very early in the Morning, the Savages began to fire on the Fort, and Veffels which lay oppofite to the eaft and weft Sides of the Fort.[2]   About 8 o'Clock the Indians called a Parley and ceafed firing, and half an Hour after, the Wain-dotes Chiefs came into the Fort, on their way to a Council where they were called by the Tawas and pro-mifed us to endeavour to foliciate and perfuade the Tawas from committing further Hoftilities.   After drinking a Glafs of Rum they went off at three o'Clock that Afternoon.   Several of the Inhabitants and four Chiefs of the Tawas, Waindotes and Chippawas and Pottawattomes came and acquainted us, that moft of

[2] The Channel of Detroit River oppofite the Fort, ran but a few Degrees South of Weft, although its general Courfe is nearly South.

all

all the Inhabitants were affembled at a Frenchmans Houfe about a Mile from the Fort, where the Savages propofed to hold a Council, and defiring Captain Campbell and another Officer to go with them to that Council, where they hoped with their Prefence and Affiftance further Hoftilities would ceafe, affuring us at the fame Time that come what would, that Capt. Campbell and the other Officers that went with him, fhould return whenever they pleafed. This Promife was affertained by the French as well as the Indian Chief, whereupon Captain Campbell and Lieutenant McDougal went off efcorted by a Number of the Inhabitants and the four Chiefs, they firft promifed to be anfwerable for their returning y^t Night.

When they arrived at the Houfe already mentioned they found the French and Indians affembled, and after counceling a long while, the Waindotes were prevailed on to fing the War Song, and this being done, it was next refolved that Captain Campbell and Lieutenant McDougall fhould be detained Prifoners, but would be indulged to lodge in a French Houfe till a French Commandant arrived from the Ilenoes, that next Day five Indians and as many Canadians would be difpatched to acquaint the Commanding Officer of the Ilonies that Detroit was in their Poffeffion and require of him to fend an Officer to Command, to whom Captain Cample and Lieutenant McDougall fhould be delivered. As for Major Gladwin he was fummoned to give up the Fort and two Veffels, &c., the Troops to ground their Arms, and they would allow as many Battoes and as much Provifion as they judged requifite for us to go to Niagara: That if thefe Propofals were not accepted of, they were a thoufand Men, and ftorm the Fort at all events, and in that Cafe every Soul of us fhould be put to the Torture. The Major returned for Anfwer,

18   that

that as foon as the two Officers they had detained were permitted to come into the Fort, he would after confulting them give a pofitive Anfwer to their Demand, but could do nothing without obtaining their Opinion.

On Wednefday the 11th, feveral Inhabitants came early in the Morning into the Fort, and advifed us by way of Friendfhip to make our Efcape aboard the Veffels, affuring us that we had no other Method by which we could preferve our Lives, as the Indians were then fifteen hundred fighting Men, and would be as many more in a few Days, and that they were fully determined to attack us in an Hours time. We told the Monf'rs that we were ready to receive them, and that every Officer and Soldier in the Fort would willingly perifh in the Defenfe of it, rather than condefcend or agree to any Terms that Savages would propofe. Upon which the French went off as I fuppofe to communicate what we had faid to their Allies, and in a little afterwards the Indians gave their ufual Hoop, and five or fix hundred began to attack the Fort on all Quarters. Indeed fome of them behaved extremely well and advanced very boldly in an open plain expofed to our Fire, and came within fixty Yards of the Fort, but upon having three Men killed and above a dozen wounded, they retired as brifkly as they advanced, and fired at three hundred Yards Diftance till feven o'Clock at Night, when they fent a Frenchman into the Fort with a Letter to the Major, defiring a ceffation of Arms, that Night, and propofing to let the Troops with their Arms aboard the Veffels, but infifting upon our giving up the Fort, leaving the French Auxilliary all the Merchandize and officers Effects, and had even the Infolence to demand a Negro Boy belonging to a Merchant to be delivered to Pondiack.

The

The Major's Reply to thefe extraordinary Propofitions was much the fame as to the firft.

Tuefday the 12th, five Frenchmen and as many Indians were fent off for the Ilinoes with Letters wrote by a Canadian agreable to Pondiacs Defire. On the 13th we were informed by the Inhabitants that Mr. Chapman, a Trader from Niagara, was taken Prifoner by the Waindotes, with five Battoes loaded with Goods.

The 21ft, one of the Veffels was ordered to fail for the Niagara, but to remain till the fixth of June at the Mouth of the River in order to advert the Battoes which we expected daily from Niagara.

Upon the 22d we were told that Enfign Paully who commanded at Sandufky was brought Prifoner by ten Tawas, who reported that they had prevailed after long Confultation with the Waindotes who lived at Sandufky to declare War againft us; that fome Days ago they came early of a Morning to the Block Houfe, and murthered every Soul therein, confifting of twenty feven Perfons, Traders included; that Meff^rs Callender and Prentice, formerly Captains in the Pennfylvania Reg^t were amongft that Number, and that they had taken one hundred Horfes loaded with Indian Goods, which with the Plunder of the Garrifon was agreed to be given the Waindotes before they condefcended to join them; that all they wanted was the Commanding Officer.

On the 29th of May, we had the Mortification to fee eight of our Battoes in the Poffeffion of the Enemy, paffing on the oppofite Shore, with feveral Soldiers Prifoners in them. When the foremoft Battoe came oppofite the Sloop, fhe fired a Gun, and the Soldiers aboard called at thofe in the Battoe, that if they paffed the Savages would kill them all, upon which they immediately

mediately feized on two Indians and threw them overboard with him and tomahawked him directly, they
being near the Shore and it quite fhoal. Another
Soldier laid hold of an Oar, and ftruck that Indian
upon the Head, of which Wound he is fince dead.
Then there remained only three Soldiers, of which two
were wounded, and although fifty Indians were on the
Bank not fixty Yards, firing upon them, the three
Soldiers efcaped aboard the Veffel, with the Battoe
loaded with eight Barrels of Provifions and gives the
following Account of their Miffortune, viz:

That two Nights before, about 10 o'Clock, they
arrived about fix Leagues from the Mouth of the River
where they encamped. That two Men went a little
from the Camp for Firewood to boil their Kettle,
when one of the two was feized on by an Indian, killed
and fcalped in an Inftant. The other Soldier ran
directly and alarmed the Camp, upon which Lieutenant
Cuyler immediately ordered to give Ammunition to
the Detachment, which confifted of one Serjeant and
feventeen Soldiers of the Royal Americans, three Serjeants and feventy-two Rank and File of the Queen's
Independent Company of Rangers. After having delivered their Ammunition, and a Difpofition made of
the Men, the Enemy came clofe to them without being
obferved, behind a Bank and fired very fmartly on
one Flank which could not fuftain the Enemys Fire
and they retired precipitately and threw the Whole in
Confufion. By that Means the Soldiers embarked
aboard the Battoes with one, two and three Oars in
each Battoe, which gave an Opportunity to the Savages
of taking them all except the two Battoes that efcaped
with Mr. Cuyler to Niagara.

Sunday the 5th of June, we were acquainted that
Fort Maimes was taken, that Enfign Holms who
                                        commanded

commanded there had been informed by two Frenchmen who arrived there the preceding Day of Detroits being attacked by the Indians, which he would hardly believe, but threatened to imprifon the French for that Report, that an Indian Woman had betrayed him out of the Fort by pretending 'that another Woman was very fick, and begged of him to come to her Cabin to let blood of her, and when he had gone a little Diftance from the Fort was fired on and killed. The Serjeant hearing the Report of the firing ran to fee what it was, and was immediately taken Prifoner. The Soldiers fhut the Gates and would have probably defended the Fort if one Walfh, a Trader who had been taken Prifoner a few Days before, had not advifed them to open the Gates, alledging that if they did not comply the Indians would fet Fire to the Fort and put them to death ; whereas, if they opened the Gates, they fhould be well treated. Whereupon the Gates were opened, and the Soldiers grounded their Arms.

On the 10th of June we heard that Enfign Schloffer the Commanding Officer at Saint Jofephs was taken Prifoner and that all the Garrifon (except three Men) were maffacred. That the Indians came on the 25th of May with a Pretence to Council, and as foon as the Chiefs had fhaken Hands with Mr. Schloffer, they feized on him, gave a Shriek and inftantly killed ten Men.

The 12th we were told that Lieut. Jenkins and all the Garrifon of Owat'anon, confifting of a Sergeant and eighteen Men were taken Prifoners and carried to the Ilonies.

The 18th a Jefuit arrived from Michillimakenac and brought a Letter from Captain Etherinton and Lieutenant Leffley, with an Account of their being taken Prifoners. That Lieutenant Jamet and twenty-one

one Soldiers. That on the 2nd the Indians were playing Ball as ufual nigh the Fort, where Captain Etherington and Lieut. Leffley happened to be looking at them, but were fuddenly feized on and carried into the Woods. At the fame Time the Savages had purpofely thrown their Ball into the Fort, as if that had happened by Accident, and followed it directly into the Fort, where a Number of their Women had Tomahawks and Spears concealed under their Blankets, which they delivered them and put the whole Garrifon to death, except thirteen Men.

The 30th we were informed that the Blockhoufe at Prefque Ifle was burned, that Enfign Chriftie and all his Garrifon, which confifted of twenty-nine Men were taken Prifoners except fix Men, who it was believed made their efcape to La Beuf.

On the Night of the 2d Inftant and Lieut. McDougall were lodged at the Houfe I have already mentioned, about two Miles from the Fort, and made a Refolution to Efcape, when it was agreed on between them that McDougall fhould fet off firft, which he did and get fafe into the Fort, but you know it was much more dangerous for Captain Campbell than for any other Perfon by Reafon that he could neither run nor fee, and being fenfible of that failing I am fure prevented him from attempting to efcape.

The 4th a Detachment was ordered to deftroy fome Breaftworks and Entrenchments the Indians had made a Quarter of a Mile from the Fort, and about twenty Indians came to attack that Party, which they engaged but were drove off in an Inftant with the Lofs of one Man killed (and two wounded) which our People fcalped and cut to Pieces. Half an Hour after the Savages carried the Man they had loft before Captain Campbell, ftriped him naked, and directly murthered

him

him in a cruel Manner, which indeed gives one Pain beyond Expreſſion, and I am ſure cannot miſs but to affect ſenſibly all his Acquaintences, although he is now out of the Queſtion.

The Indians likewiſe reported that Venango and Le Beuf is taken by the Savages.

Dated at Detroit 8th Augt 1763.

To Sir William Johnſon.

GEN. BRADSTREET'S

STATEMENT

UPON

INDIAN AFFAIRS.

INTRODUCTION.

THE following Statement upon Indian Affairs is preſerved in the Hand-writing of General John Bradſtreet, in a Volume belonging to the New York State Library, entitled *Bradſtreet and Amherſt MSS.*, beginning at Page 190. Theſe Papers were found many Years ſince in the Garret of a Houſe in Albany which Gen. Bradſtreet once inhabited, and are of un-queſtionable authenticity.

During the Indian Wars which followed the Con-queſt of Canada in 1760, General B. held the Rank of Quarter-Maſter General, and his Opportunities for judging of the Merits or Defects of the Syſtem under which Indian Affairs were managed entitle his Opinions to Reſpect. The Difficulties attending this Service are clearly and forcibly ſtated, and the Remedies which he ſuggeſts were dictated by ſound Judgment and en-forced by ſtrong Argument.

F. B. H.

GEN. BRADSTREET'S
STATEMENT.
DECEMBER 17, 1764.

A BRIEF State of our interiour Situation with the Savages, the Disadvantages occasioned by the Indian Traders following them to their Hunting Country, Castles and Villages ; the Benefit to all his Majesty's Subjects by confining the Trade to particular Posts and the Danger of fixing those Posts nearer the Colonys of New York and Quebec then St. Marys, Michilimicanac, La Bay, & the Detroit, &c., &c.

The Savages retain their Affection for the French Nation as much as ever, and have nothing more at Heart than their Return and Power in this Country, & are
ready

ready to execute any thing in their Power to anfwer
that Purpofe, and deteft the Englifh fo much, that the
Traders can not quit the eftablifhed Pofts to go &
Trade with them (as Canadians do, who run no rifk,
but on the contrary are well receiv'd) without being
murder'd and plunder'd; and Experience alfo fhews
when they employ Canadians to carry on the Trade
for them they are cheated and ruin'd; which muft in
a fhort Time put all the Indian Trade in the Hands
of the Canadians in Conjunction with the French &
Spaniards from the Miffiffippi & the Settlements of
the Illinois, who at this Time carry of great Part of
the Trade between the Miffiffippi & the great Lakes
& the Ohio.   To remedy thefe Evils and recover the
Trade which is much impair'd, the Savages debauch'd,
become Idle and neglect their Hunting by fpirituous
Liquors being conftantly carried to their Hunting
Countrys and to fix the Trade with equil Advantage
to all his Majeftys Subjects, it is imagin'd it fhould be
limited to particular Pofts & upon no Account allow
any Traders to follow the Savages to their Hunting
Country, Caftles or Villages, as it moreover gives their
Boat men & fome of themfelves a Taft for a wander-
ing & independent Life, infects them with a Habit of
Libertinifm & many of thefe Sort of Canadians remain
amongft the Savages now; from whom they are not
diftinguifhable but by their Vices & inciting them on
to Acts of Cruelty againft the Englifh; and was their
nothing to fear from the Entregues of foreign Enemies
the nearer the Pofts were fix'd to the Colonys of New
York & Quebec to more Advantage would the Trade
be carry'd on, as the Savages would then become the
principal Carriers themfelves, which is a very expenfive
Article.   But the Difadvantage of confining the Trade
to Pofts nearer the Colonys then St. Marys, Michilimicanac

micanac, La Bay and Detroit would be, the Savages of
the northweſt Side Lake Superior would find it lefs
troublefome to Trade with the Hudfons Bay Company
then to go to thofe Pofts, and thofe of La Bay, the
weſt Side Lake Superior & Lake Michigan would find
it alfo lefs difficult to go to the Miffiffippi ſhould the
French & Spaniſh Traders not go to them as they
actually do now and they would alfo foon find the way
into Lake Superior with their Merchandife—and fo
long as thofe Traders come to the Savages on the
Banks of the Wabaſh and Scioto Rivers, by the Miffiffippi and Ohio, our Traders at the Detroit & Fort
Pitt will benefit but little from them, thofe of St. Jofephs & Miames, which makes a confiderable Number
of Hunters—and to thefe Evils we may add a greater,
namely, was the Trade confin'd to Pofts as low as
Niagara, the certain Confequence would be, that all
the Furr Trade & Savages would fall into the Hands
of the French and Spaniards & it effected foon by
Means of the French Inhabitants of Detroit, Wabach,
St. Jofeph & Michilimicanac & thofe Vagabonds or
Coureurs de Bois of Canada difperf'd amongſt them,
who when left to themfelves and able to act openly &
without Fear will not fail their old Maſters ; the dreadful Confequence of which would foon be feverely felt
by the Inhabitants of the Frontiers of feveral Colonys.

From repeated Information it can admit of no
Doubt but that the French by the Miffiffippi are ufing
their beſt Endeavours to bring all the Savages to confider the Spaniards in the fame favourable light to
them as the French themfelves ; we muſt therefore loofe
Ground every Day with the Indians if we remain idle
Spectators of it ; it would be of great Ufe in helping
to prevent it as well as that of a general Confederacy
of them againſt us when attempted were we to divide
them

them by fomenting the Quarrils generally subsisting amongst them instead of making them up & turn them to our own Use & Advantage & prevent as much as possible the Intercourse of the Savages of diffirent Districts, that is, those of the north west Side Lake Superior to come down no farther than St. Mary's & Michilimicanac; those of La Bay, west Side Lake Superior & Lake Michigan to the Posts of La Bay; those of St. Josephs, Miames, Wabach & Scioto Rivers to the Detroit & Fort Pitt, & the Six Nations (if possible) to be kept from them all at the Posts of Neagara & Oswego, as the Meetings of different Nations of Indians have too often ended in making up their old Quarrils & ploting against us—and to succeed in this important Businefs, Men of Adrefs with a perfect Knowledge of the Polocy & Craft of the Savages should be employ'd.

The Number of Boats employ'd in the Indian Trade annually from this Province amounts to about 180 whose Cargoes one with the other is in Value 300 £, at the New York Prices; which makes for the whole about 100,000 £; out of which a large Deduction is to be made from the Proffits of the Trader for Transportation & other Expenfes as may be conceiv'd by the Expence of one Boat to Detroit:

3 Boatmen to Detroit,	- -	£60
Battoe, Oars, &c.,	- - -	9
Carriage over the little Falls and Fort Stanwix,		1.12
Do. Neagara,	- - -	11. 8
		£82

and to Michilimicana it amounts to 112 £, about; and innormous as this Expenfe is it bears no Proportion to that of following the Savages to their Hunting Country

Country during the Winter; which the English Merchants of Canada are no Strangers to—and to this follows the Expence of Provisions, which is always very scarce & dear at the Posts. At Michilimicanac Pork sold this Summer for two Shillings and sixpence, Bread four Shillings & Butter six Shillings the Pound, and at Detroit 5 £ a hundred weight, and this scarcity of Provisions and expensive Transportation will continue so long as the Detroit remains not properly settled; the Encroachments of the French and Spaniards not prevented; the Frontiers of several Colony's not secure from the Attacks of the Savages, nor we have the full Advantage of the Fur Trade but by Detroit being made a strong Barrier to the Colonys & that Settlement encouraged or the whole of the Missisippi in our Hands; which last will bring all the Savages dependent on us for what they want; for who ever imagines the Savages of the interior Country will remain in Peace and Friendship with us whilst the French & Spaniards possess the Missisippi will find himself mistaken'd—indeed the former has not been found perminent though very expensive—and the large Sum lately given at the Congress at Fort Stanwix will operate on the Six Nations & their Friends only. From what has been said of the Expence in carrying on this Trade, it appears the Method now practis'd is better calculated to enrich the Battoe & Canoe Men than the Merchants and is one of the Causes so many fail; the regulating this, with Justice to both, seems to be absolutely necessary; but the more Vessells are employed in this Trade to more Advantage will it be carry'd on as it may be done for half the now Expence & always with Safety against the evil Designs of any Savages.

Detroit is here mentioned as being the most proper Place for an Establishment & Barrier for the Reason

that

that its Situation being moft proper & convenient
to raife Provifions, awe and attack fuch Savages as are
moft likely to be troublefome firft, to them divide and
keep them fo, to take up the French and Spanifh
Traders that may come on our Side the Miffiffippi, for
it is to little Purpofe to fend Troops to attack Savages
and take up People protected by them from fo great Diftance as the Colonys are, to return in a few Months or
to depend on fmall Garrifons, be they ever fo well pofted,
it being out of their Power to do more than give Protection to fuch as are within their Works ; and it is as
bad Policy to fuffer the Encroachments above mention'd & the Savages to infult & murder without further Notice than giving them large Sums of Money in
Prefents to make Peace for a few Years, for which they
have always held us in Contempt & thereby encouraged
to commit frequent Depredations upon us to exact
Prefents from Time to Time to make it up. As the
Soil of the Detroit is as good as can be & plenty of it
ready for the Plow, Provifions would foon be plenty
& cheap there & the Navigation of the Lakes carry'd
on by the Inhabitants of that Place in Veffels at as
little Expence as in this Province, which would be of
great advantage to the Trade, fecurity to the Pofts as
well as leffning their Expence—and without Veffels
neither one nor the other can be faid to be fafe & fecure
from falling into the Hands of the Savages.

Should the Trade be limited to particular Pofts it
would be of advantage to eftablifh the Prices of the
Merchandife & Furrs with equal Advantage to both
Sides & to prevent Impofitions too frequently practiced
by the Traders ; and perhaps the way of doing it lefs
exceptionable to the Traders & Savages would be by two
Provincional Commiffarys of Abilities and Experience
from the Colony of New York & Quebec with the Indian
Chiefs

Chiefs in Prefence of the Officer commanding Pofts
and thofe Commiffary to refide at the Pofts, infpect
the Trade & report from Time [to Time] every thing
neceffary and fhould it appear reafonable the Traders
and Savages pay a Proportion towards the general
Security of the Interior Country, the following Dutys
may be laid by every Province connected in the Trade,
viz :

On Speritious Liquors 2s6d fterling a Gallon.

Powder,	6d	do	a Pound.
Strouds,	8s	do	a Piece.
Blankets,	1s	do	each.
Shirts,	1s	do	each.

Silver Trinkets 5 p C^t on firft Coft,
which may amount to fix or feven thoufand Pounds
fterling per annum on this Province only.

Some Court of Juftice is abfolutely neceffary to bring
Offenders to Juftice, oblige People to pay their Debts
and keep good Order, it being impoffible thofe Ends
can be anfwered by Provincial Laws fo diftant as the
Colonys are, did their Power extend fo far.

It is fubmitted, if the Defigns of our Ennemies to
draw the Savages in general on us would not be more
eafily prevented & with far lefs Expence if undertaken
before any of them commence Hoftilitys againft us,
than it can be afterwards, and if any thing can be more
effectual to anfwer this Purpofe than the Savages feeing
foon at the Detroit a refpectable Force fix'd, the Pofts
above mentioned properly eftablifhed, themfelves dif-
united & proper Meafures taking there to raife fuffi-
-cient Provifions for the full Supply of the Interior
Country. They know if the Pofts are fupplied with
Provifions from the Colonys below in Boats only they
have it always in their Power to cut off the Supply &
even the Retreat of thofe Garrifons, and on it they
chiefly

chiefly depend for Succeſs in taking them and driving
the Englifh out of the interior Country. How fatal a
ſudden & well tim'd Savage Eruption would prove
to the Englifh Indian Traders & Frontier Inhabitants
of ſeveral Colonys melancholly Experience has made
it too well known to need being mentioned here, and
if the interior Country is to remain in its preſent defenceleſs State all Laws & Regulations for the Benefit
of the Trade will be of no avail.

It would be prudent to oblige all the French &
Canadian People to remove from the Wabach, St. Joſephs, Michilimicanac & otherwiſe diſperſ'd amongſt
the Savages to the Settlement of Detroit to put an
End to the Tricks they play to our Diſadvantage.

The Nations or Tribes of Savages ſurrounding the
great Lakes that have any Knowledge of the Englifh
are at this Time in a Diſpoſition to live well with
them, reſpect them and beg for Trade & Veſſels in
every Lake, hoping thereby that Goods will be cheaper
than it can be without them. They ſtill love the
French to a great Degree and the French by the Miſſiſſippi and from the Illinois keep it up by extending
Trade to all Nations they can and ſending Emiſſarys
to propagate ſuch Tales as turn moſt to their Advantage & Prejudice to the Englifh. Theſe Savages are
numerous, proud, delight in & practice War from a
political View, knowing that ſuch as neglect keeping
up that Spirit muſt degenerate into Effeminacy & become the Prey of ſuch as do not. To inſure a laſting
Peace, gain their Affections & wean them from the
French, ſtrict Juſtice, Moderation, fair Trade, with keeping them from frequent Intercourſe with each other, &
a reſpectable Force at Detroit is the way to obtain it,
unleſs their whole dependence for the Neceſſaries of
Life depended upon the Englifh, which will never be
                                                    the

the cafe as long as the French can come up the Mif-
fiffippi in Safety, Land & extend their Trade on our
Side with Impunity, the preventing of which will in the
Execution be found difficult as the Intereft of the
Savages is to fcreen & protect them, & it is faid to be
carried on by the French Eaft India Company.

It is abfolutely neceffary to make Choice for the
eftablifhing Pofts for the Security of Trade, of fuch
Places as may be moft convenient for the Inhabitants
of each Lake to carry on their Trade with eafe to
themfelves, by which & their natural Lazinefs will
feldom go to their Neighbors & without it they will
be difcontented.

At thefe Pofts Men of Senfe, Modiration & Spirit
fhould Command, & each Detachment for the fmall
ones fhould not be lefs than one hundred good Men.
Neagara & Detroit fhould be more refpectable, the
former can not do with lefs than three Pofts upon the
Communication of fifty Men each and the latter muft
have as many to make good the Navigation to Lake
Huron, the Straits being too difficult for Veffells, fo
that Boats muft be employ'd for that Service and the
Officer commanding at Detroit fhould always have it
in his Power to detach from his Garrifon three hundred good Men befides Militia to chaftife any Nation
or Band of Savages the Inftant they deferve it, as the
taking immediate Satiffaction will make them refpect
and fear us and prevent a general War, fo that Neagara
can not difpenfe with lefs than one Battalion on the
prefent Eftablifhment & Detroit near two Battailons.

The Pofts neceffary for Lake Ontario are already
fix'd except Frontinac inftead of Fort Wm. Auguftus,[1]
the latter being ufelefs, the Navigation to it dangerous

---

[1] About three Miles below the Mouth of the Ofwegatchie. See
Note 57, Page 58.

and

and attended with great delays, and the former an excellent Harbour and from it foon into the Lake.

For Lake Erie Detroit is fufficient.

For Lake Huron Detroit and Michilimicanac.

For Lake Michigan Michilimicanac, the Bay & St. Jofephs.

For Lake Superior, Falls of St. Marys with two other Pofts at the moft convenient Places, the Inhabitants being in that Quarter numerous, particularly in the weftward of it.

Thefe Pofts of Michilimicanac, the Bay, St. Jofephs, the Falls of St. Marys with the two other Pofts upon the Banks of Lake Superior will take one Battailon, which makes four from Neagara weftward.

All Pofts upon the Banks of the Lakes from Neagara upwards to be under the control of the Officer commanding at Detroit and fhould Government judge it improper to eftablifh a Civil Government there and not encourage the Colony, ftill fome Court of Juftice is neceff'ry to the end Offenders, Inhabitants, Indians, Indian Traders and others might be brought to Juftice & punifh'd by a Law that might prevent litigious Suits & fatisfy the Savages the ftricteft Juftice is done them at all Times.

The Savages have a contemptible Opinion of all Indian Traders, it is therefore neceffary the Officer commanding at the Pofts fhould not Trade but infpect into the Trade, prevent Abufe and bring Offenders to that Juftice the Law may require; by this they will be refpected & belov'd by the Savages & have it in their Power to be of great Ufe when the Affiftance of the latter may be wanted againft his Majeftys Enemies.

The Officers at all Pofts which the Savages frequent fhould be enabled to treat Particulars, fuch as Chiefs and well affected with a little Rum, fome Pipes & Tobacco

Tobacco, with Provisions in cafes of Neceffity; they have been accuftomed to much more by the French & expect it from us, the Expence is a trifle but the Want of that may be attended with bad Confequences; for Neagara and all trading Pofts above it twenty Pounds fterling except Detroit, which fhould be thirty Pounds annually.

The Goods to be furnifhed the Savages fhould be, if poffible, as good as thofe they had from the French before the reduction of Canada, fold to them at the fame Prices or in that Proportion if not fo good, and the fame Prices given for their Skins & Peltry—and to enable us to carry on this Trade to more Advantage & greater Safety than the French did, no Tranfportation to be fuffer'd upon the Lakes but in Veffels and Government to furnifh & keep up them Veffells, the Trader paying Freight for his Goods at the Rate of one half what it would coft him if tranfported in Boats. This would overpay the Expence of the Veffells for Trade and thofe neceffary for the public Service and prevent drunken or evil minded Indians killing and plundering the Traders, which can not be avoided at Times, if the Tranfportation was carry'd on in Boats. The Number of Veffells neceffary for the Trade can not be fix'd, but by Time, but the fooner there are two or three in the Lakes Huron & Michigan with two in Lake Superior the more pleafing it will be to the Savages, as they will fee no Time is loft to put the Trade on an advantagious Footing for them. The Execution of this I take to be of great Importance towards fixing the Inclinations of the Savages in our Favor. The Savages fhould not be debar'd Spiritious Liquors; it is their darling Paffion, nay they love it fo much they will facrifice their all to obtain it and will never live in Peace with us without it, but
ftill

ſtill the Quantity each Trader ſhould be permitted to take with him ſhould be limited in the Proportion of the Goods he takes and might extend to fifteen Pounds in Spiritious Liquors to every hundred Pounds of other Goods, paying a Duty of two Shillings ſterl. per Gallon, which they can very well bear from the enormous Prices they ſell it at.

The Savages are ſubtile & the French intreguing, it therefore becomes dangerous to ſuffer the former to hord up a large Stock of Arms and Ammunition ; but this can not be prevented ſhould every Trader have it in his Power to carry with him what Quantity he may judge proper ; upon theſe Conſiderations and that the Proffits ariſing from the Sail & Returns would go a great way towards defraying the public Expence for the Protection of Trade, would it not be beſt in the Hands of Government under the Care of a Commiſſary ſubject to the Control of the Commanding Officer of each Poſt with Inſtructions as to the Quantity to be diſpoſed of annually. The Honor of Government will require theſe Articles to be good and the Prices ſhould be eſtabliſhed, and

Here I muſt notice that from the Government of Pennſylvania all the Shavanes and Delaware Indians are furniſh'd with Rifle Barrel Guns of an excellent Kind and that the Upper Nations are getting into them faſt by which they will be much leſs dependent upon us on account of the great ſaving of Powder by thoſe Guns, as it certainly diminiſhes the Demand of ſuch as have them more than Half, and in their way of carrying on War by far more prejudicial to us than any other Sort of Gun ; would it not be a public Benefit to ſtop the making and vending any more of them throughout the Colonys and prevent the Importation of any into the Colonies.

Should

Should Government judge it neceſſary to take the
ſupplying the Savages with Arms and Ammunition
into their own Hands; for the upper Lakes a Public
Magazine will be neceſſary at Detroit under proper
Officers to receive & ſend forward to the other Poſts,
as likewiſe to receive the Remittences back; and the
Commiſſary of the Outpoſts ſhould account annually
with thoſe of Detroit, ſubject to the Inſpection of the
Governor or Officer commanding there.

Should New York be thought a proper Channel for
the Conveyance up the Country, a Commiſſary ſhould
be there and one at Albany; but if on the contrary
Canada ſhould be thought beſt, Quebec & Montreal
are proper Places for Offices for this Service.

Of all the Savages upon the Continent, the moſt
knowing, the moſt intreguing, the leſs uſeful & the
greateſt Villains are thoſe moſt converſant with the
Europeans and deſerve the Attention of Government
moſt by way of Correction, and theſe are the Six Nations, Shawanes & Delawares; they are well acquainted
with the defenceleſs State of the Inhabitants who live
on the Frontiers and think they will ever have it in
their Power to diſtreſs & Plunder them; and never
ceaſe raiſing the Jealouſy of the Upper Nations againſt
us by propagating amongſt them ſuch Stories as make
them believe the Engliſh have nothing ſo much at
Heart as the Extirpation of all Savages. The apparent Deſign of the Six Nations is to keep us at War
with all Savages but themſelves that they may be employed as Mediators between us & them at a Continuation of an Expenſe to the Public too often & too
heavily felt, the Sweets of which they will never forget
nor looſe Sight of if they can poſſibly avoid it. That
of the Shawanes & Delawares is to live on killing, cap-
tivating and plundering the People inhabiting the

21   Frontiers,

Frontiers, long Experience having shown them they grow richer & live better thereby than by hunting wild Beasts.

This Campaign has fully opened the Eyes of the Upper Nations of Indians ; they are now sensible they are made use of as the Dupes & Tools of these detestable & diabolical Set, the Six Nations, Shawanes & Delawares, and it would require but little Address & Expence (the Posts and Trade properly fix'd) to engage them to cut them from the Face of the Earth (and they deserve it) or to keep the Six Nations in such Subjection as would put an End to our being any longer a kind of Tributary to them ; and their real Interest call upon them to distroy or drive the Shawanes & Delawares out of the Country they now possess on account of Hunting; this they know and would soon put either in Execution if assured his Majesty would not suffer any other Savages to live there.   Happy will it be when Savages can be punish'd by Savages, the good Effects of which the French can tell.   That we can punish them is beyond Doubt whenever Wisdom, Secrecy, Dispatch & good Troops in Numbers proportionate to the Service are employ'd.

The Pass of Neagara is of great Importance & will always be an Expence to Govern^t.   The principal Part of the Trade, if the Transportation is carry'd on in Vessells will pass that way & from its Proximity to the Geneseo Indians, a Part of the Six Nations & the greatest Savage Enemies we have, it will be difficult if not impracticable for some Time to come, for private Persons to keep up Boats & Carriage so well but that the Trade will meet with Delays; it would therefore be more safe & parmanent in the Hands of Government who only can make Transportation certain and by the Traders paying a reasonable Price for the Carriage

riage for their Goods, &c., there will be no ſtop and the public Service carry'd on there without Expence.

This Campaign upon the Lakes has alſo laid open the Hearts of the Six Nations and a black one it will appear for us if Gen[l] Gage has ſent the Papers reſpecting them to his Majeſtys Miniſters, to which I hope he has tack'd the immenſe Expence they have been at to Government this Year excluſive of Proviſions, which is immenſe alſo. It will alſo been ſeen by them Papers that the Upper Nations of Indians know that we are fully acquainted with the Tricks the Six Nations play us and I believe they do expect to hear that that Part of them call'd Geneſeo Indians get their deſerts ſoon.

The French accuſtom'd the Savages of the upper Lakes & Rivers to ſend Traders with Goods to Winter amongſt them for which Permit the Trader paid a certain Price each Time; I believe the Indians will expect it will be ſo again; ſhould Government think proper to grant it then the Trader can very well pay thirty Pounds ſterling for each large Canoe ſo permitted, which will make a conſiderable Sum annually; the Paſſ to be given at Detroit only to prevent Fraud.

I am aſſur'd by Perſons lately from the Illinois that excluſive of the French Garriſons there, the Inhabitants are 600 fighting Men, have 1000 Negroes well accuſtom'd to the Uſe of ſmall Arms, averſe to our taking Poſſeſſion of the Country & have painted us out in ſuch Colours to the numerous Savages near them that they, the latter, will certainly endeavour to prevent the Troops getting there by the Miſſiſſippi even ſhould the Indians nearer the Sea allow them to paſs, which they think they will not, unleſs well paid for it, which will not anſwer what may perhaps be expected. They add, that it is their Opinion alſo, that
all

all Attempts to get Poſſeſſion of the Illinoes with leſs than 3000 good Men will fail, and that thoſe Troops ſhould go down the Ohio River & the Expedition carry'd on with ſuch Secrecy that they may enter the Miſſiſſippi 90 Miles below Fort Charters before the Inhabitants can have Intelligence of it & Time to ap-priſe all the Savages.

I am convinced the only way to eſtabliſh ourſelves amongſt the Savages with Reſpect & Safety is to begin by coming upon them by ways unfrequented, undiſ-covered and with ſuch Force as ſhall make ſuch an Impreſſion as ſhall be laſting, and if a Body of Troops ſhould be ſent to take Poſſeſſion of the Illinoes thoſe Troops ſhould viſite all the principal Nations of Indians upon the Banks of yᵉ Miſſiſſippi as near the Sea as they live and endeavour to enter into an Alliance with all they can and purchaſe their Aid to make War upon thoſe that remain ſtubborn to bring them to Reaſon & open a free Paſſage up the River. The ſhorteſt way to carry this into Execution is by Fort Pitt, provided the Troops are not to come from Canada, but if any comes from thence the beſt way is by Neagara to Preſque Iſle upon Lake Erie.

The Colony of Detroit grows faſt and the Inhabit-ants have great Influence over the Savages; the re-moving them would occaſion a general War with the Indians, and to leave them as they now are will take a great length of Time before they become proper Brit-iſh Subjects; it is therefore humbly ſubmitted if it would not be beſt to permit & encourage Britiſh Sub-jects to ſettle there as the Increaſe of the latter would be ſo great in a few Years that they muſt ſoon become one People by Marriages, &c.

The Spirit for ſettling the Kings Subjects there ſhew itſelf fully by a Memorial of ſixty Officers ſerving in the

upper Lakes in this Campaign, praying his Majeſty
would be gracioufly pleaſ'd to permit them to ſettle
639 Farms at their own Expence, with ſuch Marks
of the Kings Royal Favour as his Majeſty may think
proper.

On receiving General Gages Orders to continue the
War againſt the Shawanes & Delawares I demanded
the Affiſtance of his Majeſtys new Subjects, the Ottawas, Chepewas, Hurons, Sakes & Potawatames ; four
Parties immediately went againſt them. One returned
with one Scalp which is fufficient for the whole to carry
on & continue the War unleff prevented by bad Management by us.

Albany, 7th Decʳ 1764.

PAPERS

RELATING TO THE

Indian Wars of 1763 and 1764,

AND THE

CONSPIRACY OF PONTIAC.

INTRODUCTION.

THE Correfpondence of Military Officers and others charged with Duties relating to Indian Affairs, during the Wars of Pontiac, neceffarily embodies a large Amount of Information concerning the Caufes which led to Hoftilities, the Alarms which thofe occafioned, the Meafures that were taken to fupprefs them, and the Opinions that were entertained as to the Changes neceffary to prevent their Continuance or Recurrence. Thefe Letters place before us in vivid Colours, the Condition of the Country, its Refources and its Wants, and narrate, without Ornament, the fimple Facts which their Writers wifhed to communicate. A Portion of thefe Papers are copied from the Bradftreet and Amherft Manufcripts, and moft of the Remainder from the Manufcripts of Sir William Johnfon, in the State Library. In making the Selection we have avoided as much as poffible including thofe ever before printed.

F. B. H.

P A P E R S

RELATING TO THE

Indian Wars of 1763 and 1764.

Letter from Gen. Amherſt to Col. Bradſtreet.

[Bradſtreet and Amherſt MSS, p. 132.]

NEW YORK, 22ᵈ June, 1763.

IR : Your Expreſs arrived here laſt Night and delivered me your Letter of the 19ᵗʰ with thoſe Encloſed; the Anſwers to which I now tranſmit you, that you may forward them by the firſt ſafe Opportunity that offers.

You do very right to be prepared for puſhing up Proviſions to Fort Stanwix, which I would have you do tho' I am in Hope we ſhall have ample Supplys for the Upper Poſts from Fort Wm. Auguſtus.

I ſend Orders to Captain Winepreſs to march with his Company to Fort Ontario, as I now order about forty

forty Men of the 42d & 77th Regiments, who are fit for Garrifon Duty to Albany, where they will remain under the Command of a Captain of the 77ᵗʰ Regᵗ who will fucceed Capt. Winneprefs in the Command of the Garrifon.   There is likewife a Subaltern of the 77th, with a Lieut: and three Serjeants of the Independents.

Major Gladwin writes me of the 14th May, that the Detroit was invefted by a large Body of Indians ; but that the Garrifon were in high Spirits & he was in Hopes of being able to defend the Place untill he received fome Succour from Niagara, & Major Wilkins acquaints me he had immediately on the Arrival of the Schooner from the Detroit, fent off a Reinforcement of fifty Men with a Lieutenant and non-commiffioned Officers, which I truft will have arrived in Time to fave the Place.

I well know that you are always ready, however I think it neceffary to acquaint you to be ready for moving at a moments Warning, as if the Savages are not quickly reduced I believe I fhall employ you on a Command, which, I am certain will be agreeable to you.

> I am, Sir,
> Your moft obedient Servant,

Jeff. Amhert

Col. Bradftreet,
    D. Q. M. G.
    P. S.   Since I wrote the foregoing Mr. Leake has
                                                deliver'd

deliver'd me a Return of the Provifions, which, by the laft Returns, were at Fort Wm. Auguftus, Ofwego & Niagara, &c., of which I enclofe you a Copy, whereby you will fee, that the Quantities at thefe Pofts are very confiderable.   J. A.

With Major Duncan's Letter I received one from Major Wilkins to Captain Dalyell, which miffed him by the Way, of the 3d Inftant : Nothing new then at Niagara ; but one of the Men that were miffing, found, as I feared, dead & *fcalped*, near the Fort above the Falls.

Altho' none of the Letters require Anfwers at prefent, I think it beft to order the Poft to return ; and I have directed Mr. Colden to order the Rider, to make more hafte than they have lately done and to be more ready to fet out from Albany, as the Service may require them, without waiting for any fixed Time.

Before I received your Letter I had apply'd to the Lt. Governor (finding that my Endeavors to accommodate Matters with the Perfons employed by the Elders & Deacons had no Effect, altho' I had fpoke particularly to the Chief Juftice for that Purpofe) to give the neceffary Directions to the Attorney-General, not only to defend your Suit, but to profecute the Corporation of Albany, for pulling down his Majeftys Fence, &c.

I am, Sir,
Your moft obedient Servant,
JEFF. AMHERST.

CoL Braadftreet,
D. Q. M. G. Albany.   P. S.

P. S. I this Moment receive a Petition from one Crifp, which I enclofe that you may be fo good to give an Anfwer. I imagine that his Claim is not juft or it would have been paid.   J. A.

NEW

NEW YORK, 20th July, 1763.

SIR:

THE Poft came in laft Night with your Letter of
the 15th Inftant, and brought me likewife Letters from Major Duncan & Captain Loring, advifing
me of the latters Arrival at Fort Ontario, on the 5th,
with the Sailors, and that he had fitted out the Johnfon
Snow, ready to proceed to Fort Wm. Auguftus for
Provifions.   Himfelf & the reft of the Seamen were to
fail in the Schooner to Niagara.

The Same to the Same.

[Bradftreet and Amherft MSS., p. 134.]

NEW YORK, 7th Auguft, 1763.

SIR:

LAST Night I received your Letter of the 1ft Inftant.

You did very right to furnifh Sir William Johnfon
with what Provifions he required, for the Ufe of the
Indians.

I have no Objecton to your fending two or three
Oxen, at a Time, to Fort Stanwix, for the Ufe of that
Garrifon, as you fay you can fupply them cheaper than
they can be got from New England. Lt. Colonel
Campbell muft take Care that there is a particular
Account kept of what is iffued, according to Orders,
as there is no Commiffary from the Crown at that
Poft, the Contractors Commiffary will be only to be
paid for the Flour; unlefs you fell the Cattle to the
Contractors.

The

The Daſtardly Behaviour of the Batteau Men is particularly unlucky at this Time; for I have been impatiently waiting to hear of the Arrival of the Engineers Stores at Oſwego: I hope when you ſent them back, they have proceeded with all imaginable Expedition.

I am, Sir,
Your moſt obedient Servant,
JEFF. AMHERST.

Col. Bradſtreet,

The Same to the Same.

[Bradſtreet and Amherſt MSS., p. 135.]

NEW YORK, 18th Septbr, 1763.

SIR:

I AM to own your Letter of the 12th Inſtant and I approve of your having ſupplyed Sir William Johnſon the Proviſions you mention as he expected to have a Conference at his Houſe with the Six Nation Indians.

Any Bedding that may be wanted hereafter for the Garriſons I can ſupply from hence, as there is a great Quantity now in Store, which came from *Martinique* and the *Havana*, but what you have forwarded to Oſwego, will be ſo much the nearer for being ſent to the Detroit, &c.

I am, Sir,
Your moſt obedient Servant,
JEFF. AMHERST.

Col. Bradſtreet,
    D. Q. M. G.

The Same to the Same.

[Bradftreet and Amherft MSS., p. 136.]

NEW YORK, 24th September, 1763.

SIR:

I AM to own Your Letter of the 10th Inftant; I have not yet come to the Determination with regard to the fmall Pofts on the Communication to Fort George: I can keep one Man only in each of them, which I will contrive to do, to continue the Poffeffion; but you may fend a Proportion of Candles for the Garrifons of Crown Point, Ticonderoga, Fort George & Fort Edward; the three laft will have one Company in each; and there will be four Companys at Crown Point.

I enclofe you a Copy of Publick Orders, which have been given here, & which I fend now to all the Pofts, for making Stoppages to all the Provifions that may be iffued to the Troops, in purfuance of Directions I have received from the Lords of the Treafury: It has already taken place in Canada, and I have ordered the Stoppages to commence at Albany, the Dependent Pofts & the Communication to Fort George inclufively on the 1ft October, for Crown Point & Ticonderoga are to be garrifoned by Troops from Canada. The Orders are to be made publick at all the other Pofts; but I have thought proper to continue an Allowance to the Troops at Fort Stanwix & the dependent Pofts & to the feveral Garrifons above, as I think it would be hard to put them to Stoppages until the *Indian War* is entirely quelled & that they are on the fame Footing with the other Troops: This Regulation does not affect the Provincials who muft

be

be fubfifted, as ufual, untill the Service will permit them to be fent to their refpective Homes.

I enclofe you a Packett addreffed to Lt. Colonel Elliott, containing Difpatches for Canada, which you will forward by one of your People, on purpofe, to Crown Point; fending at the fame Time the Letters to the commanding Officers at Fort Edward & Fort George. When the Companys from Canada arrive at Crown Point & Ticonderoga, Lt. Colonel Elliott, with the Men of the 55th (Leaving compleat Companys at Fort George & Fort Edward), will move down to Albany, where he will remain till further Orders.

> I am, Sir,
> > Your moft obedient Servant,
> > > JEFF. AMHERST.

Colonel Bradftreet,
> D. Q. M. G., Albany.

The Same to the Same.

NEW YORK, 28 Septb., 1763.

SIR :

A VESSEL having arrived here with the Cloathing for the feveral Reg^ts in this Country, I am fending that for the Corps above as faft as poffible to Albany, that no Time may be loft in forwarding it before the Winter fets in. One Sloop is already loaded & will fail to morrow Morning : Enfign Crofthwaite, who is going to Albany, has the Care of the Cloathing in her & will deliver you the Bill of Lading; fo that you will order the Cloathing to be landed & put into the Store at Albany, fending the enclofed Letter to Fort Stanwix & Crown Point, as I have directed the Commanding Officers at thofe Pofts to fend Qr.

Mafters & proper Partys to conduct the Cloathing to
their refpective Pofts ; the 17th, 46th & 80th to Fort
Stanwix ; from whence the two former will be forwarded to Ofwego, for which I write to Major Duncan;
and from thence to Niagara, &c., and the Cloathing for
the other Corps muft be fent with the Party that comes
from Crown Point.   Two other Sloops will take the
Whole from hence; and you will pay the Hire at the
ufual Rate & according to what you may think juft &
reafonable.   Swits's Sloop, which fails to-morrow, has
got many other Things, I am told, on board ; fo that
he ought to be paid accordingly ; and I fhall tranfmit
you Bills of Lading of the others when they are loaded.

I am, Sir,
Your moft obedient Servant,
JEFF. AMHERST.

Colonel Bradftreet,
D. Q. M. G. Albany.

Letter from Alexander Duncan to Sir Wm. Johnfon.

[MSS. of Sir William Johnfon, vii.]

FORT ONTARIO, 1ft Octob., 1763.

SIR :

A FEW Days ago I was favored with your Letter
of the 17th ultimo and vefterday that of the 26th
reached my Hands.

I have forwarded your Letter to Major Moncrieff,
from whom I have received a Letter dated 26th ultimo
at Niagara in which he informs, that they were then
preparing to fet out for Detroit, but that they were
obliged to carry the Provifions over the Portage on
Men's Shoulders and that it would be the 5th or 6th
October

October before they would be able to fed out. I have
sent sixteen Oxen which are with them before now,
there is likewife a Reinforcement of 260 Men that I
reckon have got to Niagara this Day, thefe I hope
will enable Major Wilkins to fed out fooner and
ftronger than he expected; the whole are under his
Command I imagine will exceed 600 Men, they go in
Battoes & carry fo much Provifions as they can.

You will no doubt have heared that the Savages attacked the Schooner going up the River to Detroit on
the 3d ultimo, the Mafter of the Veffel & one Seaman
were killed & three others wounded, but the Savages
were beat off; they had once got upon the Bowfprit
and have hacked and cut the Veffel a great dale on the
Bows & under the Stern; there was only twelve Men
on board the Schooner at the beginning of the Affair,
three of whom were fick. The Indians acknowledge
to have left eight Men & many wounded & by fome
of their Canoes overfetting have loft fixty Stand of
Arms.

Several Canoes have lately arrived here from Canada
with Paffports (to go to Detroit with Ammunition &
Indian Goods) from General Gage; I have taken the
Paffes from the Traders & fecured the Ammunition &
Goods in the Fort. The People in thefe Canoes in-
form me that feveral Traders have got Paffports to go
up Grand Riviere and that one Canoe is gone to
Toronto. I have informed Lt. Col. Browning of the
latter, that he may fend a Party & bring away the
Traders from Toronto. Here follows a Copy of the
Preamble to one of thefe Paffports..

" By the Honble Genl. Gage, &c., &c. Whereas
" Meffrs. Wells & Wade have reprefented to me, that
" it is probable that the Savages are difperfed from
" about Detroit, and therefore demand Permiffion to

" fend a Canoe there under fuch Regulations as I fhall
" think neceffary to be given."

It is not eafy to account for Mr. Gages Conduct on
this Occafion, but I have fend Copys of all the Paffports
that have fallen into my Hands to Sir Jeffrey Amherft,
let thofe two Gentlemen fettle that Affair. Six Canoes
came here five of which were loaded, the other had put
their Loading on board the Sloop at Fort William
Auguftus and they have no lefs than 75 Barrels of
Gunpowder befides, &c.

Every thing continues quiet here.

I am, Sir,

Your moft obedient humble Servant,

Alex Duncan

To Sir William Johnfon.

Letter from General Amherft to Colonel Bradftreet.

NEW YORK, 1ft October, 1763.

SIR:

AS the laft Sloop with the Cloathing is not yet
failed I take the Opportunity of fending this by
her (as fhe may reach Albany before the Poft) to acknowledge your Letters of the 25th & 26th September by Captain Sowers ; and to approve entirely of your
Readinefs in forwarding the Oxen, Carts, &c. for
Niagara : Your getting the *Tyers,* &c. made at Albany
has likewife my Approbation ; and as they muft be in
want of Provender for the Cattle during the Winter,
they not having had an Opportunity to make any Hay,

I

I fhould be glad you could forward to Niagara a Sufficiency of Corn, which you tell me you can do.

In a late Letter to Lt. Colonel Elliot I directed him
to fend down the Remainder of the Detachment of the
17th Regiment, immediately on the Arrival of the
Companys from Montreal, which I conclude he will
have done ; and that Captain Morris will have proceeded to Fort Stanwix; but fhould Captain Morris
with that Detachment be at Albany on Receipt hereof
or arrive afterwards you will acquaint him that it is my
Orders he proceeds, without Delay, to Fort Stanwix ;
as Lt. Colonel Campbell has at Prefent rather too thin
a Garrifon ; efpecially as, from the Accounts I have
received of the late Affair on the Carrying Place at
Niagara, there is Reafon to fufpect that the Body of
Savages who cut off our Convoy were moftly Senecas.
I hope the other Five Nations are not privy to this
Affair ; altho' it is hard to fay who are our Friends or
Foes.   The whole Race of Savages feem to be, more
or lefs, concerned in this treacherous Infurrection.

           I am, Sir,
                Your moft obedient Servant,
                        JEFF. AMHERST.

Colonel Bradftreet,
   D. Q. M. G.

Letter from Capt. Daniel Claus to Sir Wm. Johnfon.

                MONTREAL, 1ft October, 1763.

    HON. SIR :

I HOPE mine of the 23d ultimo, by Capt. Brown,
    came fafe to Hand, fince which I had a Deputation
from the Miffifageys living about Toronto; their
Meffage confifted of a large String and a Belt of about

2000 Wampum, by the former they expreffed their great Concern on acc^t of the prefent unhappy Difturbances about Detroit, &c., and that they abhorred and detefted it and therefore had fince the Beginning kept out of the way in the Environs of Cataracqui, that at the fame Time they were thereby reduced to the greateft Diftrefs for want of their Neceffaries being brought among them, and therefore requefted & implored the General to let ye Trader La Farge alias Tawaniawe the Swegachie interpreter, who ufed to fupply them heretofore with Neceffaries come to their Village this Seafon that they might not be prevented from this Winters Hunt for want of Ammunition, &c. ——— the Belt.

Genl. Gage without Hefitation replied them that as to their Profeffions he could or would not fo far doubt them, tho' he was fure of fome Canoes having been purfued by Miffifagey Ind^s and when overtaken & found they were French were told that they took to be Englifh whom they lay in wait for. However be that as it would he fhould not give them an Anfwer upon their Meffage, that if they wanted to exculpate themfelves they muft addrefs themfelves to you as the principal Perfon of their Affairs who only had the Power from the King to hear & fettle fuch Matters & as to fending a Perfon to trade among them he would never agree to it, neither was it in his Power, and fo fent them away. They were 3 in Number and had with them a Pany who deferted from hence when this Place was taken and being found out by his Mafter was taken from them by him upon the Gen^{ls} Order and put into the Provofts. A Frenchman that came from Niagara this Sumer informed the General that he was purfued by f^d Pany and coming up to him with his Knife in his Hand told him that if he was an Englifhman would loofe his Life.

I

I afterward examin'd the Frenchman, whether any of thefe Ind^s were in Company with the Pany but he was fure they were not.

I then fpoke to them in my Room, and made them as much fenfible as I could of the heinous Behaviour of thofe Nations that occafioned the prefent Difturbances, and that they muft attribute every Inconveniency they now labored under to them only, and endure it till fuch a Time as proper Satiffaction was given for their vile & inconfiderate Actions, etc.

I had their Arms mended for them and gave them a little Ammunition, Tobacco & Rum and difmiffed them, tho' they expected fome Cloathing, being in a Manner naked; I alfo gave them a Paffport to go your way in cafe their Nation would fend them.

I impatiently wait for the Return of the Caghnawageys as well on account of knowing the Determination of the 6 Nations who I hear had a numerous Congrefs at your Houfe, as my Deftination for the enfuing Winter.

This goes by Maj^r Abercrombie who I hear is to be one Genl. Amherft's Family.

I am, with the greateft Refpect and Compliments to the Family,
Hon. Sir,
Your moft dutyfull
and obedient Serv.

To the Honble Sir William Johnfon, Bart.
I beg leave to trouble you with the enclofure.

Letter from Maj. Robert Rogers to Sir Wm. Johnson.

DETROIT, October 7th, 1763.

SIR:

MAJOR Gladwin has told me that he will enclose you all the Proceedings at this Place since the Date of my last Letter, as also every particular Account concerning the Indian War, the first beginning, &c.

For these Reasons and as I think it would come more correct from him than from me, I defer mentioning any other Particulars relative to our Condition at this Place.

McCormick will deliver you this Letter, he has a Bill on Col. Croghan. I should be obliged to you if you would gett him the Money, for it would serve me greatly to make my Payments speedily.

Aaron the Mohawk Indian came into the Fort this Day, Daniel and Jacob is also in this Garrison but I have not any Intelligence from them but what Major Gladwin will communicate, tho' I soon shall & some that they tell me & no man shall at this Place know but myself, but you shall have it in full from me, and one of the Indians you sent up will convey the said Account, the other four is now in Sandusky where there is a grand Council, but will return in a day or two; the Schooner sails directly, therefore I can not send to you their private Information, but surely will do it by themselves the first Opportunity.

There is about one thousand Indians in this Settlement at present waiting for some Troops that is coming up; I wish they may not get a Flogging.

I beg you'll be so kind as to inform Mrs. Rogers if there is any likelyhood of my coming down this Fall, for

for my Part I know nothing of the Difpofition for this Place at prefent, neither does Major Gladwin.

I am Sir, Your moft obed^t

Humble Servant.

To Sir William Johnfon.

The Same to the Same.

DETROIT, Octob. 7th, 1763.

SIR:

SINCE I wrote my Letter, Aaron the Mohawk has come in and tells me that he was in the Council yefterday and that all the Nations here he fays the Indian War begun through the Five Nations and that fince the Belt came here that Aaron fays he told you was brought by one Indian laft Fall, that a fecond Belt came laft March and told the Indians to begin, and with that a Tomahawk was delivered and the Indians that brought this Belt from the Five Nations told and affur'd the Indians that they would begin at the Time the Corn was planted. The five Nations was to ftrike from Niagara to Schenectady and the Taways and other Nations to take the upper Pofts on the Lakes, that the Senecas and Cahugees were the People that fent this Meffage and further told them that they would meet them at the Windotes town early this Spring.

Aaron

Aaron tells me that the Hurons were obliged to ftrike the Englifh as they were threatened by the Toways and other Nations and that the Toways now tells the Hurons if they attempt to make Peace without their Confent or Advice they will directly deftroy them, and that if they attempt to come to the Fort they will be confidered by them as Englifhmen.

Aaron fays that they have feen our Troops that are coming from Niagara at the Long Point on the north Shore, and that all the Savages here are determined to attack them at Point a Plee.

Aaron fays he will lett you know further foon and what he has told you now you may depend upon is true, that the Hurons defire that you may know that the Taways and other Nations on the Lake are now their Mafters, their Numbers being fo fmall they can't help themfelves, they are going to the Huron River about thirty Miles from this Fort, where they intend to winter, and the Taways are refolv'd to winter at Miame River, the other four Indians that came up with Aaron are gone to Sandufky.

            I am, Sir,
                Your moft humble Servant,
                        ROBERT ROGERS.

Endorfed. Wrote to Jn Glen, Efqr. for 15 Barrels Pork & Flour in Proportion, 5 to be fent to Cherry Valley, 5 to Conradt Franks, 5 to Caghnawagey.

Memorandum. 10 Pr Strouds, 6 do. Aurora, 6 do. Blankets, 540 Shirts; 12 ps Stocking Stuff, 108 lb. Vermillion, 719 lb. Verdigreafe, 100 Pipe watches, 8 Groce of Knives, 20 Yds Ribbon, 6 ps Silk handkerchiefs, 11 groce Rings, 10 lbs Beeds.

Letter from Sir William Johnson to Colonel Eyre.

JOHNSON HALL, Octbr 13th, 1763.

DEAR SIR :

I AM to thank you for your Favor of the 3d Inft., altho' the Want of the *Packet*, as you obferved, muft prevent your having any material News. I moft heartily wifh whenever it arrives it may bring the News of their being perfectly acquainted in England with the Commencement of our Indian War, as without that they will be unable to take any proper Meafures & the firft News which was fent Home in June poffibly did not appear very interefting.

About 2 Days ago I had an Account that a confiderable Body of Indians are affembling at the Sufquehana with Defign to deftroy this Country from Schenectady upwards, or elfe to fall upon Efopus or Shamokin, &c. Both the former I look upon to be in their Power & therefore believe it is probable they will put one of them in Execution ; for my part I can not fee what will prevent their Succefs, as you know the Nature of the Country People fufficiently to fuppofe they can not be kept in a Body for any Time, but muft follow their feveral Occupations, fo that I have only to rely on the Hopes of fome previous Intelligence & on the prefent favorable Difpofition of all the Nations (except Senecas) many of whom are ready and defirous to join our Troops, but how long they may continue in this Difpofition is uncertain, as the great Succefs of our Enemys & the fmall Oppofition they have hitherto met with renders our Friends very apprehenfive of their Refentment from their daily Threats and may occafion their Defectn, efpecially as we are not able to give any neceffary Succour which

might enable them to withftand our Enemins.   I have
from feveral Hands the Particulars of our unlucky
Affair at Niagara by which it appears that our Troops
were attacked in fuch a difadvantagious Situation that
they were hurried down the fteep Cliffs near La Platon
unable to make any Refiftance & moft of them perifhed, many of them were found fticking in the Forks
of Trees; the Senecas of Chenefeo (who were the Principals in this Affair) have not brought in any Scalps,
with only one Man wounded on their Side.   This is
particularly unlucky at this Time and I fear will be
followed by more fuch blows if the greateft Care be
not taken.

I fhall expe６t when any thing occurs that you will
let me have the Pleafure of hearing from you, as

I am,

with Sincerity, &c.

Col. Eyre.

Letter from Sir Wm. Johnfon to Lieut. Gov. Colden.

JOHNSON HALL, O６tob. 13th, 1763.

DEAR SIR:

I HAVE juft received an Account, that a confiderable Body of Indians from towards the Ohio & the
Seneca Country are affembling on the Sufquehanna
and that they are deftined to fall either on Shamokin,
Efopus, or to deftroy the Mohawk River Settlements
from Schene６tady upwards, the firft of thefe Places is
capable of making a Defence, but I can fee little to
prevent their Succefs againft the two latter, particularly
in thefe Parts from the fad State of the Militia and
the great Want of Ammunition, &c.

I have acquainted Col. Hardenbergh of the Danger
of

of the Settlement of Efopus and as I have no doubt that one of thefe Defigns will be put in immediate Execution, muft beg the Favour of hearing from you thereon as alfo of your Anfwer to mine of the 10th of Aug. laft concerning the Vacancies & Additions necef-fary for this Regiment.

In the mean Time I fhall take every effectual Meafure for the obtaining the neceffary Intelligence on which the Safety of this important Frontier muft chiefly depend, and on Warning of the Enemy's Ap-proach fhall make the beft Difpofition the Nature of the Country will admit of.

The many Succeffes of our Enemies, together with their large Number, may prove of dangerous Confe-quence by influencing our Friends to joyn them thro' fear of their Power, Vicinity & Refentment, efpecially as we are not able to afford them the Affiftance which Allies fhould require, but I fhall continue to ufe all my Endeavors to prevent a Defection, which as Mat-ters now ftand muft prove the Deftruction of this Country as well as to cut off fo effential a Communi-cation to the Lakes.

I hope to have the Pleafure of your Anfwer and

I am with great fincerity

& Efteem, &c.

Lt. Governor Colden.

Letter from Gen. Amherft to Lieut. Gov. Colden.

NEW YORK, 15th October, 1763.

SIR :

IN a Letter I have this Moment received from Sir William Johnfon of the 6th Inftant, among other Intelligence concerning the bad Intentions of the In-

dians, he fays he has learnt, " that the Senecas & De-
" lawares were now daily marching to *Kaghraandote* on
" the Sufquehana, a Place appointed for their Ren-
" dezvous ; that when all were affembled their Leader,
" *Quaghquoandax*, would then agree to fall on one of
" the following Places, namely, Shamokin, Efopus or
" Cherry Valley ; and the Mohawk River from Sche-
" nectady upwards." I therefore think it highly neceffary to give you this Notice, that you may take
proper Steps for putting the Militia on their Guard as
it is abfolutely impoffible for me to fpare one Man from
the Pofts above ; for I have pufhed on every Man I
could fpare to Niagara & the Detroit ; and you know
I have none below. Sir William Johnfon, I doubt
not, will take every Precaution in his Power for pro-
tecting the Settlements on the Mohawk River. But
the Inhabitants everywhere on the Frontiers can not
be too much on their Guard & indeed the only thing
they have to do is to be unanimous in repelling by
Force any Attemps that may be made by the Savages.

I am with great Regard,

Sir, Your moft obedient,

Humble Servant,

JEFF. AMHERST.

Hon^{bl} Lt. Governor Colden.

Letter from David Vanderheyden to Sir Wm. Johnfon.

SIR :

I AM this Moment inform'd by Robert Lanfingh,
who came laft Night from the *Groote Imbogt*[1] that
one *Dirk Ehl* at that Place had rec'd a Letter from a

---

[1] The *Groote Imbogt* (or Great Bend) was on the Hudfon River, juft below the Mouth of the Catskill Creek, on the weft Side,

Kinfman

Kinfman, living fomewhere on Delaware River, informing him that about 60 Families were deftroy'd thereabout.

I fear that the Indians that have now been to N. York with Saml Pruyn are Spy's, tho' they behaved very complifant & civil to me & my Houfe : my Negro Wench tells me this Morning, that the youngeft of them, who talks the beft Englifh, had told her Hufband, Capt. Stephn Schuyler's Negro, that the Indians were all join'd, & that they did not fear the great Guns but enjon'd him to keep it Secret as the Negros would be in no Danger. And by fome Traders I am inform'd that he is the fame that caufed a Difturbance at Ofwego & Niagara laft Spring a Year.

I communicate thefe out of Zeal for the Service and am with unfeign'd Regard,
Sir, your Honor's
moft obedient humble Servant.

Dird van Den Heyden

Albany, the 19th October, 1763, a 8 A. M.
To the Honble Sir William Johnfon, Bt.
at Johnfon Hall.

Letter from F. Decouagne to Sir William Johnfon.

NIAGARA, Octob. 22d, 1763.
HONORABLE SIR :

IN your laft you defired to know whether Daniel & the reft of the Indians was gone to Detroit, the former has been up with two Parties & has the Character of a good Man from every one, but moft People give an indifferent Acc^t of Aron. There has been no Indians here; the Traders at this Poſt are all Suttlers. Major Wilkins is gone with the laſt Partie & has taken with him all the Belts and Bands Wampham to the Wapagamat Indians. I dont learn by any Accounts that the ſ'd Indians have done any Miſchief at preſent. I have no more to relate at this Juncture than have ſent encloſed Mr. Stedmans Acc^t of what happen'd the 19th & 20th Inſt., the ſ'd Perſon being preſent at the whole Affair.

I have an Intention to go as I think wou'd be proper amongſt ſome of the Wapagamats to get Intelligence but believe it will be very dangerous, therefore beg your Inſtructions by the firſt Opportunity.

I am, Sir,
Your moſt Obed^t Hum^l Servt

[signature]

SIR :
I have further to inform you that all the Canadians who have Paſſes from General Gage to Trade are ſtopp'd at the different Poſts.

To the Hon. Sir William Johnſon, Bt.,
    at Johnſon Hall.

Letter from General Amherst to Colonel Bradstreet.

[Bradstreet and Amherst MSS., p. 141.]

NEW YORK, 29th October, 1763.

SIR:

I ARRIVED here on Thursday Morning and gave immediate Orders for getting ready the Iron Work for the Schooners that are intended to be built for the Service of Lake Erie, &c. A sufficiency for one of 60 Tons, with the Rigging will be sent on Saturday next, & Preparation shall be made for two more & sent up as fast as possible. I need not desire you to forward the whole in the best. Manner you can.

This will be delivered to you by *Bogardus* in whose Sloop Mr. Napier has shipt the Bedding as per the enclosed Invoice & Receipt, and you will please to receive the Whole and order them to be safely stored to be ready for supplying any of the Posts above: Tho' some of them have been used, Mr. Napier assures me they are as clean, sweet and good as if they had not been used. As Mr. Napier is accomptable for this Bedding, it will be necessary that you send him a proper Receipt for them.

Lt. Colonel Campbell writes me, that the Bridges on the Communication between Fort Stanwix & the Flatts[1] were broke down by the Oxen that were lately sent up; and that if they are not repaired before the Winter, the Roads will be impassable for Sledges: I have wrote to Sir William Johnson on this Head & requested him to endeavor to get the Inhabitants to effect this usefull Service; but if you can anyways lend a helping Hand it will be so much the better, for I

---

[1] German Flats.

fear

fear we can not depend much on what the Country People will do, without they are preffed to do it.

I am, Sir,
Your moft obedient Servant.
JEFF. AMHERST.

Colonel Bradftreet,
D. Q. M. G.

The Same to the Same.

NEW YORK, 30th October, 1763.

SIR:

IN all Probability the Sloop with the Beding will be at Albany before the Poft reaches you. I however enclofe you a Duplicate of my Letter that went by her & I likewife tranfmit you a Lift of the Ironworks that are getting ready for the Schooner, and which with the Rigging, will, I hope be embarked from hence on Saturday next.

I enclofe a Packett addreffed to Governor Burton at Montreal, which you will pleafe to forward by the firft fafe Opportunity; and likewife a Letter for Major General Gage which you will keep until he arrives at Albany, where you will foon fee him, as I imagine he is on the Route by this Time & it might mifs him, were you to fend it on.

On my Arrival here, I applyed to the Lt. Governor regarding the ruinous Condition of the Fort at Albany & reprefented to him how neceffary it was to have it repaired in Time, as 'tis Shamefull to fee it: he has promifed to make Application to his Affembly for that Purpofe; but as the Fort is going in the mean Time to Ruin & that we may always want to keep a few Men there, I would have you order the Mafonry or
the

the Parapets to be repaired, if it can be done at a fmall
Expence, as it will be too late before the Affembly will
determine.   The Coping them with wood, as the north
Curtain is & the Work in the Infide of the Fort, may
be done later in the Seafon, & I hope will be done at
the Expence of the Province.

I am, Sir,
Your moft obedient Servant,
JEFF. AMHERST.

Col. Bradftreet,
D. Q. M. G.

The Same to the Same.

NEW YORK, 1ft November, 1763.

SIR:

THIS will be delivered to you by Lieut. Godwin,
whom I fend to Albany, with a non-commiffioned Officer & three Men of the Royal Artillery,
which are all that I can fpare from hence, & I think
they may be ufefull in forwarding any Artillery Stores
that may be fent to the upper Pofts, or giving their
Affiftance to other Services at Albany, and I write to
Lt. Colonel Elliot accordingly.

To avoid any Difputes about Quarters, I would
have you provide Lieut. Goodwin with a Room in
the Hofpital.

I have this Moment received your Letter of the
26th October, and with it I have one from Major
Gladwin of the 7th October.   Every thing as well as
we could expect at the Detroit: Moncrieffe, with the
Reinforcements, juft fetting off on Lake Erie the 14th
and I hope they will arrive in Time to give the Bar-
barians

barians a Check before the Winter fets in, tho' it is too late to expeƈt much.

I have applyed to the Provinces of New York & Jerfey, for two thoufand Men, to be raifed early in the Spring, 1400 from New York & 600 from the Jerfeys. Five Companys of the former, of 60 Men each, to be raifed immediately for the Proteƈtion of the Communication between Albany & Ofwego. How far my Requeft will be granted I know not; but I fhall acquaint you, as foon as I receive the Governors Anfwer. In the meantime I would have you make the neceffary Preparations for the new Boats, fhould the one you are building anfwer, of which you will be the beft Judge, and you muft be fure of your Succefs.

I may now acquaint you that His Majefty having been gracioufly pleafed to give me Permiffion to return to England, Major General Gages, with whom I am to leave the Command of the Troops & who will foon be at Albany on his way hither, will have full Directions concerning the future Operations; and you may confult with him regarding the new Boats, as well as the Preparations for the other Matters; for by the Time he arrives here I fhall be able to judge of what Affiftance may be expeƈted from the Provinces and we muft prepare accordingly. I have ordered two light Six Pounders to Albany.

I am, Sir,
Your moft obedient Servant,
JEFF. AMHERST.

Colonel Bradftreet,
    D. Q. M. G., Albany.

Extraƈt

*Extract of a Letter from William Edgar at Detroit
to Sir William Johnson.*

Novb. 1ft, 1763.

I HAVE lately received a Letter from Hombach
which came by an Officer from Illenois, who
brought a Belt & Letter to the Savages, with the
Account of the Peace, between England and France,
which neither the Savages nor the French *here* believed till now.   In Confequence of which, our moft
implacable Enemys, the Ottawas (who were the only
Nation here difpofed for continuing the War, all
the reft having begged forgivenefs for what they have
done, of our worthy Commandant) are now, with
the others, fuing for Peace, in the moft abject Manner.
Mr. Prentice is very well at Sandufky, as is Mr. Winfton, at St. Jofephs, and from the prefent Difpofition
of the Savages, I apprehend they will foon bring them
in.

*Letter from Sir William Johnson to the Authorities
at German Flats.*

Novbr 3d, 1763.

Gentlemn :

AS I underftand that fome Chenopfco[1] Indians
(who are now our Enemies) make a Practice of
coming to the German Flatts to purchafe Powder &
other Things wh you know is not allowed, befides,
when there, they have an Opportunity of making their
Remarks & feeing our Strength, you fhould in order

---

[1] Genefee.

to

to prevent yᵉ like for the Future, take up all such as you find of that Nation & send them Prisoners to Albany under a good Guard, first being certain that they are our Enemies—not doubting but that yʳ own Prudence will lead you both to do every thing of that Kind with Propriety & Discretion. I need add no more.

Letter to Justices Frank & Harkemer to apprehend any Chenupscos who may come to the Flatts.

Letter from Volkert P. Douw to Sir Wm. Johnson.

ALBANY, Novemb. 3d, 1763.

SIR:

I THOUGHT it not improper at this Time to acquaint you as being Commissioner of Indian Affairs that last Night arrived here three Tennesie Indians directly from there Castle as they say; they also say they waited on you as they passed in there way to Albany of which I doubt much; they have a small Quantity of Beaver with them but no Person chuses to Trade with them without Liberty. I am at a loss how to act with regard to those Indians and should be glad of your Direction therein by the Return of the Bearer.

I am, Sir,

Your most Humˡ Servant,

Volkert P. Douw,

To Sir William Jonson, Barnit.

Orders

Orders iſſued by Captain Guy Johnſon to the Garri-
ſon at Schenectady.

ORDERS.

AS the Safety and Protection of Schenectady depends
in a great Meaſure on the keep of a good Guard
in the Town, it is Sir Wm. Johnſons Orders that the
Commanding Officer of the ſecond Bataillon of Militia for the County of Albany do immediately appoint
a Guard confiſting of a Subaltern, Serj't, Corporal and
twenty Men to mount at the Block Houſe in the
Albany Street and to be regularly relieved every 24
Hours till further Orders, which Guard is to poſt
Centinels at ſuch Places as the Commanding Officer
of the Battaillon ſhall judge beſt, the Centinels to be
regularly relieved by the Corporal of the Guard every
two Hours and the Officer to let no more than two
Men be at any Time abſent from the Guard.   Every
Evening at Sunſet the Officer of the Guard is to have
his Men under Arms, the Roll called & Mens Arms,
&c. examined & ſee that they are furniſhed with 12
Rounds of Powder & Ball, no Perſon is to be abſent
on pain of Puniſhment and the Town Major is at the
Time he thinks neceſſary to viſit the Guards & Centinels & make a Report thereof to the Commanding
Officer.   The Serjeant of the Guard to viſit the Centinels frequently during the Night and the Officer on
being relieved to make a Report of the Guard in
Writing to the Commanding Officer who is to ſee
theſe Orders ſtrictly complied with.

In caſe of an Alarm the Militia are to aſſemble at
the Dutch Church and there to follow ſuch Orders as
they ſhall receive from the Commanding Officer for
the Protection of the Town, the Guard turning out &
continuing

continuing under Arms until they ſhall receive the Commanding Officers Orders.

And the Commanding Officer is to tranſmit in writing to Sir Wm. Johnſon a Return of the ſtate of the Blockhouſe and other Fortifications about the Town, as alſo of the Number, State & Quality of the Cannon & Ammunition, &c., immediately.

Johnſon Hall, Nov'r 3d, 1763.

[signature: G. Johnson Capt & Adjutant of the Regt of Albe militia]

Col. Vanſlyke, &c.

Letter from Gavin Cochrane to Sir Wm. Johnſon.

DEAR SIR:

I CAME here yeſterday & had the Pleaſure to find all your Friends here well—the Battoe is in a Hurry to go down which prevents my having the Pleaſure of waiting on you.   Capt. Daniel, at parting, preſſed me much to give an Account of his Behaviour whilſt with me when I was guarding the Wreck; I was there above a Fortnight & in all that Time he was but once drunk, always at my Elbow, & very Induſtrious to do every thing to ingratiate himſelf with me, and ſo was Jacob, who was with him.   We were fired at for near two Hours by 25 or 30 Indians, as they gueſſed from the Tracks afterwards & Daniel kept cloſe by me & ſhowed great Zeal—we loſt 3 Men; the Enemy came very near but we could not get one Shot at them—the Behaviour of Aaron, &c. occaſioned me to be ſollicited not to ſend Daniel up with the Schooner, but I ſent him ; nor will I believe the Mohawks in general difhoneſt.

Fatigue & Cold gave me an Illneſs which tho' I have not yet quite recovered I am pretty well, only in a very bad Weather I am pretty ſure ſtill of an Ague Fit.   I am ſo far on my Way to New York.

The Troops for Detroit, about 600 Men under Major Wilkins got out from the Head of the Rapids at the Entrance into Lake Erie the 20th of October. Two Boats were fired upon at embarking there & all in them except a Serj^t killed or wounded ; five were killed & one died of his Wounds, as did alſo Lt. Johnſon ; there were a good Body of Men ſtill aſhore who purſued & engaged in the Woods for ſome Time & than returned in good Order to the Boats.   This is the Serjeants Account who remained unhurt, who ſaid he ſaw this at a Diſtance but knows no other Particulars.

I don't know whether it is worth mentioning to you that whilſt I was at Fort Stanwix I was told a Squaw of the Oneidas that had juſt come ſaid there was a Report amongſt them that 20 of their Young Men had been killed by our People in the Cheroquee Country & that the Oneydas were holding a Council about it.   I am, with great Sincerity,
        Dear Sir,
          Your moſt obedient & very humble Servt.

Gavin Cochrane

Fort Johnſon, Novb. 5th, 1763.
The Number in the two Boats that were fired upon were 14 excluſive of the Officers.
        26   Letter

Letter from General Amherſt to Colonel Bradſtreet.

NEW YORK, 6th November, 1763.

SIR :

I HAD laſt Night your Letter of the 31ſt Octοber : The Account given by *Silverheels*, I believe, is too true and I am not ſurpriſed the Inhabitants on the Mohawk River are alarmed : They can not be too much on their guard, until they can get an additional Aſſiſtance, which I hope the Province will furniſh, when the Aſſembly meets.

I have mentioned to the Lt. Governor how neceſſary it will be to get a Law paſſed for impreſſing Carriages, as well as billeting the Troops on this Occaſion. But whether he can bring it to bear, or not, I know not.[1]

I am very glad to find you have ſuch Hopes of the Boat anſwering ; but am ſorry to hear you have ſuch bad Reports of the Stuff fit for building Boats at Oſwego ; however I am apt to think the Batteaus from Canada may anſwer ; General Gage will know that.

[1] This Law was not paſſed. The only Acts paſſed by the General Aſſembly of New York with reference to the Wars of Pontiac were the following :

"An Act providing for three hundred effective Men, excluſive of Officers, to be employed againſt the Enemy Indians, and for one hundred and ſeventy-three Men, Officers included, to garriſon the ſeveral Forts on the Frontiers of this Colony, in ſuch Manner as the Commander-in-Chief of all his Majeſty's Forces in North America ſhall think proper, and alſo for three hundred effective Men, excluſive of Officers, to guard the weſtern Frontiers of the Colony under the Direction of the Governor or Commander-in-Chief thereof. Paſſed Dec. 13, 1763."

"An Act providing for one hundred and eighty Men, excluſive of Officers, to be employed againſt the Enemy Indians and other Purpoſes therein mentioned." Paſſed April 21, 1764.

General

General Gage, in all Probability will be with you before this reaches Albany, and as he has no Family with him, I hope he will have found all the Affiftance he could require on the Route.

The Sloop with the Iron work, &c., as mentioned in my laft, failed on the 4th. , I enclofe you a Lift of the Whole, but the Mafter went off without figning the Invoice of the Sails, Cables & Anchors : you have his Receipt therewith for the Iron work, and you will pleafe to take care that he delivers the Whole, agreeable to the enclofed Lift. I need not defire you to forward them in the beft Manner you can.

As Captain Loring, I imagine, will be down foon, I would chufe to wait for his Opinion of the Size of the other Veffel, before I fent the Materials ; but fhould he not come foon, I fhall order Iron work, &c. to be forwarded for the fame Kind of Schooner as the one for which the Materials are now fent.

I am, Sir,
Your moft obedt. Servant,
JEFF. AMHERST.

Colonel Bradftreet,
D. Q. M. G. Albany.

Message of Lieutenant Governor Colden to the General Assembly of New York.[1]

[Gaine's Journal of General Assembly, ii, 720.]

Gentlemen of the Council and General Assembly.

THE great and desireable Work of Peace, being by the Wisdom and Magnanimity of our gracious Sovereign, happily accomplished since your Recess; I cordially congratulate you on this joyful Event, so highly glorious to his Majesty, and extensively Beneficial to his People. His American Subjects, who will derive from it a Security, unknown since the first Establishment of these Colonies, must receive this Mark of the royal Attention to their Interest and Safety, with the warmest Sentiments of Loyalty, Gratitude and Affection.

The Enjoyment of solid Tranquility is however unhappily suspended by the daring and unprovoked Attacks of some of the Western Tribes of Indians, who under the specious Appearance of Friendship, have treacherously surprized some of our remote Posts, and are in open War, renewing with relentless Cruelty, that Horror and Desolation among the defenceless Inhabitants, from which they were so recently delivered.

To suppress this dangerous Defection, pregnant with the most fatal Evils, before it becomes more extensive and formidable, is our indispensable Duty.

The Preservation of our own Frontier, should be our first and immediate Care, every Motive of Policy,

---

[1] The General Assembly of New York met on the 8th of November, 1763, and on the Day following the Lieutenant Governor addressed to them the preceding Message relating to the Indian War.

Justice

Juſtice and Humanity, unitedly demanding the Protection of our fellow Subjects, whoſe diſtant and dif-
perſed Situation muſt otherwiſe leave them an eaſy
Prey to mercileſs Savages.

But barely to defend ourſelves would be giving the
Enemy every Advantage, and expoſe us to perpetual
diſquietude. It is neceſſary a Force ſhould be raiſed,
ſufficient to chaſtiſe theſe faithleſs People, that feeling
the Weight of our Reſentment, they may be awed for
future by the Fear of Puniſhment ; experience evinc-
ing, that deſtitute of every juſt and humane Principle,
nothing elſe can ſecure us againſt their continual
Ravages and Depredations.

Since then, not only the Proſperity of the Colony,
but the very Exiſtence of a great Part of it, depend on
the moſt active and ſpirited Meaſures, no Arguments
can be wanting to animate you to a vigorous Exertion
of your Strength in the Accompliſhment of this eſſen-
tial Object.

I ſhall therefore content myſelf with laying before
you a Letter I received from his Excellency Sir Jeffrey
Amherſt, Commander in Chief of his Majeſty's Forces,
preſſing this Government to furniſh a Proportion of
Men, to proceed early in the Spring in conjunction
with the regular Troops, on this important Service.
Did the Subject require it, his ſuperior Abilities, would
render it unneceſſary for me to enforce, what he ſo
wiſely urges for ſubduing that reſtleſs, fierce and cruel
Spirit of the Savages, the Source of the moſt dreadful
Calamities.

Gentlemen of the General Aſſembly,

I flattered myſelf the ordinary Support of his Majeſty's Government, would have been the only Aid
required of you at this Time. But the unexpected
Revolt

Revolt of the Indians, renders a much greater Expence unavoidable. Befides providing for the Company now pofted at Fort Ontario, Niagara and Detroit, which General Monckton, by the Advice of his Majefty's Council, a few Days before his Departure, directed to be continued on that Service, I earneftly recommend you will grant the neceffary Supplies for raifing, cloathing and paying, a Body of Forces, fufficient with the other Troops, to avert the Dangers we fear; avenge the Injuries we have received; and convince the Savages of our Ability to compel them to Submiffion.

Gentlemen of the Council and General Affembly,

The Enemy have already infefted the Border of Orange and Ulfter, and though I am confident of the Spirit and Activity of the Militia, yet as this Duty will foon be too feverely felt, I affure myfelf, you will enable me to eafe them; and by the moft vigorous Refolutions in this important Conjuncture, fecure to yourfelves the great Advantages of a Peace, peculiarly calculated for the Happinefs of America.

CADWALLADER COLDEN.

Fort George, New York, Nov. 9, 1763.

And then the Letter mentioned in his Honour's Speech from Sir Jeffrey Amherft, was read, in the Words following, that is to fay,

NEW YORK, October 30, 1763.

SIR:

ON a due Confideration of the moft probable Meafures for crufhing the prefent Infurrection of the Indians, and punifhing the Guilty as they deferve, I find it abfolutely neceffary to make Application to the Provinces moft nearly concerned, that a refpectable Body of Men may be raifed, fo as to proceed early

in the Spring, in Conjunction with such regular Troops
as can be collected, to put in Execution such offensive
Operations as may be judged most effectual for reducing the Savages, and securing Peace and Quiet to the
Settlements hereafter.

I am in great Hopes that the Provinces to the
Southward will chearfully raise such Quotas, as may be
required of them, for reducing the Delawares, Shawa-
nese, and other Tribes on that Side; and as I intend
to assemble a respectable Body of Men early in the
Spring at Niagara, for the Punishment of the Senecas
and other Savages on Lake Erie, &c. who have so
treacherously commenced and are now carrying on
Hostilities against us, I think it but reasonable that
the Provinces of New York and Jersey, should contribute their Shares towards a Service of so much Consequence to the future Security of their respective Inhabitants; and therefore I am now to lay before you,
a Requisition, which I am persuaded will not only
meet with a proper Reception from you, but that you
will enforce the same to your Council and Assembly,
backed with such Arguments (if any Arguments can
be necessary on such an Occasion) as will at once remove every Obstacle that could be started to a Com-
pliance therewith.

The Proportion I must demand from your Province
is fourteen hundred Men, exclusive of commissioned
Officers, twelve hundred to be divided in four Corps
of five Companys each, commanded by a Field Officer,
who may have the Rank of Major; and each Company to consist of a Captain, and two Subalterns and
sixty Men, including three Serjeants and three Corporals; the other two hundred to have a Field Officer,
and to consist of four Companies of fifty Men each,
with the commissioned and non-commissioned Officers

as

as above; for the Service on which they will be employed requires that there fhould be a good many
Officers; the Men to be cloathed, but in a light Manner; a cloth Jacket, flannel Waiftcoat, Leggins, &c.
will be full fufficient; and it will be neceffary that the
whole are raifed and ready to proceed to Albany by
the firft of March next.

But as the Settlements on the Mohawk River, are
open to the Enemy, and that it is not in my Power at
prefent to fpare Regulars for their Protection, fo much
as I wifh to do, I muft recommend it to you, to ufe
your Influence with the Affembly to raife five Companies of the above mentioned Quota with the utmoft
Expedition, that they may be pofted during the Winter, on the Communication between Albany and Ofwego, and be ready for any Service they may be called
for, which may be a great Means of preventing any
Incurfions that might be attempted by the Savages,
and give that Confidence to the Inhabitants, which is
fo neceffary to enable them to repel, by Force in Cafe
of an Attack.

Particular Care fhould be taken that in recruiting
the Men, none fhould be raifed but fuch as are able
bodied; neither too young nor too old, but fit for the
moft active and alert Service.

Although by an Order from Home, the regular
Troops are fubject to a Stoppage for the Provifions
iffued to them, belonging to the Crown, yet upon this
Occafion I will take upon me to order Provifions to
the Provincial Troops, that fhall be raifed and take
the Field; and they fhall likewife be provided with
Arms, unlefs any of them chufe to bring their own
Arms, for which they fhall have the fame allowance as
was made in former Campaigns, fhould any of them be
                                                    loft

loft, or damaged in actual Service. Tents will alfo be furnifhed to them as formerly.

The Time of Service may be limited to the firft of November, although it is much to be hoped, every Thing will be finifhed long before that Period, in which Cafe the Men will be fent back to the Province.

I am, with great Regard Sir,
Your moft obedient humble Servant,
JEFFREY AMHERST.
A true Copy, examined by G. Banyer, D. Sec.

●

Letter from Captain Gerret A. Lanfingh to Sir William Johnfon.

[MSS. of Sir William Johnfon, vii.]

SIR:

AGREABLE to your Orders I have been round the Town to revue the Condition and State of the Fort, Blockhoufes, Cannon, Amanition, &c., likewife the Stockagadefs; as for the Fort is but in a verry confetreable Condition, whants a good Teal of preparing and the Blockhoufe at the Widow Van Eps at the North Side of the Town is unfit for Service, no Shimble in nor Flowr, at the Blockhoufe at Daniel De Graff at the fouthweft End of the town is entirely unfit for Service is ready to fall down. The Block- houfe at Mr. Ryner Mynders whants lettle repairing. As to the Block Houfe on the South End of Albany Street is fit to keep a Wacht in, and the Block Houfe which formley ufe to ftand at Mr. Thomas Nixfon Door is intirely takeing away and no more of, and as for Stoagadeges about the Town there is about feventy of them moftly rotton; as for Cannon in the Fort

27   that

that belongs to it there is none fit for Service, there is no Cannon in the Block Houfes not a fingle one, and there is a few Cannon lying up the Albany Hill unfit for Service which has been takeing out of the Fort and Blockhoufe and have been tryed by Soldier & Conductors of the Royall Artellery and is found to be condemned; as for Powder there is two Cafk of about 50 Wieght each which belongs to the Townfhip of Schenectady likewife 30 Wieght grave Schot and about feventy or eighty fmall Hand Granades.

         I am Sir

            Your moft obe^d humbl Servt

Gerret a Lanving Capt

To Sir Wm. Johnfon, Bar^t.

       [*Endorfement on Back of Letter.*]

    Capt. Lanfinghs Return of ye State of ye Blockhouses, &c. at Schenectady.

    A Return of Condition & State of the Fortification of the Townfhip of Schenectady. Novbr. 11th, 1763.

Letter from T. De Couagne to Sir William Johnfon.

[MSS. of Sir William Johnfon, viii.]

          NIAGARA, 27th of Novbr, 1763.

SR:

I HAVE rec'd your Letter dated Novbr ye 3d, 1763, wherein you write me word to be more particular or circumftantial than hitherto. You may depend I do everything to ye utmoft of my Power for my Employer

ployer, likewife for his Majeftys Service, yᵉ Troops is come back thath was going to Ditroit with yᵉ Lofs of one hundred Men, yᵉ got within lefs than one hundred Miles was caft away and loft there Ammunition was forft to return for Want; yᵉ had to I am inform'd, but eight Rounds a Man thath yᵉ could not proceed & have fpoke to yᵉ Officer Commanding, Major Browning, about yᵉ Indians coming in, he has give out an Order thath yᵉ muft not fire upon any fmall Party of Indians upon no Account & thath on their march in fight of yᵉ Garrifon he fays if yᵉ fhould fall in with Fort Slhoffer he cant be accountable what happens as they are daily killing our People.   In yr Letter you fay you do not underftand what I mean by yᵉ Voifeagamigate, Sr he is yᵉ chief Man North & Weft upon Lake Ontario and fo far upon Lake Erie as yᵉ big River, which is fixty Miles from Little Niagara, yᵉ Troops goes fifhing every Day and no body hurt. I can't promife the do no mifchief in there own Country but what they do otherwife I can not tell.

Sr, I have wrote you word before of Major Wilkins taken fome Belts of Wampum from heare; he is come back, I have fpoke to Colonel Browning for to gett them.   In yᵉ next Letter I fhall fend Word if Collonel has rec'd.

                                        DE COUAGNE.

Sir yᵉ Indians is arrived this Day from Detroit which you will yᵉ News more particular from them are yᵉ Veffel fails emediately.

Letter from Aaron the Mohawk to Sir Wm. Johnson.

[MSS. of Sir William Johnson, viii.]

FORT PITT, 1ft Decemr, 1763.

SIR:

HAVING been fent Exprefs by Major Gladwin from De Troite to this Place, on arriving at Sandufky meeting with about 300 Shany and Delaware Indians, who ware at the fame Time holding a great Counfill and by which I underftood and was told by them the breaking out of this Warr was occafioned by the Seneca Indians who went about with a bloody Belt and Tomahawk to all the Nations engag'd in this Troubles. The Taways alfo expreffly told me that the Senecas were the Beginners of this Warr, they alfo defired me (the old Men of the Delawar's & Shanees) to acquaint you that if you defire, that they would come down to you, and fwear before you that this Warr was begun by the Senecas. The old Men of the Wiandots Nation want very much to fee you, and if you defire they will come immediately, you being pleaf'd to let them know. I had the Miffortune to be rob'd of 4000 of Wampom, a Tamihok and all the Powder and Ball I had by the Delawar's, Shanees & the Five Nations.

> Sir, Remain with great Refpect,
> Your Obedient Humble Servant.

AARON.

Letter from John Stuart[1] to Sir William Johnson.

[MSS. of Sir William Johnson, viii.]

CHARLES TOWN, 10th December, 1763.[2]
SIR :

I AM now to acknowledge the receipt of both your Favors of 24th July and 2d September, which my being at the Congress with the Indians in this District prevented my receiving and answering sooner. I have a grateful Sense of your polite and friendly Expressions, and shall cheerfully embrace every Opportunity of cultivating a Correspondence with, and rendering you any agreeable Service. I am sincerely sorry for the Rupture with the Indians in your Department, which is attended with so much Bloodshed and Desolation and necessarily with so much Trouble to you.

Immediately after the Receipt of your last Letter, I wrote to the Cherokee Nation, to know if they would send some Parties against the Northern Indians according to their Proposal to me at the Congress. As soon as I receive an Answer I shall communicate it to you. Some Officers of the Independent Companies in this Province, who are on the Point of being reduced, have offered to accompany such *Cherokees* as can be prevailed upon to go and act jointly with his Majesty's Forces against the Northern Tribes. It would be a delicate Point to propose anything of this Nature to the *Creeks* at this Juncture, when they are apt to construe every Proposal as containing some hidden Design ; the Impressions left on their Minds by the French, and their Jealousy on account of the late

[1] Mr. Stuart was Superintendent of Indian Affairs in the Southern Department,

[2] Received Feb. 15, 1764.

Cession

Ceſſion of Florida and Louiſiana, not being as yet totally effaced.

The *Chaɛtaws* have but newly entered into the Covenant of Friendſhip with us. Their Country is a vaſt Diſtance, I ſhall endeavor as ſoon as poſſible to inform myſelf of their Diſpoſition and the Practicability of engaging them to ſend Parties as you propoſe.

The *Chickaſaws* are perpetually at War with the Northern Indians, but then they only act defenſively, being reduced to 450 Men at moſt, and ſurrounded by great Nations with whom they never are upon Terms of ſincere Friendſhip, for which Reaſon they dare not weaken themſelves by ſending out ſtrong Parties, ſo far as they are able their Friendſhip and Attachment to us may be depended upon.

The *Catawbas* are willing and brave, but reduced by War and Sickneſs to 60 or 70 Gunmen. The Northern Indians infeſted them all laſt Summer, killed and carried off ſeveral of them.

This may be depended on that I ſhall take every Meaſure to induce Parties from the Northern Nations within my Department to go and act jointly with his Majeſty's Troops employed againſt the Nations at War with us, and ſhall be extreamly glad to hear from you and receive the General's Inſtructions relative to my Conduct in this Matter.

Our Conferences at the late Congreſs ended with the moſt friendly Appearance. The Indians of every Nation went away well ſatiſfied, and made the ſtrongeſt Profeſſions of Attachment to the Britiſh Intereſt. They are all appraiſed of the War between the Northern Indians and us, but know nothing of the particular Events.

A minute Journal of the Proceedings at the Congreſs

grefs is now in the Prefs.   As foon I can be furnifhed with a Copy for you I fhall fend it.

The *Tafcaroras* inhabit a Tract of 10,000 Acres of Land laid out for them in North Carolina. I have wrote to Governor Dobbs for a particular Account of them and of their Situation with refpect to Debts or whatever elfe may hinder or retard their going to join their People. Governor Dobbs told me when at the Congrefs, that they confifted of about one hundred Men able to bear Arms, Women and Children in Proportion.

I am now to inform you, that on my return from Augufta, I received a Letter from the Right Honble the Lords of Trade declaratory of His Majefty's Orders, that the Agents for Indian Affairs fhould correfpond with their Lordfhips in all Matters regarding their Departments, and fhould tranfmit them all fuch Information as they fhould require. In Confequence they have required from me a regular and conftant Correfpondence upon thofe Points. Their Lordfhips have likewife directed me to tranfmit to them as foon as poffible, a full and particular Report of the State of Indian Affairs within this Department, and an accurate Defcription of the feveral Nations of Indians, their different Interefts, Claims and Difpofitions and what will in my Judgment be a proper Plan for the future Management and Direction of thefe important Interefts.

The Tafk impofed upon us I confider as arduous and what requires very mature Confideration, on which I have not as yet been able to turn my Thoughts, having a multiplicity of Affairs to fettle in confequence of the late Congrefs, it will give me the greateft Pleafure to coincide with you in Opinion, but to form *a general Plan* by which a Trade to the Indian Countries
may

may be at the fame Time *well regulated* and *free* to all his Majefty's Subjects, is not very eafy. It will give me great Pleafure to hear from you foon, being with moft fincere Regard,
     Sir,
        Your moft obedient humble Servant,

John Stuart

Letter from T. De Couagne to Sir William Johnfon.

[MSS. of Sir William Johnfon, viii.]

TRANSLATION.

NIAGARA, 15th X^{ber} 1763.

SIR :

SINCE my laft which I had the Honor of writing to you, by which I have mentioned the Accident which happened to Major Wilkin's Party which has retreated, Major Rogers arrived with his Corps and two Mohawks, Daniel and Jacob, two Days after.

The Commandant has fent the Man named Jacob with a Ranger to Detroit, and Daniel has decided to join the Party returning with Major Rogers, to rejoin you, and who can relate to you all that has happened in thefe Parts, as well as what has become of the other Mohawk. He has told me that the Man named Ouapacamigatte a Miffiffague had a Paffport from the
                           Commandant

Commandant at Detroit to come hither with a Meffage, and I believe it would be apropos if the Commandant would confent that I fhould fend him with one or two others to fpeak with you upon this Bufinefs. I believe that there is not here this Winter any Indian whom I could fend for fome Time. And I remember nothing further of which to appraife you. There are Parties croffing every Day to the other Side of the River upon the Lands of the Miffiffagaes but they have not returned with any Scalps.

The Man named Roffin . . . . a Seneca of whom you fpeak in your Letter has not arrived. I have fpoken to his two Sifters about him in a way that has flattered them much.

I have the honor to be with profound Refp^ct
Sir, Your very humble and much
obliged Servant,
DE COUAGNE.

It it impoffible at this Moment to write to you in Englifh, as every body is engaged, and I can not find a Secretary.

Letter from Colonel Bradſtreet to General Gage.

[Bradftreet and Amherft MSS., p. 169.]

ALBANY, 20th Decr, 1767.

SIR :

I RETURN your Excellency, enclof'd, the Papers you fent me relating to fmall Arms taken by my Order at Ofwego for the Indians in 1764—with my Certificate of the Number. Thofe Gentlemens Accounts & Affidavits you will pleafe to obferve fix the Time of my ordering thofe fmall Arms to be taken in

1763—near twelve Months before my Arrival at Ofwego.

I am,

JNO. BRADSTREET.

His Ex. Genl. Gage, &c. &c. &c.

Letter from Sir Wm. Johnfon to Major Gen. Gage.

[MSS. of Sir William Johnfon, viii.]

JOHNSON HALL, Decr 23, 1763.

DEAR SIR :

YOUR Excellency's Favors of the 30th ult. & 1ft of this inft. were accompanied with two Letters from the Lords of Trade, the one of Septr and the other of October laft, enclofing me one of the King's Proclamations, and expreffing Approbation of His Majefty & his Minifter and that of their Lordfhips on my late reprefentations, as alfo his Majefty's reliance on my Endeavors to bring Matters to a happy Iffue, and his Orders that I fhould .caufe the Proclamation therewith tranfmitted to be made publick and ftrictly complied with throughout my Jurifdiction.

I am hopeful that on receipt of my laft Letter, their Lordfhips will be able ftill further to contribute towards the falutary Points in view relative to Indians as I apprehend fome Additions may be added to the Royal Proclamation, which at prefent does not contain more with regard to them than has been already communicated to them by virtue of former Orders, &c. tranfmitted to America. This Proclamation does not relieve their prefent Grievances which are many, being calculated only to prevent the like hereafter, altho' there are numberlefs Inftances of Tracts which have indeed

indeed been purchafed but in the moft illegal and fraudulent Manner, all of which demand Redrefs.

I have made at this Meeting the beft ufe in my Power of his Majefty's Proclamation for the convincing the Indians here of his gracious and favorable Difpofition to do them Juftice, and fhall communicate the fame to all the reft.

The Indians have been here for feveral Days to the Amount of 230, are now moftly departed for their refpective Nations, for which Purpofe I have difmiffed them with a Prefent. They are accompanied by feveral of the yet friendly Senecas from *Kanadafego*[1] as alfo by three Deputies fent from *Chenaffio*, to defire to be informed of our prefent Refolution, and to know whether the Offer of Peace which they have now made will be accepted of, in which they are feconded by all the reft who earneftly defire the fame might be taken into Confideration and after reprefenting the Manner in which the Senecas of Chenaffio had been led into the War, intimated that fhould we now receive them into our Friendfhip the Generofity of the Indians would cheerfully join us in any Operations againft the reft, particularly againft the *Shawanefe* and *Delawares*, whom they reprefented as the principal Authors of all the late Troubles, to which after giving them ye moft fevere Reprimand in ye Prefence of all ye reft, I anfwered them, that I could do nothing therein, but would lay the fame before you. I muft therefore requeft your Direction and Sentiments thereon.

This was the chief Purport of the late Conference, the reft of their Speeches confifting of a Repetition of their Promifes and Affurances of their unvariable Attachment to his Majefty.

[1] Near Geneva, Ontario County,   N Y.

On

On this Subject I muſt beg leave to offer my Opinion that the 5 friendly Nations muſt naturally be very uneaſy at any Attempt againſt the Senecas, as they are a Part of their Confederacy, however juſtly they may deſerve our Reſentment, but I am confident that the whole would readily joyn againſt their perfidious Dependents, the *Shawaneſe* and *Delawares*, as well as any others who have acted as Principals in the War. The Hurons of Detroit from the concurring Accounts of all Perſons were with the utmoſt Difficulty and by ſevere Threats, perſuaded to engage in the War by the Ottawas under Pondiac, who with the before mentioned *Shawaneſe* and *Delawares* have ſufficiently ſhown themſelves as Principals in the War.

I imagine that any Hoſtilities committed in or about Pennſylvania and Jerſey muſt be done by the Delawares.[1] All thoſe of that Nation who have lately become our Enemies, have lately removed from the Suſquehanna to the Ohio amongſt the Shawaneſe, and thoſe who remain on or about the Suſquehanna, particularly from its Source down to *Owegy* are our friends, and here I cannot help remarking that the abſurdity of moſt of the Acc'ts received from the Provinces is apt to give a very unjuſt Idea of Indⁿ Affairs. For inſtance, in one of the late New York papers you muſt have obſerved it is inſinuated that a Party who defeated Capt. *Weſtbrook* on the Borders of *Penſilvania* confiſted of Mohocks, which they pretended to know from their Caps, and Manner of cutting their Hair. The Fidelity of the Mohocks deſerves a better Return, and the Folly of ſuch Repreſentations ſhould certainly be removed, leaſt it come to the Knowledge of our

---

[1] The following Sentence is here interlined in the original Draft without apparent Connection with the Text: "*Wyalooſin* is an Indian Town a confiderable Diſtance from any Settlement."

friendly

friendly Tribes who might entertain much Rancor from fuch a Falfity.   The Mohocks do not wear Caps, nor any Nation of the Confederacy except the Senecas and fome Cayugas, the former learned that Practice from their vicinity to *Niagara,* where fuch were ufually worn during the Winter, neither are the Authors of that Paragraph or any other Perfons capable of diftinguifh-ing one of thefe Caps from another or knowing to what Nation it belonged any more than they are of difcern-ing one Blanket from another.

The Houfe of Affembly have been very moderate in their Refolves.   I have received from the Lieuten-ant Governor in confequence thereof fome blank Com-miffions for raifing two Companies of 50 Men each to be ftationed at *Schohare* and *Cherry Valley* which I fhall give to fuch Perfons as I fhall judge beft qualified to anfwer their Intention.

I am informed by Letter from Niagara that Wabbi-commicot, Chief of the numerous Nation of the Chipe-weighs who accompanied me to the Detroit in 1761, and has fince behaved very well on his Part and pre-vented Numbers of his People from joyning againft us, propofes to vifit me fhortly on public Bufinefs, which if he does, or that I am attended by any other diftᵗ or Enemy Indians, indeed I fhall be glad to have your Sentiments concerning my Behavior on that Occafion and in what Manner you think it most ne-ceffary to treat them.

I am, &c.

Letter from Sir Wm. Johnſon to Lieut. Gov. Colden.

[MSS. of Sir William Johnſon, viii.]

JOHNSON HALL, Decr 24th, 1763.

DEAR SIR:

I AM juſt favored with your Letter of the 7th Inſt. encloſing me two Captain's Warrants & 2 Commiſſions as alſo three Lieutenants Warrants & 4 Commiſſions, from which I conclude that 'twas a Lieuts Warrant which was given to Mr. *Ten Eyke*. The reſt of the Warrants ſhall be given to ſuch Perſons as I judge will anſwer the public Expectations in the moſt expeditious and moſt effectual Manner. The Companies when raiſed ſhall be muſtered agreable to your Directions, but the ſmall pay of the Officers in a Country where People are accuſtomed to high Wages and where Men are now raiſing by Col. Bradſtreet at much higher Rates, will I fear greatly retard their completing, and I am a good deal ſurpriſed how your Letter and encloſures could have been ſo long by the Way.

The Indians who had been with me from all the 6 Natˢ for ſeveral Days are juſt departing for their reſpective Habitations. They numbered 230, and were accompanied by ſeveral of the yet friendly Senecas from *Kanadaſego* as alſo by three Deputies ſent from the *Chenuſſio* requeſting to be informed of our preſent Reſolutions and to know whether Offers of Peace will be accepted of or not. In this they were ſeconded by the reſt of the Nations who after repreſenting the Manner in which the *Enemy Senecas* had been drawn into the War, intimated that ſhould they now be received into our Friendſhip the whole of the Six Nations

tions would heartily joyn us againſt the reſt of our
Enemies particularly againſt the Shawaneſe and Delawares whom they repreſented as the principal Authors
of all the late Troubles, and I know the Diſpoſition
of theſe People ſo well as to foreſee that any Attempt
againſt the Senecas muſt naturally create uneaſineſs
amongſt the reſt of the Confederacy, particularly the
Cayugas and Onondagas who are more connected with
them than any of yᵉ reſt.

I have juſt received two Letters from the Lords of
Trade (one dated in Septr the other in October laſt)
encloſing me the King's Proclamation and expreſſing
the Approbation of his Majeſty and his Miniſters and
that of their Lordſhips on my late Repreſentations as
alſo his Majeſty's Reliance on my Endeavors to bring
Matters to a happy Iſſue, and his royal Orders that I
ſhould cauſe the Proclamation therewith tranſmitted to
publiſhed and ſtrictly complied with throughout my
Juriſdiction, and I am hopeful that within a ſmall
Period of Time things may be ſettled on a ſtill more
ſatiſſactory Plan.

I am a Stranger to what Cauſe the Aſſembly attribute the unhappy Rupture, which is not a general Defection of the Six Nations as is inſiſted, nor indeed of
any others except yᵉ Shawneſe, ſome of the Ottawaes
and Chippawaies, alſo Delawares. I ſhall not take
upon me to point out the original Parſimony, &c. to
which the firſt Defection of the Indians can with Juſtice and Certainty be attributed but only obſerve as I
did in a former Letter that the Indians (whoſe Friendſhip was never cultivated by the Engliſh with that
Attention, Expenſe and Aſſiduity with which the
French obtained their Favors) were for many Years
jealous of our growing Power, were repeatedly aſſured
by the French (who were at the Pains of having many
                                                    proper

proper Emiſſaries among them) that ſo ſoon as we became Maſters of this Country we ſhould immediately
treat them with Neglect, hem them in with Poſts and
Forts, encroach upon their Lands and finally deſtroy
them, all which after the Reduction of Canada ſeemed
to appear too clearly to the Indians who thereby loſt
the great Advantages reſulting from the Poſſeſſion
which the French formerly had of Poſts and Trade in
their Country, neither of which they could have ever
enjoyed but for the Notice they took of the Indians
and the Preſents they beſtowed ſo bountifully upon
them, which however expenſive they wiſely foreſaw was
infinitely cheaper and much more effectual than the
keeping of a large Body of regular Troops in their
ſeverall Countries which however conſiderable could
not protect Trade or cover Settlements, but muſt remain cooped up in their Garriſons or elſe be expoſed
to the Ambuſcades & Surpriſes of an Enemy over whom
from the Nature and Situation of their Country no
important Advantage can be gained.

From a Senſe of theſe Truths the French choſe the
moſt reaſonable and moſt promiſing Plan, a Plan which
has endeared their Memory to moſt of the Indian Nations who would I fear generally go over to them in Caſe
they ever got Footing again in this Country, and who
were repeatedly exhorted and encouraged by the French
(from Motives of Intereſt and Diſlike which they will
always poſſeſs) to fall upon us by repreſenting that
their Liberties and Country were in yᵉ utmoſt Danger
and that a Fleet and Army, was arrived at Quebec, and
an Army coming by way of the Miſſiſſippi to their Aſſiſtance, all which the Indians were perſuaded to credit
until their Meſſengers ſent to the Ilinois returned and
contradicted the Report ſo induſtriouſly propagated
by the French, which imediately ſtruck at our Trade,

gave

gave them fome diftant Hopes of a reëftablifhment by embroiling our Affairs and drew down the valuable Fur Trade by the way of the Ilyones & Miffiffipi and the Indˢ once embarked in the Quarrel were eafily induced by their Succefs and Advantages of Plunder to continue their Ravages.   In the midft of which however I have the Satiffaction to find that my un-wearied Labors hath hitherto preferved the whole Confederacy (Chenuffeos excepted) with many other Nations and thereby fecured this very important Com-munication to the Lakes, alfo that by the River St. Lawrence, together with thefe Weftern Frontiers from the Fate which hath attended the neighboring Colonies, to effect thefe important Ends, as I have facrificed all my Tranquility and domeftic Concerns fo I have the Pleafure to find myfelf rewarded in the favorable Sen-timents with which his Majefty and the Miniftry have been lately pleafed to exprefs themfelves concerning my Labors for the public Welfare.

The prefent unhappy Rupture was long forefeen and frequently reprefented by me, but I had the Mor-tification to find that it did not meet with fufficient Credit, which Neglect at length brought on the Calami-ties in which we are involved and from which I appre-hend we can never be free unlefs we remove the Jeal-oufies which the Indˢ entertain of us, and purchafe their Friendfhip with Favors and Notice, which Friendfhip once obtained and eftablifhed will enable us to withdraw our Expenfes by imperceptible Degrees.

Thefe are my Sentiments on the prefent State of Indian Affairs and the Caufes to which the Hoftilities are certainly to be attributed and I hope they may tend to the further Information of any who may be defirous to enquire into the Subject.

The Petition which you fent me I was informed of
29   fome

fome Time ago and that Geo: Klock a Perfon of an infamous Character at Conajoharie had made it his Bufinefs to procure it figned by fev¹ Perfons (the greater Part of whom I know to be his Relations and Retainers, and his own Name is erafed at the Head of them) whom he perfuaded thereto on Promife of Rewards and of procuring them Commiffions, which the ignorant People readily believed, I have however fent for the Officers complained of and fhall tranfmit you my further Inquiries therein.

I am Sir, &c,

Letter from the Rev. Samuel Dunlop¹ to Sir William Johnfon.

[MSS. of Sir William Johnfon, viii.]

CHERRY VALLEY, Decemr 25th, 1763.

HONOURED Sr:

NOT Reflecting upon you, becaufe perhaps the Matter does not lye alltogether within the compafs of your Power, we the Inhabitants of Cherry Valley, think we are deferted, we hope not of God, but we think in a great Meafure of Man, and expofed to the mercylefs Infults of our Enemies without Covert or Relief.

¹ In 1738, John Lindefay and others procured a Patent of 8000 Acres in what is now Cherry Valley, and foon after Mr. L. met in New York the Rev. Samuel Dunlop and prevailed on him to vifit the Tract, offering him feveral hundred Acres upon Condition of his ufing his Influence with his Friends to fettle upon the Land. The Propofition was accepted and Mr. Dunlop vifited Londonderry in New Hampfhire, where feveral of his Acqaintances refided, and induced Numbers to emigrate to the new Tract. Mr. D. was a Native of the North of Ireland, and had traveled quite extenfively in the Colo-

You

You know General Amherſt was condemned for not making ſome Proviſion for the Safety of the Inhabitants by covering the Frontiers, and it was expected when he reſigned that General Gadge and your Honour, or the Perſons to whom the Care and Management of theſe Things were committed (you know beſt who they were) wou'd have made an alteration before now. But Things ſeem to remain in ſtatu quo, with the poor and unhappy Fronteers and the Council of the Heathen held ſome Time agoe ſeems to have had its accompliſhment againſt all the Places they intended, us only in this Quarter eſcaped. Matters appear darker and darker with us, and the Time now ſeems to be at Hand to fetch us the intended Blow, and Schoharry's being warned off we take to be a bad Omen of our aproaching Ruin.

And if Mȧn neither can nor will help us, may Allmighty God, either ward off the Blow or endow us with that Firmneſs of Spirit that may make us bear the Thoughts of Death without Amazement, and bring our Minds to an equal Poize between the ſtrong Inclinations of Nature to live, and the Dictates of Reaſon and Religion that ſhould make us willing to die when he pleaſes.

Death and a deſtroying Enemy may curtail a few Years of this mortal Life, from thoſe of us that are old,

---

nies, particularly in the South. He left Ireland under an Engagement of Marriage which he returned and fulfilled. He opened a School for the Inſtruction of Boys, at Cherry Valley, and has the Honor of beginning the firſt Grammar School Weſt of Albany within this State.

In the memorable Maſſacre of November 11, 1778, Mr. Dunlop's Wife was killed, but himſelf and Daughter were ſpared by Little Aaron, a Mohawk of the Aquago Branch. He was releaſed ſoon after, but the combined Effects of Age, Fear, and Cold, led to a Decline, which terminated in Death about a Year after.—*Campbell's Hiſtory of Tryon Co.*

but

but thanks be to God can never deſtroy our immortal
Life.   But it's a Pity the young and riſing Generation
ſhould be cutt off, and the Hand of the Heathen
embrewed in their Blood, who if ſpared, might make
ſome Figure in the World and be uſefull to Genera-
tions to come, and therefore, if you can mediate any
Timous Relief I beg you may.

For it is but a poor Redreſs to come to our Aſſiſtance
when dead, and to bury our ma[n]gled Corps when
we are gone, which is but too often the ſenſeleſs Cuſtom of the Country where we live, tho tis the beſt
Redreſs the Caſe will then admit of.   But the Matter
is to ſecure againſt the Blow beforehand and therefore
once more I would beg of you Honourable Sʳ that you
would mediate ſome Relief for us, or ſome way to
ſecure us if in your Power before it be too late.   And
if we fall, as Chriſt prayed for his Enemies, Father
forgive them for they know not what they do, ſo I
pray God our Blood may never be laid to their Charge
who had it in their Power to help us and did it not.
Pleaſe to give my kind Compliments to Capt. Guy
Johnſon & all your good Family.   I add no more, but
remain Sr your

Humble Supplicant,

Letter from Sir William Johnſon to Lieutenant Governor Colden.

[MSS. of Sir William Johnſon, viii.]

JOHNSON HALL, Decʳ 30, 1763.

DEAR SIR :

YESTERDAY I was favored with your Letter of the 19th Inſt. in anſwer to mine of the 5th.

I have received particular Information of all the late Tranſactions at the *Detroit*, as well from the Officers as from one of the Mohocks (whom with others I ſent there to be of any Service in their Power), who is juſt returned from thence charged with ſeveral Belts, &c. to me.

As the chief Cauſe of the Hoſtilities committed by the Indians was intended to procure themſelves Redreſs of ſome Wrongs, and to obtain a better treatment, together with occaſional Gifts and Rewards, for the admitting Poſts in their Country, I am of Opinion their Offers of Peace ariſe principally from an Expectation that they will for the Future obtain theſe deſired Ends which they could not get by any other Means than by having recourſe to Arms, having found all amicable Proceedings ineffectual.

For this Reaſon I conclude they have made their late Offers, and I likewiſe believe they would abide by their Promiſes if we for the Future gratify their Expectations, but I am fully convinced they will never preſerve Peace on any other Terms.

They know their own Strength and Situation too well to be as yet apprehenſive of our Reſentment, and they will never want Ammunition whilſt the French can ſupply them by the Variety of Communications open

open to the weſtern Indians and beyond our Power to
ſhut.

The Five Nations have had no Occaſion to alter their
Behavior, which as it has ſaved this Communication
and the Frontiers of this Part of yᵉ Province, juſtly
entitled them to all neceſſary Supplies for themſelves ;
more they did not require, nor are they ſo well affected
to theſe Nations who have made War upon us as to
give them any Ammunition even tho' they had plenty.
Indeed the Indians are very chary of Powder, and
although they often waſte it when they have plenty
(yet that has not been ſince the Surrender of Canada)
yet they are not ſo weak as to part with it to others,
beſides they have never had more than a bare ſuffi-
ciency, often expended before their hunting Seaſon was
near over.

If therefore they ſhould be denied Ammunition it
would immediately confirm them in the Sentiments
which greatly contributed to produce the Defection of
the reſt, and would counteract all my Endeavors to
remove that too general Opinion for the ſuſpecting
their Sincerity wᵈ make them dangerous Enemies, and
of this I have had repeated Experience.

I wrote you pretty fully in mine of 24th by which
you will ſee the Difficulties which may ariſe in puniſh-
ing the *Chenaſſios* and the Advantages which will attend
our turning our Arms againſt the reſt of our Enemies,
which will equally anſwer the important Purpoſe of
giving them a juſt Idea of our Abilities and Reſentment.

As I am well acquainted with the Inclinations of
the friendly Indians I know the lengths they are to be
truſted on the Article of Ammunition, of which I am
certain they will make no bad Uſe. It is an Article
ſo hard to be procured here, that I have not had it in
my

my Power to give them what they ſtood in yᵉ greateſt need of, and the Trade being now over they can have little if any from that Quarter, altho' I muſt confeſs the Danger they have run from the Attachment to which we have hitherto own the Safety of theſe Parts ſufficiently merits ſuch a Return from us as will ſhew them that they are not loſers by their Fidelity.

From what I have heard from the Senecas, as well as from the good Diſpoſition of the reſt, I ſhould be induced to hope that that theſe Frontiers might enjoy a State of Tranquility, at leaſt for a Time, but as this muſt be very uncertain (eſpecially if the Peace offered by the Senecas is not accepted of), I apprehend the two Companies for theſe Frontiers may not be amiſs but I fear they cannot be eaſily raiſed at this Time, as I have offered the Warrants to ſevˡ who declined accepting of them, by Reaſon of the lowneſs of the Officer's Pay, and the Bounty now offered in Albany, &c. for raiſing Men for other Service. Be aſſured I ſhall give you imediate Notice in caſe there appears a Proſpect for compleating them, at well as give you any further Intelligence which may come to my Knowledge worthy your Information, and I have a particular Pleaſure in aſſuring you how much I am,

Dr Sir, &c,

Memorial of Indian Traders.

[MSS. of Sir William Johnson, viii.]

[Copy.]

TO his Excellency Thomas Gage, Commander-in-Chief of His Majefty's Forces in America, &c. &c.
May it pleafe your Excellency as we conceive fome Hopes from the Accounts we have from D'troit of having a Peace with the Indians in the Spring, and as your Excellency has the ordering of every thing on the Continent, knowing your Inclination of ferving every Perfon to the utmoft of your Power, and your Excellency's Defire ftrictly to adhere to the good of his Majefty's Subjects, we humbly beg leave to Petition your Excellency and reprefent to you the Misfortunes we have labored under from the Plunder that was made by the Indians at the Time that the Forts were furprifed, and to hint to you what we think may be to our private Advantage without any Detriment to the Nation and wherein our Loffes may be in fome Meafure repaid without any Retardment to the publick Peace. According to the Cuftom of Trading feveral Indian Nations having taken up Goods upon Credit to a very confiderable amount, and are all of them capable of making Payment for the fame, fome of them having heard nothing of the Indian Warr had brought their Peltrys to Difcharge their Debts, but on feeing the Diftrefs we were in their good Intentions were laid afide and they took a Part with our Enemies. Thefe are the Indians who have been moft diftreffed during the Time the Warr has continued, and we hear are moft defirous of bringing Things to an End. The Ottawas, the Chipaways, the Miamis, the Pouteouta-
mis,

Saguinaw, Iroquis, &c. with all the Indians who trade on Lake Superior. If your Excellency thinks proper, when they propofe Terms of Peace, to mention to them to pay their Debts, if your Excellency thinks it will be no Detriment to the Publick Good it will make us fome Retalliation for the exceffive Loffes we have fuftained, will put us again on a good Footing for Trade and will relieve from great Diftrefs your Excellency's Petitioners, and moft dutiful & obed^t Serv^{ts}.   Signed,

Ja's Howard,	Hen'y Bostwick,
Jno. Chinn,	Forrest Outres,
Edwd Chinn,	Gorsen Levy,
James Stanly Goddard,	Holmes & Memsen.

Dated 30th Decr 1763.

Letter from T. De Couagne to Sir William Johnfon.

[MSS. of Sir William Johnfon, viii.]

Sir :

I HAVE the Honor to acquaint you on the 20th of Novr I got hear from the Seneke Caftles the Chiefs promifed me that they would fend the Horfes here. The Seneke Indians comes in evry Day, brings in Bevers and Vennifon and behaves very well, as alfo the Miffafagoes. I have no more to add, but if any thing happen fhall inform you, fo conclude.

Y^r moft hum^l Servt to command.

De Couagne.

Niagara, Jan'ry 4th, 1764.

30

Letter from Sir Wm. Johnfon to Lieut. Gov. Colden.

[MSS. of Sir William Johnfon, viii.]

JOHNSON HALL, Jan'y 12th, 1764.

DEAR SIR :

A GREAT Indifpofition under which I have labored for feveral Days, and from which I am not yet recovered, prevented my anfwering your Favor of the 28th ult° fooner.

In my Letter of the 30th ult° I gave you my Sentiments on the Reafons which induced the Indians to propofe an Accommodation, as alfo concerning the Article of Ammunition, reprefenting that none received any but thofe on whofe Confidence I might perfectly rely and to whom a Refusal might prove of dangerous Confequence, and that even the trifle of Ammunition which they received was too little and too much valued by them to part with. In my Letter of the 24th ult° I acquainted you with the Occafion of my having been vifited by the 5 Nations accompanied by fome Seneca Deputies.

Laft Week arrived here feveral of the Senecas on the fame Errand as before, whom I acquainted that I was not as yet authorized to treat with them on Terms of Peace, they were followed by the 5 Nations amounting to near 300, who came to repeat their Offers of taking fuch fteps againft our Enemies as I fhould direct, to which I have affured them in the beft Manner I could. But thefe Senecas having come contrary to my Defire and not being defirous to give any Satiffaction farther than a Promife of affifting us againft the reft, I have accordingly difmiffed them until I hear from General Gage. I however apprehended a white Man now amongft them, and who was formerly delivered

livered up but went back to the Indians and has had
as I am informed the Treachery to act againſt us in
the late Operations of our Enemies particularly at
Niagara Carrying Place, I ſhall therefore commit him
to Jail.

The Generality of the People have certainly great
Reaſon to be irritated againſt the Indians, and I am
glad to find ſuch a Spirit of Alertneſs as you expreſs
amongſt them, tho' I fear they will not find it an eaſy
Matter to puniſh thoſe who really deſerve it, and the
falling upon thoſe yet our Friends and who are conſe-
quently not aware of any ſuch Deſign, would I apprehend be very imprudent as well as diſagreeable to you
ſince it muſt inevitibly involve us in a general Quarrel.

The general Thirſt for Revenge ſo juſtly raiſed
amongſt our People may without proper Inſtructions
direct itſelf to a wrong Quarter as was lately the caſe
in *Penſilvania,* to prevent which, as well as to promote
the Succeſs of all the hearty Volunteers I muſt obſerve
that the greateſt Part of our Enemies are removed a
great way up the Cayuga or Tohicon [?] Branch of
Suſquehanna. Thoſe of *Wawilooſin* (our Friends) are
gone chiefly to Philadelphia and the reſt are removed
to *Chughnot* on the *Suſquehanna,* ſo that our Enemies
chiefly reſide from Diaoga[1] up that Branch, viz⟶ *Sing-
ſink, Pepiquaghquey,* &c. The meeting of theſe our
Enemies is very uncertain, as they have not made any
long Reſidence at any Place ſince the Commencement
of Hoſtilities, but the Indians of Caneſtio, a Village
between Chenuſſio & Fort Auguſta, who are chiefly
Renegadoes of proflicate Fellows from ſevˡ Nations,
& who murdered the two Traders in Novʳ 1762,[2] are

---

[1] Tioga.
[2] Upon learning of theſe Mur-   ders Sir William Johnſon ſent up
Lieut. Johnſon to attend a Meeting
very

very proper Subjects of our Refentment and have been Principals in carrying on Hoftilities.

I heartily wifh that whatever Party goes out, may be able to ftrike fuch a Blow as will give the Indians in general a good Opinion of our Abilities, but to give any Hopes of Succefs in my Opinion it will be neceffary that they fhould at leaft confift of 400 Men, and thofe expert and well qualified for the Service, acquainted with the Woods and furnifhed with Snow Shoes and all other neceffary Articles. The diftreffing and annoying the Enemy in Winter if well conducted muft prove very ufeful. I am now preparing fome Parties of trufty Indians for that Purpofe of which I hope the General will approve.

As the Trade by Reafon of the War hath been at an end for fome Time I apprehend it will not be thought advifable to grant any Paffes till Matters are better fettled, whenever that may happen I am humbly of Opinion that you will judge it neceffary the Traders fhould give Security for their fair Dealings, and alfo be permitted to trade at the principal Pofts only, as *Fort Stanwix, Ontario, Niagara,* &c. At thefe Pofts they will be in the moft fecurity and their Conduct can be beft enquired into, which if juftly blameable and fo reprefented by the com^(dg) Officer they may forfeit their Recognizance, for the indulging them in a liberty of trading in the Indian's Country or at their Caftles, will always produce Complaints from the latter, of Frauds and Extortion, as well as render the Traders liable to be murdered, and their Effects feized on any future Quarrel which may happen.

called at Onondaga to infift on the immediate Apprehenfion of the guilty Parties, but the upper Nations did not attend and the reft of the Indians could do nothing but promife that if the Senecas did not apprehend the Murderers they would themfelves go in queft of them—*Letters of Sir William Johnfon to Lieut. Colonel Wm. Eyre and Gov. Monckton.*

With fome Difficulty I have got Perfons to accept of the Warrᵗˢ for raifing the 2 Companies for the Security of this Frontier, and I am juft now informed they are almoft compleated with good Men. I fhall accordingly have them muftered and report to you thereon.

As Lt. Johnfon, who by his Majefty's Proclamation is entitled to a Grant of Land, is defirous to know the Limits within which you confider the fame may be granted, I muft requeft the Favour of your informing me on that Head, alfo your Directions concerning the Steps he is to take therein and whether he is entitled to his Share as Captain of the Provincials in 1758, or is to abide by his Title as Lieut. of the Independent Companies.

I am with very perfect efteem, &c.

P. S. I have great Reafon to apprehend that many mercenary Perfons inhabiting along the River fell Ammunition and other Articles to the Senecas, I could heartily wifh you could interpofe your Authority to prevent the like for the Future.

Letter from Sir William Johnfon to the Commanding Officers of the New York Provincials at German Flats.

[MSS. of Sir William Johnfon, viii.]

JOHNSON HALL, Jan'y 19th, 1764.

SIR:

AS fome Deputies from the Senecas, our Enemies, who have been here with a Meffage from their Nation to me, are now returning Home and being probably not fo well difpofed as they pretend, may be induced

duced to do some Mischief at or about the German Flatts, these are therefore to desire you will be sufficiently on your guard to prevent them, and in Case they should attempt Injury the Persons or Properties of the Inhabitants or the Troops under your Command, you will immediately seize upon them (taking Care that none escape) and send them down Prisoners to Albany, under a strong Guard, sufficient to prevent them from getting off.

In Case you find it necessary to take this Step it will require the utmost Precaution to be taken to prevent the greater Part of them from escaping, which will in a great Measure defeat the Design proposed by making them Prisoners.

I am Sir your most humble Servt.

P. S. The Inhabitants will enable you to distinguish the Senecas, who are upwards of 20, but it will not be prudent to mention my Name as the Occasion of their being apprehended at this Juncture. Should any of the Inhabitants sell them any Ammunition, Clothing or other Necessaries, you will immediately give me Notice thereof, and also prevent them for the Future from trading with any Indians who have been in Arms against the English.

Letter from John Stuart to Sir William Johnson.

[MSS. of Sir William Johnson, viii.]

CHARLES TOWN, 16th January, 1764.

SIR :

SINCE my last of 10th December I have not had the Pleasure of hearing from you.

I have not as yet received any Information about the

the Tufcarora Indians, as foon as I do, you may depend on its being communicated to you.

On the 24th ultimo 14 of our back Settlers upon Long Cane River were murdered, and we have fince found out by feven Creeks, who for fome Years paft refided in the Cherokee Nation. The Creeks have fent me a Talk upon the Occafion and difclaim the Murder and the Murderers, who fay they, the Cherokees ought to kill to fhow their Innocence. I have fent off Talks to all the Nations within my Diftrict, but I muft acquaint you that in this Department every Governor acts as if he were fole Agent, they will hardly be directed by each other and do not confult me, fo that it is odds but we counteract each other ; this requires fome Regulation.

By next Opportunity I will write you fully, it being my Intention to keep you regularly informed of the Occurrences within the Department.

I am with great Refpect,
Sir, your moft obedient
Humble Servant,
JOHN STUART.

Letter from Sir Wm. Johnfon to Lieut. Gov. Penn.

[MSS. of Sir William Johnfon, viii.]

JOHNSON HALL, Jany 20th, 1764.

SIR :

I HAD the Favor of your Letter of the 31ft ult. and fifth of this inft., together with the Enclofures, and I heartily congratulate you on your Arrival to your Government, wifhing that your Appointment may prove to your entire Satiffaction,

The

The Steps you have taken to difcover thofe rafh Offenders were certainly very judicious as well as highly neceffary and I am hopefull they may be attended with Succefs for bringing them to Juftice.

I apprehend that after their firft Offence in murder-ing the 6 Indians at Coneftoga their miftaken Refent-ment would have ended, and that firft Act was fufficient to create much uneafinefs amongft all the Indians, but their laft public Infult to the Laws and the Govern-ment itfelf certainly demands the moft ftrict Enquiry as well as the fevereft Punifhment.

You may be affured I fhall ufe every Argument with the Six Nations, for removing the unfavorable Ideas which they muft certainly entertain of fuch a Proceed-ing, as well as to fatisfy them that your Government highly difapproves of it and will feverely punifh the Offenders, but I am aware of their Sentiments on the Subject and [am] greatly apprehenfive it will ftagger the Affections of the 5 hitherto well affected Nations, who confider the Indians of your Government as con-nected with them and under their Protection, and as the murdered have been all along peaceably inclined, the friendly Indians in thefe Parts may be induced to doubt our Faith and Sincerity toward themfelves from the unhappy Fate of our late Friends in Pennfilvania, which will caufe them to expect the fame Treatment whenever it is in our Power to deftroy them. This I fear may greatly check the Ardor they have lately ex-preffed to me of affifting us againft our Enemies and even fpirit up many to obtain Revenge within your Government.

The Threats which the riotous Parties have fince thrown out, that they would deftroy the Indians in the Neighborhood and under the Protection of Philadel-phia, favors fo much of Madnefs that I cannot acc't for

for them. Your gratifying the Indians Requeft thereon
of coming to me muft therefore appear pleafing to
them, but I have juft received a Letter from Lieut.
Gov. *Colden* informing me that the Council "have
advifed him not to admit them into this Province."
This will probably prevent me from feeing them, and
I heartily wifh their return back may not expofe them
to frefh Infults, which would certainly occafion a
general Defection.

Several Deputies from the Enemy Senecas have
been lately with me here, making fome friendly Offers
of Peace, but I am convinced that nothing but a good
Treatment accompanied with occafional Favors will
ever enfure a lafting Peace from the jealous Sentiments
which our Enemies entertain of the Englifh and the
Prefents the French have accuftomed them to, for the
Toleration the Indians afforded them in their Country
infomuch that any future Neglect on our Parts will
immediately produce a difcontent and apprehenfion of
our Defigns which will inevitably occafion a renewal
of Hoftilities, fo that a Peace made with thefe People
without proper fubfequent Steps to remove thefe Jeal-
oufies and eftablifh a good Opinion with the Indians
is always liable to be violated to the great Detriment
of Trade and the certain Deftruction of the Frontier
Inhabitants wth their Dwellings, and the Expence in
which the Crown muft be involved to fup'prefs fuch
Devaftations will certainly am^t to a much greater Sum
(indep^t of the Lofs the Provinces muft fuftain) than
would conciliate the Affections of the Ind^s and enable
us to extend our Settlements and Trade with the utmoft Security.

I heartily wifh that the Law you have propofed may
be agreed to by the *Affembly*, as it appears to me highly

neceffary

neceffary and effential as well to the Credit as the Safety of the Province.

  I am with great Efteem
    Sir, Your moft obed^t humble Servt

Letter from Sir Wm. Johnfon to Lieut. Col. Eyre.

[MSS. of Sir William Johnfon, viii.]

JOHNSON HALL, Jany 29th, 1764.

DEAR SIR :

I THANK you for your interefting Letter of the 7th Inft. which I would have fooner anfwered but for the Bufinefs in wch I have been engaged for this Fortnight paft with a large Number of the 5 Nations and fome Seneca Deputies.

  It would have given me much Pleafure to have feen you on your Return from *Niagara.* I difpatched a Letter in anfwer to yours, with Directions that it might be left at *Ontario* till you came back, which I hope you received altho' I underftand you did not return by that Poft.

  I cannot but coincide in Opinion with you on the greateft Part of what you have mentioned on Ind^n Affairs, and I could wifh for the good of the Public that every.Perfon had been of the fame way of thinking, which might have proved a Means of preventing the many Loffes we have lately felt.

  The Caufes to which the Defection of the Indians may be attributed are: Firft. Their Jealoufy of our growing Power, and occupancy of the Outpofts where they neither met with the fame Treatment nor reaped any of the Advantages which they enjoyed in the Time of the French. Secondly. The Reports induftrioufly
          propogated

propogated by many of the French, tending to fet our Defigns in the moft odious Light and to reprefent the Indians as being on the Brink of being enflaved.

It will not appear extraordinary that the French who had purchafed the Ind^s Favour at a high Price fhould obtain Credit from fuch a Reprefentation, efpecially when there were but too many concurring Circumftances to ftrengthen the Belief of a People naturally credulous and jealous of their Liberties.   The Indians began with Remonftrances, reprefented many Grievances and demanded Redrefs.   Their Complaints I communicated from Time to Time with my Sentiments and Apprehenfions thereon, but the inconfiderable Opinion too univerfally entertained, of their fmall Power and Abilities occafioned it to be treated with Negleƈt.   To particularize all their Complaints would exceed the Bounds of a Letter ; it will be fufficient to obferve that I declared it as my Opinion that the Indians would not be totally negleƈted, but that (after redrefs of their Grievances) we fhould cultivate to the utmoft of our Power a good Underftanding with them, at leaft until we became more formidable and our Frontiers better eftablifhed, and this I thought we could effeƈt at an Expenfe infinitely lefs than any other Method, and on Principles the beft adapted for fecuring Peace, promoting Trade and encreafing our Frontiers.

The Expence, Difficulty and Dangers attending other Expedients, the ftagnation of Trade, deftruƈtion of our Pofts and Frontiers, and the fmall Advantages to be gained by a War with us, are now obvious to moft People, and are fo well reprefented in your Letter that they need not to be enlarged upon.

The Difficulty and even Impoffibility of fecuring our Communications or maintaining our Outpofts

contrary

contrary to the Indians Inclinations is very clear to me, but I am pretty certain we can purchafe all thefe Advantages and fecure their Inclinations by a proper Treatment which will gain us a fufficient Credit with them, and awe of this Country, as it will remove all their Prejudices and which no other Steps can effect. The inland fmall Pofts don't appear to me very necef- fary, they are too great a Temptation to the Ind^a when- ever they are induced to quarrel, and from their Dif- tance and difficulty of obtaining Succours muft always fall into their Hands. The fame Reafons induce me to think, that the Perfons and Property of Traders would be fafe amongft them, for whilft there are any French there, they will certainly thro' Jealoufy pro- mote a Quarrel, and even were there none there the Expence of tranfporting Goods is fo great, that they muft fell at a Price which would not be agreable to the Indians as well as be guilty of many Frauds not in the Power of an Officer to difcover or prevent. Whereas the Indians (who think little of going a great way to purchafe Neceffaries) would find them cheaper at our large Pofts, and the Traders would be lefs expofed to Rifque.

Wherever we can have a good Communication by Water, we might tolerably well maintain Pofts, and if fome fmall Veffels are kept up on *Lake Erie, Detroit* or even *Michilimackinac* might be kept up, the latter being well fituated for drawing down the northern Furs. After all that can be faid, we fhall be liable to many Broils, till the French Inhabitants and Jefuits are re- moved, the latter (being no longer a Society in France) we might very well appropriate their Lands to his Majefty's Ufe. I dare fay they would be fufficient to endow a *Bifhoprick* in Canada, and for good Miffiona- ries, and I imagine an Epifcopal Foundation in that
Country

Country would greatly contribute to bring over the French, and make good Subjects of them in Time.

The late Offers of Peace made by some of the Nations has been greatly promoted by the Attachment the 5 *Nations, Indians of Canada,* &c. have manifested during the Course of the War, which makes our Enemies dread they will accompany our Troops against them in the Spring, for they have much more Reason to fear Indians than the best Troops in the World.

Indeed the beforement^d Nations have made me so many Offers of Service that I have no doubt of their Sincerity, and I am now sending out a confiderable Party of *Oneidas* and *Tufcaroras* who I hope will greatly diftrefs our Enemies, as well as convince them that we are not without *Allies* of their own fort. This will likewife contribute to difunite them, a Circumftance too important to be neglected.

Whenever the prefent unhappy Trouble fhall be ended by an Accomodation, I truft fuch Meafures will be taken at Home as may enfure a lafting Peace to the Northern Colonies, on which Subject I have lately received fome Letters from the *Lords of Trade* expreff-ing his Majefty's favourable Sentiments and thofe of their Lordfhips concerning my late Reprefentations.

I am heartily forry to hear that the Animofities in England have not fubfided, as fuch Party Differences muft greatly prejudice public Affairs and tend to divert the Attention of the Miniftry from many important Objects of public Concern.

Letter

Letter from John R. Hanſen to Sir Wm. Johnſon.

[MSS. of Sir William Johnſon, viii.]

SCHOHARIE, Capt. Thos. Eckkers,
Feby 1ſt, 1764.

HONOURED SIR:

AFTER Lt. Coll. Van Derhyden's muſtering my Men, I immediately march'd for this Place where I arrived with my Men 28th of January, and have proceeded perſuant to your Order in getting the Men quartered in the moſt convenient Manner with the Advice of the Juſtices and Capts of Militia.

I have ſince ſent one of my Lts to the uppermoſt Part of *Scohare* with a Command of 16 Men, which was judged moſt neceſſary, whom I have order'd to be ſtation'd in the beſt Manner the Situation of that Part would permitt off.

The remainder 34 Men I have with Advice quartered within a Mile hereabout, if there ſhou'd be any Occation to ſend out Scouting Parties there's no Poſſibility of getting any Snow Shoes, at this Place, if they ſhou'd be wanted.

I am, Honoured Sir,
Yours at Command,

JOHN R. HANSEN.

To the Honble Sir Wm. Johnſon, Bart.

Extract

Extract from a Letter from Ferrall Wade to Sir William Johnson.

[MSS. of Sir William Johnson, viii.]

PHILAD^a Feby 6th, 1764.

SIR :

YOUR Fav^r of the 5th Jany was handed me a few Days ago, which I fhould have anfwered before now but being in continual Alarms on account of a Numb^r of People comeing from the Frontiers in Arms with an Intent to murder all the Indians in this City and under the Protection of this Government, but the Opofition they met with by moft Part of the Inhabitants being in a Pofture of Defence obliged them to return as they came, excepting two, which was apointed to lay fome Grievances before the Government.

*   *   *   *

Letter from Sir William Johnfon to Gen. Burton.

[MSS. of Sir William Johnfon, viii.]

JOHNSON HALL, Feby 11th, 1764.

SIR :

CAPT. Claus, my Deputy for Canada will deliver you this, as I would not fend him to this Duty without doing myfelf the Pleafure of writing you, as well as giving you fome Account of the prefent State of Affairs in this Quarter.

The Indians of five out of the fix Nations who from the Commencement of the prefent Indian War have fhewn great Zeal and Attachment towards the Englifh have thereby preferved thefe Frontiers and the important

ant Communication to Ontario, both of which muſt
have inevitably fallen but for their Fidelity.   As I am
now impowered to comply with their Requeſt of going
upon Service, I have accordingly equipped a party of
near 200 Indians accompanied by fev[l] Indian Officers,
&c. who marched two Days ago (nothwithſtanding the
Snow is here 3 Feet deep) againſt the Delawares, Shawanefe and others our Enemies in that Quarter, and I
have great Hopes that their Operations will be attended
with Succeſs, as it muſt appear evident that they are
the beſt calculated to go in queſt of one another, and
that the engaging them as Party's in the War, will
effectually create a Diviſion among them w'ch will
prove a great Check to their Power hereafter.

As the Indians of Canada have likewife acted a very
good Part and made me Offers of Service when here
laſt Year, I ſhall likewife put their Zeal to a Trial, nothing doubting but it muſt ſtrike a great Damp on the
Spirits of our (hitherto elated) Enemies, when they
fee the Strength of our Alliances and that they are
liable to be attacked on all Sides even by their own
Sort, which will greatly contribute to the Succeſs of
the approaching Campaign, and make our Enemies
very cautious how they violate a Peace hereafter with a
People who can employ one Nation againſt another.

Capt. Claus will give you any further Particulars
neceſſary for your Information on the prefent Poſture
of Affairs in the Indian Department.

I fincerely wiſh you an eafy and agreable Government and remain with much eſteem,

Sir, &c,

Letter

Letter from *Thomas McKee to Sir William Johnſon.*

[MSS. of Sir William Johnſon, viii.]

HON. SIR:

M Y Son returned Home the 1ſt Inſt, when I was honoured with your Warrant, Inſtructions and Favour of the 3d January. I was extremely ſorry to hear of your Indiſpoſition & ſincerely hope you had a ſpeedy Recovery.

I make no doubt but my Son at that Time informed you of the Conduct of the Frontier Inhabitants of this Province[1] who murdered ſix Conniſtogo Indians at

---

[1] The Diſorders here alluded to have been known in Hiſtory as the Paxton Riots, from having originated in the little Town of Paxton on the Eaſt Bank of the Suſquehanna, a Place which had been burned, and many of its Inhabitants butchered in 1755. A Band of Rangers had been formed here under the Auſpices of the Rev. John Elder, under the Command of Matthew Smith. The irritation of Feeling towards the domeſticated Indians on the Suſquehanna, in Conſequence of ſome Murders by unknown Parties, led the Government to gather the Moravian Indian Converts of Nain, and Wecquetank near the Lehigh, and of Wyaluſing near Wyoming, numbering about 140 Perſons, to Philadelphia for Protection. It required all its Strength to protect the defenceleſs and peaceful Indians from the ferocious Abuſe of the excited Frontiermen, and as they paſſed on their way to the Aſylum provided they were everywhere threatened, and at Germantown came nigh being murdered by the Mob that followed them. They were marched to the Barracks but the Soldiers refuſed to receive them and boldly ſet the Governor's Orders at defiance. After ſtanding ſeveral Hours before the Barracks ſurrounded by the inſulting Mob, they were marched down the Street and conducted to Providence Iſland below the City, where Buildings were haſtily prepared for them by the Quakers.

About the Middle of December, 1763, it was reported to Smith, Leader of the Paxton Rangers, that an Indian who had committed ſome Depredations, had been traced to Caneſtoga, a ſmall Iroquois Settlement near the Suſquehanna, and not far from Lancaſter. Without waiting for a Confirmation of the Story or its Circumſtances, a Reſolution was at once formed, with the Con-

their

their Town near Lancaster, being all that were at Home at that Time except two Boys who made their Escape from them. The remaining Part fourteen in Number, Women and Children, being dispers'd through the Country were seized by the Sheriff and Magistrates of the County and confined in the Work house of Lancaster, in order to guard them, but upon the back Inhabitants receiving Information of this, they again

sequences detailed in the above Letter. Mr. Elder used all his Influence to divert his Neighbours from their barbarous Purpose, as they were about to set out for Lancaster, but with the Fury of Demons they rushed forward on their Errand of Blood. Breaking into the Jail on the 27th of December, they murdered fourteen Men, Women and Children. Before the Magistrates and Citizens could be rallied the white Savages were gone, and nothing remained to be done but to give decent Burial to the mangled and mutilated Remains of these friendly Natives. The News of this Outrage quickly spread through the Country and aroused the Quakers in particular to loud and bitter Denunciations of the Act. The Memory of Indian Murders, still fresh throughout the frontier Counties, led many to sympathize with the Rioters, to which they were rather instigated than deterred by the indiscriminate and sweeping Abuse of the Quakers, which included not only the Rioters themselves, but the whole Presbyterian Sect. Emboldened by this Sentiment, the guilty Parties openly proclaimed their Achievement as in the highest Degree meritorious, defended it by Reason and Scripture, and defied the civil Authorities in any Attempt at Punishment.

They even went further, and reeking with the Blood of the passive Victims of their Fury, they resolved to complete the Work of Death upon the Moravian Indians gathered at Philadelphia. An armed Mob marched towards that City at about the last of December, with the avowed Purpose of Murder, if not of overturning the Government and expelling the Quakers, whose Sympathies with the Indians were bitterly denounced and whose Motives were unscrupulously impugned. At Midnight on the 4th of January, the Authorities, hearing of the Approach of this Party, hastily marched the Indians through the Streets, and having been supplied by their Friends with a few Necessaries, they were escorted to Trenton, and from thence to Amboy, with the View of sending them to the Protection of Sir William Johnson; but before notifying either him or the Government of New York of this Intention or asking Permission.

At Amboy they were met by a positive Order from the Governor

assembled

affembled themfelves in a Body and came down armed
to Lancafter, broke open the Work houfe and in a
moft inhuman Manner butchered the whole, fparing
neither Women or Children, an Action I look upon
not inferior to any of the Cruelties committed by the
Savages fince the Commencement of the late or prefent War.   As to my Knowledge thefe Indians have
lived all their Lives within eight Miles of Lancafter,

of New York, forbidding their Entrance into that Province, and foon
after from the Governor of New Jerfey, requiring them to leave the Territory of that Province. They were
marched back to Philadelphia under
a Guard of Regulars, and quartered
in the Barracks where the Soldiers,
conquered by the meek Endurance
and patient Suffering of the Indians,
received them. The Paxton Boys
hearing of the Return of their Victims, rallied in great Numbers, the
City was thrown into Uproar, and
for feveral Days it was the Scene of
intenfe Excitement, and active Preparation for Defenfe. The Ad-
vance of the Infurgents was checked
by this Show of Refiftance, and the
Affair finally ended in Negotiation.

The humane and fagacious Sir
William Johnfon, perceiving the
Perils that would attend the March
of thefe Indians through the Interior,
upon application immediately de-
vifed a Plan for their removal from
Amboy to Albany, and their Support among his friendly Indians
until the Tumult was over. The
Victims of thefe Riots, fhut up in
their Barracks, fuffered dreadfully
from the Small Pox, which deftroyed a third of their Number. In
about a Year after their Arrival,

quiet having been reftored in the
back Settlements, and Peace with all
the Northern Tribes, thefe Converts
were allowed to return with their
Miffionaries to their wafted Fields,
and the Sites of their burned Cabins,
on the Banks of the Sufquehanna.

The Government was too fenfible of the exafperated Feeling which
prevailed in the Interior to attempt
any Arrefts until nearly eight Years
after, when Lazarus Stewart was
apprehended on a Charge of murdering the Indians at Coneftoga.

Learning that his Trial was to
come off in Philadelphia, where
Conviction would have been certain,
he broke Jail, called a Number of
old Affociates around him, and fetting the Provincial Government of
Pennfylvania at Defiance, withdrew
to Wyoming and joined the Con-
necticut Settlers in that Valley. It
is not improbable that the Defola-
tion of that Settlement by the Indians and their Tory Companions
in the Revolution, a few Years after,
may have had fome Connection
with their Knowledge of the Retreat
of the former Butchers of their
Kindred. *(Parkman's Pontiac;
Lofkiel; Hazard's Pa. Regifter;
Rupp's York and Lancafter; Sparks's
Franklin.)*

in

in Peace and Quietnefs with their Neighbours, and I do not believe were ever concerned againft us.

The Government made fome faint Efforts to find the Heads of thefe People, which only encourage their Impudence, as I am informed a few Days agoe, to the Number of three hundred affembled themfelves in Arms and came down to Philadᵃ in order to cut off fome Indians the Government have here, but upon fome Promifes being made them by the Government, they have diffuaded them from murdering thofe in Philadᵃ and they are return'd Home again, and they now carry Things to great Length as to threaten the Lives of fundry private People who have not agreed with them in Opinions but condemned this as a moft deteftable Murder, and not only contrary to the Laws of Government but Chriftianity, and every thing that ought to diftinguifh us from Savages, as this leaves us no Room to find Fault with their killing our innocent People in cold Blood, as they may now fay we are fatiated in the fame Manner on them. I fhould be far from efpoufing their Caufe did I not think they were innocent, as no Perfon has fuffered more by the Savages than I have done, and I fhould have thought the People who have thus behaved more excufable if they had cut off in Philadᵃ maintain'd at the Public Expence, as there is fome Reafon to believe that fome of thefe have acted againft us. But the others in a Manner were become white People, and expected the fame Protection from us. I thought proper to acquaint your Hoʳ with this Affair, as you might perhaps want to acquaint the Indians with the true Circumftances relating to it.

My Son prefents his Compliments to your Honour and begs if you have not fent a Warant for his Accᵗ that you would be kind enough to forward one as foon as it may be convenient to you & if it likewife fuits
                                                          your

your Conveniency I ſhould be glad your Honʳ would accompany it with one to me for ſome Money, as I am really at preſent in Neceſſity.

I have nothing further to add, but that I am with greateſt Reſpeƈt, your Honour's
        moſt obedient and very humble Servant,

Part of a Letter from Colonel Bradſtreet to General Amherſt.

[Bradſtreet and Amherſt MSS., p. 146.]

ALBANY, 20th Feb. 1764.

DEAR SIR:

YOUR Excellency's Favor of the 13th Inſtant was delivered me yeſterday. The Boats for 2000 Men only have long ſince been built and I direƈtly ſtopt building any more untill your farther Direƈtions.

To fix the Number of Carriages [at] the Carrying Place at Niagara, it will be neceſſary to know whether you would have all the Proviſions, Stores, &c. tranſ- ported acroſs before the Troops proceed to any other Service, and what Number of Days you would have taken up on that Service only.   Genˡ Amherſt talk'd to me of leaving 600 Men at the Poſt to the weſtward of Neagara with 18 Month Proviſions; if that is ſtill to be the Caſe, and our whole Numbers amount to no more than 2000, it will require about 6000 Barrells (for your Ex. knows we ſhould not count by Ounces but

but give a proper Allowance for the Kind of Service) which will take 50 Ox Carts 15 Days to carry it a crofs at a full Load of 8 Barrells each Trip, exclufive of every thing for the Veffels & Pofts to be eftablifhed; but if Accidents, which we certainly muft expect from the Diftance the Cattle have to go & the badnefs of great Part of the Road, of which Major Moncrief can inform you, the Time required would be much longer.

As for the Boats I fhall begin to provide as many Horfes & Carriages as fhall be fufficient to carrying them over with the Baggage of Troops in Proportion to the Ox Carts. By this your Excellency fees it is moft probable the Tranfportation at Neagara will laft three Weeks at leaft; a long Time indeed, but it would be impertinent in me to urge to one fo well in-form'd as you are of their Treachery and good Senfe of the Savages the abfolute Neceffity of entering this inland Country with a Difpatch hitherto thought by them impracticable in us, and more particularly fo fhould our Strength fall fo prodigioufly fhort of the Threats denounced againft them & the Pains taken to let them know it and therefore doubt not you will think it neceffary to direct me to augment the Number of Carriages to do the Work in the Number of Days you fhall judge we ought to remain on that Carrying Place.

I take it for granted I muft provide Teamfters & Waggons, but in this I fhall not act untill I receive your Exls Directions upon it.

I hope Gov. Murray[1] will not difappoint you, and I alfo hope the Eaftern Affemblys will think no Credit ought to be given to an Indian Peace but what comes

[1] JAMES MURRAY had been ap-pointed Governor of Canada on the 21ft of November previous. He re-mained in Office until June, 1766.

to their . . . . directly from you, which I am perfuaded they need not expect this Spring.

Letter from Henry Monture, Wm. Hare and John Johnston to Sir William Johnson.

[MSS. of Sir William Johnfon, viii.]

KAUNAWAU KOHARE, Feb. 21, 1764.

SIR WILLIAM:

SIR: The Bearer hereof pleafe to deliver eight Dollars for which we war forc'd to do for the good of the Service, for a Hog for the Warriours to make a Feaft as we could not do any otherwafe as'tha faid it was a cuftomary Thing and they hope Sir William would not make any Differance now, and pleafe to fend Paper and Sealing Wax up to their Prieft as I have ufed fome of his Paper and Wax. A Quire and Stick of Sealing Wax. Pleafe to fend no more, but we remain

Your humb^{le} Serv^{ts}

HENRY MONTURE,
WILLIAM HARE,
JOHN JOHNSTON.

The Same to the Same.

[MSS. of Sir William Johnfon, vii.]

KUANA WAHOHARE, Feb. 21, 1764.

SIR WILLIAM:

AFTER our Refpects to you we muft inform you of the Reafon of our detainment here, at this Place, we being in great Confufion here ever fince our Arrival for Reafon why, becaufe one Conokuiafi and one big
Nichols

Nichols of Oneida haft fent two Belts through the Six Nations to the Sinackefs to tell them of all our Defigns and force this Caftle to likewife comply with their evil Purpofes, and one young Warrior called Wyyautaukeen from old Oneida has faid he would very foon fcalp fome white People and then immediately fly to the Six Nations, and there is one of the Head Warriors call'd Cut the Pumpkin has fent Word he will meet us at Teurogoa to try what we are, and he wifhes to fee Jacob the Mikouder[1] of Stockbridge as he is fo long a coming when he could have the Impudence to pretend to withftand him. Laft Evening we received yours dated the 12th Inftant wherein we acquainted the Indians your giving your Love to theire Warriors and Chiefs and then your Defire of their exciting themfelves in this Affair, depending which fhould never be forgot, and would redound unto their Credit hereafter, and your Defire of our pufhing on and not delaying our Time in Things of no Confequence or Moment, and likewife the hearty Wifhes of all the Governors and Chiefs of the Country and Prayer of all good People.

The Anfwer of the Indians to your Letter :

Friend and loving Brother Wawaukaugee, we return you Thanks for your good Will and Complement to us and likewife the Complement of the Governors and Chiefs. We fhould have been fet out before had it not been for them Belts fent by Conokgoraffe and Nichols as we had Reafons to think what would be the Confequences that might likely attend us and this Body of our Enemy coming down againft us, for which Reafons Brother, we muft acquaint you that yefterday our Chief Warrior Cowaha fet out for Onandaug in order to fee if the upper Nations would come down at the re-

---

[1] Mohegan.

quest

queft of them Belts and he to try his beft to alter there
Minds and fend them back, and at his Return they
imagen the whole Party will joyn us.   However tomorrow Morning early we fet [out] from this on our March
for Auqquage and what Warriors have a Mind to joyn
us to proceed and the reft to follow us as foon as Go-
waha returns.   Thefe Indians defire you would fend
for thefe Fellows to know the Meaning of their fending
this Belt and let fome of thefe Indians come down alfo
along with them that he may hear what they have to fay
for themfelves.   The aforefaid Cut the Pumpkin fent
Word by Capt. Monture to come along as he would be
very glad to fee him, and we hope Sir William will hurry
all of them that is behind to pufh up to Auqquage
to joyn us fo as in Cafe of a Retreat that we will be
able to pufh on them again and indeavour to rout
them.   The Indians of this Caftle requeft of Sir William that you would be fo good as to fupply their
Women with Provifions if required at Fort Stanwix
in a reafonable Manner and that what few Men there
is left accordingly you will fupply them with Fire Arms
and Ammunition, and fuch Things as they will be
fhort of in cafe of an Attack.

No more at prefent, but our Advice to you, to be
on your guard in and on every Part of the Mohawk
River, Schohary, Stone Rauby and Cherry Vally.
We remain your fincear and ever devoted hum¹ Servᵗˢ
till Death.

HENRY MONTURE,
WILLIAM HARE,
JOHN JOHNSTON.

33   Letter

Letter from Robert McKeen[1] to Sir Wm. Johnson.

[MSS. of Sir William Johnson, viii.]

CHERRY VALLEY, February 25th, 1764.

SIR:

I HAVE thought proper to acquaint you with the prefent State of my Company and have the Pleafure to acquaint you that they are all in a good State and in high Spirits.

I have kept a regular Guard at Capt. Wells[1] ever fince I arrived at this Settlement, and reviews my Men every Week and has them ftationed in the beft Manner I could for the Protection of this Settlement.

I fhould be glad if your Honour wou'd let me know if it is neceffary to fend a monthly Return to the Lt. Governor.

I am Sir your moft Humble Servt

Robert McKeen

[1] Captain McKEAN refided at Cherry Valley and early in 1776 raifed a Company of Rangers for the Protection of that Place. He was an enterprifing and fearlefs Partizan, and was mortally wounded in the Summer of 1781 in an Expedition againft a Tory Band in the Border of Schoharie Co.—*Campbell's Tryon Co.*

[2] Mr. ROBERT WELLS and his Family perifhed in the Maffacre of Cherry Valley, Nov. 11, 1778. The Family confifted of himfelf, his Mother and Wife, and four Children, his Brother and Sifter and three Domefticks, not one of them efcaped excepting John, one of the Children, who happened to be abfent at School at Schenectady. A Tory boafted that he killed Mr. Wells while at Prayer.—*Campbell's Tryon Co.*

P. S.

P. S. In Cafe of an Alarm my Men is always in readinefs to affemble at the Place appointed for an alarm Poft.

A monthly Return of Captain Robert McKeans Company of Provincials now lying at Cherry Valley, Febuary 25th, 1764.

Prefent for Duty.

Captain, - - - - - 1
Lieutenants, - - - - 2
Rank and File, - - - 50
Total, - - - 53

ROBERT McKEEN, Capt.

Letter from Sir Wm. Johnfon to Gov. John Penn.

[MSS. of Sir William Johnfon, viii.]

JOHNSON HALL, Feby 27th, 1764.

SIR :

THE Exprefs delivered me your Favor of the 7th laft Night concerning the perfecuted Indians now in Philadelphia. The Rancours with which they have been purfued by the Rioters is as extraordinary as it may be dangerous to the Public, and leaft their Defigns might be put in Execution I cannot but approve of your Propofal of fending them hither, for fhould they fall a Sacrifice to unjuft Refentment it muft certainly occafion a Breach with all the Friend Indians.

The fending them thro' the back Parts of the Country at this Time might fubject them to the Infults of the Rioters, neither would it be practicable. I think the fafeft and beft Way would be, what you propofe of fending them by Water from Amboy to Albany, after which I fhall difpofe of them (altho' it will bring
fome

fome Expenfe on the Crown) amongft the Friend Indians whilft the prefent Ferment continues. I fhall accordingly write immediately to Governor Colden, and reprefent the Neceffity of removing thefe Indians for a Time, as highly effential to our Interefts and the public Safety, and I fhall requeft the Governor in cafe ehe Government has no Objection to their coming to give you Notice that no Time may be loft.

I am Sir your moft obed^t & moft Humble Servt

To the Hon'ble Govr Penn.

.

Letter from Sir Wm. Johnfon to Lieut. Gov. Colden.

[MSS. of Sir William Johnfon, viii.]

JOHNSON HALL, Feb'y 28th, 1764.
DEAR SIR :

I HAVE juft received your Favour of the 17th Inft. as alfo a Letter pr Exprefs from Govr Penn reprefenting the late audacious Attempts of the Rioters to murder the Indians under the Protection of Philadelphia, as alfo his Apprehenfions concerning their future Safety there, on which acc't he propofes fending them by Land thro' his Government or elfe by Water from Amboy to Albany. The former may fubject them to too many Infults and Hazards, and as I am well fatiffied that fhould thefe Indians or any of them fall a Sacrifice after what has already happened, it will prove highly prejudicial to our Affairs as well as dangerous to the public Security, I cannot avoid recommending the Propofal of tranfporting them by Water to Albany, after which I fhall difpofe of them amongft the Indians here till matters are accommodated. If it is judged advifable

advifable a Line from you to Govr Penn will enable him to take the neceffary Steps without lofs of Time.

Whenever any thing farther tranfpires relative to Mr. Lydius,[1] I fhall let you know it. I am told that one of his Sons has been lately thro' the Country in Company of a Juftice of the Peace to obtain Affidavits for what Purpofe I know not, but probably in fupport of his Claims.

Ifle la Motte[2] is fuppofed to be to the fouthward of the 45th Degree of Latitude, but perhaps on future Obfervations it may appear in the *Quebec* Government. The Lands above the Great Falls on Otter Creek may be good tho' a good deal out of the way for fmall a Tract.[3] There is a fmall Piece of Land within about

---

[1] Among the extravagant Grants of Land made by Governor Fletcher which have rendered his Name a Synonym for Corruption, and occafioned among other Things his Recall and Difgrace, was that of a 'Tract covering eight hundred and forty fquare Miles in the prefent County of Wafhington, N. Y. and the fouthern Part of Vermont. This Tract was granted Sept. 3, 1696, to the Rev. Godfredius Dellius, Minifter at Albany, for the annual Rent of one Raccoon Skin, payable annually, on the Feaft Day of the Annunciation, at the City of New York. The Grant was annulled by the General Affembly of the Colony, May 12, 1699, but Dellius denied the Authority of that Body, and continued to regard the Claim as valid. He foon after fold his Claim in Holland to the Rev. John Lydius, his Succeffor in the Paftoral relation at Albany. His Son, Col.

Lydius, to give additional Claim to this Title, made a Settlement on the Hudfon at Fort Edward and engaged in Trade with the Indians. In 1744 this Houfe was captured and burned by the Indians, and a Son was carried Prifoner to Canada. The Writer refers in the Text to Efforts made by this Family to fubftantiate their Title to this Tract. *(Tranfactions of N. Y. State Ag. Soc., vol. viii.)*

[2] Now in Vermont, forming a Part of Grand Ifle County. It lies in Lat. 44° 57m. and Long. 3° 41m. E. from Wafhington. It is 28 Miles N. W. from Burlington, 13 Weft from St. Albans, and contains 4,620 Acres. It was firft fettled about 1785, and is celebrated for its extenfive Limeftone Quarries, which afford a black Marble.

[3] It will be remembered that at

3

3 Miles of Lake George, on the Road leading from Fort Edward. Pleafe to inform me whether it can be granted, but I find at the back of my Patent here and at 10 or 12 Miles from the River, a fmall Piece which is an Intervale and I fhould be greatly obliged to you if you would grant it, on the Indians confenting thereto. Lieut. Johnfon[1] will have a Certificate fhortly from Gen. Gage as you defire.

There are now feveral Partys marched againft the Enemy,[2] one of thefe amounts to about 200 Indians, many more are collecting to follow them and my whole Time is occupied in Conferences, in fitting out Parties, &c. The Indians will not be difcouraged by the Rigors of the Seafon. The Pofts I have fent them to are the Forks and Branches of Ohio and Sufquehanna, where many of our Enemies refide, and the Alacrity which our Friend Indians manifeft gives me great Reafon to hope I fhall fhortly have the Pleafure of acquainting you that they have in a great Meafure deftroyed and removed thefe dangerous Enemies who have infefted the neighboring Frontiers.

I am, &c.

P. S. One Mr. Tice of Schenectady has been mentioned to me as a very proper Perfon for a Provincial Comp[y] I muft beg leave to recommend him to your Notice, fho[d] fuch be raifed, as he has ferved as an Officer for fome Years.

this Period the Colony of New York claimed Jurifdiction over the Territory embraced in the prefent State of Vermont, and were granting Lands in lavifh Profufion, in Quantities of a whole Townfhip at a Time. Sir William Johnfon was peculiarly favored in thefe Allotments of the King's Domain.

[1] Referring to Sir John Johnfon's Son.

[2] The Succefs of one of thefe Parties is related in a fucceeding Letter, dated March 2, 1764.

Letter

Letter from Henry Monture, Wm. Hare and John Johnston to Sir William Johnson.

[MSS. of Sir William Johnson, viii.]

AUQOUGE,[1] Feb. 28, 1764.

SIR WILLIAM:

WE have the Pleasure to inform you of some Part of our Success, which if failed of some Parts of the Mohawk River must unavoidably suffer, as we suspect Cherry Vally or Schoharey.

The Prisoners we send to you as a Token of our prosicuting your Instructions as far as we are able; the Commander Sir William will singal out and several of them as principal Murderers during the War and reward them according to their Desert. The Woman bringing down we adjudge as Scheme that they might not be suspected they are Murderers that has been and they have come some of them from Kanisteo. So we leave Sir William to act as he pleases.

We remain your ever Devoted and hum^l Ser^ts

HENRY MONTURE,
JOHN JOHNSTON,
WILLIAM HARE.

Please to excuse the Pen and Haste, one of the Prisoners a young Man had the Impudence to bring some English Prisoners through this Place.

---

[1] Endorsed Oghquago, and variously written as Onohoghwage, Auqoage, Oucqoago, Oghquaga, &c. It was situated on the East Branch of the Susquehanna in the present Town of Windsor, Broome Co., N. Y. The Hills here slope gently towards the River on both Sides, forming a beautiful Vale of three or four Miles in Length, and from a Mile to a Mile and a half in Width, where the Indians resided in great Numbers prior to and during the Revolutionary War,

The

The Same to the Same.

[MSS. of Sir William Johnſon, viii.]

AUQOAUGE, Feb. 28, 1764.

SIR WILLIAM:

THIS Day with Pleaſure we can acquaint you of our Proceedings and Succeſs, after our Arrival, which we ſhall deliver to you in the following Maner from the Indians:

After our Love and Reſpect to you as Governor & Chief, and then to the Commander of the ſeveral different Places in America. Firſt three Days after our Arrival at this our Settlement we were informed that a Body of our Enemies were arrived here and going down under ſome Pretence to the River, but on the contrary we ſuſpect to do Damage as they formerly have done to kill, burn and deſtroy, being noted for murdering, notorious Villains. Laſt Night we ſeized ſeven of there chief Warriors here in our Caſtle and the famous Captain Bull of their Party, after ſome little Reſiſtance, bound them Hand and Feet. This Morning we all ſet out for their Encampment, and unbeknowing to them about Day, ſeized eleven Men of there Warrors and eight Women and three Children, which make twenty-nine in Number.

And now Brother you ſee our Fidelity in opening the Door and we hope you will conſider our Care, and that we lay expoſed to Cenſure and ill Will of all Nations that are not found in the Cauſe. We hope you will look into our Caſe and liſten to us as well as we liſten to you, as we think we are equally bound to each other. Conſider Brother that this our Settlement and Chininga and Chuknut are our Bounderies of
Friendſhip

Friendfhip fo as we expect you will liften to our Re-queft, that is to fend a Party of Men to Conawa Ro-hare[1] at Oneida and another Party to this our Settle-ment at Auqqoage of a Safeguard for our Women and Children, and to hurry all Partys of Warriors to come to our Affiftance immediately as we are very weak at prefent and make no delay. So after our Arrival we found all our Warriors as redy to execute and defign as we were ready to propofe, but we are forry to think that the Oneidas differ fo much in their way of think-ing and that is one of the Reafons we requeft a fafe Guard, and when we heard the Sound of our Brother Warriors coming from you and from Conawa Rohare it revived our Spirits and was like a pleafing Toy to a Child or like a Phyfick that refrefh a fick or weak Bodye, fo as tho we are delay'd from proceding untill we get more Affiftance.

You ufed to fay that your Body was light and it was only the Word for you to fay March, and every one muft comply and you was never fhort of Provi-fion.

Tomorrow we fend the Prifoners by the way of Onida, for the Reafon that perhaps that fome of the Friends of the Prifoners may meet each other and breed a Quarrel. No more, but we remain

Your trufty Brother Indians.

Attefted by us,
    HENRY MONTURE,
    WILLIAM HARE,
    JOHN JOHNSTON.

---

[1] Stated in a fubfequent Letter, dated March 2, 1764, to be within twelve Miles of Oneida Lake. See p. 262.

Letter

Letter from Sir Wm. Johnson to Maj. General Gage.

[MSS. of Sir William Johnfon, viii.]

JOHNSON HALL, March 1ft, 1764.

DEAR SIR:

I HAVE had the Pleafure of your Letters of the 13th and 20th ult⁰ and embrace the firft Opportunity which Time has permitted of anfwering them.

The exact Number of Indians who may accompany the Army muft be uncertain, nor is it poffible to know how many they will confift of. The prefent Spirit amongft them gives me great Hopes of a powerful Affiftance and I fhall ufe every Endeavour in my Power to keep it up for this Purpofe. I apprehend however that I may rely with Confidence on the Attendance of 4 or 500, perhaps they may be twice that Number, but it will greatly depend on Circumftances and the Time I fnall have given me to collect them with the help of feveral proper Indian Officers who muft neceffarily be appointed for that Purpofe. The Friend Indians in general will readily joyn either againft the weftern Nations or the Shawanefe and Delawares, and if Affairs are not fpeedily fettled between us and the Senecas, I have no doubt but they will march alfo againft them.

I apprehend the Shawanefe and Delawares will fuffer greatly from the Partys I have already fent out, and fhall continue to fend againft them, which will make eafy Work for the Troops on the Campaign. Thefe two Nations appear the moft determined but their Party decreafes, many of them have already fallen off on hearing the determination of our Friends and I am hopeful they will (as Affairs are now circumftanced) be unable

unable to perfuade the weftern Nations to renew Hoftilities, efpecially as the latter will fhortly difcover that
fuch a Proceeding muft involve them in a War with
the Friend Indians, which they would by no means
relifh.   The like Reafons will (I hope) have the fame
Effect on the Senecas which will prove of great Service
to us, as the Indians in general would certainly proceed with greater Alacrity againft the reft.

Many Steps have already been taken by the Friend
Indians to bring over the Senecas, to which their In-
activity for fome Time paft muft be chiefly attributed,
and I truft that the Belts and Meffages lately fent to
them will be productive of an Accommodation of
which I expect to have Notice in a very fhort Time,
as the upper Nations will fhortly be down.   I mean to
treat with them outwardly as a mifguided People whom
we are defirous to compaffionate and forgive on certain
Terms rather than to give them any Confidence in
their Abilities by expreffing a Defire to promote a
Peace with them, and I truft this Conduct will have a
good Effect.

I have fent out fev¹ Partys fince the firft and fhall
continue to do fo, as I have the Pleafure to find that
our Enemies are already greatly alarmed at the Refolutions of the reft.

Letter

Letter from Henry Monture, William Hare and John Johnston to Sir William Johnson.

[MSS. of Sir William Johnson, viii.]

OUCQOAGO. March 21, 1764.

SIR WILLIAM:

THIS Day the Prisoners set out for your House by the way of Oneida, and all the Oneidas that came with us likewise return with them, as they said they had fulfilled your Pleasure by taken of so many Prisoners and chief Warriors. Yestarday we rec^d your two Letters by an Onida, the one dated the 21 of Feb'y and the other the 23d of Feb'y, wherein we acquainted them of your Concern for their Wellfare and your Desire of our proceeding. They were very glad and made Answer that they had done according to your Will, which would be a welcome Sight for you to see so many of your sworn Enemies, as they had but one Belt they thought they could return with Honour. They pres^d very hard for us to come along with them in Company, but we consider of our Errand refused, knowing at least Sir that we was short as yet for the good Work now in Hand before us. We then remain here untill such Times as the Arrival of other Forces to joyn that we may strick the Blow to Purpose, which Sir you will not neglect sending us a Reinforcement as soon and as quick as possible, if you should think proper to send us a Body of two hundred Whites to joyn the Body of Indians you are about to send us, we think with Gods help we may destroy a great Part of their Settlements along the Dioago[1] River, the Ouqoagos are very harty and only wait for any thing of a party to joyn

[1] Tioga.

that

that they may ftrick the Blow as they fay their Work is as yet before them.   There is here in Store fix Barrells of Flour and about a hundred Weight of Sugar belonging to Mr. Wells of Cherry Vally, which Sugar would be very ufefull for any Body of Men to make Ouquickare and the Flour likewife in Cafe required. We fend you one Capt Bull, the famous Head Warrior belonging to the Sqoafhcutter, a great Villain, and the reft of his Crew of Warriors.   We hope Sir William will not take any Excufes from them but punifh them with Severity as they deferve.   Two Brothers, Fidlers, excepted, being by all Accounts not Party concerned, as Capt. Monture knows them very well.   As to our fpeedy Return it is uncertain, as Sir William muft judge by Circumftances, but you may depend on our prefling it on as far and as faft as poffible we can, and with Gods help we hope is fhort of give you pleafant Detail of our Succefs.   We remain your ever devoted and

Hum^l Serv^ts till Death.

HENRY MONTURE,
WILLIAM HARE,
JOHN JOHNSTON.

P. S. Be fo good as to forward the Party.   The Prieft of the Parifh here gives his Complim^ts to you and all his Family.

Letter

Letter from Sir William Johnson to Col. Bradstreet.

[From the Original in the Poſſeſſion of M. M. Jones, Eſq. of Utica.]

JOHNSON HALL, March 2, 1764, }
At Night. }

DEAR SIR:

IT gives me great Pleaſure that I now inform you of the Succeſs of the firſt Party I lately ſent out againſt our Enemy, an Expreſs being juſt arrived with Letters acquainting me that on the 26th ultᵒ in the Evening, near the main Branch of Suſqehanna, as they were purſuing their Rout, they received Advice that a large Party of our Enemys the Delawares, were encamped at a ſmall Diſtance on their way againſt ſome of the Settlements hereabouts, upon which Intelligence they made an expeditious March to their Encampment, which they ſurrounded at Daybreak, then ruſhing upon the Delawares (who were ſurpriſed and unable to make a Defence) they made them all Priſoners to the Number of 41, including their Chief, *Capt. Bull*, Son of Teedyuſcung, and one who has diſcovered great Inveteracy againſt the Engliſh, and led ſeveral Partys againſt them during the preſent Indian War. They are all faſt bound and may be expected here under an Eſcort in a few Days.

The Indians of Onoghquagey and Canawaroghere, the latter within twelve Miles of Oneida Lake, are very uneaſy leaſt our Enemys ſhould take Advantage of the Abſence of their Men, and deſtroy their Familys, on which Account they are very ſolicitous for a Guard till their Men return, & I apprehend if their Requeſt is complied with, it will give new Spirits to the Partys and encourage more to go on Service.

I

I have therefore mentioned it to the General, and am of Opinion it may be eafily done by Partys from the Provincials at German Flatts.

I am of Opinion it will be beft to fend the Prifoners to New York as the beft Place of Security, there to remain till fomething be done with them.

I am with great Refpect,
Sir, your moft obedient
humble Servant,
Wm. Johnson.

Letter from Capt. John R. Hanfen to Sir William Johnfon.

[MSS. of Sir William Johnfon, viii.]

Capt. Eckerfon's, Wisersdorp,[1] March 12, 1764.

HONOURED SIR:

RECEIVED yours of the 3d Inft. and have fince proceeded according to your Directions, in dif-patching a Serg^t with 10 Men of my Comp^y and 6 of the Militia in Company with 6 Indians for Ouaghquago laft Saturday. Yeftarday five of the Indians, all Mohawks, returned here to me, with two Indians which they fay are their Prifoners, and told me for what Reafon they had taken them, they at firft refufed to tell me, and infifted that I fhould take them and fend them down to your Honour, and if I would not that they would immediately kill them. I then re-quefted of the Head of them, one Jofeph a Sachem, that he would fend one or two of his Men along with

---

1 Weifer's Dorp was on the Site of the prefent Village of Middle-burgh, Schoharie Co. It was named from Conrad Weifer, a prominent early German Settler,

the

the Prifoners to your Honour. He told me he could not do that for he was afraid if he did not go off with his Warriors and our Men to Onoghquago that his Brethren there would fuffer.

He then cautioned me in particular about the Prifoners and in particular againft one of thefe named *George O'Moke* and faid that the faid *O'Moke* had threatened one of their old Indians and a Squaw and fay'd as foon as the young Men their Warriors was gone againft their Brethren the *Delawares,* that they then would kill their Wifes and Children here. This Morning two of the Mohawks again returned to me, who having heard that I fhould have ordered the Prifoners to be unty'd and fay'd if I order'd any fuch Thing and the Prifoners fhould efcape, that they would be afraid to go to Onoghquago for fear of the feverall Threats made by the Prifoners.

The Serg^t who I have gave the Command of thofe Men affigned for Onoghquago I have gave particular Inftructions agreable to my own Inftructions received from your Honour; the Serg^t is pretty well acquainted with the Indian Tongue. His Inftructions are, that he fhall act no farther than what is agreeable to Heads of that Tribe or as your Honour may further direct him.

The remaining Part of my Comp^y are all fitt for Duty. I have placed fo the beft Advantage in Cafe of an Attack with our Arms in the beft Manner. The Company having never received any Pay yet fince they have been raifed caufes an infinite Trouble, notwith-ftanding all I can do to the contrary to prevent it.

I am Honoured Sir,
    your moft obedient Servt to Command.
                    JOHN R. HANSEN.
To the Honour^{ble} Sir Wm. Johnfon, Bart.

                                        Extract

Extract of a Letter from Sir William Johnson to Lieutenant Governor Colden.

[MSS. of Sir William Johnson, viii.]

JOHNSON HALL, March 16th, 1764.

DEAR SIR :

I HAVE had the Pleasure of your very kind Favor of the 19th Inst. and in Addition to the Success of my first Party, I have the Pleasure to acquaint you that another Party of only ten headed by Thos. King, which I had lately sent out, met with a Party of nine Delawares, who were singing their War Song against the English, on which they imediately killed and scalped one and took three Prisoners, who are now on their way here. This is a small Affair, but as 'tis the first who has been killed by our Indians, it will prove of some Consequence, and I have Reason to expect good News daily from the other Partys.

The first Prisoners taken arrived here yestarday, and this Morning I sent down 14 Men of them to the Care of Coll. Elliot at Albany. One of the stoutest remains wounded at Aughquago, and I was obliged to give them People 5 Prisoners for their good Behavior, others to the Oneidas, Tuscaroras, Onondagas and Mohawks, and to detain 4 myself which I distributed amongst the most deserving to replace Persons deceased, for which Purpose the rest were given according to the Indian Custom.

The Consternation our Enemies are in on acc't of our employing Indians against them is very great, and will I hope soon be the Means of bringing the disaffected to our Terms. Near 400 Senecas, &c. are coming here to make some Proposals, as the Onogh-

quago's

quago's are very Apprehenfive that their Familys may fuffer by the Enemy in the Abfence of their Warriors, I thought it very neceffary at this Time to comply with their Requeft of a Guard, and accordingly fent them an Officer and 30 Men from the Cherry Valley and Schohare Garrifons with 6 Militia, and the General having given me the Direction of the future Security. Thefe Deputies with Numb^{rs} from the Five Friendly Nations now here, amount to about 500. From the latter I fhall fend out feveral Partys amongft the Shawanees and Delawares, who are the only Nations at prefent that have not made any Offers of Accomodation.

I received feveral Letters in Autumn and the begining of Winter from the Lords of Trade, one of which contained Orders of a like Nature with thofe you mention, which I anfwered fome Time ago as well as I could under fo much Hurry and Bufinefs. As I underftand the Board have the Regulation of Trade, &c. under prefent Confideration, I apprehend it may be too late to lay Matters of that Nature before them fo as to anf^r the Defign. All that I thought neceffary on that Head was, that the Indian Trade fhould be free to all his Majefty's Subjects and carried on at only the principal Outpofts, where the Traders fhould be under tha Protection of the Garrifon and thereby avoid the Rifque they often run of being robbed and murdered, their Goods being a great Temptation to Indians if they are in the Indian Villages, and fuch Robbery or Murder might prove the Foundation of a future War, as the Indians feldom ftop at the firft Crimes, neither is it eafy to perfuade them to make any Reftitution. Another Matter of Confideration is, that the Traders at the principal Garrifons by being under the Eye of the Comd^g Officer would not be fo ready to overreach
them,

them, fearing a Difcovery, whereas in their Villages
they are often impofed upon and apt to redrefs themfelves.   The Commanding Officer could alfo banifh the
Trader on Proof of Extortion.   The reft I obferved
to their Lordfhips regarded the State of the Department, the Interefts, Difpofitions and Numbers of the
Indians.

I am much obliged to you for the Particulars you
communicated concerning the Nations to the fouthward, as alfo about the Tufcaroras, and fhould be glad
to hear further from you on that Head.

It gave me Concern to hear of the Hoftilities committed by the fouthern Ind^s & I heartily wifh a fpeedy
Stop may be put to them as well as that the fev^l Governors may act fuch a Part as may enable you to bring
them to Reafon, for whilft People act upon different
Plans it is impoffible for a Superintendant to difcharge
his Truft as he would wifh.   The French are probably
at the Bottom of the Affair, as they have been to the
northward, for it gives them fenfible Pleafure to foment
Differences between the Ind^s and us, from which they
are apt to flatter themfelves with reaping an Advantage.

I fhall not omit acquainting you in a little Time,
with any material Tranfactions in this Quarter, and am,
&c.

Letter

Letter from Sir William Johnson to John Stuart.

[MSS. of Sir William Johnson, viii.]

JOHNSON HALL, March 18, 1764.

SIR :

I HAVE had the favour of your Letters of the 10th Dec^r & 16th January laft, which I fhould fooner have anf^d but for the extraordinary Hurry and Bufinefs I have been engaged in, the great Refort of Indians and the Variety of their Affairs occupying my whole Time, nor efpecially at this Seafon can they be neglected with Prudence.

Since the Command of the Army devolved upon General Gage I have been impowered to make ufe of the Services of the friendly Nations ag^ft our Enemys, and have fent out in different Partys above 300 of them. The firft of thefe Partys furprifed at the North Branch of Sufquehanna 41 Delawares with their Chief. I deliver'd over fev^l of them amongft thofe who attached to our Intereft to replace their deceafed Relations, and fent 14 of them with their Chief to Albany under a Guard, from whence they will be forwarded to New York. A fmall Party of 10 has fince fallen in with a fcalping Party of 9 Enemys (who feemed deftined againft fome of the Frontiers of Penfilvania), of thefe they killed one and made three Prifoners, whom I daily expect. The killing of this Indian by a Party of their own Sort will greatly promote the Caufe and intereft our Friends more heartily in our Behalf.

Thefe Partys have already fhown their Importance, the Enemy are greatly alarmed, Numbers have retired towards the Twightwees, and the reft knowing that Indians are beft calculated to deftroy them, have for-
faken

faken their Caftles and will fhortly be reduced to great extremity if not totally fubdued.

The Chenuffios and other Enemy Senecas have fent me feveral Deputys from each of their Towns with Propofals of Peace, which will not be granted them but on Terms moft adventageous to our Provincials at the German Flatts. I have ordered Aughquago to be reinforced by a Detachment of a Capt. 2 Subs and 60 Men, and fent the like Number to Canowwaroghere, a Village of Oneidas, whofe Men are all going out againft the Enemy. Thefe Garrifons for the Indians will not be required for above 4 or 5 Weeks and will greatly forward the Service by the Encouragement it will give the Indians.

I cannot but agree in Opinion with the Council, that the Wyaloofins, &c. might give bad Impreffions to the reft, but I was determined and prepared to guard againft that and hoped to be able to remove any unjuft Sufpicion they might conceive having (without vanity I may fay it) a greater Influence now over the many Nations in our Alliance than ever. However as General Gage informs me that he has propofed an Afylum for them in Burlington Barracks, I think it will anfwer very well for the prefent.

Capt. Duncan[1] of Schenectady has requefted I would reprefent to you his Requeft, whether he may have his Proportion of Land, he fold out of the 44th Regiment, but thinks he may claim fome Title on account of the Service he performed laft Year, as will appear from Lt. Campbells Certificate.

*   *   *   *

---

[1] JOHN DUNCAN, a Merchant of the City of Schenectady. He died at Albany, on the 5th May, 1791, aged 69 Years.

Extract

Extract of a Letter from His Excellency the Honble Major General Gage to Major Gladwin, Commanding at the Detroit, dated New York, 23d March, 1764.

[MSS. of Sir William Johnſon, viii.]

YOU will there be informed, I accepted of the Propoſals of Peace, which the Indians of Detroit had made you, and I am now to deſire, if you find the Savages amicably diſpoſed, and ſincerely inclined to conclude a Peace with us in earneſt, that you would give them Notice in a proper Manner to repair to Niagara by the End of June, at which Time Sir William Johnſon will be there to meet them. You will beſt know what is moſt proper to do, on ſuch an Occaſion, ſhall therefore add, that it may be neceſſary to acquaint them that the Repreſentatives they ſend to this Buſineſs need not be apprehenſive of receiving any Inſults from the Troops which they will probably meet in their way, as when we find they are ſincere in their Overtures the Troops will have Orders not to moleſt them, and they ſhould likewiſe have Notice to collect all the Priſoners and Deſerters which they may have amongſt them, who ſhould all be delivered up to us on this Occaſion. If you think of any Propoſals proper for Sir William Johnſon to make on this Occaſion of Peace, you will write to Sir William on that Head.

Letter

Letter from John Campbell to Sir William Johnson.

[MSS. of Sir William Johnson, viii.]

FORT STANWIX, MARCH, 31, 1764.

SIR :

I AM favoured with your Letter of the 17th March, concerning the Women of the Oneida Village, called Canowoarohere, being in great Diſtreſs for the Want of Proviſion on account of the Abſence of their Men. I have therefore agreable to your Letter this Day ſupplyed the Women of ſaid Village with a Quantity of Proviſions ſuppoſed to ſerve them till the Return of their Men, which I dare ſay will meet with the Generals Approbation, it being ſo very neceſſary and prudent to treat them with Civility at this preſent Juncture, which is the moſt effectual Method of gaining their Affection and of cours to promote the good of the Service.

I had the Satiſfaction of ſeeing Capt. Bull when the Priſoners paſſed here, whom I think the beſt looking Indian I ever ſaw. He is quite the fine Gentleman.

The Succeſs that attends the Partys that you have ſent out gives me infinite Pleaſure, as it muſt to every Perſon that has the good of the Service at Heart, and heartily wiſh that the like good Fortune may conſtantly accompany your unwearied Attention to his Majeſtys Service.

I hope Mr. Johnſon has remembered to apologize my going away ſo abruptly from your Houſe the Morning I left it without my paying my Reſpects to you, which I beg you will excuſe as I was afraid of diſturbing you ſo early in the Morning.

I am with the greateſt Eſteem Sir, your moſt obedient, humble Servant.   JOHN CAMPBELL.

P. S.

P. S. I have received Orders from the Gen^{ll} to be in Readiness to take the Field with the 17th Regiment next Campaign.

Letter from Whitham Marsh to Sir William Johnson.

[MSS. of Sir William Johnson, viii.]

BAYARD HALL, Ap^l 2d, 1764. }
¾ p. Merid. }

SIR :

ALTHO I had not the Happiness of receiving some more agreeable News by Capt. Post, yet I cannot help acquainting you that last Monday I visited Capt. Bull in Jail. He confesses the Shawaneze are Rascals, and that the Chenussaes sent for him and other Delawares. This was confirmed in the Morning of this Day in presence Mr. Nic's Bayard, Senr at the Jail by *Joe Newtimas*, who may remember at Easton. When I asked whether any *white Men* of Pennsylvania (you well know who I mean) had desired them (ye Delawares) to strike us, Joe answered, *he did not understand the Question.* Bull owned there were 22 Ind^s who made Inroads into the Jerseys, by whom poor Westbroke (at whose House we lay'd) was killed. I much want to get at the Bottom of the Delaware Scheme, I am sure some *quaking Devils* originated the Business, Excuse me Sir, for saying no more now, as the Post Rider waits in the Entry. I am with all due Deference and Respects to yor Families y^r

Most obed^t & humble Servt

WITHAM MARSH.

P. S. Darlington sends by me when I embark a great Curiosity of Shellwork. It is a Grotto.

Letter

Letter from Colonel Bradſtreet to General Amherſt.

ALBANY, 6th April, 1764.

DEAR SIR:

I HAVE received your Excellencys Packett of the 1ſt Inſtant and ſhall obay your Commands in every thing in my Power.   I have already inform'd your Excellency that Major Hogan could not enliſt but ſixty Men to ſerve to the firſt of May, & that they were not fit for Service; and I may now add, that they cant get any more this way, nor have they try'd for ſome Time paſt.

That I may know the exact Number of Boats to take from Schenectady, I beg to know if there is any more Troops to go beſides the following, viz:

17th Regiment,	314 including the Draughts.
Yorkers,	300
Connecticut,	250
Jerſeys,	240
Canada,	300
	1404

I ſet the 17th Regiment at 314, as I am aſſur'd they can not at this Time make out but 140 Men fit to go on Service, but they have ſome which may do in Garriſon.

What Exploits may be expected of 1400 Men, one half of them new raiſed Provincials, and the half of the other half but lately the Subjects of the French King, acting in the Center of the Savages ſurrounding the great Lakes, known to be our inveterate Enemies, I know not, but ſure I am, if the whole were of the beſt Troops his Majeſty has, the Number is far from being equal to

36   Service;

Service; however it is my Duty to obay and to doe the beft I can for the Service. After the 55th has given 174 Men to the 17th, they will have about 230 good Men left. If I could be allowed two Detachments of 50 each out of them, to be replaced from the Provincials, it would be of great fervice, but your Excellency is the beft Judge and I hope will excufe this Liberty.

I mentioned your Excellency there was but 50 Barr^s of Powder here, including what was fent from New York, fince which Sir Wm. Johnfon has had ten Barrells. I beg to be allow'd fufficient for the Service and Practice.

There is no mufkets arriv'd from New York yet & but 300 in Store here.

Permit me to afk your Excellency if there is to be no kind of Staff allowed us.

Letter from Colonel Bradftreet to Major Duncan.

ALBANY, 30th April, 1764.

DEAR SIR:

SEVEN Days after the Letters from Neagara got here I received a Letter from Col. Browning, by which I find it abfolutely neceffary to fend the Grenadiers & another Company of the 55th Regiment from hence to Neagara, they are compleat to 45 Rank & File with two Subalterns to each, and I muft beg of you to add to them as many Officers & non-commiffioned Officers as you poffibly can from your Garrifon, and to make them in every refpect, as refpectable as poffible. I fuppofe Capt. Daly will join his Company as foon as poffible after knowing it has gone on Service.

Some

Some York Provincials are alſo on their way to you, but in order to get up the Boats I am obliged to ſend them half man'd; then you'l pleaſe alſo to ſend on to Neagara and you will be the beſt Judge what Proviſions to put in each Boat, of the whole, as they leave you.

If the Canadian Battoe Men ſhould have made their ſecond Trip from Swegache[1] before I get up and any Proviſions remains there pray ſend them back for it, or at leaſt as many of them as will be ſufficient to bring it away, and let the others puſh on to Neagara, not only to land their Proviſions at the Landing but to be employ'd in carrying the Proviſions at the Fort to Landing, &c. and if any make the third Trip they muſt do the ſame if you think it neceſſary and ſafe.

Pray endeavour to get an exact State of all the Proviſions from Swegache to Neagara as ſoon as you can, that we may provide in Time if more is wanted.

By Miſtake Lieut. Grant has taken a new Mainſail belonging to the Schooner on the Onida Lake; be ſo good to write for it by the firſt Conveyance and ſend it her.

Pray caution all the Detachments that leave you for Neagara to be watchful, for it may poſſibly happen if the Savages find they can't do much to the People employ'd at the Veſſells or on the Carrying Place they will endeavor to ſurpriſe our People on ſome Place on the Banks of Lake Ontario.

Pleaſe to let me know if the Canadian Battoe Men have Arms, if they have not and that you can ſupply

[1] Oſwegatchie, now Ogdenſburgh, St. Lawrence Co., N. Y. A flouriſhing Indian Miſſion at this Place, formed in 1749 by Francis Picquet, a Sulpitian Prieſt, was moſtly broken up by the Conqueſt of 1760. There was a ſtrongly fortified Iſland in the River three Miles below, and as it lay at the Foot of Navigation from the Lake this Station poſſeſſed great Importance.

them

them that go to Neagara with the Provifions, pray do it.

Sir Wm. Johnfon tells me he has fent fome Friend Indians to affift at Neagara which will prevent your being troubled with fo many as was firft intended. I make no doubt but the Draughts & Yorkers are near leaving Ofwego for Neagara and that you gave the Arms with the Draughts. I will fettle it with the Artillery Officer and Col. Campbell will give the proper Receipt for them when he gets to Ofwego.

Major Duncan.

Letter from Colonel Bradftreet to General Amherft.

NEAGARA, 4th Auguft, 1764.

DEAR SIR:

THE Indians of the Bay, thofe of Arbrecroche, fome Cheppawas & Miffiffages now here have fo fettled Matters with Sir William Johnfon, that he acquainted me he thought it abfolutely neceffary to fend thofe People Home well fatiffied, and that it could not be done without allowing them to trade for every thing, except Arms & Ammunition, which has been allowed them as you will fee by the enclofed Order & Regulations. The Prices were fix'd by three Indian Traders & infpected by Sir William. For the greater Security of the Troops to be pofted at Michilimicanac, I thought advifable to defire Sir William to tell the above Savages they need not expect Trade to extend fo far as this Country without Pofts & Garrifons to Protect the Traders and fee that Juftice is done them; on which they defired Michilimicanac fhould be reëftablifhed and that they would endeavor to protect it.

As

As to the Genefea Indians a Meffage arrived at
Ofwego from them before we left it to Sir William
Johnfon, defiring four Boats with Provifions fhould
be fent them to Irondequoit in which Part of them
would proceed with all the Englifh Prifoners they had
to this Place. The Boats & Provifions by Sir Williams defire I ordered thither directly, but they were
fo far from keeping their Words, that they were not
there to receive them, but on being fent to, fent Men
& Horfes for the Provifions. For fome Time after
this, the Accounts we had from them were, that they
feem'd more inclinable not to keep the Peace they
made laft Winter but continue the War; but at length
they finding the Troops remaining here & fufpecting
it was on their Account and having no Time to hunt
for Provifions & thereby ftarving, they took the Refolution to fet out for this Place in different Parties, and
the 18th Inftant we were informed of their being on
the way, but that they were bringing but four of our
People inftead of thirty which they had Prifoners
amongft them with many other Circumftances fhowing
plainly Neceffity only makes them fubmit more than
Inclination; whereupon Sir William & myfelf were of
Opinion, that fuffering any longer fuch Infults might or
would be attended with bad Confequences, at this Time
in particular, as the Eyes of the upper Nations was
upon us and would judge of our Strength & Spirit from
what pafs'd upon this Occafion, and that it was for his
Majeftys Service we fhould fend them Word that unlefs they would punctually fulfill every Article they
promif'd at the making the Peace laft Winter, they
had no Bufinefs and that we did not defire to fee them;
and determin'd alfo, if they return'd, it was abfolutely
neceffary to march againft them and treat them as they
deferve. It appears to me, the true Caufe or Reafon
for

for this Conduct of the Senecas proceeds from their utter Abhorrence to us, that they do not think the other Part of the Six Nations in general will hurt them, that we live a great Diftance from them & that the Shawanes, Delawares & their Friends can do them great Damage, and confequently it is their Intereft to be well with the latter. But to return to their Conduct; on the 21ft July they fent in two Men here to tell us, that upon receiving the Meffage we fent them, they had fent off Runners to bring in all the Prifoners and that the principal Part of their Men, Women and Children would be here the 23d, and on that Day came in about 60 Men with about 150 Women & Children, and faid the Remainder would immediately follow and do every thing that could be defired of them; but they did not arrive untill the 1ft Inftant with nine Prifoners only; nor would they have been here then had they not fear'd we fhould march againft them, which they were feveral times given to underftand. The 2d Sir William Johnfon called them together, they acknowledged their Faults and infift on it that they will be very good for the Time to come, and that they will deliver up the King and War Chief of the Delawares and Shawanes & be amenable for the future Conduct of the Reft which they took under their Protection this Spring, provided we grant them Peace alfo, which is agreed to. I expect to fee this Place clear of Savages in a Day or two fo as to be able to proceed with Troops to the weftward; and I think it prudent to take with me as many Indian Warriors as will go, it being certain the Savages round Detroit, &c. will take it much amifs in them, which if properly managed will be of infinite Service to the Nation whenever either thofe to the weftward or five Nations break out again; their additional Expence in going on will only

be

be Provifions, and altho' one half or more may be
fufpected of loving their own Color better than us,
ftill I think it my Duty to rifk it for the Advantages
which may attend it hereafter. It will be impoffible
to know the Numbers of them until they are in the
Boats.

Letter from Colonel Bradftreet to General Amherft.

NIAGARA, 5th Auguft, 1764.

DEAR SIR:

I HAVE received your Excellency's Letter of the
2d Inftant and I will fend to the Savages of the
Illinois as foon as I get to Detroit and fhall not fail to
do all I can for Pontiac. You will fee by the inclofed
Letter from Major Gladwin, the Sandufky Savages
have lately offer'd to make Peace ; had I not been
ftopt here, I fhould not have received that Letter &
perhaps might have had the good Fortune to have cut
up that Band, which I think would have been more
for the Public good than making Peace with them.

From very good Information I find it impoffible to
get to the Siotio River by Water, but from Prifq Ifle
Shataquau and fo round by Fort Pitt, which would
take up fo much Time ; even was there Water at this
Seafon, which there is not for many Miles at firft fetting off, that I do not think we fhall have time to undertake it, and I have great Reafon to think Major
Gladwin has been mifinformed, when told that the
Shawanes & Delawares Indians were but two Days
march from Sandufky, as the fame Savages who gave
him the Information now tell me that they are ftill at
their old Caftle near the Ohio, except a few, and this
is confirmed by others. But you may depend upon
my

my marching to them by Land if it is poſſible for us to undertake it, which perhaps may be about the Time Col. Bouquett on the move this way.

I am not without Hopes of falling on Mr. Pondiac's Friends and ſhall puſh firſt for that.   The Putewatamas have alſo offeerd Peace, which I am ſorry for, as I think I could not well fail of making them repent of what they have done as well as thoſe of Sanduſky, if not prevented by being ſo late.

Untill I came here no Place of Security for the Veſſels of this and of Lake Erie was found ' and they were under the Neceſſity of coming to anchor in the open Lake & expoſed to every Storm & to be loſt ; add to this they had more than twenty Miles to ſend for their Loading ; but on examining the north Shore a proper Place has been found to ſecure the Veſſells by the help of a Wharf juſt above the Rapids ; a Poſt is now building there & all that can be done towards finiſhing under our Circumſtances this Seaſon will be done ; and to avoid giving Offence to the Senecas Savages to whom the Land belongs, I hǎve deſired S. Wm. Johnſon to aſk it of them and they have granted it.

I encloſe your Exl Returns of the Troops with a Plan & Report of what we have done for the Security of the Carrying Place & Veſſells from hence to the Rapids on Lake Erie.

P. S. I can not diſcarge the Teamſter & Waggoner altho' that Buſineſs is done, being obliged to employ them at clearing the Wood of each Side the Road over the Carrying Place, Battoeing Proviſions to Fort Erie, making Hay, &c. and have employ which is ab- ſolutely neceſſary for many more than I had then.

This Inſtant I have received the encloſed from Ma- jor Gladwin, ſaying the Outawas aſk Peace & have
brought

brought in three Prifoners. Fear has brought all thefe Civilities about, but how long they will laft when the Danger is over Time muft tell. The enclofed Staff of the Baker here will appear ftrong to your Exl. and believe you will approve of my ordering the Man to be paid no more than what he receives from the Troops & direct Mr. Lake to pay it being a great Saving to the Crown.

Col B. to the General, Niagara.

Letter from Colonel Bradftreet to General Gage.

PRESQUE ISLE, 14 Aug. 1764.

DEAR SIR:

AGREEABLE to your Inftructions to grant Peace & His Majeftys Protection to fuch Savages who fhall lay down their Arms & beg for Peace, I enclofe you what has pafs'd between me & the Deputys of all the Nations of Indians, who inhabit the Lands of Sandufky, Scioto Plains, Mufkinhem, the Ohio, Prefque Ifle, &c. and your Excellency may depend upon my marching to the Plains of Scioto if I find they intend to play me the leaft foul Trick. Surrounded as I fhall foon be by Numbers of Savages who afk Peace from Fear only, makes it impoffible for me to fix any other Plan than acting as Circumftances occafion, fo that I can now only fay that I fhall do every thing in my Power for the Honor of His Majeftys Arms & the Benefit of the Nation.   I am, &c.

J. BRADSTREET.

P. S. I fend this by the way of Fort Pitt; out of 574 Indians which was faid at Niagara I fhould have with me, we have 255, 100 of whom belong to Canada.

His Excell. Gen. Gage,

Letter

Letter from Colonel Bradſtreet to Gov. John Penn.

[Bradſtreet and Amherſt MSS., p. 155.]

PRESQUE ISLE, 14 AUG. 1764,

To Governor Penn.

SIR :

AS it may be agreeable to you and the People under your Government to know as ſoon as poſſible
of the Peace concluded with all the Nations of Indians,
who have done you ſo much Damage, I encloſe you a
Copy of what has paſſed on the Occaſion.

I am, &c.

JNO. BRADSTREET.

P. S. Perhaps under preſent Circumſtances of the
Troops acting from your Quarter and the advanc'd
Seaſon, it may be agreeable to the ſouthern Govern-
ments to have early Information of this Affair in which
you will pleaſe ſo act as may be moſt agreeable to you.

Letter from Colonel Bradſtreet to Colonel Bouquett.

[Bradſtreet and Amherſt MSS., p. 159.]

PRESQUE ISLE, 14th Aug. 1764.

SIR :

AGREEABLE to Gen. Gages Orders to me to
grant Peace and His Majeſtys Protection to all
Savages that may lay down their Arms & beg for Peace,
I encloſe you what has paſſ'd between me and the
Deputys of all the Nations of Indians who inhabit the
Lands of Sanduſky, the Scioto Plains, Muſkinham,
the Ohio, near this Place, &c. and doubt not if you

are

are in readynefs to march you will firft receive Gen. Gages Directions how you are to act after his receiving my Letters and Articles of Peace.

I am, &c.

JNO. BRADSTREET.

Col. Bouquett.

PRESQUE ISLE. 14th Aug. 1764.

SIR :

I SEND you enclof'd Copy of a Peace I have made with all the Nations of Savages upon the Banks of the Ohio, Scioto Plains, &., &c., &c., and Letters for Gen. Gage, &c. which I muft defire you to forward with the utmoft Difpatch.

I am, &c.

JNO. BRADSTREET.

Letter from Colonel Bradftreet to Sir Wm. Johnfon.

[Bradftreet and Amherft MSS.]

DETROIT, 28th Aug. 1764.

DEAR SIR :

I HAVE only Time to fay by Major Gladwin we have fhown the Savages in this Quarter we could have cut them up in Part at leaft had they not afk'd Peace, that the Outawas, Petewatamas, &c. Chepewas are to be all   in fix or feven Days to end the general Peace & comply with every thing I demand, amongft which Bondeac is to be given up to be fent down to the Seacoaft & maintain'd at his Majeftys Expence the Remainder of his Days.   Major Gladwin will tell your Ex. the fad State of this Place refpecting the Quarters

for

for the Troops.   I fhall do all I can towards building
Barracks, it being abfolutely neceffary.   The Troops
you ordered for to Garrifon Michilimicanack with two
Companys of fifty Men each which I have raifed out
of the Inhabitants here, go of to morrow and one of
the Veffells fhall be got into Lake Huron, tho' no
more than fix feet Water is as yet found over the Barr
in Lake St. Clair, and no Pains fhall be wanting to
know how to fix the Navigation from Neagara Falls
to Michigan Lake, &c.

Inclofed you have a Copy of the Peace made with
the Shawanes, &c. and I fhall be at Sandufky at the
Time appointed for the Chiefs & Prifoners to be there
& to march againft them to Scioto if they do not fulfill their Engagements.

From very good Information I found neceffary to
give the Inhabitants & Savages of the Elliones & the
Nations on this Side of it to the Miames to know
that unlefs they carry themfelves well to His Majeftys
Troops who were to take Poffeffion of that Country,
they might expect to hear from us and yᵉ Savages of
the Six Nations, thofe of Canada, the Shawanes, &c.
that we have made Peace with, together with the Nations furrounding this Place foon, for which Purpofe
I have fent Capt. Morris of 17ᵗʰ Regiment and Savages
with the ufual Belts.   Should Capt Morris fucceed he
is to pufh on to all the Nations of Savages on the
Banks of the Miffifippi to the Sea, as your Ex. will
fee by his Inftructions a Copy of which is herein enclofed, as alfo the Oath the Inhabitants are to take.

Letter

Letter from Colonel Bradftreet to Lieut. Sinclair.

DETROIT, 12th Sept. 1764.

SIR:

YOU are hereby requir'd and directed the Beginning of May next to receive on board the Schooner Gladwin a Load of Provifions for the Garrifon of Michilimicanack & with it proceed to that Place, and as foon as you have delivered it you are to fail for the Bottom of the Bay where we had a Fort, & from thence round the Lake Michigan, fteering up the River St. Jofephs as far as you can, making throughout the whole Voyage fuch Remarks & Obfervations as the Importance of the Service you are ordered on requires for the Safety of the future Navigation of thofe Lakes, obferving the fame on Lake Huron, the whole of which you will report in Writing to Lt. Col. Campbell or Officer commanding here on your Return and receive from him Directions for your further Conduct.

As you will doubtlefs fee many Savages before you return you will inform them, that the Reafon of your failing round thofe Lakes is to find out if it is practicable for Veffels agreeable to my Promife to them at Neagara.

I am, &c.

J. B.

Lt. Sinclair.

Letter

Letter from Col. Bradſtreet to Lt. Col. Campbell.

[Bradſtreet and Amherſt MSS., p. 155.]

SANDUSKY, 10th Oct. 1764.

To Lt. Col. Campbell.

SIR:

YOUR Letter by Chain, without Date, I have received and I have great Pleaſure to find you have in ſo ſhort a Time gained ſo much Influence over the Indians as you mention. I doubt not but you will improve it as His Majeſtys Service much requires it at this Time to correct the Shawanes & Delawares; but I muſt obſerve for the good of the Service, that it is abſolutely neceſſary that every Perſon that may have Influence with the Indians ſhould be employ'd to gain their Affection and to engage them not only to keep the Peace with us but act for us againſt the Kings Enemies. The Savages love the Inhabitants of Detroit in general and the latter may by gentle Treatment be brought to exert themſelves in our Favor with the former with little or no Expence to Government; but after all, Affability & Attention in the Officer commanding at Detroit is abſolutely neceſſary, to the Savages in general, particularly thoſe going out to War, without which all will go wrong. You will pleaſe to uſe your utmoſt Endeavours to make up & ſend out againſt the Shawanes & Delawares all the Parties of Indians in Friendſhip with us you can poſſibly collect & continue it until further Orders, unleſs you ſhall receive Letters from Col. Bouquett telling you to deſiſt, he having made Peace with thoſe two Nations of Savages, the Shawanes & Delawares, & you are to fit out all ſuch Parties as you ſend out againſt thoſe

two

two Nations in the Manner the French did thofe Indians they fent to War, and pay for every Scalp or Prifoner brought in by them, you fend out four Blankets, four fhirts, four Pair of Stockings and one Pound of Paint. The Goods wanted for this Service you are to pur-chafe as Occafion requires and add it to your other public Accounts. You will alfo employ fuch of the Inhabitants of Detroit in each Party as you think can be trufted. Mr. Royome, that was with Capt. Morris, offers his Service. I fhall fend you what I can from Niagara this Fall, & fet off for that Place this Day. Much depends upon the Manner you receive thofe Indians now going againft the Delawares on their Re-turn; if they do any thing pay them for each Scalp or Prifoner as above mentioned, & if not fuccefful be kind & give them what will fend them Home fatiffied, with fome Rum to the Chief of the Party. At the Requeft of the Ottawas, Chepewas, etc. I have appointed *Chain* an Interpreter to thofe Nations, he is much beloved by them & will be of great ufe in getting Parties to go out & go with them when neceffary. You will allow him one Mans Provifion to be given to his Mother when he is on Service & pay him the fame Pay and in the fame way as you do the other Interpreters. You have enclofed Copy of my Letter to the Officer com-manding the Places at Fort Chefter with the Inftruc-tions to Godfroy & Maifonville whom I order thither &·when they return the latter may proceed to me with the Anfwer if he thinks proper, otherwife you will for-ward the Officers Letter and the Anfwer from the In-dian Nations they fpeake with.

You have the Copy of the Peace, &c. with the Hu-rons on   of this Place to be added to the one made at Detroit, and it being highly neceffary to ac-quaint all the Nations of Indians we poffibly can that
                                                                our

our continuing the War with the Shawanes, &c. is owing to their fending out Parties, killing and taking our People Prifoners after having fued for Peace and neglecting to come to Sandufky with their Prifoners & Chiefs to ratify that Peace agreeable to their . . . . . .

You will therefore ufe every Means in your Power for that Purpofe, and I fend an Order to Mr. Morfac having great Influence, he being well acquainted with the upper Nations, to proceed to the Falls of St. Marys for that Purpofe, alfo as you will fee by the Copy of his Inftructions herein enclofed, all Paffes that I thought proper to give when I left Detroit for carrying on the Ind^n Trade you will allow to be carry'd into Execution, giving Inftructions to the People to acquaint all the Indians when they go of the perfiduous Behaviour of the Shawanes & Delawares, and to ufe their utmoft Endeavours to prevent any bad Impreffions being on them by the . . . .

F I N I S .

INDEX.

Johnfon

Robinſon

LIST OF SUBSCRIBERS.

J. Carson Brevoort, Efq., Brooklyn, *large paper*,		2
John Carter Brown, Efq., Providence,	do	1
Hon. Alex. Campbell, Kingfton, Canada,	do	1
James Lenox, Efq., New York,	do	1
William Menzies, Efq., New York,	do	1
George C. Anthon, Efq., do	*fmall paper*,	1
Prof. Charles Anthon, do	do	1
John Anthon, Efq., do	do	1
S. Alofsen, Efq., Jerfey City,	do	1
George Bancroft, Efq., New York,	do	1
Samuel L. M. Barlow, Efq., do	do	1
J. W. Bouton & Co., do	do	2
J. Carson Brevoort, Efq., Brooklyn,	do	10
Charles I. Bushnell, Efq., New York,	do	1
Wm. J. Davis, Efq., New York,	do	1
H. B. Dawson, Efq., do	do	1
John Fowler, Jr., do	do	1
B. H. Hall, Efq., Troy,	do	1
Chas. E. Hammett, Jr., Efq., Newport,	do	1
Wm. Howard Hart, Efq., Troy,	do	1
James B. Kirker, Efq., New York,	do	1
H. S. McCall, Efq., Albany,	do	1
John B. Moreau, Efq., New York,	do	1
Henry Nicoll, Efq., do	do	1
Charles B. Norton, Efq., do	do	5
Dr. E. B. O'Callaghan, Albany,	do	1

M. O'Conor, Efq., New York,	*fmall paper*,	1
Francis Parkman, Efq., Bofton,	do	1
J. R. Paxton, Efq., Philadelphia,	do	1
Hon. G. W. Pratt, New York,	do	1
Hon. J. V. L. Pruyn, Albany,	do	1
Joel Rathbone, Efq., do	do	1
Francis Raymond, Efq., Detroit,	do	6
C. B. Richardson, Efq., New York,	do	3
Geo. W. Riggs, Jr., Efq., Wafhington,	do	1
Winthrop Sargent, Efq., Philadelphia,	do	1
J. G. Shea, Efq., New York,	do	1
J. Austin Stevens, Jr., Efq., New York,	do	1
Robert Townsend, Efq., Albany,	do	2
Franklin Townsend, Efq., do	do	1
Dr. Howard Townsend, do	do	1
Gen. Frederick Townsend, do	do	1
W. B. Trask, Efq., Bofton,	do	2
Hon. Wm. Tuthill, Efq., Tipton, Iowa,	do	1
C. J. Walker, Efq., Detroit,	do	1
W. H. Whitmore, Efq., Bofton,	do	1
H. Austin Whitney, Efq., do	do	1
Joseph Willard, Efq., do	do	1
Bifhop John Williams, Middletown, Ct.,	do	1
Hon. W. A. Young, Albany,	do	1
Am. Antiquarian Soc., Worcefter, Mafs.,	do	1
Aftor Library, New York,	do	1
Maine Hiftorical Society,	do	1
Mercantile Lib. Affociation, Baltimore,	do	1
Military Academy at Weft Point,	do	1
New York State Library, Albany,	do	1
Wifconfin Hiftorical Society, Madifon,	do	1

www.ingramcontent.com/pod-product-compliance
Lightning Source LLC
Chambersburg PA
CBHW020934030726
47496CB00005B/1185